The Holy Doves

L.E. Austen

Published 2024 by Jason Music Publishing
408 Phoenix Avenue NW, Albuquerque, NM 87107
http://jasonsmusicpublishing.com

Title: The Holy Doves
Thrillers Suspense
Thrillers Religious
Historical Thriller
Magical Realism
Historical fiction

ISBN 978-1-7351855-2-1

Printed and bound in the United States of America

THE HOLY DOVES
Prologue

The Light will herald humanity's salvation or its destruction. The choice mankind's alone.

—The Secret Gospel of Judith the Elder

<u>Castle Cockaigne</u>

Lying to yourself is infinitely easier than lying to others, Inanna thought as she pulled open the door to her husband's office. People do it constantly, never considering that everything they believe about themselves is almost always wrong. She had to wipe every trace of her true intentions from her mind. She could do it.

Unfortunately, lying to her husband was incredibly difficult if he paid little attention to another person's words. She had learned long ago to tell him only the truths that wouldn't overly upset him while deliberately skimming over anything that might. She hoped he wouldn't notice.

Luckily, he was distracted by the stack of oversized ledgers piled on every corner of his desk as he barked orders at the ever-present crowd of sycophant assistants, who swirled around him while awaiting his slightest pronouncement, ready to do his bidding without question. She found them all so irritating.

She stood quietly until Jehovah lifted his eyes, noticed her waiting, and quickly gestured for his assistants to leave.

Inanna watched with amusement as he struggled to remember if she had mentioned that she was coming to see him. He took one

1

last wistful look at his accounting books before walking around the desk to stand beside her.

"I am surprised to see you, Inanna," he said, "Did you make an appointment?"

"I am your wife and equal partner. Why would I need an appointment to see my husband?"

"Of course," answered Jehovah. "It's just that you rarely visit my office. I thought this paperwork bored you beyond belief."

"It does, but without your unparalleled skill as an administrator, the Universe would be chaos." She said as she smoothed a nonexistent wrinkle from her ivory Chanel suit and tucked a stray white hair behind her ear. "I too often neglect to compliment you on your diligence."

He glanced at his overflowing inbox. "You do know that ninety-eight percent of my time is devoted to cleaning up the messes you have created. I wish you'd learn a little restraint."

"I'll work on it, I promise," she answered, knowing she wouldn't.

He glanced at her appearance and shook his head. "I take it you're visiting Earth."

"I'm visiting Princess Celeste. She happens to live there now that she's retired. I'm meeting a couple of new designers in Los Angeles who are quite innovative, and I thought I'd pop in to see Dolce and Gabbana in Italy to take a peek at next year's collection just for fun."

"What else?"

"What do you mean 'what else?'"

He stared at her sternly. "You know what I mean. We had an agreement not to interfere. A bet is a bet."

She smiled with a look of such sweetness that it would have melted any heart other than his. "I will not betray the terms of our wager. You have my word."

"It does not please me to say it, but humanity has been a disaster from the beginning. It's best to end it before they cause even greater harm."

"It does please you to say it, my dear. You are thrilled that my plan hasn't worked exactly as I envisioned."

"Numbers don't lie, Inanna."

"Giving humans free will, intelligence, and curiosity should have turned out much better than it has."

"I told you it was a terrible idea."

"You did. I hope they will change for the better."

"In my experience, hope dies in the face of reality."

"Not always. Sometimes hope prevails."

"I don't know why I even try," Jehovah grumbled.

"Then don't. You've never been skilled at compromise."

Jehovah sighed. "Give Princess Celeste my regards. Tell Gabriel I want him to accompany you to keep you out of trouble."

It was best to let her do whatever she wanted. He found a certain satisfaction in knowing he could hold the disaster over her for all eternity.

"An excellent idea, dear. Thank you. I will speak with him at once," she answered as she turned her head and mouthed 'hello' to Gabriel, who was waiting in the hallway with a stack of vintage Louis Vuitton luggage at his feet.

"Inanna?" Jehovah said as she stepped into the hallway. "Be careful. It's dangerous down there." In a rare moment of emotion, his voice cracked ever so slightly. "You are the best part of me," he said quietly.

She turned back to look at him. "And you are the best part of me, dearest. I'll be back before you have time to miss me."

◆ ◆ ◆

An expression of disdained boredom marred Gabriel's perfect face as he picked up the luggage. He was displeased that Inanna had involved him once again in her scheme to influence the wager's outcome, but there was no way he could refuse her. After all, she was the mother of them all.

"Let's do this," Inanna said as she nodded slightly.

Gabriel closed his eyes as the Light swirled around them and grew in intensity until it engulfed them in a blinding brilliance. It was best, he decided, not to think about how Jehovah would react if he found out what they were doing.

Chapter 1
Day One

Midnight: The Light Bria Tanaka

You were born a child of light's wonderful secret, and you return to the beauty you have always been.

—Aberjhani

<u>Los Angeles, California</u>

"It's almost midnight, Theo. We need to get some rest," Bria said as she released her sun-streaked brown hair from the clip on the top of her head, which formed a wavy halo around her face.

"What's-her-name is going to be here at 9 a.m."

"Inanna. Her name is Inanna. I can't believe that you can't remember her name. We've been working on this collection for the last two months. It has to be perfect."

"And it is. Each piece is classic and yet has the modern Cross and Tanaka twist. That's what attracted her attention at the LA Fashion Forward Show in the first place. We're good."

Theo pursed his lips. "She needs to buy every single piece of the collection, Bri. If not, we'll both have to take jobs at Mickey D's to pay the rent. I'm not joking. Cross and Tanaka will stop being 'up-and-coming' and become 'down-and-out.' Everything depends on Inanna."

"Stop being such a drama queen–," Bria started as a blinding flash of light filled the midnight sky. She staggered as it shot through her like an electric shock, and her knees buckled beneath her. She struggled to keep herself upright, shaking and gasping to catch her breath. The Light disappeared as quickly as it appeared. Her body slowly slid to the floor, her head dropping to her chest.

"OMG, Bri," Theo said as he ran to her side, "what's wrong? Are you sick?"

"The Light! An amazingly light filled the sky. Then it shot through me, engulfed me. My entire body is still tingling like I've been poked with a million little needles."

"Bri, what are you talking about? I didn't see anything. There wasn't a light in the sky."

"I saw it, Theo!" she stubbornly answered. There's no way anyone could have missed it. It was this searing blast of blinding white light!!"

Theo shook his head. "I promised you I didn't see it. Maybe it was a UFO sent just for you. They're coming back, I heard."

Bria struggled to her feet, using the wall to steady herself as Theo gathered everything that had fallen out of her bag. "I love you, but you're a weirdo," she said, taking her bag from him. "A UFO? Really?"

"I said maybe. Maybe it was a UFO, but we should have you checked out in the Emergency Room. Seeing a flash of light when there isn't one probably means something."

"I don't need to go to the hospital. I need to go home and sleep. I think I'm so tired that I must have imagined it. There wasn't a light that filled the universe," she said firmly as she leaned forward and kissed him on the cheek, "and if it was a UFO, it's gone now."

"Ok. You sleep. I'm going to stay a while longer and re-look at the collection one last time. It has to be perfect before we show it to Inanna.

"You need to stop worrying, Theo. She's going to love us. We're exactly what Inanna has been looking for. I've never been more sure of anything in my life."

"And you know this because?"

Bria thought about it for a second.

"I think your aliens told me," she giggled. "Don't worry. Everything's going to work out exactly as it's meant to. I promise."

◆ ◆ ◆

Midnight: The Light
Cardinal Rafael De Posada of Opus Christos

Vatican Advanced Technology Telescope (VATT)
Mount Graham International Observatory
Southern Arizona, USA

"We saw the Light!" whispered Brother Matthias, "It was just as Judith the Elder predicted."

"What?" asked Cardinal De Posada as he gestured to his aide, Father Richard, to leave his apartment in the Apostolic Palace in the Vatican. "What did you just say?"

"The James Webb Telescope recorded a flash of light that filled the Universe 13.6 billion light-years from Earth. It happened exactly as Judith the Elder's prophecy said it would."

"You saw it?" asked the Cardinal, "You saw the light?"

"Of course not," answered Brother Matthias. "Only the Holy Doves, the living descendants of the Messiah, would have seen the Light. But the telescope recorded in its entirety. I can't explain how it did, but it's indisputable proof. Judith was right."

De Posada stood and walked to the window to stare across the Vatican toward St. Peter's. "And you're sure it wasn't an exploding black hole or a comet? Is there a reasonable explanation acceptable to the scientific community?"

"We're not sure of anything. A Light filling the Universe is unprecedented. I would imagine that the powers-that-be will keep a lid on announcing the discovery until they can come up with a reasonable explanation."

"Perfect," answered Cardinal De Posada, "That gives us a little breathing room, a week or maybe two. With any luck, the Guardians of the Holy Doves are still unaware that Judith's prophecy has come to pass. If we move quickly, we will be in place and kill every Holy Dove before the Guardians can move in to protect those damn women. If the Doves are all dead, there can be no new Messiah."

I'll call Father General Scotti to let him know that Operation Holy Doves will commence immediately. Call Alberto Zayas. Tell him to go ahead and pick up Brother Joseph and get him to the Vatican. And have him contact Felix wherever he may be. He knows what to do."

Brother Matthias was silent for a moment. "We're doing the right thing, aren't we? Murder is a sin."

"*Opus Christos*, as did the Crusaders who fought to save Jerusalem from the infidels, will be blessed by God. By destroying the Holy Doves, we are saving our beloved Church and Western society. We are acting for the greater good. Your mortal soul is safe."

"You're right, of course. If the truth is revealed, it will destroy the Church, and the Western world will collapse into chaos. In God's name, we're doing what we must to save the world."

"That we are, Brother Matthias, that we are."

◆ ◆ ◆

Midnight: The Light
Brother Joseph Pirelli

Our Lady of Guadalupe Trappist Monastery
Lafayette, Oregon

Brother Joseph Pirelli sat straight up in his narrow bed and watched the glow in the sky fade into nothingness. Overcome with uneasiness, he slipped on the traditional white woolen robe and chocolate-brown apron worn by Trappist monks, stepped into the hall, and walked toward the chapel. In the dim light, Brother Joseph could see the order's oldest resident, Brother Mark, struggling with the heavy door. Brother Joseph rushed to help him.

"You saw the Light," Brother Mark whispered, his voice rough from years of disuse as he looked at Brother Joseph. "Of course, you would have, knowing as we do of your legacy."

"My legacy?" asked Joseph as he took Brother Mark's arm to help him enter the chapel.

"There's much I must tell you," Brother Mark answered as he raised his hand to reveal a silver dove pinned inside his cowl. "I–we–the Guardians of the Holy Doves," he whispered weakly, "have been watching over you since you were born. You are God's chosen son."

"I'll be right back, Brother Mark. I need to get the Abbot," answered Brother Joseph as he lowered Brother Mark onto the pew.

The elderly monk grabbed Brother Joseph's hand.

"There isn't time. St. Peter is impatiently waiting for me at the gates of heaven. Listen carefully, Joseph. You must find her, the Holy Dove, to save humanity from annihilation. Together, you are mankind's last hope," Brother Mark whispered as he released the final breath of air from his lungs and slumped lifelessly into Joseph's arms.

Chapter 2
8:13 A.M.

The Guardians of the Holy Doves

No one can bar the road to the truth, and to advance its cause, I am prepared to accept even death.
—Aleksandr Solzhenitsyn

The Guardians of the Holy Doves' Command Center
Abbey Sainte-Victoire,
Marseille, France

The Light reached deep inside the Earth, penetrating the thick concrete walls of the Guardian's hidden underground facility. It engulfed Isabella, leaving her shaken, but she shook it off. She had vowed to protect the Holy Doves with every fiber of her being. She had a job to do.

Without hesitation, she implemented the Guardian's plan to protect the living Holy Doves, the blood descendants of the First Messiah, just as Judith the Elder had done two thousand years ago when she founded the order.

She turned her swivel chair away from her computer screen when she heard Father Patrick, the Command Center's Chief Executive Officer, enter her office, followed by Jasper, the director of their IT department. "You heard the news much quicker than I expected," she said as she looked up at Father Patrick. "It wouldn't surprise me, Jasper, if you knew before I did."

"It took me 53 seconds longer. My contact at VATT had to run down to his room to find his phone. It was another two minutes before we intercepted a call placed to Cardinal De Posada."

"Meaning that *Opus Christos* knows already," said Father O'Neill. "We need to mobilize immediately to save as many Holy Doves as possible. Are the safe houses ready?"

"They should all be up and running by this evening to accommodate the Holy Doves as our operatives bring them in," said Jasper. "My team is working on that now."

"Good," said Father Patrick. "Where do we focus our initial attention?"

"The Doves on the US West Coast, Baja California in Mexico, and Western Canada need to be approached immediately," stated Jasper.

"Explain," said Father Patrick.

"Judith's prophecy stated the Holy Doves will see the light at the stroke of midnight. Thirteen minutes ago, Izzy, a verifiable Holy Dove, saw the Light. It was 8 a.m. here in France; therefore, it was Midnight in the Pacific Time Zone. Ergo, I believe the Chosen Dove will be found somewhere in that region. My team is correlating the locations of the women we know are on the West Coast. We'll contact our operatives as soon as possible to assign them as efficiently as possible."

Izzy quickly pulled up a map. "How many Holy Doves are we talking about?"

Father Patrick firmly raised his hand. "I need to remind you both that we vow to protect all the Holy Family, not just the one who will be Chosen by God. I don't disagree with your assessment, Jasper, but the life of every Dove is equally precious."

"Of course. The teams we've contacted in Israel, Eastern Canada, and most of Europe will be ready to move out within the hour. As we speak, we are issuing orders for our agents in India, Japan, China, and Sub-Saharan Africa," said Jasper. "The team is working on contacting Father Claude, Orlando, and our other operatives in the States, Mexico, and Canada, but it's the middle of the night there. We're doing our best, Father Patrick."

"It wasn't a criticism, Jasper, just a reminder," answered Father Patrick.

"I thought we'd have a few days before those bastards found out and started murdering the Holy Doves so God's child, our Savior, cannot be born," said Izzy.

"Then God has given us a clear path to follow. We must secure the Doves before *Opus Christos* finds them," answered Father Patrick as he turned and walked out of Izzy's office. "We will protect them with our lives if necessary. We will succeed or die trying. Those are the only options available if we're going to save humanity from destruction."

Izzy and Jasper waited silently as they watched Father Patrick enter the elevator at the end of the hall.

"How many Doves are we talking about?" whispered Izzy. "Fifty-three living in California, nineteen in Oregon, twenty-four in Washington, and another dozen in Western Canada," answered Jasper, understanding her question intuitively. "And we have no way of knowing the names of women from Leah's Bloodline who might be on the Pacific Coast since their records were destroyed during the Second World War,"

"With any luck, neither does *Opus Christos*. Hopefully, the names on the list were destroyed as rumored and not just lost and waiting to be found. What if Leah's list wasn't destroyed? What if *Opus Christos* knows where it is?"

"Let's hope that doesn't happen. Leah's Daughters would be 'screwed and tattooed,' as my granddaddy used to say. We've been looking for the list of her descendants for over seventy years with

no luck, but I'll work on finding it in my spare time."
"Smart ass," answered Izzy.

Chapter 3
8:15 A.M.
Bria Tanaka and Theo Cross

We are linked by blood, and blood is a memory without language.
-Joyce Carol Oates

Los Angeles, California

Bria opened the studio's front door to find Theo slumped at the reception desk, his folded arms cradling his head. His hair was matted on one side while sticking straight out on the other. A grunt escaped his lips as Bria set her bag down with a thump. A trickle of saliva glistened at the corner of his mouth.

"What time is it?" he asked.

"Oh, Sweetie, there's not enough time to fix everything wrong with you."

"Haha. I need coffee. I stayed up after you left and reviewed the entire collection again."

"And?"

"It's perfect. If Inanna doesn't like it, then she's impossible to please."

"There's the insufferable egotist I know and love," answered Bria. "You need to clean yourself up. Inanna will be here in less than an hour."

"Let's have coffee first," he insisted, looking down at his

pizza-stained shirt and sniffing his underarms. "Damn, you're right. I smell like a dorm room on a Sunday morning."

"I am," she answered, leaning forward and taking a deep breath. "OMG, Theo. A clean shirt and pants are hanging behind the storeroom door. Wash your face, brush your teeth, and do something with that bleach-blond rat's nest you call a hairstyle. And, Theo, please use deodorant, for God's sake."

"I hate you."

"No, you don't. You've loved me since pre-school. You can't help yourself."

"True. You were my first and only girlfriend. But at this moment, I don't like you."

"Don't like me all you want, just come back looking all clean and sexy for Inanna. I'll get the coffee ready," Bria said as she playfully pushed him off the chair. "Move it, Dude!"

Twenty minutes later, Theo returned in a clean outfit; his hair tamed into a stylish over-gelled sweep, his face scrubbed and glowing. He grabbed the cup of strong Italian coffee that Bria had set on the corner of the desk.

"I forgot to ask if you're feeling better after that 'I saw a bright light' episode last night. I'm the worst best friend ever," apologized Theo.

"I'm feeling terrific. Never better. You were right all along. I imagined seeing a light. It never happened."

"I'm right? That's the first time I've heard those words escape your mouth.

"Don't let it go to your head. You had to be right about something sooner or later. But don't worry, it probably won't ever happen again. The odds against it are astronomical."

Theo stuck his tongue out before he looked at his iPhone, and his eyes filled with panic.

"Oh, crap! Inanna's going to be here any second!"

"Then I guess our lives just got simpler. We don't have time to worry whether she'll like our collection, or she won't. In fourth grade, Sister Mary Francis repeatedly reminded us that our future is in God's hands. There's nothing we can do to change it."

Chapter 4
8:55 A.M.

Brother Joseph Pirelli

He is a true monk who is separated from all and united to all.
—Evagruis Ponticus , 4th-century Christian monk

<u>*Our Lady of Guadalupe Trappist Monastery,*</u>
<u>*Lafayette, Oregon*</u>

Brother Joseph sat quietly by Brother Mark's still body in the infirmary.

"We missed you at Lauds," said the Abbot as he entered the small white room.

"I apologize, Father Abbot. I didn't want his last hours on Earth to be spent alone."

"We are never alone in God, Joseph. I had not realized you had a special bond."

"A special bond? I don't think he ever spoke a dozen words to me in the last nine years."

"How strange. I awoke last night shortly before midnight," answered the Abbot, "to find Brother Mark sitting beside my bed. He said calmly that we must do all we can to help you fulfill your destiny. Then he stood and left without another word. May I ask what he said to you?"

"His words made no sense, Father Abbot. It was gibberish.

I have no idea what he meant."

The Abbot reached inside Brother Mark's cowl and removed a small silver pin. "Years ago, he asked me to ensure this pin was with him when he was buried, but he changed his mind last night. He made me promise that I would give it to you. He said you'd understand," the Abbot said.

"It's a silver dove," Brother Joseph said as he turned the pin over to study it. "I'm afraid that I have no idea what it's supposed to mean or why he asked you to give it to me."

"The Lord works in mysterious ways, Brother Joseph. I'm sure that prayer will bring you the answers you seek. However, I came to find you for another reason. You have a visitor waiting to speak with you. Alberto Zayas? He says he's an old friend. He told me that Cardinal De Posada of the Vatican sent him to request your aid in discovering the identities of an Islamic Terrorist group that is murdering Christian women. Their bodies have been left on altars all over the world. It is both an attack on and an insult to the Church. The Vatican believes you have connections to help the Church identify the perpetrators and bring them to justice. I will send him away if you wish."

Brother Joseph stood up. "No. I will see him. Years ago, we worked together on the CIA's Anti-Terrorism Team. I doubt I can help him, but I will speak with him. It's the least I can do."

Chapter 5
9 A.M.

Inanna, Bria, and Theo

I hear the wind among the trees playing the celestial symphonies.
–Henry Wadsworth Longfellow

Los Angeles, California

The roar of a powerful engine caused them to turn toward the large windows facing the street.

"It's a Lamborghini Veneno," whispered Theo excitedly, "OMG, I have to get a selfie!"

"No selfies, Theo! Promise me you're not going to act all crazy. It's just a car!"

Theo sighed. "So you're saying I can't ask to drive it?"

"Not funny," Bria said as Theo reached over and squeezed her hand nervously. "Smile and stop shaking. We need to pretend we're grown-up professionals."

The male blonde-headed driver stepped out and circled the car as they watched. He stood as straight as a soldier on review before he put his gloved hand out to help his passenger exit the vehicle.

Bria's breath caught in her throat. Inanna was, without a doubt, the most incredible creature she had ever seen or imagined she would see. Her hair was white as Norwegian snow and pulled back into a sleek chignon at the back of her neck. When she moved her head, it sparkled as if dusted with diamonds, and her iced mocha-colored skin was set off by highlighting an undertone of golden glow. Bria was mesmerized.

"Cashmere," whispered Theo as he looked at her elegant, tailored pants and swing jacket. "Albino python boots."

"Vicuna, but you're right about the boots," corrected Bria in a whisper as she stepped forward to greet their guest. "Welcome to Cross and Tanaka," she said as she opened the door. "We're excited to show you the collection we have created for you."

Inanna's smile was like a beam of sunlight breaking through the clouds. "It's nice to see you again, Theo," she said, extending her gloved hand. "You must be Bria. Theo speaks highly of your talent as a designer."

Bria blushed. "Thank you, but Theo is the driving force behind Cross and Tanaka's designs. He's the real talent."

"So he told me...several times," Inanna responded, her voice amused.

"We have the drawings and fabric suggestions ready for your review," said Bria.

"We also have a few of the designs completed and on mannikins. I believe that they are easier to visualize that way. May we offer you coffee or champagne?" asked Theo.

Inanna smiled. "It's 9 a.m., Theo," she said.

"Oh, yes. Of course. Bri, can you bring us a carafe of coffee?"

A peal of laughter escaped Inanna's lips. "Champagne, Theo! Coffee is not the way to start this wonderful adventure! It's almost cocktail hour in Paris, so I think a flute of champagne is perfectly acceptable. Theo, could you get it? I want to get to know Bria," Inanna said, ignoring the look of surprise on his face.

"Of course," Theo said, somewhat taken aback. He always assumed he was the star, and Bria was his assistant, the one who always got the coffee, or in this case, the champagne.

As Theo searched the kitchen for champagne flutes, a tray, and cloth napkins, Bria led their new client into the showroom. "My friends call me Bri," she said, "I hope you will, too. I'm sorry, but I don't remember Theo telling me your last name... Mrs.—?"

Walking to the table where the drawings and fabric swatches were laid out for her approval, Inanna picked up one or two for closer inspection before she raised her eyes to meet Bria's.

"I have a feeling, Bria, that we will soon consider each other close friends. I'm rarely wrong about that. Please call me Inanna, and I will call you Bri as your friends do."

"I am honored," answered Bria politely. "I don't think I've ever heard the name Inanna before. It's quite unusual, but I like it."

"It's an ancient name. She was the Goddess of the morning and evening stars, but enough about me. I want to learn about you, Bri. Theo thinks you're quite fascinating."

Bria laughed. "I'm afraid Theo is prejudiced. We've been best friends since we were in preschool. In reality, I'm pretty average and boring."

"I doubt that," said Inanna. "Tell me about your family. Do you have brothers and sisters?"

"I'm an only child. I live in the same house with my mother where I was born."

Inanna leaned forward to look at the medallion hanging on a silver chain around Bria's neck. "Is that St. Nicholas?"

"Yes," answered Bria as her hand lifted to touch it. "My father gave it to me a few weeks before he died. St. Nicholas is the patron saint of children. I think he gave it to me to protect me. I never take it off. That way, he's always with me. I know it's silly for a grown woman, but–."

"I don't think it's silly at all," answered Inanna. "Saint Nicholas' feast day is December 6th, I believe. Is that your birthday?"

"No. My birthday's in the spring."

"But you're Catholic?"

"My father was."

"And you and your mother?"

"Not really. I mean, my mother sent me to Catholic schools, and she does go to Mass occasionally, but I think we could call her a 'social' Catholic. I've never asked, but I think she gets lonely and attends church to be part of a community. Nearly everyone active in the parish is her age or older."

"And for the coffee and cookies afterward?"

Bria laughed. "She'd never admit it, but I think it's a good possibility."

"But she sent you to Catholic schools? Did she want you to become a nun?"

"I'm sure that never crossed her mind."

"Do you still practice your faith?" asked Inanna.

Bria paused, wondering why Inanna was so interested in her religious views. Discussions about religion could quickly become uncomfortable if you disagree with the speaker's viewpoint. She had to tread carefully.

"I'm more spiritual than religious," she answered cautiously, "I respect the beliefs of all faiths and all people equally, even those who don't believe in God."

"Interesting. I must say I agree. Since the dawn of time, there have been thousands of different human ideas about God's identity and desires. Each religion is firmly convinced that they alone speak for God until a new one supplants it. I find it to be the height of human arrogance since none come close to representing the truth," said Inanna. "I suppose the question I meant to ask is: do you believe in God?"

Bria relaxed slightly. "You mean the God that the nuns taught us about? The scary-looking old white guy with long gray hair and a bushy beard who's scowling and pointing his finger in judgment at the imperfect creatures he created? Like a growing number of people, I believe there is something bigger and better than all of us together, but honestly, I don't know who or what that is. I'm just hoping it's not the mean, scary guy."

Inanna laughed out loud. "God is a mean, scary-looking old white guy who's judgmental and vengeful? Nothing could be further from the truth," she said, "I promise you."

"That's a relief," answered Bri with a smile.

"I think," answered Inanna, " the problem with religion is that God is too immense and complex to be understood or explained by mortal man, no matter how hard they try. It can't be done."

"So you're saying that a human trying to understand God is like a flea trying to understand quantum physics? The desire may be there, but the ability is lacking?" asked Bria.

"Exactly!"

"The Wind!" said Bria in a sudden moment of insight. "God is like the wind–." She was suddenly embarrassed. "Sorry. That popped out of my mouth before I could stop it."

"I'm intrigued," encouraged Inanna, "to know how you came up with that idea."

"I was thinking that you can't see, smell, touch, hear, or taste the wind, but there is no doubt the wind exists. Maybe God is like the wind, invisible but ever-present."

Inanna smiled widely. "I've never heard the true nature of God explained better. I will probably steal it the next time I converse about God and the wind."

"I would be honored if you did," said Bria, hoping to change the subject. "My mom has rheumatoid arthritis. I moved back home to help her as much as I could. She was a pattern maker and seamstress for some of the top LA designers."

"Bria Tanaka. Tanaka. I should have made the connection. Your mother is Magdalena Tanaka. She's a legend. She was the best seamstress ever to have worked in American fashion."

"She was. Not being able to work has been hard on her. She misses her independence."

"I imagine she does. Independence is a rare gift. Most women are never allowed to experience it. How does she cope when you're working?"

"Carmen, her caregiver, is there during the day. We'd be lost without her."

"She never remarried?"

"She said she didn't need another man to make her feel complete."

"Wise woman. Is there anyone serious in your life?"

Bri laughed. "I've had a few Mr.-Right-Nows but never a Mr. Right-Forever. Maybe I'll find him someday, or maybe not. I'm not going to settle for second best."

"What about Theo? Have you ever considered him?" asked Inanna.

Bria laughed as she shook her head. "He's not boyfriend material, but, as I mentioned, we've been best friends forever. Miss Burkett, our preschool teacher, decided to put on a play, *The Princess and the Frog*, for Parents' Day. Theo was so sad–"

"Champagne!" interrupted Theo as he set the tray on the table just as a gust of wind scattered the stack of drawings onto the floor. "Where did that come from? The door and windows are closed."

"Maybe it was God?" Inanna said as she and Bri giggled at their secret joke.

"She will never tell you but," he stage-whispered as Bria bent over to gather the drawings, "I was heartbroken that she was the princess, and I was the frog. She brought the princess costume to me and said, 'I want to be the frog. It's fun to hop around.' I fell madly in love. We've been best friends ever since. Bri has a magical way of making everyone feel amazing and special. I can't explain it."

"Maybe it can't be explained," answered Inanna. "Maybe it just is."

Theo handed Inanna the flute of champagne as Bria returned the scattered sketches to the table. "You will find him, the one who will make you feel complete," Inanna whispered to Bri as she lifted her glass. "He doesn't know it yet, but he's out there waiting for you. I promise."

Chapter 6
10:15 A.M.
Felix

Evil infects the mind with self-importance and self-righteousness. It is quite effective at convincing itself that it is good. That is why the worst tyrants have risen to power by claiming they were good.

-Joseph J. Adams

Los Angeles International Airport

Felix murdered the elderly nun in the convent's chapel and draped her body across the altar just as his handler, Alberto Zayas, had ordered. Without a backward glance or remorse, he left the convent and hailed a passing taxi to take him to Logan International to catch his LA-bound flight.

He had several hours at LAX before picking up Alberto Zayas and the Trappist monk at the Van Nuys Airport. Zayas' plan, as always, was overly complicated. He, instead of Alberto, would accompany Brother Joseph to the nursing home to interview Hilmi Al-Jafri, an elderly and well-respected Islamic journalist who knew, knew the location of the secret list of Islamic terrorist groups. The plan was to frame them for the Doves' murders and divert suspicion away from *Opus Christos*. Felix was damn sure it wasn't a list of terrorists.

He understood more about *Opus Christos'* plans than Zayas

and De Posada shared with him—not that he cared. They could do any crazy thing they wanted as long as they paid him well.

While waiting in line, he pulled out his phone to review the photos and descriptions of his LA targets. He had been assigned six Holy Doves in Los Angeles. The two in the nursing home would be straightforward, a simple pillow over their faces. He'd wait for the waitress at El Coyote in the parking lot and do her when she went out for one of her many smoke breaks. Then he'd finish off the last three: the nurse at Cedars-Sinai, the fashion designer, and her mother.

He lingered over the photo of Bria Tanaka. He was intrigued by her almond-shaped hazel eyes and her golden-streaked brown hair. She reminded him of the first young woman he strangled on Cabrillo Beach years ago. It was his first kill, so it wasn't perfect. It was downright sloppy, but he was only fifteen, so he gave himself a break.

Eighteen months and five girls later, Lt. Alberto Zayas caught him dead to rights after a particularly satisfying kill. Zayas gave him a choice: life in San Quentin or join *Opus Christo* as a world-class assassin, second to none. It was a no-brainer.

Felix hated Alberto and every dumb fuck in *Opus Christos* from Cardinal De Posada on down, but he never regretted his decision. He was doing what he was born to do.

He felt a stirring of excitement as his hand slipped into his pants. As he stared at Bria's photo, he imagined her struggling beneath him, pleading pitifully as tears streamed down her face as he slowly strangled the life out of her.

He quickly revised his plan. He'd satiate his hunger by killing Bria Tanaka first. Then he'd take care of the other LA Holy Doves one by one before he moved on to his next *Opus Christos* assignment and more delicious ladies.

Chapter 7
12:25 A.M.
The Guardians of the Holy Doves

Our true self is waiting to be discovered.

-Judith the Elder

The Guardians of the Holy Doves' Command Center
Abbey Sainte-Victoire, Marseille, France

Isabella had been at *Abbey Sainte-Victoire* for three years, working directly under her friend and mentor, Father Patrick. She proudly wore a silver chain holding a gold crucifix, a Star of David, and a white enameled dove around her neck to declare her identity and lineage: a Catholic Hispanic American and a *Marrano*, a hidden Jew.

She first learned about Judith while researching a paper about the contributions of women to the founding of Christianity. An obscure comment sparked her curiosity and led her to ask her Comparative Religion professor, Father Patrick O'Neill, if he knew of any other sources, she could use to bolster her theory that the Messiah's message had been subtly modified to accommodate the cultural prejudices of the time that males were superior in God's eyes. At the same time, women of the early church were pushed into subservient roles in direct defiance of Christ's message of equality and acceptance.

Father Patrick looked at her thoughtfully for a minute, then nodded before leaning forward across his desk. "I wondered if and when you would discover the truth about your family."

"My family?"

"Yes. Your maternal line is directly descended from Sarah, the Messiah's youngest daughter."

Isabella sat there dumbfounded for a moment. "I don't know how to react to that information."

"The truth is known to only a few, but you deserve to know. The Messiah had three daughters: Leah, Rebecca, and Sarah. Judith the Elder was a close friend of the family and an early follower of the new faith. She quickly realized the girls were a serious stumbling block to the new faith's increasingly male-centric teachings."

"The Messiah was married and had three daughters?"

"Yes, but it's not the point of the story. Judith gathered eleven like-minded women around her, forming the Guardians of the Holy Doves to protect the girls. Together, they decided the girls needed to be taken far from Judea. Leah, the eldest, went to Egypt to establish the Holy Family's African branch. Rebecca, the middle child, was taken to Gaul to start the European line, and Sarah, the youngest, traveled to Antioch to begin the Asian branch of the family."

"You're saying I'm descended from Sarah?"

"Without question. Each Dove married and produced their own daughters while carefully hiding the truth of their identities. Within a few generations, the Messiah's family had forgotten their divine origins or dismissed their legacy as a family myth."

"If that's true, that the families forgot their origins, then how can you be sure I am a descendent of Sarah, a Holy Dove? It seems far-fetched, at best."

"Because the Guardians never forgot nor wavered in their commitment to God and the Holy Doves. For two thousand years, we have continued Judith's holy work. The scribes faithfully recorded the birth of each new child in Judith's Grand Accounting, always waiting for the Light, for the moment when God would call them to action to protect the Holy Dove and The Child-Who-Is-Coming."

It was at that moment that Isabella decided her path in life.

"So, how do I join the Guardians?" she asked Father Patrick.

"I brought you some decaf tea," said Father Patrick. "The kitchen staff is working frantically to keep everyone's caffeine levels on overload, and it's starting to show."

"Thanks," answered Isabella. "I need something to calm me down."

Father Patrick handed her the cup before he spoke. "You want to talk about it, Izzy?"

"No. Yes. I thought that once the Light filled the universe, *Opus Christos* would realize their outdated ideas of male superiority, wealth, and power were wrong. I thought they would see that their ideals are hateful and in opposition to God's true path for humanity."

"I wish that, too. But, Izzy, human history has been built upon one group of religious fanatics after another, committing unthinkable violence and cruelty in the name of God. *Opus Christos* is no different. They believe, as do all religious fanatics, that they alone are chosen to be God's moral and spiritual representatives on Earth. By murdering the Doves, they believe they will hide the truth and save the Church to continue as it always has. They would rather defy God than admit they are wrong."

"That's bullshit! All they want is to protect their wealth and sense of power!"

Father Patrick stretched his stocky six-foot-three-inch frame and ran his dark brown fingers inside his white clerical collar. "I agree that *Opus Christos'* philosophy is –ah– bovine excrement. But I remember what Sister Elizabeth said years ago: 'You must consider your opponent's motives and actions calmly and rationally. Only in this act of clarity will you find the path to defeat them.' It would serve us well to remember her words."

Jasper, the Guardians' IT department head, poked into Izzy's office. "Our agents are deployed and ready to secure the Doves. We're ahead of our projected schedule," he announced.

"Excellent, Jasper. Have we approached Brother Joseph?" asked Father Patrick.

"Orlando is on his way to Portland. He'll be at the monastery within four hours," answered Izzy.

"Four hours? Don't we have anyone closer?"

"First of all, it's still the middle of the night in Oregon. The monastery is not open to the public until the 6 a.m. mass. Secondly, I chose Orlando Dudley for a good reason," spoke up Izzy. "Brother Mark passed away last night soon after the Light, so that avenue of contact is closed. Brother Joseph and Orlando worked together at the CIA's Anti-Terrorism division along with Zayas. I felt Brother Joseph would accept the truth of his birthright if it came from Orlando."

"I apologize for second-guessing you, Izzy. Orlando? Have I met him?"

"About a year ago. Chinese American, five-eight, and built like a gymnast?"

Father Patrick O'Neill smiled. "Of course. Orlando Dudley. I remember thinking he must face the same reaction I get when people meet me and discover I'm a tall black man instead of a short, red-headed priest with an Irish brogue. It's funny and sad all at the same time," he said. "Have we learned of more attacks on the Doves?"

Before Izzy could respond, Jasper interrupted in his uncanny way of answering questions before they were even asked. He leaned his long, lanky body against the doorframe and pushed a lock of wayward light brown hair from his forehead before he spoke.

"We have several unconfirmed reports of the murders of Doves in Dublin, Jerusalem, and Mexico City. Felix killed a Holy Dove, an elderly nun, at the Convent of the Poor Sisters of St. Clare in Boston about eight hours ago," he said, his Texas twang belying the gravity of his words.

Father Patrick's face paled. "Are you sure it was Felix?"

"My team doesn't make mistakes," answered Jasper curtly. "We've hacked into the security tapes at Logan. We believe Felix boarded a flight to Los Angeles to meet Alberto Zayas, his *Opus Christos* handler. I'm not feeling good about this."

"I'm concerned about the LA Doves especially-," started Father Patrick.

Jasper interrupted him. "I've already pulled Father Claude out of Phoenix. He just boarded a non-stop to LAX. He'll team up with Milo as soon as he arrives. They'll approach Bria Tanaka and her mother and bring them to the Command Center as soon as possible. It's the safest course of action."

"Charter a jet. I want them here as quickly as possible."

Izzy turned to Father Patrick.

"Wait a minute! Why are we sending two of our best operatives, Milo and Father Claude, to focus on Bria Tanaka and her mother, Magdalena? There are six identified Doves in LA and over two hundred in North America. They are all in equal peril. It's irresponsible and a waste of our resources. Why Bria and Magdalena Tanaka? Why bring them here?"

"I have my reasons, Izzy," he said firmly, "Excellent reasons. First of all–."

Jasper nodded as one of his team members whispered to him before he cleared his throat loudly.

"Can I get a word in edgewise? You two can continue your adorable little spat later."

"Sorry," said Izzy and Father Patrick in unison.

"We have confirmed that Felix was on the United LA-bound flight that just landed at LAX."

"Call Milo and let him know. He'll need to be on top of his game when he picks up Father Claude," answered Father Patrick. "Remind him that Bria Tanaka and her mother are their only priority. They have to find Bria before Felix does."

"Already done," said Jasper. "We're ahead of you. But, then again, we usually are."

"Let's keep it that way, Jasper," answered Father Patrick as he swept out of Izzy's office to escape the questions about his interest in Bria Tanaka that he knew Izzy was about to ask.

Chapter 8
9:45 A.M.

Inanna, Bria, and Theo

The future depends on what you do today.

-Mahatma Gandhi

Los Angeles, California

It wasn't long before Bria and Theo relaxed in Inanna's presence. They presented each design sketch in-depth and listened as she suggested minor alterations.

"These two and the red swing coat and matching pencil skirt are yours, aren't they, Bri?" Inanna asked as she picked up two of the sketches. "And the cashmere jacket and matching slacks?"

Bria looked at Theo. "The collection is a collaborative effort."

Inanna looked at her and raised an eyebrow.

"I had the original concept for those designs," she said as she glanced at Theo, "but Theo did all the final touches."

"Don't pout, Theo. I can see your hand in them. I love the entire collection. I'll take all the pieces as soon as you finish them."

"Thank you," said Theo, releasing the breath he hadn't realized he had been holding.

"There is one change I would like, however," she said, turning to the mannequin wearing a black evening gown. "I don't wear black. So, perhaps, a different fabric?"

"Not a problem, we can certainly—" started Theo before Inanna interrupted him.

"I know exactly what I want!" she exclaimed. "I saw a bolt of fabric at Stefano and Domenico's, which would be perfect! They were saving it, but I'm sure they would give it to us if we asked."

"As in Stefano Gabbana and Domenico Dolce?" asked Theo with a catch in his voice.

"Of course, Theo. They are fashion designers like you and Bri. You must know them."

"Inanna, we're not in their league. I don't have the slightest idea of how to contact them."

"You are in their league or will be one day." She shook the design drawings she held. "I think it will be best to ask them in person."

"But they're in Italy," Theo pointed out.

"Of course they are. I'll call my pilot to prepare the jet while you and Bria gather your personal items and passports. I assume you do have passports?"

"Ah, yes," stammered Bria, "but I've never used it. I'm not even sure where it is."

"In your underwear drawer under the lacy panties and bra set, the ones with tags still on."

"I'm not going to ask you how you know that."

"It's probably best you don't."

"I'm sorry, Inanna," Bria said, ignoring Theo. "It sounds wonderful, but I can't go. My mother needs me during the night. I can't find someone on such short notice to care for her. I'm sorry."

Inanna waved her hand to dismiss Bria's concerns. "Because of her arthritis? This trip will do her a world of good. I promise. You both design beautiful clothing, but only a seamstress of your mother's caliber will know how to make your designs perfect. Tell her I will not take no for an answer."

Both Bria and Theo stared at her with their mouths open.

"Close your mouths and get moving. We're leaving for Rome in two hours," Inanna said as she stood up and swept out of the showroom without a word. She accepted her driver's outstretched hand and lowered herself into the Lamborghini.

"So," he whispered in her ear, "Is she the one?"

Inanna smiled. "Yes, Gabriel, she is the one. She's the Holy Dove."

Chapter 9
11:55 A.M.

The Guardians of the Holy Doves

There is no good reason good can't triumph over evil, if only angels will get organized along the lines of the mafia.

- Kurt Vonnegut

Guardians' Command Center
Abbey Sainte-Victoire Marseille, France

Izzy's face was devoid of color as she pulled the phone away from her ear to look at Father Patrick.

"*Opus Christos* has Brother Joseph," she said. "When Orlando arrived at the Monastery, Brother Joseph was already gone. The Abbot said he left with Alberto Zayas, Cardinal De Posada's *capo*."

"It may not be as bad as you think, Izzy. Alberto would have killed him immediately if they knew his true identity as the Son of the Doves."

Izzy started to gesture for Jasper to join them. As usual, Jasper walked into her office before she could open her mouth.

"Alberto was Brother Joseph's roommate at Notre Dame," said Jasper.

"Joseph went to the CIA Academy in Virginia after graduation. Zayas joined the Firm three years later. He was assigned to Joseph's Anti-Terrorism Task Force. When Joseph's detailed exposé about hunting down *Al Qaeda* members became a worldwide bestseller, his family was murdered in retaliation. He joined the Trappists out of either grief or remorse. Maybe both." Soon after, Alberto Zayas left the CIA under a cloud. He became an LAPD homicide detective for a while. We believe he was a member of *Opus Christos* even before he was in college, considering his close relationship with Cardinal De Posada," continued Jasper. "The question is, what's he up to?"

"I hate it when you do that," exclaimed Izzy, "I really, really hate it."

"Do what?" asked Jasper as he turned and returned to his desk without waiting for an answer.

Izzy shook her head in aggravation. "Damn mind reader," she murmured under her breath.

"Jasper's right. *Opus Christos* is planning to use Joseph for something else," said Father Patrick.

"Ask Orlando if the Abbot overheard their conversation. Maybe he knows something."

Izzy spoke into the phone and hung it up. "He'll call us back."

Jasper poked his head into Izzy's office again. "What do you need?"

Izzy stared at him for a moment before speaking. "Check all flights out of PDX and see if Zayas and Brother Joseph boarded a plane. We have to find out where they're going."

"We're already on it, Izzy. Anything else?"

"Rental cars?"

Jasper slowly closed his eyes as he filled his lungs with air and pushed it out of his nostrils in a gush. "Come on, Izzy. Give us some credit," he said as he turned and walked away. He did that a lot.

"I was afraid that something like this would happen," said

Izzy, looking sternly at Father Patrick. "We should have approached Brother Joseph a long time ago."

"The Council felt Joseph was safer in the monastery than in the outside world. We had Brother Mark to watch over him. His true identity is known to only the highest-ranking members of the Guardians," Father Patrick said as he paced across the room. "It's impossible that *Opus Christos* learned about his true identity as the Son of the Dove."

"Nearly impossible," answered Izzy, "but not impossible."

"Impossible," said Father Patrick firmly, "if *Opus Christos* had known he was the Son of the Dove, they would have killed him years ago. We're missing something."

Izzy started to respond, but they heard Jasper congratulating himself loudly. Seconds later, he popped his head into Izzy's office again.

"Private airport in Newberg, Oregon," he crowed, "a man matching Alberto's description and a Trappist monk boarded a Cessna Citation M2 20 minutes ago."

"Where are they heading?"

"They wouldn't tell me, but the M2's range is slightly over 1500 miles. Pretty much anywhere in the Western United States."

"Los Angeles?" asked Father Patrick.

"Los Angeles is within the M2's range, but so are San Francisco, Las Vegas, Seattle, Phoenix, Salt Lake City, or Denver. Dallas or Houston and, with a stop to re-fuel, all points east. The possibilities are endless."

Father Patrick thought for a minute before speaking. "Do whatever you must, Jasper; just find them. We must get Brother Joseph away from *Opus Christos* as soon as possible."

Chapter 10
11:55 A.M.
Father Claude

God considered not action but the spirit of the action. It is the intention, not the deed, wherein the merit or praise of the doer consists.

—Peter Abelard (1079–1142)

Los Angeles International Airport

Father Claude, a member of the Guardian of the Holy Doves and the Order of the Knights Templar, ran his thin fingers through his closely cropped gray hair before spraying it with a temporary Chestnut Brown coloring in the airport bathroom.

He removed the secondhand beige suit to reveal red cargo shorts and a tie-dyed tee shirt underneath. Dumping the brown leather shoes and the suit in the trash, he slipped a pair of worn blue vans from his backpack and put on a pair of mirrored Ray-Bans.

Satisfied he looked different enough, he left the men's room and wandered through the LAX arrivals area, discreetly checking for *Opus Christos* agents. Either his disguise was working, or he had shaken the man following him in Phoenix.

Five Doves had been on his list in Arizona. He had only

approached one of the Doves before Jasper re-assigned him to Los Angeles to team up with Milo to secure a young Dove named Bria Tanaka. It seemed irresponsible to him to assign two agents to one young woman, but an order was an order.

A smile crossed his face as he remembered the thin, worn-out-before-her-time woman he had surprised as she was picking worm-eaten tomatoes in a raggedy garden alongside a tumbled-down house in South Mountain outside of Phoenix. She stood up slowly and brushed the dirt from her hands.

"You coming to try and kill me, too?" she asked in a flat and monotone voice as she pulled an ancient Colt revolver from her apron pocket and pointed it at him. "Probably not one of your best ideas."

Father Claude was taken aback. "I'm a Guardian of the Holy Doves. I've been sent to save you."

She looked him up and down. "Yeah," she said, lowering the Colt, "I had a feeling I might meet one of you Guardians after I saw the Light last night."

"You know the truth of your heritage? I thought that knowledge died out centuries ago."

She shrugged. "Maybe some families forgot, or their lines died off, but we remembered."

"And, for all those centuries, not one of your family members ever shared the truth with others?"

"A few did. They were either burned at the stake as heretics or locked away as crazy. You don't claim you're a descendant of the Messiah without retribution. It's a dangerous secret."

"It would be. I'm here to offer you sanctuary before *Opus Christos* sends someone to kill you."

"A bit late for that," she answered as she stepped to the left and revealed a crumbled body hiding behind her. "I dragged the other one's body in there," she said, pointing to a rickety shed,

"I'm thinking we probably should do something about them before we leave."

Father Claude helped her bury the men in the middle of her garden. He took the silver crosses worn by *Opus Christos* members from their necks before he drove the woman to a nondescript pickup truck, waiting on a dusty back road, that would take her to safety. She never asked his name or where she was going. Maybe it didn't matter. Perhaps she was glad to escape her sad life and drunken husband.

He thought fleetingly about Jasper telling him that Felix, *Opus Christos'* most notorious assassin, was also on his way to LAX. It did complicate matters considerably, but getting the young Dove, Bria Tanaka, safely out of harm's way was paramount.

He and Milo would do whatever they had to, even if it meant facing the legendary Felix.

Chapter 11
1:30 P.M.

Bria, Theo, Magdalena, Inanna, & Gabriel

Coincidence is God's way of remaining anonymous.

-Albert Einstein

Van Nuys Airport Van Nuys, California

Theo leaped out of the Uber and grabbed their bags before he ushered Bria and Magdalena into the terminal. Within seconds, a six-foot-tall, handsome young man with perfect skin and blond ringlets surrounding his head approached them.

"You're the Lamborghini's driver!" Theo said excitedly, "I'd love to give it a spin!"

Gabriel ignored him as if he hadn't spoken. "Inanna is already aboard. Follow me," he said as he placed the bags on a cart.

With a shrug of his shoulders, Theo gestured for Magdalena and Bria to follow Gabriel as he brought up the rear. "Guess he's not talking to me," he whispered. "His loss."

"Isn't he the most beautiful man you've ever seen?" Magdalena whispered back.

"Besides me, you mean? Just wait until you see Inanna, Miss Maggi May," Theo answered as he barely missed running into a monk in a white robe covered by the brown apron of a Trappist.

"I'm so sorry, Sir, I mean Brother," stammered Theo, thanking his Catholic education for the first time. "I wasn't paying attention to where I was going. Please accept my apologies."

The monk stopped and smiled at Theo. "It was nothing, young man. "God's blessings," he said kindly, "to you and your friends."

"God's blessings to you, Brother Joseph," Gabriel answered. "You're going to need them."

◆ ◆ ◆

Brother Joseph, Alberto Zayas, and Felix

Felix was waiting at the curbside passenger loading zone for Alberto Zayas and Brother Joseph to arrive. He stood stiffly by the unmarked black Ford for several minutes until one of the airport's rent-a-cops directed him to move on. Felix flashed a forged CIA identification card and stared him down. The man walked away quickly. Nothing like good forgeries, he thought.

He watched as a young man with bleach-blonde hair stepped out of a black Uber and helped two women, one older and one younger, exit the car. Something about them felt familiar, but Felix was distracted by Alberto Zayas and the monk leaving the terminal. Alberto did not acknowledge or guide his robed companion toward the car. He didn't notice when the young man bumped into Brother Joseph. Alberto didn't even look at the young man's two female companions. A laugh escaped as Felix realized the women were Bria Tanaka and her mother, Magdalena. It amused him more than he could explain as a smirk played across his lips.

Brother Joseph followed Alberto, matching his movements step-by-step as if he had no more substance than a shadow. Still, Felix thought, there was something else inside the man, something primal and explosive. Felix almost saw it rising in translucent waves like heat from a desert roadway.

Alberto pushed past him, dropping his bag at Felix's feet before he entered the car without a word. Dismissing Felix as unimportant was a mistake, and his anger rose. There would be plenty of time to change sides, he decided. He could tell Brother Joseph the truth about *Opus Christos,* their plan to murder the Holy Doves, and how they would use him to blame Islamic terrorists.

Loyalty was always granted to the highest bidder. The Guardians, Felix was positive, had bottomless pockets.

Chapter 12
1:45 P.M.

Bria, Theo, Magdalena, Inanna, and Gabriel

Precisely because we cannot predict the moment, we must be ready at all times.

—C.S. Lewis

The Van Nuys Airport

There was something surreal about flying private instead of commercial, Theo thought as they climbed the red-carpeted stairway to the Gulfstream 650ER. No lines. No grumpy TSA agent scoped him out like he was a criminal. No long walks down corridors that never seemed to end. He stopped at the top of the stairs and sighed contentedly. He could get used to this.

Bria had been carefully watching her mother as she slowly navigated the jet's retractable stairs, but she turned around at that exact moment and laughed at Theo.

"This is going to spoil you forever, Mr. Fancy-pants," she said.

"Yup," agreed Theo as he stepped inside. "My days of Southwest flights are officially over."

Their golden-haired escort dropped their bags near a teakwood closet and turned to them.

"My name is Gabriel. We should be taking off within the next fifteen minutes," he said as he led them into the spacious main cabin.

"Oh my goodness," blurted out Magdalena as she saw the airplane's interior. The cabin, with its white carpets, matching leather chairs, and teakwood tables set with fresh white flower arrangements, looked like a photograph in *Architectural Digest.* "This must be what heaven looks like!"

"Not in the least," said Gabriel, "but it was the best I could do in the short time allowed."

Inanna appeared from the plane's rear in a vintage Dior pajama set in the palest shade of gold.

"Gabriel, stop being snippy. She meant it as a compliment," she scolded. "You must be Bri's mother, Magdalena," she said, taking Magdalena's hand, "I can see where she gets her beauty."

Magdalena blushed. "Thank you, but I'm afraid I wouldn't have held a candle to her even in my heyday. She's my beautiful little dove."

Gabriel and Inanna looked startled.

"How did you know," questioned Gabriel sharply, "that she is a Dove?"

Magdalena looked at Gabriel, confused. "A dove? As a baby, she'd lay in her cradle and coo non-stop. I called her my little dove. The nickname stuck. She's my sweet dove."

"A childhood nickname? How charming," answered Inanna as she caught Gabriel's eyes to caution him to let it go, just as an attractive older man in a well-fitting uniform interrupted them.

"Excuse me, Madam. We've received clearance to depart in fifteen minutes. May I ask you and your guests to be seated?" he asked, his Swiss-German accent subtly indicating that it wasn't a question.

"Of course, Stefan," answered Inanna as she pointed to the white leather seats.

Theo and Magdalena took the two oversized ivory leather chairs nearest the front. Theo helped Magdalena with her seatbelt as Inanna pointed to a matching set across the cabin.

"Sit with me, Bri," she said as Gabriel leaned over and helped Inanna with her seatbelt.

"I'll be back when we're cleared to move about," Gabriel said.

"See what I mean, Magdalena?" whispered Theo. "They're so beautiful; even the captain is a silver fox. I feel like I'm stuck in the middle of a fashion shoot, and I'm the before photo."

She nodded her head in agreement. "So true, Theo. They don't even look like real people."

It was several minutes before the captain's voice came over the intercom. "We have reached cruising altitude of forty-two thousand feet. Our flight time is estimated at 10 hours 41 minutes, making our arrival at approximately 3:00 a.m. tomorrow Central European Standard Time. We will have a short layover in Atlanta to refuel and do a safety check before we cross the Atlantic."

"Please feel free to move around while I prepare lunch," said Gabriel as he reentered the cabin. "Would you prefer Lobster Thermidor with rice pilaf or New York Steak with a black-pepper glaze and asparagus?"

"Can I say both?" Theo asked, got up, and walked over to the bar. Gabriel shook his head and shot him a disgusted look before he returned to the galley. "I guess that was a hard *no*," he grumbled. "Ladies, may I make you a cocktail or pour you a glass of wine?"

Bria looked at Inanna, who was struggling to undo her seatbelt. She reached over to help her.

"Is that all right?" she asked. "We don't want to step on Gabriel's toes."

"Gabriel might kiss Theo on the top of his head to have one less thing to do." She lowered her voice to a whisper. "He can be unbearably vain and lazy if you give him half a chance."

Bria giggled. "He is unbelievably beautiful, you have to admit."

"Physical beauty is fleeting at best, Bri. One should never rely upon it," answered Inanna.

"Ladies," said Theo, bowing low while balancing a tray with four crystal wine glasses, "May I offer you a Château Haut-Brion Blanc while we wait for lunch?"

"I thought you'd never ask," said Inanna, taking a glass.

"Try taking ladylike sips instead of gulping it down like a thirsty truck driver like you usually do, Bri," Theo whispered, "I can almost guarantee that we'll never be able to afford to drink Château Haut-Brion Blanc again in our natural lifetimes."

Chapter 13
1:45 P.M.
Father Claude & Milo

*In all men is evil sleeping; the good man is he who will not awaken
it, in himself or in other men.*

—Mary Renault
The Praise Singer (1978)

Los Angeles International Airport

Father Claude checked his watch before he walked to a baggage-
claim carousel. Milo was late, which was worrying since *Opus
Christos* had a heavy presence in Los Angeles. If Milo didn't show
up soon, he'd sneak away and find a quiet place to call Izzy so she
could devise an alternate plan.

He knew staying in one place was dangerous unless he wanted
to be spotted. *Opus Christos* agents would be crawling all over the
airport searching for him by now. Looking around, he noticed that
a flight from Maui, if he was right about the passengers' colorful
Hawaiian shirts and leis, had just entered the baggage area. He
picked out a willowy, raven-haired young woman struggling under
the weight of two tote bags. He walked quickly to her side.

"You've been fighting with those from the plane. I was just
too far back to offer to help you," he said, implying that he had
been on the flight from Hawaii, "Let me carry them for you."

A look of caution crossed her face for just a second, but the weight of her bags allowed her concern about his motives to pass quickly. She smiled as she handed Father Claude her bags.

"Thank you. They're cumbersome. Do you need a ride somewhere? My car's in the parking lot just over there," she said, her voice accented with a slight Spanish lilt. "It's the least I can do."

"The least I can do," Father Claude said, "is walk you safely to your car. Then I'll take a taxi to the Hyatt at the Airport, but thank you for the offer."

"I insist," she said. "It's no trouble. I'm driving right by there. I'm Maria. What's your name?"

"Thomas," answered Father Claude, "but my friends call me Thomas."

Maria laughed. "Okay, Thomas, my car's in the garage across the roadway. I have a funny feeling that this is a day we'll remember for the rest of our lives."

Father Claude thought she was a good cover. *Opus Christos* was looking for a gray-haired man in clerical garb traveling alone, not a happy couple returning from vacation. With any luck, he'd slip right under their noses.

The young woman chattered on about her vacation as she led them to a bright yellow Jeep with a white and yellow striped canvas top on the third level of the garage. Father Claude laughed as he saw it. It was a perfect getaway vehicle, so eye-catching that any professional would discount this gaudy lemon Jeep without a second glance.

He placed her tote bags through the open space where the windows should have been, lowering them to the floor behind the front seats. Then he backed away and gave her a shy little wave before turning and walking to the elevator. "Nice to have met you, Maria," he said.

"Come on, Thomas," she said, "it's silly to pay for a cab. I'm driving right by your hotel."

Father Claude smiled as he climbed into the passenger seat. "You sure it's okay?"

"It's very convenient," she said, "No problem at all."

She turned the key in the ignition, revved the engine, and smiled. The tires squealed on the warm pavement as she pulled out of the tight parking spot. He grabbed the roll bar as she started for the downward spiral that led to the ground floor, driving at a speed several times the posted limit. The Jeep leaned dangerously close to the outside concrete wall of the ramp as he planted his feet against the dashboard and tightened his grip on the roll bar.

He had seriously considered that he might not live out the week, but never once, he thought, as she took the next turn, had he imagined being crushed to death under a yellow and white Jeep on the down ramp of the LAX Parking Garage.

Suddenly, she slammed on the brakes, barely missing the rear bumper of a blue Toyota. Father Claude's body pitched forward. His knees pushed into his chest and knocked the wind out of him. Her eyes were sparkling with excitement as he raised his to meet hers.

There is a smell that precludes death, a tingling in your brain that foretells imminent danger that is unmistakable. Father Claude smelled it as the ominous hiss of a bullet sliding from the silencer registered in his conscious brain. He jerked his head toward the woman as her body slumped against the steering wheel.

The impact of a high-caliber bullet had blown away the back of her head. The yellow and white awning of the Jeep was spattered bright red, and he felt a stream of warm, sticky liquid sliding down the left side of his face and shoulders. He tugged at the jammed seatbelt that held him firmly in place. He closed his eyes and waited to hear the next deadly hiss of the silencer as a hand reached around him. He felt the cold of a steel blade against his neck as the seatbelt was cut loose.

"Father Claude, you stupid son-of-a-bitch, don't just sit there! Run!"

He did as he was told without a second thought. He ran like a son-of-a-bitch, following the man sprinting out of the garage to an old, beat-up, white Chevy cargo van already pulling away from the curb. He pushed himself beyond his endurance, increasing his speed with the last ounce of energy as he flung himself through the open cargo door. He hit the metal floor with a thud and felt the transmission vibrations as the driver shifted gears. He lay there, face down, waiting for whatever happened next.

"You know, *Padre*, it's a damn good thing that you're a priest," said the voice from the driver's seat, "because you can't pick women worth shit!"

Father Claude pushed himself up on his elbows and crawled toward the front of the van. It took him several seconds to catch his breath before he spoke.

"Milo, it's a miracle that the Guardians accepted you, considering your filthy mouth."

The young man chuckled as he reached back with his right hand to help Father Claude crawl into the passenger seat.

"You should thank your skinny little *culo* that God cares more about my heart than my language. Otherwise, they'd be picking up your shit-for-brains off the pavement instead of hers," answered Milo as he checked the outside mirrors, pushed his hair out of his eyes, and slid the van across three lanes of traffic onto an access road that was parallel to the southernmost runway.

"The damn place was crawling with beautiful women," he continued, "and who do you pick up? Goddamn Maria Veronica of Seville! After Felix, she's *Opus Christos'* top assassin, you dumb *pedazo de mierda.* You gave me a frigging heart attack! I had you well covered, and then you walked right up to Maria Veronica of Seville! Let me repeat that, Father Claude, goddamn Maria Veronica of Seville! All the *Opus Christos* agents standing around watching for you were laughing their fucking heads off!"

Father Claude patiently waited for Milo's laughter to wind down. He pulled off the bloody t-shirt and wiped splattered brains from his hair. "Happy me almost dying, amused you," he answered.

"I got her and two others, but God only knows how many of those bastards I didn't get. In case you hadn't fucking noticed, not only is *Opus Christos* going to be crawling all over LA looking for us, but my little handiwork is going to bring every cop in the state of California down our throats. Not to mention airport security and the Feds. We got a big-time major, fucking problem."

Father Claude nodded in acknowledgment, "That isn't good."

"You think? You think 'that isn't good?'" Milo asked sarcastically as he looked at Father Claude in the dim light of the van. "Shit, you're a mess."

He reached down, pulled a half-empty bottle of Evian water and a filthy rag from under the driver's seat, and poured the water over Father Claude's head before handing him the rag.

"Do me a favor, *cabrón*," Milo said, "duck the next time. *Lo entiendes?*"

Before Father Claude could respond, the van came to a screeching halt. Milo quickly opened the driver's door and beckoned him to follow.

"*Vamos, Padre,*" he said, "we've got to get rid of this van like yesterday." He pulled out his cell phone as they walked into a seedy-looking biker bar.

"Order us a couple of brewskis. The bartender's name is Skull. Tell him you're with me; he probably won't shoot you. I got a call to make."

"Izzy?"

"Who else would you suggest I call? The X-men? Hell, yes, I'm calling Izzy. Maybe she can figure out how to get us the fuck out of Dodge. After the screw-up at the airport, I'm pretty much out of ideas."

Chapter 14
2:45 P.M.

Inanna and Bria

Nearly all the best things that came to me in life have been unexpected

-Carl Sandburg

42,000 feet above Socorro, New Mexico

"That," exclaimed Theo, "was amazing. I couldn't manage another bite!"

"You ate your Lobster Thermidor and half my mother's steak," scolded Bria.

"A manly appetite for a manly man," answered Theo as he wiggled his eyebrows.

"It is a great compliment to the chef," said Inanna, turning toward Gabriel, "it was delicious."

Gabriel nodded, smiling slightly at Inanna's compliment as he removed the dishes from the table. He turned to Magdalena. "I took the liberty to make up the bedrooms. I thought you might want to rest."

"Bedrooms?"

"Oh dear," said Inanna. "In our rush to leave, I neglected to give you the grand tour. There are three suites in the front of the plane and my suite in the rear. I rarely sleep on these long trips, so hopefully, I won't bother you if I'm further back. There is a big-screen TV with Wi-Fi access in the main cabin and a few movies that have not yet been released. I hope they will interest you. If not, ask Gabriel; he can supply you with anything you want to pass the next few hours."

Magdalena stood up stiffly and placed her napkin near her plate. "A nap does sound lovely. Perhaps Gabriel could show me where I might do that?"

With Magdalena resting in her suite and Theo sprawled in front of the TV watching an action movie, Inanna turned to Bria.

"I think a coffee would be perfect right now, don't you?" she said as she looked at the DeLonghi espresso machine with a puzzled expression.

"These machines can be confusing, Inanna. Why don't I take over? It can't be much different from our Keurig at the office."

"It looked easier when I started," Inanna said with a smile. "I might have to give Gabriel a raise."

It took a couple of tries and a glance at the instruction manual, but Bria soon produced two perfect cups of espresso. She proudly passed one to Inanna.

"Shall we take these into my suite? It's quite comfortable, and we'll hear ourselves think without the background explosions of whatever awful thing Theo's watching."

"I think it's the new Avengers movie," answered Bria. "He loves all that blood and gore stuff. I don't understand it. He's a gentle guy in real life. Go figure."

"I have found that males are inexplicably fascinated by violence. It is a design flaw, as Azrael has repeatedly mentioned," she said as she led Bria to the suite at the rear of the jet.

The creams and teakwood of the main cabin were reflected in the decor of Inanna's suite, but it was somehow more ethereal and feminine. Bria felt immediately at ease as she sat down across from

Inanna. She placed her espresso on the low teakwood table between them.

"Azrael? Is that your husband?"

Inanna laughed. "No, Azrael has worked for us forever."

"What's your husband like?" asked Bria, hoping she wouldn't be offended after all the personal questions Inanna had asked earlier. "He must be quite amazing to be married to a woman like you."

"I prefer to call him my partner," answered Inanna thoughtfully. "The word 'husband' has historically implied that I am his subservient property, at least to my ear. However, some women use the term as a badge of honor; 'my husband this and my husband that.' You know the type. What would you like to know about him, Bria?"

"The regular stuff, I guess," answered Bria, relieved that Inanna didn't seem offended by her questions. "How did you meet? What's his name? How long have you been together? What does he do?"

Inanna nodded her head. "We have been together forever. I can't remember a time without him. He and I complement each other perfectly; equals but opposites in all ways. We are two halves of a single whole."

"Isn't that what they say to brides and grooms in Christian weddings? Two becomes one?"

"That does sound familiar, but I believe it's a lofty, rarely obtainable goal, " Inanna answered. "You asked me his name. He, like I, has many. I occasionally call him Joe to tease him, but he doesn't like it. It offends his dignity."

She paused to think. "But I don't think anyone calls him anything at all. He's usually called 'Sir,' or they use his title, 'Lord,' I imagine. I've never paid much attention. What does he do? Everything I choose not to do, while I do everything he chooses not to do or believes is beneath his notice."

"But you must love him to be with him so long."

"There are many definitions of love, Bri. Most have nothing to do with romance. I respect him, although he irritates me as I do him at times. I understand him, as does no one else in the universe. He attempts to understand me, which is difficult for him, but he occasionally tries."

Inanna took another sip of her espresso and smiled. "We are so very different, I'm afraid. He is ruled by logic and order, while I am driven by creativity and emotion. We see everything from opposite sides of the spectrum."

"That must be challenging," said Bria.

"It is. His solution to everything is to check the rules and regulations in one of his tens of thousands of rulebooks. He invents a new one if he can't find an applicable regulation. He hates change and resists it with every fiber of his being. I find it all a horrible waste of time and energy. I don't care a fig about his rules and regulations. I rarely overthink things. If I have an idea, I move forward to see what happens. I am fascinated by change and new ideas, especially those that surprise me."

"You're the creative one, and he administers your businesses?"

"Exactly. On rare occasions when one of my projects starts going wrong, he never wonders how to fix it. He ends it without a backward glance, while I will spend an eternity figuring out how to make things right. I get too emotionally involved to give up easily. It drives him crazy."

"He sounds interesting," said Bria.

"Believe me, he isn't," said Inanna. "He's quite boring. However, we tolerate each other's quirks. Or, more honestly, I tolerate his idiosyncrasies while he struggles to tolerate mine. I listen to his concerns and pretend that I will consider them seriously. Then, I do whatever I think is best. But, ultimately, we both understand that we would be nothing without the other."

"Do you have friends to talk to when it seems overwhelming? It helps to have someone who will listen when life gets too much."

"Not really. Everyone I know works for us in one way or another."

"Well," said Bria, reaching out and touching Inanna's hand, "If you ever need to talk, I'm willing to listen."

Inanna looked down at Bria's hand on hers. "That's sweet, Bria. I'll remember you said that. I might do it someday."

"I hope I didn't overstep by asking about your personal life," Bria said. "Sometimes, my curiosity gets the better of me. I've been told that I can occasionally ignore people's boundaries."

Inanna placed her cup on the saucer and stood. "Of course not. I rarely get to speak so frankly. I'm never sure if someone in our circle is more loyal to him than me. It was refreshing being so open and truthful for once. It also allowed me to know a bit more about you. We often learn more about a person by the questions they ask rather than by the statements they make."

She smiled and graciously extended her hand to dismiss Bria from her presence.

"Gabriel will show you to your stateroom. It's a long flight. With the time change, we will arrive in Rome early tomorrow. We have a big day ahead of us. There will be new people to meet and unexpected opportunities for you to consider. I want you to be rested and at your best."

Chapter 15
4:45 P.M.

Milo and Father Claude

Good can exist without evil, whereas evil cannot exist without good.

—St. Thomas Aquinas

Los Angeles, California

"I feel like an idiot," said Father Claude, climbing off the black Harley. He pulled off the helmet decorated with a skull and crossbones and adjusted the black leather chaps worn over his ripped jeans.

"Well, those sweet little *senoritas* at the last stoplight thought you were bitchin'," said Milo as he looked back at the candy apple red, metallic flake chopper he was riding. "Anyway, Izzy said to be on the down low. This is about as down and as low as we can go."

"You've got interesting friends, Milo."

"Best in the world," answered Milo as he ran his fingers through his brown hair, cut in California Surfer style that fell into layers of individual waves that looked seemingly unkempt but were expensively cut and styled to maintain the casual I-don't-care look. "If *Opus Christos* traces us to the bar, I guarantee they won't walk out in one piece. They might not walk out at all. It's a win-win," he said as he slapped his leg with a resounding whack and laughed.

"Let's get this show on the road, *Padre*. We've got a fashion designer and her mother to take with us if they agree to come with us or to kidnap if they don't. It will be dark enough in a half-hour to approach the house safely and sneak them out before anyone realizes what we're doing."

Forty-five minutes later, Father Claude stared at the house on West Adams where Izzy said Bria and her mother lived after a quick check at the design studio revealed it was empty and locked up tight.

"Nobody's here. Where are they?"

"Damn," answered Milo, "I left my crystal ball in my other pants. Izzy wants us to wait for them to show up. Father Patrick is adamant we secure Bria and her mother tonight." He looked up and down the block. "But we're sitting ducks on this dead-end street. We need to move the bikes."

Father Claude pointed to a walking path leading to a West Adams parking lot. "Over there?"

"We can get tacos," Milo suggested, pointing to the food truck, "while we watch the house."

"Good idea. The parking lot at the end of the street gives us a decent vantage point, and we won't be scaring the neighbors sitting in front of their houses in these ridiculous outfits."

"This is LA, dude. We're the height of style," said Milo as he glanced down at his studded Levi jacket, "and I look smoking hot," he said as he pulled his visor down, "You, not so much."

"You can say what you like," Milo said minutes later, leaning against the motorcycle, his mouth full of *carne adovada burrito,* "but there ain't nothing better than good old American home cooking."

"Except this is Mexican food from a bright green and orange food truck."

"We're in LA, Bro. This is SoCal food at its best; our version of American home cooking."

Father Claude looked at Bria's house and dropped his taco. "Milo, someone's going in the gate, but I don't think it's Bria or Magdalena. Maybe the housekeeper?"

"Because she's Mexican?" asked Milo, "That's more than a little offensive, *Pendejo*."

"No, Milo, because she's carrying a vacuum."

"Yeah, okay, there is that. One of us should go and talk to her."

"Really, Milo? Looking like this? She'll double-lock the door and call the cops as soon as she takes one look at us. Come up with something better."

The woman opened the front door and walked down the steps, followed by a tiny black and white dog on a pink leash. Milo looked around quickly at the other people waiting for tacos.

"Give me a second," he said as he pulled out his wallet. He returned in a moment, leading a brown mutt of questionable parentage. "Say hello to *Chula*," he said. "The most expensive rental dog in LA. $100 for 20 minutes. I'm going to take this cutie on a walk. Watch and learn, Father Claude."

When the papillon completed his business, the woman turned and ran head-on into Milo. Father Claude could tell by her body language that Milo was making an impression on her as he fumbled with *Chula's* leash, which wrapped around his ankles and tripped him. She laughed at his clumsiness and bent down to help him. It soon seemed that she was more interested in Milo than the dogs.

He lost sight of them briefly as a black Nissan with darkened windows drove slowly down the block and pulled into the driveway next door to Bria's. The man, his face covered with a hoodie and laden with several large grocery bags, got out and walked toward the back of the house.

Just a neighbor returning home after work decided Father

Claude. He relaxed as he watched Milo and the woman pull out their phones to exchange numbers. He shook his head. Milo was irrepressible.

A few minutes later, Milo returned the rental dog, shook the owner's hand, and walked over to Father Claude. He retrieved the bottle of Corona sitting on the picnic table and took a long sip.

"She's the housekeeper, Carmen. She's walking the dog because Bria and her mother left on the last-minute trip to Rome with an important client," Milo reported.

"Rome, Italy? They went to Italy? We need to let Izzy know so she can book us a flight tonight."

"I'm ready," said Milo, pulling his passport from his back pocket.

"You carry your passport on you?"

Milo smiled as he dropped the empty beer bottle into the recycling bin.

"It's Southern California, Bro. You never know when you might end up at a party in Tijuana. Easy to get into Mexico. Bitch to get out without your papers. A smart man is always ready to party."

A loud explosion shook the house, breaking all the windows and shattering the door. Shards of wood and glass flew in the air but miraculously missed Carmen as she bent over to release Kilo's leash at the front gate. It was almost as if God was watching, she thought, as she crossed herself before bursting into tears.

As Milo and Father Claude ran toward the house, the front porch burst into flames, and the black Nissan pulled out of the driveway next door. The driver stuck his arm out the window and flipped them off before he sped away.

"Oh shit," said Milo as he sprinted toward Bria's house with Father Claude close behind him, "That was Felix."

Chapter 16
6:30 P.M.

Brother Joseph, Felix, Hilmi Al-Jafri

The size of the lie is a definite factor in causing it to be believed for the vast masses [are) easy prey to a big lie.

—Adolf Hitler
Mein Kampf

Altria Senior Care Home,
Pasadena, California

A blast of cool air hit Brother Joseph and Felix as soon as they entered the Nursing Home's lobby. They walked towards the glassed-in window, where a heavy-set black woman was seated behind the desk. She reached up and slid the window open, the glass grating on the metal framework.

"Hilmi Al-Jafri? Hand your weapons over. I'll return them after your visit."

Brother Joseph looked at her with admiration. "You knew whom we wished to visit even though we have never been here before."

"Experience," she said, "Mr. Al-Jafri's visitors are in a class by themselves."

"Please be assured, " he turned to Felix, "we have no weapons. I'm an old friend of Hilmi."

She pulled herself upright and didn't hide her aura of disbelief. "You and Mr. Al-Jafri are friends? You're a Catholic monk." She pointed her chin at Felix. "And you smell like a cop. Hilmi's ninety-two, for goodness' sake. What could have that old man done to have the cops sniffing around?"

"As I said, we are friends."

She glanced at the clock. "You have about half an hour until his dinner. I wouldn't expect much if I were you. He's not all there most of the time. He probably won't remember you."

Hilmi Al-Jafri was sitting in a wheelchair and staring out the window into the courtyard garden. He seemed so much smaller than Brother Joseph remembered. He stood patiently waiting for Hilmi to turn and acknowledge their presence. In Islamic circles, Al-Jafri was an honored elder. To approach without being bidden to do so would have been disrespectful to his advanced age and position.

Al-Jafri slowly unfolded his hands and beckoned them forward without turning to look at his visitors. Joseph bent down and gently touched his cheek to the older man's, the traditional greeting honoring him as his elder and teacher. Silently, he stood waiting for Al-Jafri to speak.

His voice, when he finally spoke, was unwavering. "I knew an old friend was coming, but my angel is a trickster. He holds back pieces of his knowledge. I wasn't sure it would be you."

Joseph lowered himself to kneeling so as not to tower over Al-Jafri.

"Your flight? It was comfortable?"

Brother Joseph showed no surprise at Al-Jafri's question. "Quite comfortable."

Hilmi Al-Jafri laughed. "You keep me humble, Joseph. You have been missed."

"As have you, my friend."

"I have little time left for polite small talk and less to be consumed by curiosity. My angel spoke only in riddles to tell me of your coming."

"I have questions."

"We all have questions, Joseph. What makes you think I have the answers?"

"It is only my hope. "

Felix moved impatiently, shifting his weight from one side to the other, bored with the ritual politeness of conversation between the two men.

"The little I know is of no interest to the police."

"I need your wisdom, Hilmi. Many innocent women have died. Many more may die. The officer knows more than I do. It would be helpful if we listen to what he tells us."

At Joseph's nod, Felix began to detail the murders as a look of concern spread across Hilmi's face. Felix spoke of the women in scattered places across the globe, their bodies left in Catholic Churches. He said that the CIA believed an unnamed Islamic terrorist group was responsible for the murders.

Al-Jafri's body sunk a little deeper in the chair, and he grew smaller, almost as if he were willing himself to disappear.

"These are not men who believe in Allah," said Hilmi as he glanced defiantly at Felix. "Your friend is looking down the wrong pathway, Joseph. I know nothing that will help him."

Brother Joseph turned to Felix. "We will learn more if I speak with him alone. Give us a moment," he whispered as he ushered Felix into the hall and closed the door behind him.

"He works for Alberto, doesn't he?" asked Hilmi. "Alberto is a zealot who despises the modern changes made to your faith. My angel does not trust him, nor should you."

"Your angel is insightful," Brother Joseph said, "but I need your help to find the murderers of these innocent women. We believe there is a record, a list, of radical Islamic group members that may be harboring these murderers. We understand it was smuggled out of Afghanistan years ago. We have been told you know where the list may be found."

"I have heard there is a list as you describe, Joseph," Hilmi answered quietly. "The rumors are many, but the truth is elusive. It is equally possible that such a list never existed at all."

"The Vatican believes it does, my friend, as does the American government. Anything you have heard, even the rumors, may lead us to the murderers of innocent women. I am asking for your help."

Hilmi was silent for a moment. "I heard that Idris Turabi, Bin Laden's right-hand man years ago, had such a list, but it was stolen from him," he said, "Turabi's third wife fell into a fit of jealousy when he took his fourth, a girl much younger than herself. She vowed to punish him for putting her aside."

Soon after the wedding, she returned to Yemen to attend her father's funeral. She could not read but knew her husband had said the list was of inestimable value. She never arrived home. Several days later, Turabi realized that she and the list were missing. He sent his men to find her."

"Did they?"

"Find her? It took months, but they did. She was in Cuba, of all places. It was a clever move, I suppose. Who would think to look for a Yemeni woman there?"

"And they found the list?"

"They did not. She denied she had taken it, but they killed her anyway as a fitting punishment for a wife who had deceived her husband."

Joseph sat quietly.

"You are not the first to ask me what I know of this list," Al-Jafri sighed. "I do not."

"You have never lied to me, my friend."

Al-Jafri was lost in thought for a moment. "I have heard that after the pope visited Cuba, the property of the Church was returned to the Vatican as an act of goodwill."

"I don't understand what you are telling me," responded Joseph.

"Turabi's wife helped pack the crates in the warehouse destined for the Vatican before her husband's men found her. If I were looking for the elusive list, I would look in the Vatican."

"Are you sure?"

"Joseph, my friend, I have clearly said I am not. I do not know if such a list exists, or if it does, that it contains the names of men you seek. I had even heard that the names were of women, but no woman could be important enough to create such interest." Hilmi stopped speaking for a moment to catch his breath. "However, if I believed such a list existed, I would start with Rafael De Posada."

"Cardinal Rafael De Posada? He is an essential member of the Curia," said Joseph, neglecting to mention that he had been sent to speak with Hilmi by Cardinal De Posada's order.

"Rafael's family lost everything after the revolution. They never got over it. I suspect that Rafael's dedication to the Church was predicated upon his desire to regain the wealth and power his family lost. He arranged the pope's visit and negotiated the repatriation of the Church's property held by the Cuban government. I was told that every crate shipped to the Vatican was labeled with De Posada's name and delivered directly to him. It has been said that many of the valuable items mysteriously vanished during shipping. Possibly into the Cardinal's many bank accounts."

"And you believe this information reliable?" asked Brother Joseph.

"The Vatican didn't become the richest institution in the

history of the world by being careless with its wealth and possessions. Cardinal De Posada has made many enemies as he clawed his way into the highest level of your Church," continued Hilmi, "so this information may not be reliable. My source is often more interested in telling a good story than the truth. Search the Vatican for the answers, Joseph."

"You are a wise man, Hilmi. Thank you for speaking with me." Joseph patted him on his shoulder before he turned to leave him to his solitude but turned back when Hilmi called his name.

"Joseph," Hilmi said, "My angel says to tell you God will be by your side, but you will face great peril. Sometimes, my angel is a jokester. I will pray for you anyway."

Chapter 17
6:30 P.M.

Izzy, Jasper, Father Patrick

We are not necessarily doubting that God will do the best for us; how painful will the best turn out to be?

— *C.S. Lewis*

Guardians' Command Center
Abbey Sainte-Victoire Marseille, France

Jasper's iPhone began ringing as he entered Izzy's office. He gestured his apologies as he answered.

"Shit!" he exclaimed, throwing the phone on the desk.

Father Patrick and Izzy looked up in surprise.

"Milo and Father Claude ran into an unexpected problem. Father Claude connected with Maria Veronica of Seville, the *Opus Christos'* assassin, at LAX. I'm not sure how that happened. Milo was laughing too hard to tell me. Milo took her and two other *Opus Christos* goons out," answered Jasper.

"What?" asked Father Patrick.

"Somehow, the entire incident was ignored. There was no law enforcement involvement or news coverage. It was like it never happened," said Jasper.

"*Opus Christos* must have covered it up. Are Father Claude and Milo okay?" Izzy asked.

"Milo said he was glad he has friends in low places. They were hanging out in a biker bar half the afternoon, waiting for a new 'ride' to be delivered. The van with their phones inside was towed to a junkyard and compacted. Milo said the van and dog rental will be on his next expense report."

Father Patrick gave him a questioning look. "Why do I feel there's more?"

"Oh, there's more, and it just gets better," answered Jasper. "They were staking out Bria and her mother's house since the design studio was empty. Milo scored a dog to walk so he could talk to the housekeeper, Carmen, who told him Bria, Magdalena, and Theo left on a last-minute trip to Rome with a rich new client on her private jet."

"They're on their way to Rome with a person or persons unknown?" Father Patrick asked.

"That's what Milo said. It just gets better. Bria's house exploded."

"Bria's house exploded?" asked Izzy. "That doesn't sound like Felix, not his style."

"True, but Father Claude is sure it was Felix, and Milo agrees," said Jasper, raising his hand to stop Father Patrick's questions. " But we're not done yet. I just received a report from a contact at LAPD that a Trappist monk and Felix visited Hilmi Al-Jafri in his nursing home, where he's lived for the last two years. Soon after they left, the aide brought Hilmi Al-Jafri his dinner and found his dead body."

"Felix murdered Hilmi?" asked Father Patrick, "What did Hilmi tell them?"

Jasper shook his head. "The official cause of death is a heart attack. The nurse said that Hilmi's door was closed, so no one heard what they talked about, but she heard the monk say they needed to book flights to Rome once they returned to the hotel."

"Jasper," said Izzy, "check all the hotels in LA for a monk who checked in sometime today. Zayas will stash Brother Joseph somewhere until they can get on a flight."

"My team's already on it, but there are hundreds of hotels in the Los Angeles area," answered Jasper, turning to leave, "and before you ask, we've already booked the flights to Rome for Milo and Father Claude on the next flight out of LAX."

"It's a bit more than a coincidence, don't you think," asked Izzy, "that Bria's on a private jet on her way to Rome and Brother Joseph is on his way there or soon will be?"

"God works in mysterious ways," said Father Patrick as he stood to leave. "Inform the Rome and the Vatican teams to expect them sometime tomorrow. Milo's the lead on this operation. I'll make some calls and see if we can get additional backup. We'll need all the help we can get to secure Bria and Brother Joseph before *Opus Christos* figures out who they are."

Chapter 18
10:45 P.M.
Felix and Alberto

When it comes to controlling human beings, there is no better instrument than lies. Because, you see, humans live by beliefs. And beliefs can be manipulated.

—Michael Ende

<u>*Los Angeles, California*</u>

Felix pulled the black Nissan into the Hyatt's curving driveway. He tossed the keys in a high arc to the athletic-looking young man in the short red jacket, who jumped up to catch them. He smiled at Alberto Zayas, who stood in the lobby waiting for him.

Alberto made a show of pushing up the left sleeve to glance at his gold Rolex. He took several steps forward, firmly placed his hand under Felix's bent elbow, and guided him toward the bank of gleaming glass elevators. Neither man said a word as they waited for one of the glass elevators to be cleared of its passengers. With a shove to Felix's chest, Alberto pressed the button to the top floor.

"Where the fuck," he said, his voice icy as he emphasized the last word, "have you been, Felix? You were ordered to guard Brother Joseph." He leaned over and pressed the elevator's emergency button, and it came to a quick halt.

Felix instinctively moved for his Beretta, hidden in the waistband of his pants, but Alberto was ahead of him. He pinned Felix firmly to the elevator's glass wall. The barrel of the Astra 9 mm was positioned squarely between Felix's eyes as his gun clattered to the floor. Alberto kicked the gun to the far corner of the elevator without moving his eyes from Felix's. If there had ever been a moment in their relationship when Alberto Zayas felt he could kill Felix, it was now. He stepped away, his arm fully extended with the gun's barrel boring a hole in Felix's forehead. He stood there for a minute before pulling the gun away and holstering it.

Felix felt a thin line of sweat dripping down his forehead. He raised his hand to wipe it off but quickly thought better. "I was doing my job. I've been taking care of the Doves," he stammered.

Alberto stared at him a moment before he spoke. "If anything had happened to Brother Joseph while you were ignoring my orders, I swear, you little shit, I would have blown your brains out myself."

He bent down, picked up Felix's Beretta, and secured it in his waistband. He then turned to look at the elevator's glass windows to see if the gun had damaged the lines of his suit.

"Two first-class tickets are waiting at the Delta counter at LAX for the 1:50 flight to Rome. Diplomatic passports will be at the hotel's front desk for you and Brother Joseph, so you'll not need the unimpressive forgery you have hidden in your suitcase. Don't bother to look," he said, patting his jacket pocket. "Cardinal De Posada and Superior General Scotti have been informed that you will arrive tomorrow. A Vatican official will escort you through Italian customs," Alberto said as he pushed the emergency button, causing the elevator to jump back into operation, "Keep on your toes. Father Claude and Milo are in town."

"I saw them. Those two assholes were riding motorcycles and acting like they were all bad. They don't scare me," Felix answered as he decided not to tell Zayas that he had seen Bria and her mother leaving Los Angeles at the Van Nuys airport.

Alberto gestured for Felix to stand back as he exited the elevator, "Milo and Father Claude should scare you. Every Guardian should scare you. One more screw-up, and I swear I'll call Izzy and tell her exactly how to find you."

The door had nearly closed when he thrust his hand between the doors, causing them to jump back open. "You are not indispensable, Felix. There are a million more sick bastards like you who won't be such a pain in my ass. I'll take you out without a second thought. That's a promise, not a threat."

Chapter 19
Day Two
2 A.M.
Inanna, Bria, Theo, and Magdalena

A great sign appeared in the sky: a woman clothed with the sun,
With the moon under her feet and on her head, a crown of twelve
stars.

—Apocalypse 12:1

<u>Palazzo Di Luca</u>
<u>Rome, Italy</u>

Inanna's presence seemed to change the air around her. Theo glanced at her, sitting elegantly in the back of the limousine, holding Magdalena's swollen hands between hers.

Getting through Italian customs, usually a nightmare, was a breeze. They were ushered into a private VIP line where a handsome young customs officer stamped their documents without looking at them. He was too busy staring at Inanna, mesmerized by her every move.

Within the hour, they pulled through the massive iron gates guarding a magnificent stone building on the Via Della Pilotta. The courtyard gardens were manicured to perfection, the landscape lights twinkling, making it seem like a fairy tale castle.

"This hotel is amazing!" Theo said, taking in the marble exterior. "I could live here forever!"

Gabriel frowned. "Prince Gianni Di Luca wouldn't be pleased. This is his private home."

"This is someone's house? It's bigger than Buckingham Palace!"

Inanna smiled at Theo. "I believe it is. The Prince and his mother, Princess Celeste, are dear friends. He's generously offered his home to us for as long as we need it. The family had collected artwork and furniture for the last five hundred years. I believe you'll find the interior more impressive."

"I'm not sure that's possible," answered Theo, staring at the marble stairs.

"There will be time to explore it later, but I suggest Gabriel shows you to your suites. It would be best to rest a bit, as it promises to be an eventful day. I'll meet you in the Music Room," she continued as she glanced at her vintage Cartier watch, "at eight a.m. for coffee and breakfast. We're scheduled to meet Domenico and Stefano at eleven. Gabriel has reserved a helicopter to take us to Milan."

She turned and took Magdalena's hand. "I'm relying on your expertise to assess the suitability of my chosen fabric. Domenico and Stefano admire the quality of your work and are excited to meet you."

Magdalena's eyes grew wide. "I don't know what to say. They know my work? I'm shocked."

"You shouldn't be," answered Inanna. "I will leave you in Gabriel's capable hands. I noticed that bedroom lights in Princess Celeste's private apartments were on. She is quite elderly and sleeps fitfully. She will be hurt if I do not go over immediately and pay my respects."

"Theo and Bri. Don't forget to bring your portfolios in the morning. Dolce and Gabbana will want to see examples of your work."

As Theo, Bria, and Magdalena climbed the wide marble stairs behind Gabriel, Magdalena turned to Bria and whispered, "How in the world would anybody in Italy know me?"

Bria smiled, "Your couture work for Bob Mackie, Tom Ford, and other American designers is known for your unerring skill and precision. Of course, they know you, Mom. You're a star."

"*The* Dolce and Gabbana?" asked Magdalena, her voice shaking. "You're joking, right?"

"Miss Maggie May," said Theo as he crossed himself. "We don't joke about D&G."

Chapter 20
8:30 A.M.

Izzy, Father Patrick, and Jasper

When the solution is simple, God is answering.

-Albert Einstein

Guardians' Command Center
Abbey Sainte-Victoire Marseille, France

Izzy looked up to see Father Patrick hurrying toward her office.

"You should have sent someone down to wake me several hours ago," he scolded.

"We would have called you if needed, but we're still waiting for information."

"Any word about Brother Joseph?" he asked as he pulled a chair and sat across from her.

"Brother Joseph and a companion boarded the Delta red-eye flight to Rome using diplomatic passports. They have a layover in Frankfurt but should arrive in Rome later this evening. The second man may be Felix from the description we got from the boarding crew, but Jasper says Delta's booking system is, I quote, 'a real bitch.' He needs more time to breach their system."

Father Patrick thought for a moment. "Is Alberto traveling with them?"

"The ground crew only mentioned two men traveling together. He may be on his way to Rome, but I'm guessing he's still in LA running the *Opus Christos* operation in the Americas."

"Let's see if we can confirm that one way or another. Have Milo and Father Claude left for Rome yet?" asked Father Patrick.

"They are booked on the next American flight. It's non-stop, so they'll arrive soon after Brother Joseph and Felix have landed. The flight was fully booked, but Jasper pulled some strings. Neilson and Toshi will meet them at the airport with weapons."

Father Patrick looked at Izzy. "Any idea why they're in Rome?"

"We're trying to figure that out, but there are some pretty interesting ideas."

Father Patrick was silent for a second. "Sorry. I switched gears without telling you. I meant Bria, Theo, and Magdalena. Why are they in Rome? What's the name of the client they are traveling with? Don't Italian customs ask why people visit Italy? Ask Jasper to reach out to his contacts at Da Vinci and see if he can learn anything."

Less than fifteen minutes later, Jasper poked his head into Father Patrick's office. "They came in on a private jet at two a.m. this morning. They passed through Da Vinci's VIP Customs like royalty. Bria, Theo, and Magdalena's passports were run-of-the-mill, but the passport for the other woman was weird. I've never seen anything like it."

"What do you mean, weird?" Father Patrick asked Jasper.

"The Vatican issued it. In a single name. There was no surname and no birthdate."

"What was the name?" asked Father Patrick.

Jasper looked down at his notes. "Inanna," he said, "no surname. Just Inanna."

"Inanna?" Father Patrick's voice shook as his face drained of color. "Bria's with Inanna? Oh, My Holy God! Jasper, I don't care what you have to do or how much it costs; find out everything you can about where they are, who they are seeing, and what they're doing. We have no time to waste."

He turned to Izzy. "Pull every agent you can from the field and get them to Rome immediately. We're on full alert from this point forward. If Inanna's involved, things are about to get deadly serious."

Chapter 21
5:30 P.M.

Inanna, Bria, Theo, and Magdalena

We know what we are but know not what we may be.
*   –William Shakespeare*

Palazzo Di Luca
Rome, Italy

Inanna smiled indulgently as she sipped chilled Campari. As always, she had enjoyed the day spent with Stefano and Domenico in their Milan showroom. She had even ordered a few new outfits while Theo, Bria, and Magdalena occupied the workshop.

She quietly watched the three as they laughed in the corner of the Grand Salon. With Inanna's consent, they were giddy from the rare opportunity to explore Dolce and Gabbana's fabric vault and the freedom to take precisely what they needed to finish their collection. To Bria, Theo, and Magdalena's credit, they acted professionally while they discussed their designs in depth with the staff of Dolce and Gabbana. If they were star-struck, it never showed, but now, their pent-up excitement was released; they were as silly as teenage girls after a dance.

"I love Stefano!" said Theo, "Domenico is great, but Stefano took a real interest in our portfolio. I think they were impressed."

"I think they were surprised," answered Bria. I don't think they expected to see high-fashion design aesthetics from two American kids from Los Angeles!"

"And the fabric vault!" said Magdalena. "I've worked with some of the most expensive fabrics in the world, but I've never seen anything like it. The fabric Inanna chose, the ombre silk, going from gold to cream, was unbelievable! It will look like she's walking in a halo of dawn sunlight. Theo, I insist I cut and fabricate that evening gown. I wouldn't trust anyone else with it."

Bria looked at her mother, "Mom, that's so nice. I would trust no one else more than you, but I worry about your hands. You can supervise. Ok?"

"I can do it, Bri. My joints don't hurt at all, not even a little bit," she said as she wiggled her fingers and grinned. "I haven't felt this well in years. Maybe it's the air in Rome?"

Bria started to answer when she noticed Inanna watching and nudged them both to calm down.

"I'm so glad you enjoyed yourselves," said Inanna as she stood and walked over to them. "You deserve it. You're hard-working and very talented. I predict great things for all of you."

"Thank you, Inanna, for the most wonderful and amazing day in my life," said Theo, looking at Bria and Magdalena to include them. "We were hoping that we could invite you out to dinner. It's not much we know, but we'd like to thank you for all you have done for us."

They could see that their offer touched her. "That's so nice of you. More often than not, people expect me to do things for them. It is rare for anyone to ask if there is something they could do for me. I appreciate the offer, I truly do, but Gabriel has been cooking all day to prepare a special dinner. I don't want to be the one to tell him we won't be here to eat it, and neither do you. He can be, shall we say, a bit difficult, and if he gets his feathers ruffled, believe me, he will be impossible."

The meal was out of this world, and they all pushed away from the table in total satisfaction.

"That was amazing, Gabriel," said Bria as he entered with a large tray of Italian pastries. Theo groaned loudly at the sight of the desserts.

Gabriel shot him a look. "Too much?" he asked.

"No, no," answered Theo, "just perfect, actually. Place it right here," he said, patting the table in front of him, "I'll share with the ladies…maybe…if they ask me nicely."

Gabriel placed the tray on the table with a growl, "You'd better. I'll be watching," he said as he cleared the dishes and brought a pot of strong Italian coffee to set in front of Inanna while giving Theo dirty looks. When he left the dining room, they all broke out in gales of laughter.

"I told you he can be difficult, didn't I? See what I have to put up with?" asked Inanna.

"You could fire him, you know."

"I couldn't, actually," Inanna answered. "He's been with us forever, and he's one of few of our staff whom Joe trusts. I would never hear the end of it if I even suggested firing him."

There was an awkward silence until Inanna spoke again, changing the subject smoothly.

"Stefano is viewing the collections of a few other young designers tomorrow. He was wondering if you would like to come with him. It would be an opportunity to make valuable connections."

"That would be amazing!" they shouted in unison.

"I assumed you would, so I've already accepted for you, Theo and Magdalena." She paused for a minute as she sipped her coffee. "Bri, I plan to visit some people I have known for a long time. I was hoping you would be kind enough to accompany me. A few of them can be a bit dour and grumpy. I hoped your youthful charm would cheer them up and make my visits more bearable. That is, of course, if you wouldn't mind spending more time with me."

"I would love to meet your friends," said Bria, hiding her disappointment perfectly.

Inanna stood up, "Perhaps the word 'friends' is an overstatement. Except for Princess Celeste, the visits are more of an obligation, but tongues will wag if they discover I was in Rome and didn't visit them."

"I would be honored," answered Bria, "to meet them."

Inanna rose. "Not as honored as they will be to meet you, I promise."

Chapter 22
9:45 P.M.

Neilson and Toshi

The martyrs have damaged the truth.

—Frederick Nietzsche

<u>Rome, Italy</u>

Neilson and Toshi were staking out customs at Da Vinci to confirm that Brother Joseph and Felix had been on Delta flight 356. It had arrived forty-five minutes earlier, but neither man had gone through customs with the rest of the passengers. Neilson approached a Delta flight attendant leaving the 'Flight Crews Only' area.

"Excuse me," he said as he opened his jacket to show her a badge. "US State Department."

She turned to his voice and smiled, "You're American?"

Neilson nodded. "We were sent to pick up two men from your Los Angeles flight 356. I'm afraid we might have missed them. They were first-class passengers. One of them is a monk."

"I remember them. I didn't know the monk and his companion were that important until we stopped on the tarmac, and a portable stairway was brought to the plane. Two security officers escorted them off the plane to a white limousine that whisked them away."

"Did you notice what company's limo it was?"

She looked at Neilson strangely. "It was the pope's limousine. I thought you guys at the State Department would have known that."

He shrugged his shoulders. "Government jobs," he said as if that explained everything. Neilson thought that if the pope sent his limo to pick up Felix and Brother Joseph, it must mean that the pope was a member of *Opus Christos*. This couldn't be good. He had to call Izzy immediately.

Felix, Brother Joseph, Father Richard, and Cardinal De Posada

Felix sighed as he melted into the white leather backseat of the Papal limousine. After a sixteen-hour flight, Brother Joseph would have appreciated the chance to stretch his legs even if it meant a long walk to the customs line, but he didn't have a say.

"Welcome to Rome," the priest sitting beside the driver said as he turned to look at them. "I am Father Richard, Cardinal De Posada's aide. His Excellency apologizes that he could not meet you personally, but he had several appointments that were impossible to cancel. He wished me to convey that the murder of innocent Christian women in our holy sanctuaries by Islamic terrorists is an abomination neither he nor the Church can ignore. I will accommodate your every need while you are a guest of the Vatican. Your rooms are ready, so you may rest before you meet with the Cardinal at 8 a.m. At that time, he can discuss the situation more fully."

"Thank Cardinal De Posada for his kindness," said Brother Joseph, "but I would like to begin as soon as possible."

"That is impossible. The Cardinal's schedule cannot be altered. However, I have assembled the original packing lists of

His Excellency's possessions shipped from Cuba. I can provide them with the Cardinal's permission this evening."

"I was told that all the items sent from Cuba belonged to the Church."

"Most of the possessions received from Cuba did belong to the Church, but the Cardinal was allowed to claim some of his family's possessions left in their country estate outside Havana. I'm sure that he will be more than happy to allow you to search through his family's keepsakes along with the items belonging to the Church that he was able to recover. One of the advantages of the Vatican," Father Richard smiled, "is that our archivists have a mania for filing every little piece of paper they can find. I am well-versed in their methods and will be at your full disposal during your search to find those responsible for this assault on our Church."

Father Richard glanced in the mirror and caught Brother Joseph's eyes as they drove slowly off the tarmac. "The Cardinal also wishes me to tell you that Hilmi Al-Jafri died shortly after you left him. His Excellency knew him slightly when he lived in New York."

"God is most merciful," said Brother Joseph as he bowed his head, "I'm sure that the gates of heaven will open to greet him. He will be with God. I rejoice for him."

"But," said Felix, speaking up for the first time, "he wasn't a Catholic. He wasn't even a Christian. Only those who have accepted Jesus can go to heaven. Alberto Zayas said–."
Brother Joseph interrupted him. His voice was low and measured, and he said the subject was not open for discussion.

"Perhaps the Church is incorrect in this one instance." He turned his head and looked out the limousine window.

"Your Excellency?" whispered Father Richard.

Cardinal De Posada was napping with a book in his lap, but he immediately opened his eyes.

"What's wrong?" he asked.

"Nothing is wrong, Your Excellency. You asked that I report to you when I returned."

The Cardinal sank back onto his overstuffed chair. "Water," he said curtly.

"Yes, Your Excellency," He quickly poured a glass from the carafe and handed it to him.

De Posada drank it in one gulp and thrust the glass back at Father Richard. He waved his hand up and down impatiently. "Well?" he asked.

"It went as you requested, Your Excellency. The air traffic controller was more than cooperative. The airplane stopped on the tarmac."

"Of course, they were cooperative. What else did you expect? It was the pontiff's limousine." snapped Cardinal De Posada, "Were there any Guardians at the airport?"

"Father Seward reported that he saw a man speaking with one of the flight attendants from the flight, but I already had Brother Joseph and Felix in tow. I saw no reason to endanger Father Seward by telling him to approach the man. I hope that was the correct decision, Your Excellency."

"Whether or not it is the correct decision is immaterial at this point, Father Richard. But, for your information, it was not the correct decision, nor was it your decision to make. I would have liked to know what the stewardess told him."

"Of course, Your Excellency," answered Father Richard as he nodded in apology. "Brother Joseph asked if he could speak with you this evening."

"I will meet Brother Joseph tomorrow at my convenience. It would not be wise to act as if we are desperate for his help. It's best to keep him off balance," said Cardinal De Posada as he answered his phone and dismissed his aide with a wave.

He waited until he heard his bedroom door shut before he spoke, "No, Alberto, there is no reason for you to come. Father Claude and Milo are, as I'm sure you know, in Federal custody in Atlanta, Georgia," he continued, his tone sharp, "I am not without my resources."

"But there is no reason for the Guardians to gather in Rome," answered Alberto Zayas, "unless they have reason to believe that the young woman, Bria, is of special importance. I should be there."

"We are well aware of Bria. We are searching for her as we speak. Meanwhile, please stay in the States and run the American operation. Felix will continue assisting Brother Joseph in finding Leah's List. I trust that you will do as you are told without further trying to question my authority," the Cardinal said before he disconnected the phone.

Chapter 23
10:15 P.M.

Izzy, Father Patrick, and Jasper

No matter how hard you fight the darkness, every light casts a shadow, and the closer you get to the light, the darker that shadow becomes.

—Plato

Guardians' Command Center
Abbey Sainte-Victoire Marseille, France

"The pope's limo, Neilson? I'll see if Jasper can hack into the tarmac's cameras. Thanks."

"Jasper!" Izzy shouted.

"Yes?" whispered a voice behind her, making her jump and twirl around simultaneously to face Jasper.

"What the–?"

"Get Father Patrick down here," said Jasper, "We've got a problem. Maybe he knows somebody high up in the Federal Aviation Administration. I've exhausted every contact I have to no avail."

❖ ❖ ❖

"Thank you, Senator," said Father Patrick, "I'll wait for your call." He hung up the phone and turned to Izzy and Jasper. "The LAX- Da Vinci non-stop flight was diverted to Atlanta mid-flight with a 'minor mechanical problem.' Homeland Security pulled Father Claude and Milo off the flight when they landed. They're being held in federal custody while the FAA investigates how two suspected white nationalist terrorists awaiting trial and on the no-fly list were allowed to board a plane destined out of the country."

"What?" exclaimed Izzy.

"De Posada outplayed us," said Jasper. "How did he learn Milo and Father Claude were on their way to Rome so quickly?"

"The same way," suggested Father Patrick, "that you identified that Felix and Brother Joseph were on their way to the Vatican on the Delta flight, or our system was compromised."

"No way! Our system is impossible to hack. I designed it myself."

"Could *Opus Christos* have developed an IT department that rivals ours?"

"Possibly, but only a handful of programmers could do something that complex."

"Check with your contacts. Maybe one of them has heard some rumblings about a hacker or programmer doing something funky or suddenly living large," said Izzy. "I'll do the same."

Father Patrick's cell phone chimed. He listened for a moment before responding. "Thank you, Senator," he said. "Tell Bob I'm looking forward to beating him at golf the next time I'm in the States."

He blew out a gust of air as Izzy and Jasper stared at him. "The Senator spoke to the Director of the FAA. They quickly realized that Father Claude and Milo didn't match the photos of the men on the no-fly list. Their database was hacked after the flight was airborne. Their images were replaced with photos of Father

Claude and Milo. An arrest order was issued to pick them up as soon as they landed."

"Impressive," said Jasper, "I've hacked the FAA once or twice just to poke around, but it was difficult even for me. That narrows the possibilities about who had the chops to pull it off."

"It's going to take a few hours to release them, " Father Patrick answered. "The Senator is going to the federal detention center outside Atlanta. She'll raise holy hell until Milo and Father Claude are under her protection. She'll threaten that a breach of the FAA computers has put the security of the United States in serious jeopardy and result in a full Senate hearing if they aren't released immediately. Izzy, charter a private jet in Atlanta. Use the Senator's name. Have it waiting on the Tarmac and ready to leave at a moment's notice. Hopefully, *Opus Christos* will think they're still in custody and out of the game. Jasper, how quickly can you get new passports to them?"

"Real or fake?"

Father Patrick shrugged his shoulder. "Good enough to get them past customs officials."

"Real but expertly altered would be best. I'm on it," answered Jasper.

"What do you need me to do?" asked Izzy.

"It will be late tomorrow afternoon before Milo and Father Claude will be in Rome. I'll bribe our way into the secure customs area. Toshi can slip the new passports to Father Claude and Milo to present to the Italian customs officials," said Jasper.

"Who else can we get to Rome? We'll need everyone you can spare to search for Bria and Brother Joseph," interrupted Father Patrick.

"Lilliana is in Sicily with Gabriella. Either one of them would be a good choice to find Bria."

"Can we pull them both, Izzy?"

"There are a few Doves in southern Italy that we haven't been able to find, but if Gabriella and Lilliana can't find them, there's a good chance *Opus Christos* won't be successful either."

"Can we get someone familiar with the Vatican to approach Brother Joseph?"

"That's a bit more difficult," answered Izzy. "Several nuns stationed in the Vatican are Guardians, but it's contraindicated to involve them at this point. Pablo? He's in Madrid. It's not that far away. His uncle is in the Curia. Maybe a spur-of-the-moment family visit? Lucas is in London. He worked as a summer tour guide at the Vatican in college, so he knows it well. I can get them both to Rome."

"Do it," said Father Patrick.

Chapter 24
Day Three
7:15 A.M.
Bria and Inanna

I love Her like a mother, and She embraces me as Her own child. She will not cast me away.
                              —Makeda, Queen of Sheba (1000 BCE)

Palazzo Di Luca
Rome, Italy

Inanna walked into the sitting room as Bria spoke quietly on her phone.

"Is everything all right?" she asked as soon as Bria ended the call.

"No, it isn't. Our housekeeper, Carmen, called. She was upset, so I didn't understand everything she was trying to tell me, but I think there was some gang violence at our house. The police have roped off the entire block but aren't saying much. Carmen said that Molotov cocktails or something destroyed the front porch and windows. It damaged our neighbor's house, too. It was a miracle no one was killed."

"Living with the constant incidents of random gun violence in the States must be frightening."

"I guess we make ourselves believe it will never be us or anyone we know. If we didn't fool ourselves and turn a blind eye to reality, maybe we'd stand up together and say, 'Enough is enough.'"

"I won't let anything happen to you, Theo, or Magdalena. I'm sure your house is insured and can be repaired. Most importantly, Carmen and Kilo weren't harmed."

"How did you know my mother's dog is named Kilo?"

"Didn't you mention him?" asked Inanna.

"I don't think so. Maybe my mom did?"

Inanna nodded her head. "That must have been it," she said calmly.

"I hope you are not disappointed that I asked you to stay with me instead of returning to Milan."

"I'm not disappointed at all. Theo and my mom will represent Cross and Tanaka perfectly."

"I have no doubt, but perhaps you should have gone, too. You are a full partner in the firm."

"I don't think of myself as a full partner. Theo is the one who keeps us going."

"You're stronger than you believe, Bri," Inanna replied. "I know I'm being selfish, but I'm glad we'll have some alone time to get to know each other better."

"Me, too," Bria said as she took a cup of coffee and chose a pastry from the plate Gabriel had set between them. He looked at them both with a look of barely controlled aggravation.

"Ladies, the car will be here in fifteen minutes. You need to pick up the pace. Time and aristocratic elderly Italian women wait for no one. Not even you two," he said sternly as he slammed the kitchen door.

"Move it now, or I'll tell the car to leave. You can walk for all I care!" he shouted through the closed door.

"Bossy," said Bria.

"And difficult," added Inanna as they both giggled.

Chapter 25
8:25 A.M.

Pope Peter

When anyone questions the Church, they are to be opposed in all ways. For, even if they should say something true, you should not agree with them. The true truth is only according to the faith.
—Bishop Clement of Alexandria

Vatican City

Pope Peter's hands shook as he struggled to tie the long laces of his Nike running shoes. The two young men stationed at his apartment on the third floor of the Apostolic Palace stepped aside and followed him as he swiftly walked down the long corridor, headed for the marble stairway that led down and out to the Via St. Anne. He stopped at the bottom of the marble steps, stretching his legs to limber himself up. He looked to his left and right as if trying to decide his route.

For centuries, the men elected to the supreme and infallible position as pontiff, the head of the Roman Catholic Church, have been set firmly in their archaic belief that they had the right to absolute power in God's name. Pope Peter, at fifty-three, was one of the youngest men, if one discounts the child popes of the Middle Ages, to sit on the Throne of Peter. He was also one of the most educated and liberal-minded men ever elected by the Curia to the position.

"Your Eminence," said a voice behind him, "The gates open to the public in 35 minutes."

He turned to face a young, dark-haired man dressed in the Swiss Guard's distinctive, multicolored uniform. "Thank you," he answered, "I'm well aware of the time."

The Swiss Guard had found guarding Pope Peter challenging. They had hoped he would behave as befitted his position as had the much older men whom the Curia had elected to fill the role of pope, but Peter's daily runs and rock music had thrown them into a tizzy. After several long and tiresome discussions, he agreed to restrict himself to the Vatican grounds, wear jogging pants instead of shorts, and wear a long-sleeved shirt instead of a tee. He would run in the early mornings and late evenings when no tourists were around. In exchange, it was agreed that the guards would remain at arm's length as long as he informed them of his intended routes. Pope Peter turned and answered the young man's unasked question.

"Up past the Pio-Clementine Museum, around the Pontifical Academy, and back again."

"Thank you, Your Eminence," he said as he began speaking into the tiny microphone hanging from his earpiece. Pope Peter might not see his bodyguards, but he knew they would always be nearby.

He ran, willing himself not to think about the meeting an hour earlier. He should have realized when he saw Cardinal De Posada and Superior General Scotti enter his apartments together that nothing good would come of it.

Together, they were the three fabled popes of the Catholic Church: the White, the Red, and the Black. Each held a pivotal position in balancing the reins of power within the infrastructure of the Roman Catholic Church and were often at odds.

He was Peter of Rome, traditionally dressed in pristine, ivory papal robes, the White pope. Elected by the Curia, he is the legitimate heir to the Throne of Peter the Fisherman. As such, he was considered by the faithful to be both supreme and infallible in all spiritual matters.

Rafael De Posada was the Red pope, resplendent in his scarlet Cardinal's vestments as the Cardinal Prefect of the Congregation of the Evangelization of Peoples with authority over all mission territories. More than once in the long, turbulent history of the Catholic Church, the Red Pope had endeavored to outflank the White Pope and had won.

Enrico Scotti, somberly dressed in black, is the Superior General of the Society of Jesus, the Black pope. He equally held the power to checkmate the pontiff's desires as the Jesuits are influential in the secular and intellectual world. It was a delicate balance that had erupted into conflict more than once in the Church's long history.

But who could have imagined, thought Pope Peter as he ran without noticing his surroundings, the magnitude of the information the two men had left at his feet the first thing this morning? If even half of what they had revealed earlier were true, then his entire world, the Roman Catholic Church, and everything he had ever believed to be true was about to come tumbling down around his ears.

He felt a wave of anger shoot through his body as he remembered the smug way Cardinal De Posada dared to speak to him and how the Superior General's wizened face wrinkled in a self-satisfied smirk when he pushed an ornate casket filled with damning proof across the table as they stood up, breaking the traditional protocol that they wouldn't rise until the pontiff had dismissed them.

As a parting shot, Cardinal De Posada leaned over Peter's chair to whisper that destroying the ancient documents secured in the casket was useless. They were only a tiny part of the incriminating documents in the Vatican's secret archives.

Peter picked up his pace, pushing himself beyond his endurance, hoping the additional stress on his body would pressure him to find a solution or kill him. Either outcome seemed equally acceptable at the moment.

Chapter 26
11:00 A.M.

Father Patrick, Jasper, & Izzy

The truth will be shut out if you shut your door to all errors.
—Rabindranath Tagore (1861–1941)

Guardians' Command Center
Abbey Sainte-Victoire
Marseille, France

Katie, the supervisor of Facility Operations, was also the resident mother hen to the entire staff of the Command Center. She focused her ice-blue eyes to stare Father Patrick down when he asked her if she knew where Izzy had gone.

"I've paged her twice, but she hasn't answered," he asked.

"Father Patrick," scolded Katie, "the poor girl has barely slept or eaten since the Light. She's pushing herself too hard, and you're not helping. I confiscated her phone and forced her to take a catnap which," she paused as she checked her watch, "should be over in about 15 minutes."

Before Father Patrick could reply, Izzy walked into the office, a lock of hair flattened against her face and her clothes wrinkled, but she appeared more rested than she had two hours earlier.

"If you promise me to eat a decent meal, I will declare my role as 'mother hen' officially over."

"When do you think that will be?" Izzy asked suspiciously.

Katie laughed.

"Eight hours tops. Consider yourself lucky. Fran and Martin in the documents department have been putting up with me for twenty-five years. Between us, there's something seriously wrong with them. Give them an ancient parchment to translate, and they forget about eating and sleeping until I go down and force them to stop by disconnecting the electricity to their lab."

She turned to wag her finger at Father Patrick before she left.

"Don't you browbeat this girl until she's eaten. I have friends everywhere. I'll know if you do," she said as she turned to look Izzy over.

"Grooming is as important as food and sleep, Izzy. After your meal, you will return to your room, shower, wash your hair, and change your clothes. I'll be back in an hour to check," she ordered as she swept out of the office.

Father Patrick stuck out his tongue at her back, making Izzy laugh, but he waited until Izzy ate her sandwich before he spoke. Being on Katie's bad side wasn't something one did lightly; it was a lesson that he learned the hard way and, wisely, never forgot.

"Any leads on the whereabouts of Bria and Inanna?" he asked.

"Jasper's team was working on it. They were scouring every hotel within a hundred-mile radius of Rome," answered Izzy between bites.

"They're wasting their time. Inanna will only be found if she wants to be found. Bria is safe as long as she's with her. What about Brother Joseph?"

Jasper sauntered in and casually stole a French fry from Izzy's plate.

"We know from Sister Bernadette," he answered, "that he's with Felix and Cardinal De Posada's aide, Father Richard. They are searching the storerooms at the Vatican Museums. She's working on finding out more if she can."

"But why bring him to the Vatican?" asked Father Patrick. "Why take him to speak with Hilmi?"

"Maybe," Izzy said, taking a drink of her soda, "they're using his reputation as an expert on terrorism? Bringing him to Rome only makes sense if *Opus Christos* is trying to divert attention from themselves by blaming Islamic terrorism for the Doves' murders. Could they use Brother Joseph to convince the pope that the Islamic groups have declared a holy war against Christianity?"

"I think *Opus Christos* is having him look for something else," said Jasper as he stole another fry from Izzy's plate. "It's the only thing that makes sense."

Father Patrick lifted his eyebrows as if to question his assessment.

"What if Joseph is looking for the list of Leah's Doves?"

"I was wondering the same thing, Jasper," said Izzy. "If *Opus Christos* is intent upon murdering all the Doves, they would move Heaven and Earth to find Leah's List. What if the Islamic terrorist thing is just a red herring to get Brother Joseph to search for Leah's List without knowing what he's looking for? It would explain why Opus Christos took him to speak with Hilmi Al-Jafri."

"Except Leah's List was destroyed when the Nazis torched the blocks around our monastery in Marseille in 1942," answered Father Patrick.

"But what if the Nazis found it before they burnt the monastery?" suggested Jasper. "What if they realized what it was? They could have used it to blackmail Pope Pius XII into keeping quiet about their atrocities against humanity in WWII."

Father Patrick thought for a moment. "There have always been questions why Pius XII never condemned the Nazis and the holocaust. We know he was aware of the Nazi's activities as it was happening, but he never spoke out."

"So it's possible the Vatican has Leah's List?"

"Possible and probable are two very different things, Izzy. We know the Nazis never discovered the vault in the cave under the monastery where the documents and relics were stored. There's a slight chance they might have seized the documents, including Leah's List, which the monks couldn't secure in the underground vault before the fire destroyed them. It's possible, I suppose."

Chapter 27
4:30 P.M.

Bria, Inanna, and Gabriel

Remember today, for it is the beginning of always.
>   *—Albert Einstein*

Palazzo Di Luca
Rome, Italy

Hours later, after visiting Inanna's friends, punctuated by quick stops at several elegant boutiques, Bria and Inanna returned to the *Palazzo* happy but tired.

Gabriel was waiting inside the front door with a tray holding two ice-cold glasses of Prosecco. They dropped their bags on the floor and slipped off their shoes before gratefully accepting the offered drinks. In a graceful move, he swept up the bags and shoes before he disappeared down the hall.

"How does he do that?" asked Bria.

"Years of practice. If I didn't know better, I'd think he could read my mind."

Bria smiled. "I enjoyed meeting your friends. They're all angels!"

Inanna nearly choked on her sip of Prosecco. "Did Gabriel tell you they were angels?"

Bria shook her head, a bit confused. "Gabriel? He barely lowers himself to speak to me unless it's absolutely necessary. I can't imagine him liking anyone enough to call them an angel. It's an English term sometimes used to describe a person who is especially sweet and kind."

Inanna visibly relaxed. "Yes, you're right. They are angels. Even the grumpy ones."

Inanna returned to the library an hour later, wearing a fitted pale blue coat and matching hat and carrying a small Louis Vuitton bag. "I'm afraid I will miss Gabriel's dinner this evening. I must be on my way home," she said apologetically.

Bria put her book down and walked to Inanna's side. "Is everything okay?"

"Everything is fine, or it will be. Joe is in one of his moods over a tiny indiscretion of mine and insists we need to discuss it immediately. The longer I keep him waiting, the more intractable he becomes. He is quite unreasonable when he believes I have done something that doesn't conform to his rigid expectations."

Bria wrapped her arms around her, "I'm sure everything will work out fine, Inanna. Call if you need to talk. It doesn't matter what time it is; I'll answer."

"Thank you, Bri," answered Inanna, pulling away from the hug, "Your concern is touching and appreciated. We made a bet ages ago, and he thinks I am trying to influence the outcome, which is ridiculous. I have realized that regardless of the consequences, people will do exactly what they want. Perhaps the combination of intelligence and free will was ill-advised."

"True. I've been surprised by people's behavior time and time again."

"He needs to rail and thunder while I listen. I doubt he cares about the outcome as long as he can see a solution that won't overly tax his patience. Then, we both walk away as firmly committed to our opinions as we always have been. It is a waste of his effort and my time," she shrugged, "but it's too late to change him."

Bria put out her arms and engulfed Inanna in a tight hug. "I'll miss you. Call if you need me."

"Your mother is correct," Inanna whispered, "you are the sweetest of all the Doves."

Chapter 28
6:00 P.M.

Pope Peter

When the truth is hidden by lies, they shout from underneath, and then it will be clear to you which is true and which is a lie.
*   –Kamaran Ihsan Salih*

Vatican City

Pope Peter could no longer put off the unthinkable chore that faced him. He walked over to the desk in the papal apartment's study and took the wooden box out of the drawer, which he had hidden after the meeting with De Posada and Scotti. It was heavier than he remembered, and he almost dropped it. Slowly and carefully, he lifted it to the desktop and studied it.

The seal of Pope Clement V was broken, and the seal of the Third Reich was placed over it. Pope Pius XII's seal was affixed over them both. He cut the seals with his Swiss Army knife and opened the box. Gently, he picked the ancient yellowing parchment off the top. Luckily, it was in Latin. Ignoring the pounding of his heart, he began to read:

I am Caiaphas, High Priest of the
Temple in Jerusalem, on the third day of the
fifth month in the year 3799.

*As he commanded, we condemned Jesus,
our King, to death. His rebellion against
Rome had failed. He ordered us to surrender
him to the Romans. He understood that he
would be condemned as a traitor and
crucified. He did this to save us all from the
anger of the Roman oppressors occupying our
land.*

*He asked only one thing of us: that we
protect his family. His mother, Mary, and two
younger sisters are well-protected on
Hippicus's estate. His brothers, James and
John, are in Syria. Simon, a Rabbi, is in
Nabatea.*

*The Messiah's beloved three daughters
are hidden far away to protect them from
those who would seek to destroy them and end
the Messiah's bloodline.*

*With God's blessings, they will grow
into strong women and pass the blood of God
to many generations. With God's mercy, the
Holy Family will forgive us.*

Peter felt the blood rush from his head. Cardinal De Posada
and Superior General Scotti had told the truth. For centuries, the
Church had deliberately modified the Messiah's message to amass
wealth, power, and domination. They subjugated women and
people of other races, started holy wars, and destroyed entire
cultures without remorse, knowing full well that they were hiding
the truth from their followers. Millions died needlessly to empower
and enrich the Church.

If the truth were revealed, at this point, it would destroy the foundations of the Church and call into question everything he believed and loved. He could do nothing to stop *Opus Christos* and save the faith if Cardinal De Posada and Superior General Scotti revealed the truth as they threatened. He had no choice but to do as they demanded.

He was Peter of Rome. The Prophecies of St. Malachy were true. He was destined to be the last pope of the Roman Catholic Church. He was as damned by action as by no action at all. He lowered his head into his folded arms and began to weep.

Chapter 29
6:00 P.M.
Bria and Gabriel

The glories of creation are in your very cells; you are made of the same mind stuff as the angels, the stars, and God himself.

—Deepak Chopra

Palazzo Di Luca
Rome, Italy

Gabriel rolled his eyes as he entered the library and waited for Bria to finish her call.

"Of course, Theo," said Bria, "it's an amazing opportunity. You guys will have a fabulous time!"

"Why don't you get on the train and join us?" asked Theo, "It's only a three-hour trip to Milan. You could be here by 9:00 at the latest. This is Italy. You'll be just in time for dinner. Stefano found us a gorgeous suite. It's big enough for all of us. Come on! We'll have a ball."

"Sounds fun, but I'm exhausted. Inanna and I spent the entire day running all over Rome. We were visiting her countless friends when she wasn't shopping at expensive boutiques."

"Understand. Being nice for hours on end is exhausting," said Theo. "I'm running on adrenaline myself. Your mom, however, is more energetic than both of us put together. It's like her arthritis has magically disappeared. She's amazing." Theo lowered his voice to a whisper, "Stefano wants to invest."

"In your next collection?"

"In our Design Studio. Cross and Tanaka? We're a partnership, remember? We'll talk about his ideas tomorrow. He's waiting downstairs to take us to some fancy restaurant. Love you. Your mom says she loves you, too. Got to go!"

Oh darn, thought Bria, I didn't have time to tell him that Inanna had left, a thought that suddenly had her wondering how they would get back to Los Angeles. Maybe she should be looking for hotel rooms now that Inanna had left.

"Ah," said Gabriel, "I see you're off the phone. I wasn't sure if that was possible for someone your age. When you're not texting or talking, you're staring at the screen endlessly.

"Inanna asked me to tell you that the jet is at your disposal whenever you choose to return home to America. You are welcome to stay here as long as you desire. Prince Di Luca is showing his four classic Ferraris at a series of car shows, so it's available for your use."

Inanna was right. He does read minds, she thought.

"That is incredibly kind of them both," Bria answered, "I'm surprised you didn't go with her."

"I have several important tasks to complete before I return home. Don't worry about Inanna. They have a huge staff. I doubt I will be missed."

"Gabriel," blurted Bria, "I have an idea. What would you say if I invited you for a pizza, a bottle of wine, and a walk around Rome? I haven't seen much and would like to do the tourist thing before we leave."

"I would say that it would be ill-advised," he answered, "but I would also say I would love to have someone else cook for me for once. Seeing something other than these gaudy surroundings would be nice. You're paying, right?"

"I'm taking that as a yes?"

Gabriel almost smiled. "I supposed it is. Yes, although I'm sure I will regret it sooner or later."

"This place is perfect!" said Bria, looking around La Pratolina. "I love the checkered tablecloths. It feels so rustic and authentic. How did you find it?"

"You wanted pizza. La Pratolina has the best. One would have to live in a cave not to know that."

She raised her glass of red wine. "To Gabriel and Inanna."

They clinked glasses and drank. Bria's eyes watered, and she coughed.

"It's strong," she croaked, which made Gabriel laugh.

"This is Nebbiolo. The tannins add bitterness and astringency, making Nebbiolo quite complex in flavor. It's called Italy's prize possession."

She wiped the tears away. "Maybe it's an acquired taste?"

"Luckily," said Gabriel, "all you have to do is drink the rest of the glass and have another. I can guarantee you'll acquire a taste. Humans always enjoy everything that isn't good for them."

Chapter 30
6:00 P.M.

Neilson, Toshi and Father Claude

Coincidence is the language of the stars, for something to happen, so many forces have to be put into action.

—Paulo Coelho

Rome, Italy

Neilson and Toshi were waiting outside Da Vinci when Father Claude and Milo exited the airport. Father Claude immediately recognized them from the photos Jasper had texted.

Toshi was leaning against the hood of the taxicab, smoking a cigarette, while Neilson was stationed near the trunk pretending to polish a dirty spot. It looked casual enough to the average observer, but Father Claude knew they were ready to respond if *Opus Christos* had anyone waiting to move on them. He nodded to Neilson as he and Milo quickly approached the car and jumped in.

Toshi drove like he was on the NASCAR circuit, cutting in and out between cars, while Neilson leaned over the seat to watch the cars behind them before he finally spoke.

"I think we got away clean," Toshi said calmly. "If *Opus Christos* was staking out the airport, we slipped in and out without them noticing, wouldn't you say, Neilson?"

"Well, nobody followed us," Neilson answered as he stuck his hand over the seat. "I'm Neilson. Toshi is the one who is steering this rusted piece of junk like he's an American teenager in a muscle car on the Pasadena Freeway. I'm hoping you are Father Claude and Milo. If not, we've just scared the hell out of two American businessmen," he laughed.

Neilson picked up the duffle bag at his feet and threw it over the seat. "Izzy had us bring you a change of clothes. We're heading to Hotel La Rovere. It's on a residential street, so it's off the beaten path a bit, but the Vatican is only a seven-minute walk away."

"Perfect," said Father Claude, looking over at Milo. "Does that work for you?"

"As long as I can lie on a real bed instead of a lumpy cot, I'm good. I've just got to ask: have you ever tried to eat the goddamn *merda* they pass off as food in federal prisons? I'm starving. I could eat—"

Father Claude raised his hand to stop him. "I don't want to know, Milo!"

Toshi looked shocked, but Neilson laughed out loud. "I know what you're talking about. I was in county jail once as a kid. The food was total crap."

"Okay, boys," said Toshi, "enough of the potty mouths. I understand why Izzy assigned us the way she did. Father Claude, we're a team. Milo, you will be partnered with Neilson."

"All good," said Milo, turning to Neilson, "but I need to eat something that doesn't taste like cardboard. Italian sounds like a damn fine idea. Wouldn't you say, *compatriota*? Any ideas, Toshi?"

"Milo," interrupted Father Claude, "what happened to your Spanglish?"

"We're not in LA anymore, Dorothy. When in Rome... Right, *Amico*?"

"There's a great pizza place, La Pratolina, not too far away," said Toshi. "It's still early for dinner in Rome. I bet we can get seated if we hurry."

"If that's all you can come up with, then, *dannazione*," said Milo, "I guess the best pizza in all of Rome will have to do."

◆ ◆ ◆

Milo, Bria and Gabriel

"That was amazing!' commented Bria as she wiped a dab of sauce off her chin. "The crust reminded me of San Francisco sourdough bread, but it wasn't greasy like American pizza, and you were right. This wine keeps getting better and better with every sip."

"Should we order another bottle?" suggested Gabriel. "The night is young."

"We probably shouldn't, but let's do it anyway. We only live once!"

"Truer words were never spoken," answered Gabriel as he motioned to the server.

Gabriel seemed more relaxed than Bria had ever seen him, but after the fourth time the waiter had come by to check if they had finally placed a credit card on the bill, it was apparent that their welcome had worn thin. Bria looked over at the people impatiently waiting in the small lobby.

"Should we walk back?" she asked as she placed her credit card on the table and raised her arm to signal the waiter that they had finally taken his not-so-subtle hint.

Gabriel took a last sip of wine. "There's an amazing *Gelateria* on the way, but it's closing soon. We won't make it in time if we walk. I suggest we take a cab."

"Do they make bittersweet chocolate?"

"They do. Although once you see their selection of fresh fruit flavors, you might change your mind," he said as he stood up.

"Gabriel?" Bria said as they stood at the taxi stand in front of the restaurant, "This has been fun. You're a nice guy, no matter how much you try to hide it."

Gabriel laughed. "Not really, but good red wine turns me almost human." He moved to her left side and pointed toward the waiting car. "Don't worry. I'll get back to my true self before too long."

◆ ◆ ◆

Neilson, Toshi, Father Claude and Milo

Toshi pulled the car into the last remaining parking spot across the street from La Pratolina. Father Claude and Milo, now dressed in buttoned-down white shirts and faded Levi's, melted into the crowd, wandering the streets and enjoying the warm Roman evening. Neilson and Toshi held back, standing by the car while carefully checking the area before they moved to join them.

"Good," said Toshi as he scanned the restaurant's entrance. "It doesn't look too crowded—only a fifteen to twenty-minute wait, I'm guessing."

He whirled at the sound of gunshots as Neilson, Father Claude, and Milo hit the ground while the crowd scattered, screaming as they fled. As he heard a car speed away, Father Claude looked up and saw a beautiful young woman being pushed into a taxicab by a tall blond man. He jumped up, realizing it was Bria. He began running after the cab, only to be tackled to the ground.

Milo pulled him up and pushed him in the opposite direction. "We have to get out of here before *Opus Christos* takes another run at us. We've been made."

"You don't understand, Milo! That was Bria getting into the

taxi. We need to follow her!"

"No!' shouted Milo. "Getting us killed doesn't help Bria. We've found her once, so we'll find her again, *Stronzo*!"

Father Claude turned his head as the taxi pulled into the heavy stream of early evening traffic to see Bria, who had turned to look back through the rear window. Their eyes caught each other's before Milo forcibly shoved Father Claude forward to follow Toshi toward a dark alley bordering La Pratolina.

Neilson had been hit, and Toshi struggled to get off the sidewalk as blood flowed down his left leg. They needed to get away before Neilson bled to death or *Opus Christos* returned.

◆ ◆ ◆

Bria and Gabriel

"That man was shot! We need to go back and help him, Gabriel," Bria shouted.

"Inanna told me to protect you," answered Gabriel firmly, "and, damn it, that's what I'm doing!"

"No, *Signorina,* I don't go back. You don't go back. Mafia or street– how do you say?– gangs," said the cab driver in broken English as he looked at her in the mirror, "We do nothing. We see nothing. We say nothing. We stay alive."

She looked over at Gabriel. "When the good do nothing," she said, "evil wins."

Gabriel shrugged. "It always does," he said. "It is the one constant in the history of humanity. That's why demons don't exist. They would be redundant. Humanity does better at being consistently evil than any devil could even begin to imagine."

Chapter 31
8:00 P.M.
Izzy and Jasper

Religion supports and perpetuates the social organization it reflects.

—Riane Eisler
The Chalice and the Blade

Guardians' Command Center, Abbey Sainte-Victoire Marseille, France

Jasper picked up the phone on the first ring. He nodded before walking to Izzy's office.

"You better take it, Izzy. It's Father Claude," he said as he handed her the phone.

"Where are you?" she asked before Father Claude said a word.

"Presently, we are in an alley near the Vatican, a block or two north of Via de Scipioni. La Pratolina restaurant is about two blocks south of us—multiple gunshots from a nondescript car without license plates. Neilson was hit in the leg. He's profusely bleeding, so we won't get much farther unless we leave him. That's not going to happen."

"Crap! *Opus Christos*?"

"That would be my guess, but it happened too fast to ID anybody. Right now, Milo and Toshi are standing guard at either end of the alley, but we need help to get out of here."

Jasper popped into Izzy's office, "Dhabi is on his way. Five minutes tops."

"Sit tight," said Izzy, ignoring Jasper's self-satisfied look, "Jasper has sent help. Dhabi should be there in a few minutes."

"Dhabi? I've never heard of him."

"It would have surprised me if you had. He's a member of the *Mehdi of Islam*. They have offered their support in our fight against *Opus Christos*, and we have accepted their assistance."

"Fine. Just tell him to hurry. We're hiding behind a dumpster that smells like cat litter mixed with rotten fish guts," answered Father Claude, "Izzy, I saw Bria getting into a taxicab with a tall blond-headed man right after the shots rang out. I'm positive it was her, but the man wasn't Theo."

"I'll see if we can find out who he is and where the cab took them," Izzy answered.

"Jasper," she shouted, "Father Claude saw Bria get in a cab with an unknown man, tall and blond. We need to locate a taxi that might have picked up a couple of passengers from La Pratolina in the last 15 minutes and know exactly where they dropped the passengers off."

Who's the man Father Claude saw with Bria? Where are Theo and Bria's mother? And, more importantly, who is Inanna, the mysterious woman Father Patrick has been steadfast in his refusal to discuss? Izzy needed answers, and she needed them now if they were going to find Bria and save her from *Opus Christos*.

Chapter 32
8:00 P.M.
Inanna and Joe

In God, the characteristics of men and women that we admire in men and women are combined.
That's been a traditional Catholic teaching that God is the combination of opposites.

-Andrew Greeley

Castle Cockaigne

Inanna squared her shoulders and inhaled deeply before opening the massive door to her husband's office. He was hunched over an oversized ledger, his face set in its usual grumpy scowl. He quickly gestured for his assistants to leave.

"Inanna, where have you been?"

"I am surprised you took your nose out of your ledgers long enough to notice I wasn't here."

He stood and walked around the desk to stand by her side. "I don't remember discussing you going on another of your ill-conceived trips. I disapprove of your behavior."

"I don't remember that I had to ask for your approval. I'm quite sure I don't."

He grunted a sound she knew was as close to laughter as he could make.

"I am an equal partner in this endeavor," she continued, "in case you've forgotten."

"Forgotten?" He glanced at his overflowing inbox. "Ninety-nine percent of my time is devoted
to clean up the messes you make with your outrageous ideas."

She shrugged. "I admit that a few, a very few, have been less successful than others, but you can't deny they are all innovative and creative."

"One, in particular, is both stupid and dangerous. I fear to ask, but what were you doing?"

"I left you a note, Joe," she said, privately tickled that he shuddered at the use of her nickname for him, "If you had bothered to read it, you would know that I visited Princess Celeste and a few other old friends." She smiled as she slipped off her calfskin gloves.

"Inanna, you are quite exasperating. Nothing you do is logical or well thought out."

"I'm sorry I upset you," she apologized, although they both knew she didn't mean it.

He stared at her sternly. "You promised not to interfere with the outcome. A bet is a bet."

She smiled with such sweetness that it would have melted any heart other than his. "I would never betray the terms of our wager. I understand exactly what I can and cannot do."

He shook his head and returned his gaze toward the open ledger on his desk. There was no talking to her. It was best to let her do whatever she wanted and wait for the ensuing disaster. Then, he could hold it over her head for all eternity. The thought of it made him almost smile.

Chapter 33
8:20 P.M.

Milo, Father Claude, and Dhabi

Where did Christ come from? From God and a woman! Man had nothing to do with Him.

—Sojourner Truth (1851)

Rome, Italy

Father Claude was crouching in the dark alley next to Neilson when he heard the metallic rattle of an old Mercedes diesel engine approaching slowly.

He watched as Milo stepped up to the car, spoke to the driver, and jumped in the passenger seat. The headlights shut off as the Mercedes navigated the narrow, unlit alley. He whistled an all-clear to Toshi, stationed at the end of the alley, to stand down as he struggled to get Neilson to his feet before he stepped out from behind the overflowing dumpster. Thumping his fist on the Mercedes' roof, he pulled open the rear door and pushed Neilson inside.

"Let's get out of here," he said to the handsome Arab man sitting in the driver's seat.

Dhabi nodded, flipped on the Mercedes headlights, and quickly pulled out of the alley, stopping only to pick up Toshi before he took a hard right into traffic. He glanced back in the rearview mirror.

"Where do you want to go?" Dhabi asked.

Father Claude looked at Milo, who had climbed over the passenger seat and wrapped a towel around Neilson's leg to stanch the bleeding.

"I'm not sure," he answered.

"Lucky for you, I am," said Dhabi simply as he turned down another dark alley to merge onto a busy boulevard.

After forty minutes of hairpin turns and narrow alleys, Dhabi stopped the Mercedes in front of one of the most dilapidated buildings Father Claude had ever seen. Milo leaned over Neilson's sleeping form, leaning on his shoulder, and shook him awake.

"Dhabi," Father Claude said, staring at the building that looked like it might crumble down at the slightest gust of wind, "is it safe?"

Dhabi turned in his seat and looked back at him. Then he shrugged his shoulders and smiled. "For you? No. This is the Arab neighborhood. Strangers are not welcome," he said, stepping out of the Mercedes. He turned and walked to the wooden door cracked with age and neglect. He produced a key from his pocket and turned it in the lock. "Luckily, I am not a stranger."

"Come," he said as he gestured them through the door that led to a passage that ran along the side of the building. He fumbled to find the light switch. A twenty-five-watt bulb hanging precariously from long exposed wire dangling from the high stone ceiling flickered on and off before it jumped to life. A dim glow bathed the long passageway in half-shadows.

Dhabi beckoned them to follow him down the hallway toward the rear of the building and stopped before a door covered in peeling brown paint. His hand searched the top of the wooden door jamb to produce a heavy old-fashioned key before ushering them inside.

"It doesn't look like much. Lay Neilson on the table," he instructed Milo and Toshi, carrying him. "I'll see what I can do about his gunshot wound," he said as he gathered supplies in the bathroom.

Milo noticed an ancient refrigerator in the corner of the room. "You got something to eat? We were rudely interrupted before we could order pizza."

"Help yourself. There's not much, but maybe enough for sandwiches," answered Dhabi from inside the bathroom. "Let me take care of Neilson first; then, I'll run out and get something."

Dhabi turned to Father Claude after he treated and bound Neilson's wound. "The bullet nicked an artery but didn't break any bones. He's lost a lot of blood, but I was able to stitch it up. He'll be sore in the morning, but I've seen worse," he said as he moved toward the door, "Let him rest. I will get you something to eat before I speak with Izzy to see what she wants us to do to assist you."

"Assist us? You're not a Guardian?" asked Father Claude.

"He is a member of the *Mahdi of Islam*," blurted out Milo as all eyes turned to him.

Dhabi looked surprised. "You know the *Mahdi*?"

"Not personally, of course, but my great-grandfather knew the previous *Mahdi* during the Second World War. They blew up railroad tracks together to stop Rommel's troops. The Guardians and the *Mahdi of Islam* worked together at the time to save their sacred texts from the Nazi looters."

"Your great-grandfather was a Guardian?" asked Father Claude.

"My family has been Guardians for over seven hundred years," answered Milo quietly.

Dhabi smiled incredulously. "Your great-grandfather was Merle? My grandfather spoke of him often. He always wondered if your great-grandfather survived the war. He said he had never met a braver or more reckless fool of a man."

Milo laughed. "I think your grandfather had him pegged. He was a crazy bastard, always up for a new adventure until the day he died."

Father Claude slapped Milo on the back. "That explains a lot, Milo. As my grandmother would say, the nut didn't fall too far from the tree." He turned to Dhabi. "I'm sorry I've never heard of you, but I'm glad you're on our side."

"There is no reason you would have heard of us, Father Claude, but the *Mahdi* is almost as ancient as the Guardians. We share much of the same knowledge and many of the same concerns, but often for different reasons. Our objectives rarely align, but it has happened over the centuries."

"But, how–?" asked Father Claude.

"We've been watching *Opus Christos* for several years. Fanatics of all faiths are dangerous men. After the Light of God exploded in the heavens three nights ago, the *Mahdi* offered our services to the Guardians, and your Grand Council accepted our support. *Opus Christos* seeks to blame Islam for the Doves' deaths. We cannot allow a falsehood that is a grievous insult to our faith to go unpunished, nor do we wish to embroil the world in another war.

"What is the saying? An enemy of my enemy is my friend? Together, we are stronger than we are apart. We will fight the evil that is *Opus Christos* as one before they destroy us all," Dhabi said as he opened the door. "Our prophets may be different, but have no doubt, gentlemen, we serve the same truth and the same God."

Chapter 34
Day Four
7:30 A.M.

Izzy, Jasper and Father Patrick

Annihilation itself is no death to evil. Only good where evil was, is evil dead.
An evil thing must live with its evil until it chooses to be good. That alone is the slaying of evil.

—George MacDonald

Guardians' Command Center
Abbey Sainte-Victoire Marseille, France

Izzy was staring at her computer screen when Father Patrick entered her office.

"What do I need to know?" asked Father Patrick. "Katie threatened to snatch me bald if I didn't demand you get a decent night's sleep. I will take over as best I can."

"I'm fine," Izzy said, suppressing a yawn. You should have awakened me."

"Be that as it may, I'm more afraid of Katie than I am of you. You needed a decent meal and a night of uninterrupted sleep."

Izzy started to argue and then thought better of it. "OK, fine. Jasper's team is pretty much on top of everything. Dhabi was able to pick up Father Claude, Milo, and Toshi. Neilson was shot, but it's a relatively minor injury. He's in pain, but Dhabi managed to care for his wound without calling a doctor."

"Was it an attack by *Opus Christos*?" asked Father Patrick.

"We're unsure if it was *Opus Christos* or random street violence. Either is possible. The police were on the scene quickly, but the witnesses didn't have much to contribute. Fear of the Mafia is greater than their desire for justice."

"Have we identified the man with Bria when she left the restaurant?"

"I haven't confirmed it was Bria, Father Patrick," answered Izzy. "Father Claude believes it was, but it could have been a woman who looked like her. But, yes, we tracked them down. The cab driver said he dropped the woman and her companion off at a *gelato* shop. We can't find evidence that they called another cab, a city bus, or an Uber. They must be staying near enough to the *gelato* store to walk."

Father Patrick nodded his head. "That's progress. At least we have narrowed down the search area," he responded. "Who do we have on their way to Rome? We need to bring in everyone we can."

"That's another problem. Multiple airports worldwide have closed down after receiving multiple terrorist threats. International travel is at a standstill at the moment. Until they reopen, I can't get more of our agents to Rome. We're going to have to rely on the assistance of the *Mahdi* to a greater extent than we had hoped if we're going to find Bria."

"Is *Opus Christos* behind the threats and airports being shut down?"

"That's a fair assessment," answered Izzy. "It plays well into *Opus Christos'* plan if they are going to have the Church accuse Islamic terrorists of the Doves' murders."

"You're jumping ahead of yourself, Izzy. We don't know that's *Opus Christos'* plan."

"It's the only thing that makes sense, Father Patrick. Why else would they bring Brother Joseph, an internationally known expert in Islamic terrorism, to the Vatican? Why did Felix kill Al-Jafri, a respected elder in the Islamic community, unless it's to rile up the radical fringe on both sides? *Opus Christos* plans to blame Islam for the death of the Doves."

"I'm not saying you're wrong, Izzy. I'm saying we have no proof that's what they're doing."

"We've tracked down Bria's mother to Milan," Izzy continued after a moment of silence, "She used her credit card at a restaurant this morning. I'm assuming that Theo is with her since she purchased two meals. I've sent Orlando to Milan to find them. He'll kidnap them, if necessary, and bring them here. We can apologize later."

"No," said Father Patrick, "we don't want to do anything that might frighten them." He thought for a moment. "Have Orlando tell them that Inanna sent him to bring them here since she and Bria changed their plans and have already arrived at *Sainte-Victoire.*"

"You've mentioned Inanna before. Who is she? The Abbot of the Grand Council?"

Father Patrick laughed. "I doubt it, but it may be a possibility. Even I don't know who the Abbot is, but if Inanna is who I think she is, she's a force to be reckoned with. If not, then she was named for her. That alone makes her formidable."

"Should I put a team out to search for her?" asked Izzy.

"I promise you that Inanna cannot be found unless she chooses to present herself. We must concentrate on what we can do and not waste time chasing rainbows. Where are Father Claude and Toshi?" He asked, changing the subject.

"They're playing tourists at the Vatican to try and get a lead on Brother Joseph. I don't think they'll be able to approach him, but with luck, we'll have a visual to confirm he's there. Milo, Neilson, and Dhabi are looking for Bria. That's about it, I think," answered Izzy

"Anything else I need to know?"

Father Patrick didn't answer for a moment. "There's one more development that may or may not help validate your theory about *Opus Christos* and the pontiff. We don't have enough information to assess the situation properly."

"Hold that thought for a second," Izzy said, calling Jasper to join them.

"I spoke to Sister Bernadette," started Father Patrick. "While cleaning Pope Peter's apartments, she found a box of ancient parchment hiding in his desk drawer. She's sure it wasn't there before Cardinal De Posada and Superior General Scotti visited earlier."

"Blackmail?" asked Jasper.

"Let me get this clear," interjected Izzy. "You're saying that Pope Peter is willingly aligned with *Opus Christos,* or are you saying he's being blackmailed to support their agenda?"

"Sister Bernadette believes the latter is more possible than the former. There were broken seals of Clement V and the Third Reich on the box. She has no idea if Peter has seen the documents or knows what they are. He's been secluded all day in his private chapel," said Father Patrick.

"I imagine they are damning to the Church, or De Posada and Scotti wouldn't have shared them otherwise," replied Jasper firmly. "Pope Peter is being blackmailed."

"So," answered Izzy, "what will we do about it?"

"I spoke with Martin in our documents department. He suggested that he and his team gather some obvious forgeries from third to twelfth-century parchments. The idea would be to replace the original documents with our obvious forgeries," offered Father Patrick.

"Obvious fakes will make *Opus Christos* look like fools if they try to use them against the Church," said Jasper. "I can charter a helicopter to bring Lucas here to pick up the forgeries, transport them to the Vatican, and exchange them with the documents in the casket. I like it."

"Lucas is the perfect choice," said Izzy. "He worked at the Vatican for several summers as an English language guide. He knows the layout."

"Believe it or not, Sister Bernadette was his mother's roommate at Holy Oak. She's known Lucas since he was a baby. She trusts him," added Father Patrick, "I'll ask her to exchange the forgeries for the real documents. Lucas can bring the originals back here for translation and conservation."

"Can you think of anything we're missing, Izzy?"

"A hundred thousand things," she said, "but we can only do what we can."

"Yes," answered Father Patrick, "and we all can pray to God and hope we're heard."

Chapter 35
7:30 A.M.

Cardinal De Posada, Brother Joseph,
Felix and Father Richard

*People of privilege will always risk their complete destruction
rather than surrender any material part of their advantage.*
—John Kenneth Galbraith

<u>Vatican City</u>

Father Richard was surprised when Cardinal De Posada entered the
cavernous basement storage room. He bowed his balding head as
he reached over and touched Brother Joseph's sleeve. Joseph
looked up and quickly dropped the documents in his hands back
into the carton. He stood, lowered his eyes, and waited for Cardinal
De Posada to walk across the cement floor toward them.

"Your Excellency," Brother Joseph said humbly as he raised
his eyes to look at the Cardinal.

"You've started early. It's not even 8 a.m."

"I did not wish to waste time, Your Excellency. There are
innocent lives at stake."

"I fear that there are no innocent lives in the world," answered
Cardinal De Posada, "but we must continue the fight to bring the
people to the true faith, don't you agree?" His attention was
distracted by the papers sitting on the table.

"My high school diploma," he said, not waiting to hear the answer to his previous question. "I had forgotten that evidence of my youth still existed. I would have imagined it all destroyed years ago as worthless junk." He smiled at Brother Joseph, "I hope there's nothing indiscreet inside these boxes. I shouldn't want my childhood mistakes to embarrass me."

Brother Joseph recognized it for what it was—an attempt on Cardinal De Posada's part to humanize their relationship. In the hierarchy of the Church, there was an insurmountable chasm between their respective positions that couldn't be breached, even if the Cardinal wanted to pretend it could be.

"I am not looking for indiscretions, Your Excellency," Brother Joseph answered humbly, "I am sure I would not find them even if I were."

Cardinal De Posada smiled and turned to Father Richard.

"I understand from the nuns that our guests have not eaten a proper breakfast," he said.

Father Richard blushed. "I brought coffee and pastries, Your Excellency. We began searching through the crates, and it slipped my mind." He turned to Brother Joseph. "I would be glad to–."

Cardinal De Posada interrupted, "Perhaps it would be better if you and—?" He looked straight at Felix, who had just entered, carrying two wooden boxes from the basement.

"Special Agent Felix-." Felix paused a second to remember his pseudonym, "Blanc."

"Special Agent Blanc," Cardinal De Posada continued smoothly, "go with Father Richard to the kitchen and get some scrambled eggs, Prosciutto, and a pot of espresso. I shouldn't like Brother Joseph to think I'm an inconsiderate host."

As he watched Felix and Father Richard leave the basement, he turned to Brother Joseph.

"I was shocked to have been told that Hilmi Al-Jafri was your friend," he said, "I knew Al-Jafri when I was much younger. I have no doubt you will find his hand involved in these horrendous murders. He is no less a murderer of women and children than those he taught to murder. I hope your memory of your friendship will not sway you when the evidence of his involvement comes forth."

"I seek the truth, Your Excellency," replied Brother Joseph, "if Hilmi was involved, I will find the proof." The lessons of obedience he had taken into his heart over the last nine years as a Trappist held fast. To question one's superiors challenged the Church itself. To question the Church questions God. Brother Joseph was not yet at the point where such a thought would have crossed his mind.

Chapter 36
9:45 A.M.
Milo and Dhabi

*If the work of God would be comprehended by reason, it would be
no longer wonderful, and faith would have no merit.*
—Pope Gregory I (530–604 CE)

Rome, Italy

Milo had decided they would begin their search for Bria in the
neighborhood near the gelato shop. As Neilson waited at the coffee
shop across the street for the rest of the team to arrive, Dhabi
excused himself and ran across the street to speak to an older man
who was unlocking the door of the gelato store. He watched as the
two men waved their arms around in sweeping gestures and ended
with a vigorous handshake before he ran back across the street.

"He remembers her. She's a beautiful American with honey-
colored streaks in her hair and sparkling eyes. She seemed upset.
He thought they had had a lover's quarrel. He said she was so
beautiful and sad he couldn't refuse her even though they were
already closed. They took their gelato and walked down the street."

"Did he say in which direction they went?" asked Milo. "That
would be as helpful as hell."

"Not exactly, but she did ask how far it was to *Palazzo Di
Luca.*"

Milo shook his head, "No idea what that is. A hotel? A

nightclub? A restaurant?"

Dhabi looked at the two taxicabs that had pulled up in front of the coffee shop.

"It's one of the few palaces that are still privately owned. The Di Luca family has lived there for more than 600 years: old money and old titles. The art collection is worth hundreds of millions of dollars, so the security is top-notch. If she's there, our work will be cut out for us."

"If it's not a major problem, I've got no interest in tackling it. Let's figure out how we do what we need to do," answered Milo. "Neilson, we got people to see, places to go. Shake a leg, *il cavaliere.*"

"Not funny, Milo," grumbled Neilson as he limped to the cab. "It hurts like a son-of-a-bitch."

◆ ◆ ◆

Milo, Neilson and Dhabi
10:00 A.M.

The two cabs, one with Milo and Dhabi and the other carrying Neilson and two of Dhabi's men, pulled up to face the mammoth stone building.

"*Santa Merda,*" said Milo, "this pile of stone is a private home? The damn thing is a block long, and the security looks space-age techno. We'll never be able to sneak in there unannounced."

"Hold on, my friend," said Dhabi as he slipped out of the cab. "I think Allah just smiled at us."

Milo watched as Dhabi approached the second of two trucks waiting at the gate. He jumped on the running board to greet the driver with a hearty handshake.

"I've got a way in," he said as he slid back inside the cab and threw Milo a pair of overalls. "We're about to become part of the crew unloading the boxes that need to be delivered inside. Neilson, stay in the cab. You're the lookout. Call Milo if you see anything suspicious."

Chapter 37
10:00 A.M.

Bria and Gabriel

Reputation is what men and women think of us; character is what God and angels know of us.

—Thomas Paine

<u>Palazzo Di Luca</u>
<u>Rome, Italy</u>

Bria woke with a raging headache. Drinking wine had never bothered her before, but she had never drunk Nebbiolo, she thought as she threw back the bedcover. It was also the first time she had ever put away an entire bottle by herself, so she was lucky that a headache was the worst of her problems.

Opening the curtains, she was surprised by a beehive of activity in the courtyard. There were moving trucks and men unloading large crates and cumbersome boxes. She quickly dressed in pink sweats and a comfy jean jacket. She pulled her hair into a ponytail before rushing downstairs to find Gabriel fussing at the movers and sending them, with growing irritation, in different directions with every new crate. The sweet Gabriel of last night had disappeared. He had warned her that his momentary attack of kindness was due to the amount of wine and pizza he had consumed, so she wasn't surprised.

"Ah, Your Royal Highness," Gabriel said mockingly when he

noticed her standing on the stairs, "so very kind of you to wake up and grace us with your sparkling presence."

"What's going on?" she asked, ignoring his sarcastic tone. She quickly moved as two men carrying large crates gestured for her to get out of their way.

"Inanna is what's going on. As usual, her gifts to her hosts go overboard."

"All this?" Bria questioned.

Gabriel looked at her with a dismissive roll of his eyes.

"You can't believe that Inanna consults me regarding her every move. However," he said as he looked over at the tower of boxes, "from the labels and size of the crates, I would say it's artwork. As you may have noticed, the Prince's extensive collection leans toward excessive. More is never enough."

They were interrupted by a man, his blue workman's shirt discolored with sweat stains. He barked in Italian, pushing a clipboard toward Gabriel while leering at Bria. She couldn't understand a single word, but she understood his meaning. Gabriel responded sharply as he signed the Bill of Lading and turned his back on the man, dismissing him, as another delivery man accidentally bumped into Bria. Keeping his face down, the man turned quickly and mumbled an apology.

"One wonders," Gabriel said, "what it is that allows men, no matter how unappealing, to believe that a beautiful young woman will find them attractive? It boggles my mind."

"Years of their mother's unrealistic admiration?" Bria suggested.

Gabriel laughed out loud. "You may be on to something," he said as he looked at the boxes. "We must postpone our visit to the Vatican until this afternoon. The Prince's curator and staff will be here shortly to uncrate and hang these paintings. Inanna insisted that I remain until they are finished."

"Okay, not a problem. Maybe I'll visit a few museums or wander around Rome."

"Inanna suggested that you pay a visit to Princess Celeste. She is housebound due to her age. Inanna said that the Princess enjoyed your company and would like to spend more time with you."

"Of course. I would be happy to do that. I'll grab a coffee and some toast first."

Gabriel looked her over head to toe with a questioning look.

"Yes," answered Bria, "I'll make myself presentable."

"One never knows with Americans," he mumbled as she turned toward the kitchen.

"I heard that!" she said over her shoulder.

"I wanted you to," he answered back.

Chapter 38
12:10 P.M.

Brother Joseph, Felix, and Father Richard

It is piously spoken that the Scriptures cannot lie. But none will deny that they are frequently abstruse and their true meaning difficult to discover.

—Galileo (1564–1642)

Vatican City

Shortly after noon, Father Richard returned to check Brother Joseph and Felix's progress. He gasped at the photos of crucified and murdered women pinned to the walls. He diverted his eyes to the long table in the middle of the room where Brother Joseph was leaning with his head down.

"Brother Joseph?" he said, trying to keep his voice steady. "His Excellency begs your indulgence. His meetings with the bankers are taking longer than expected."

Brother Joseph nodded. "It's quite all right, Father Richard. Special Agent Blanc and I have been busy chasing our tails, so we have nothing concrete to share with him."

Father Richard looked at him strangely. "I'm sorry, but I'm afraid my understanding of English is not quite what I thought. Chasing our tails?"

"Wasting our time," he said with a sigh. "We've checked everything in these boxes. If there's a list of potential terrorists, it's not here." Brother Joseph glanced at the photos taped to the walls, "I thought that if we came from another perspective, we might see something that ties the choice of victims together, but we're not seeing it."

He turned back to look at Father Richard. "We've done all we can here. We will need access to every packing crate that Cardinal De Posada brought with him from Cuba, every item that the Cardinal donated to the library, and we'll also need access to His Excellency's private quarters to examine his library and possessions there."

"I will ask His Excellency as soon as he is available," Father Richard said.

"Father Richard," said Brother Joseph firmly, "His Excellency has already agreed to open up all his belongings to us. We cannot wait for his meetings to conclude. I want to inspect the Cardinal's apartment immediately. Can that be arranged?"

"I will have to speak with him," answered Father Richard equally firmly, "when he finishes his meeting. Until then, I suggest that we continue at the library. Although I must warn you, the librarians are very protective of every document and book housed there. Unless the Cardinal has personally instructed them to provide access to his collection, I promise your requests will be ignored."

Brother Joseph shook his head in frustration. "Impress upon the Cardinal that time is of the essence. There is a killer or a group of killers targeting Catholic women. Every minute we delay puts an innocent woman at risk."

"I can make no promises," answered Father Richard, "I know the Cardinal well. We will see him as he wishes and when he wishes. To expect anything else would be a waste of your time."

Chapter 39
12:15 P.M.
Bria and Princess Celeste

*It is not because angels are holier than men or devils that makes
them angels, but because they do not expect holiness from one
another.*

—William Blake

Princess Celeste's Apartments, Palazzo Di Luca
Rome, Italy

"I am so pleased," said Princess Celeste, an elegant woman of
indeterminate but considerable age. Her ebony hair, cut into a
stylish chin-length bob, swayed as she walked, "that you came for
lunch."

"I'm pleased that you invited me, Princess. I can think of
nothing else I'd rather do."

Princess Celeste laughed. "You would probably prefer to
explore Rome with your friends, but thank you for saying that. I
can see why Inanna is so taken with you."

Bria grabbed the Princess's soft hand and held it gently. "Even
if I had plans, Princess, I would have gladly changed them. My
friend Theo and my mother are in Milan again today. Your
invitation was quite welcomed. Gabriel had planned to take me to

145

the Vatican, but Inanna sent a few paintings to your son. Gabriel is waiting for the curator's staff to uncrate and hang them. I was as free as a bird."

"The Prince Di Luca? Oh no, he is not my son. I never had children, but I've watched over him since his birth," Princess Celeste answered as she led Bria to a bright, sunny room with large French doors that overlooked a private garden. "He's quite dear to my heart."

"This is lovely," exclaimed Bria, looking around at the ivory-cushioned furniture and the large green plants decorating the room. "You've brought the outside indoors!"

Princess Celeste beamed at the compliment. "We call it the Garden Room," she said, "We redecorated it when it became difficult for me to climb the steep marble steps to the courtyard and gardens. The Prince came up with this brilliant idea. I quite love it. I'll have Lorenzo serve our lunch here if that's okay with you. I find the dining room overly formal and rather intimidating."

The luncheon was superb, and the conversation light and entertaining, but Bria noticed that the Princess ate sparingly and only sipped her sparkling white wine.

"Would you like to see the apartment?" asked the Princess. She started rising when Bria placed her napkin beside her plate.

"I'm afraid that these chairs are heavy and difficult to move," the Princess said as Bria quickly rose and helped her from her chair, "unless Lorenzo is here to help me."

"Have you considered replacing them with wicker? They would enhance the illusion that this is an extension of the outdoors and would be lighter to manage if you have to move the chairs yourself."

"What a clever idea, Bria! I will have Lorenzo text the Prince this afternoon and have him order them," she said. "I like to walk a bit after a meal, but I'm afraid I'm just the slightest bit vain. I don't like asking the staff for help up and down the stairs."

"I would be happy to help you."

"Thank you," said Princess Celeste, "but I have devised a route in and out of the rooms on this floor. Come. I'll show you," she said as she led Bria through the butler's pantry, where glassed cabinets were filled with elegant china and crystal glassware.

They stopped in the kitchen to thank Lorenzo for the delicious luncheon before exiting another door leading into the formal dining room. A long table was lined with gilded chairs and tall ornate candelabras. The gilded walls were covered with paintings of monumental proportions. Bria was not an expert in Renaissance paintings, but she recognized the works of Caravaggio, Botticelli, and Tintoretto. Following the Princess's lead, they walked around the table twice, as was the Princess' routine.

They strolled down the long gallery as Princess Celeste paused in front of a painting of a young woman. "Lady with an Ermine by Leonardo da Vinci," she said reverentially, "it's either the original or a preliminary study. There's a controversy between the Prince and the Czartoryski Museum in Krakow as to which is which. Not that it matters to me. Either way, it's one of my favorites."

Bria stood back and stared at it for a minute. "Yes, I can see why you like it. She seems calm and serene, but I see her strength and determination the more I look at her."

Princess Celeste nodded her head. "Exactly! She's a mystery like so many of Leonardo's women. She reminds me quite a bit of you."

"I don't see it. We don't look anything alike."

"Not so much the physical appearance, dear; it is the look in her eyes as if she is waiting for her fate to present itself. It's her quiet strength and confidence."

Bria leaned forward to examine the painting more closely.

"Of course, you are much more interesting-looking than she. Forgive an old lady if this is rude, but where does your family originate? I can't quite figure it out."

"I'm asked that all the time. I usually reply with a single word: human. I think that should be enough, but I get confused looks when I answer that way."

"That's a perfect answer," said Princess Celeste as she moved away from the painting. You should stick with it. It's simple but accurate."

"But, to answer your question, my father's mother was Greek and Algerian. His father was Japanese and Basque. My mother is English, Swedish, and Hungarian, with some Jewish blood thrown in. I'm a bit of everything."

"I think you should stick to your first answer. The world would be better if everyone answered 'human' and left it at that," the Princess said as she gestured for Bria to follow.

They slowly walked around the room's perimeter before duplicating the process in one room after another, discussing the paintings and furniture until they returned to the Garden Room.

Lorenzo looked up as they entered. "I hope you had a pleasant walk, Princess. Gabriel was here a few minutes ago to drop off a painting that Inanna included in the shipment. It was supposed to be delivered here to you," he shrugged, "but the moving men were too lazy to make a second stop."

He turned to Bria. "Gabriel asked that I inform you that he will take you to the Vatican in about an hour. He suggested you wait in the garden as the Princess needs her rest in the afternoon."

The Princess's eyes flashed with anger. "Not only was that rude to my guest, Lorenzo, but neither you nor Gabriel has the right to decide what I do or behave. I may be an elderly woman, but no mere man should try to bully me! My mother was Lilith. It's best you both never forget that."

"Please accept my apology," Lorenzo said, looking at Princess Celeste. He blinked his eyes and allowed a smile to cross his lips as if he was a naughty little boy who believed his charm alone would melt her heart, but it didn't calm Princess Celeste's ire a bit.

"God created men and women as equals," she stated firmly, not appeased. "God didn't make men and women subservient nor men superior. I will not be devalued or told what to do by you or any other man!"

Lorenzo bowed his head to hide his anger at being publicly scolded and left the room without comment. Bria watched him go and wondered what had just happened. Princess Celeste certainly wasn't the gentle, little, aristocratic lady she had appeared to be.

"I'm sorry, Bria," the Princess said, turning to her. "My behavior was inexcusable. I should have controlled myself, but I despise being treated like a senseless child incapable of making wise decisions."

"I liked you from the minute I met you, but Princess," she said before she threw her arms around a surprised Princess Celeste, "you stood up for yourself like a rockstar! Bravo!"

Princess Celeste laughed and hugged Bria a little tighter.

"A question, though, Princess. You said that Lilith was your mother. Should I know who she is?"

"That, my dear, is a question for another time. For now, let's unwrap the painting Inanna sent. She is exceedingly generous and has exquisite taste. I'm sure whatever she's chosen will be a welcomed addition to my meager little collection. "

Chapter 40
2 P.M.

Father Claude and Toshi

There is nothing more important than appearing to be religious.
—Niccolo Machiavelli

Vatican City

Father Claude and Toshi, dressed as members of the Roman
Catholic clergy, had spent the morning wandering the vast
expanses of the Vatican grounds, searching for Brother Joseph.
They carefully timed their movements to coincide with a surge of
tourists to melt unnoticed into the growing crowds.

They searched St. Peter's Basilica and the Gallery of
Tapestries by tagging along with a group of Spanish tourists. They
bought tickets for the Vatican Library and the Sistine Chapel while
trailing closely behind a guided tour of devout Catholic ladies from
Brazil and shorts and tee shirt-clad Americans. Their plan seemed
to work so far as no one glanced at them.

Father Claude found the Vatican Library an assault on his
visual senses. Every inch of the wall and ceiling was either painted
with religious scenes and portraits of angels and saints or gilded in
gold.

Luckily, their tour members were so engrossed in the
ostentatious display of the Church's wealth that no one noticed

Father Claude and Toshi were not a part of their original group.

Father Claude pointed to a glass case that contained a display of 14th-century hand-painted Bibles. A young nun caught Toshi's eye while examining the documents in a lighted case. After a moment, she smiled at a British naval officer standing next to them as he touched the brim of his hat and nodded back to her. Ignoring Father Claude and Toshi, she moved to the next case without looking at them.

Toshi stared down the long gallery as a red-garbed figure rapidly approached them. Father Claude tried to get his attention by whispering his name to no avail as Toshi's muscles tensed like a panther, ready to pounce upon a chosen prey. The cardinal was less than twenty feet away when Father Claude unpinned the tiny white dove pin hidden inside the cuff of his left sleeve.

He glanced up and saw that the cardinal was nearly on top of them as he reached over and thrust the sharp end of the pin into the flesh of Toshi's right hand. It was just enough to break his spell. He yelped and turned away as the cardinal glanced at them.

"Holy Mary," whispered Father Claude as soon as they were out of earshot, "that's Cardinal De Posada of *Opus Christos*."

"Yes," answered Toshi, "let's hope he didn't recognize us as easily as you recognized him."

"He's too absorbed in himself to notice anyone else," the British Naval officer beside them whispered. "Stay as you are. I believe the monk with him is Brother Joseph unless other Trappist monks are now visiting the Vatican." He turned his head slightly. "Lean over the display to hide your faces. They are coming back this way. I'll meet you outside at the cafe in twenty minutes," he whispered as he slipped away, "and be careful. *Opus Christos* agents are swarming all over the Vatican looking for us."

◆ ◆ ◆

Bria & Gabriel

After spending time in the Palazzo Di Luca, Bria found the elaborate ornamentation of the Vatican Library ornate but not overwhelming. She wasn't as awe-inspired by the profusion of murals and gilding as she might have once been. She and Gabriel stood patiently in a short line at the other end of the Vatican Library, waiting to enter the Sistine Chapel.

"Is it worth standing in this crowd?" asked Gabriel snappishly.

"It is. I'm looking forward to seeing the ceilings Michelangelo painted."

"I would be surprised if you knew the truth behind the ceiling. It is not as it seems."

"Go on," said Bria, understanding that Gabriel was most comfortable when he felt he knew more than anyone else.

"Michelangelo never considered himself a painter; he wanted to focus on sculpture."

"I knew that."

Gabriel huffed before he continued. "However, Pope Julius II insisted that Michelangelo take the commission despite their intense dislike of each other. Julius pushed Michelangelo to complete the ceiling even though it almost killed him. Julius didn't care. He wanted what he wanted, but in the end, Michelangelo got revenge.

"The ceiling murals in the Sistine Chapel are Old Testament or Jewish stories rather than depictions of New Testament or Christian stories. Pope Julius II and several other Church dignitaries of the time are depicted as sinners in the scenes of hell. It's as insulting as it is-."

"Who is that?" Bria interrupted Gabriel's long-winded

152

explanation as she stared at a group of men walking toward them.

Gabriel glanced over his shoulder, "The cardinal?"

"No, the other one, the man in the white robe with the brown apron, speaking to the cardinal."

"The Trappist monk?"

"It's weird, but I feel I should know him."

"Impossible," said Gabriel as he moved his body between Bria and the men as they passed. "The Trappists are a sequestered order. They rarely, if ever, leave their monasteries."

"If they're sequestered, what is he doing here?"

Gabriel shrugged his shoulders. "I have no idea," he said as their group shuffled closer to the entrance to the Sistine Chapel. Gabriel dismissed them and took it as an opportunity to continue his story about Michelangelo and Pope Julius II.

◆ ◆ ◆

3:15 P.M.

Father Claude, Toshi, & Lucas

Father Claude and Toshi, seated at a small table outside the Vatican Cafe, were drinking iced coffee when the British Naval officer sat beside them. He put a black briefcase on the vacant chair and pulled out an English newspaper. Without turning, he spoke quietly.

"You must be Father Claude and Toshi. I'm Lucas. Izzy and Father Patrick send regards."

Toshi looked around before he answered, but no one seemed interested in them.

"How did you spot us?"

"You mean, besides the fact that Izzy texted me your photos? I've had someone watching the rathole you call a hideout. You might want to think about that. I found it easily, so *Opus Christos*

153

isn't far behind. I was coming to the Vatican anyway. It was easy to track you once you entered the library."

"Izzy sent you to follow us?" asked Father Claude, slightly offended.

Lucas lifted the newspaper as if reading it and turned his head slightly to see them from the side of his eye. "Of course not," he said as he reached out and tapped the briefcase beside him. "I thought it wise to recognize each other if bullets started flying. I don't want to be a victim of friendly fire."

Toshi nodded, "Smart. Did you see where Cardinal De Posada went with Brother Joseph? We need to contact Brother Joseph without the cardinal's knowledge."

"They entered the Sistine Chapel, but they were able to walk right through, bypassing the line for tourists," answered Lucas. "I couldn't follow them, but I noticed a couple waiting in line that fit the descriptions of the Dove, Bria, and the man she was seen with last night. They stood out because he deliberately moved his body to shield her from Cardinal De Posada's view as they passed. Who is he?"

"Tall, curly, blonde hair, very handsome?"

Lucas nodded his head.

"We know who he is, more or less. We don't know what he is, if that makes any sense."

"Sounds reasonable, but I suggest you find out," said Lucas as he picked up the briefcase and stood up, "I think he's important."

3:30 P.M.

Cardinal De Posada, Brother Joseph and Father Richard

After impressing upon the head librarian that he expected total cooperation from the library staff, Cardinal De Posada, with Brother Joseph trailing behind him, entered the storeroom under the Sistine Chapel where Father Richard and Felix were working.

He stopped to watch Father Richard removing the brown paper on the backside of a large painting with a utility knife. Felix was in the corner of the room, examining the construction of a large chest of drawers as he ran his hands over the interior surfaces. He looked over at Brother Joseph.

"Searching a room and destroying it are two different things," the cardinal said, looking at the stacks of papers scattered on the table, "I take it there is no sign of the fabled list. I told you Hilmi Al-Jafri was a liar. I promise you that the list that the pontiff is insisting you find didn't arrive here in my possessions. You need to search elsewhere."

Brother Joseph began to respond and then thought better of it. Despite his growing dislike of Cardinal De Posada, he could not forget their respective ranks and positions. Nodding his head in acknowledgment, he walked over to Father Richard to help steady the large painting as Father Richard pried out the tiny nails holding the stretched canvas to the frame to discover nothing was hidden inside. This painting was the last item listed on the manifest of the cardinal's possessions stored in the cellar under the Sistine Chapel.

"We still need to search several other storerooms. This is just one of many. Perhaps–," started Father Richard before the cardinal interrupted him.

"I understand you wish to search my private apartments,

Brother Joseph," said Cardinal De Posada. "It is a waste of your time and, more importantly, a great inconvenience to me, but since His Eminence himself requested that you be given free rein to search for the list of Islamic terrorist groups who are targeting Christian women, I have no choice but to comply. I will see you at 6 P.M. this evening," he continued as he swept out of the storeroom. "Be prompt. I am a very busy man."

Chapter 41
4:45 P.M.

The Guardians and the *Mahdi of Islam*

The death sentence is a necessary and efficacious means for the church to attain its ends when rebels against it disturb the ecclesiastical unity.

—Theo XIII (1810–1903)

Rome, Italy

"Something's wrong," said Dhabi, "Neilson missed his check-in. Fatima isn't answering her phone."

Milo looked down from his position on the roof across from the *Palazzo Di Luca*. He lifted the binoculars. "Both of their cars are still in place, but I don't see any movement. Neilson probably nodded off. I was worried about those painkillers."

"That's why I backed him up with Fatima."

"I'm going down to check on them."

"Okay. Walk by like you're just going to the store."

Milo stroked the Beretta in his shoulder harness. "Really? My family has been Guardians for seven hundred years, and you're telling me to 'walk like I'm just going to the store?' I'm a goddamn professional trained by the best. I'll take it a step further. I'll go to the goddamn store. How do you like them apples?"

"Milo, why are you going to buy apples? We have more

serious issues, at the moment."

"Up yours, Dhabi. I'll get back to you in a few."

5 P.M.
Bria and Gabriel

"Would you like to stop for a glass of wine before we return to the *palazzo*?" Gabriel asked Bria as they passed through the Viale Vaticano after a long afternoon of touring the Vatican.

Bria laughed. "As long as it's not *Nebbiolo*. I'm sticking to white wine for a while."

"You seemed to enjoy it at the time."

"After the first glass, yes, but after I drank a whole bottle? It was more that it didn't like me the next morning."

"Well," said Gabriel, looking her up and down critically, "that does explain a lot."

"Meow."

"I don't understand what that's supposed to mean."

Bria smiled sweetly. "It means you're a catty little bitch. I didn't look that bad."

Gabriel arched an eyebrow. "You looked horrible, like something your cat dragged in. See? I know snarky American expressions, too."

"Just for that," said Bria, as she linked her arm inside Gabriel's bent elbow, "It's going to be a very expensive white wine, and you're going to pay for it."

"That seems fair enough. If you admit you looked awful, I'll throw in some garlic bread."

"Dream on," answered Bria laughingly. "That ain't never going to happen, fool."

Milo

Milo borrowed a wicker shopping basket sitting by one of the apartment doors before he walked out of the building. He bent over and tied his shoes to check the block in both directions. It looked clear, but he was ready to react just in case. He casually glanced inside Neilson's car as he walked by, swinging the shopping basket. After a few minutes, he returned, walking down the opposite side of the street with the basket filled with bread, cheese, and apples.

He stood in front of Fatima's van and turned his head as if checking for traffic before he crossed the street and entered the apartment building. He returned the basket, still full of groceries, to the apartment door where he had borrowed it before climbing the stairs to the roof. He leaned against the short parapet and punched a number into his burner cell phone.

"They're both dead. Headshots: clear and right in the middle of the forehead. I don't know how they got past us."

Dhabi cursed in Arabic before he spoke. "It was the parking meter lady. She was slowly driving by in that stupid little cart. I didn't even look at her twice."

"Shit," said Milo, "she was sixty years old if she was a day. Sneaky bastards."

Bria and Gabriel

Bria and Gabriel sat at a window table in the cafe, waiting for the waiter.

"Oh darn!" she said as she searched her bag, "I was supposed to check on my mother about half an hour ago. I forgot to charge my phone. It's dead. She's going to be worried if I don't call her."

Gabriel pulled his iPhone from his jacket pocket.

"Here, use mine," he said/.

"Thanks. I'm going outside. It's too noisy in here. If you order before I get back, it better be white, and it better be expensive. Forget the garlic bread. I looked great for first thing in the morning, even after all the wine you forced me to drink last night."

Two glasses of white wine and a large platter of garlic bread were sitting on the table when Bria returned from making her phone call. She rolled her eyes at Gabriel and sat down across from him. He lifted the platter and offered her a piece.

"Oh no," she said, sipping the wine, "it's all yours. I'm not admitting a thing."

"The waiter just brought it over with the compliments of the house. It's their thing, I guess."

"Really?" asked Bria as she grabbed a slice and took a big bite. "OMG, this is the best!"

"Not really." Gabriel chuckled, "He came over, shook his head, and said that I was a brave man to go out with a woman who looked so awful in the morning. I deserved all the garlic bread I could eat."

"You're a jerk, Gabriel, do you know that?"

"It's part of my charm, don't you think?"

"Absolutely... not. But this is perfect garlic bread. The best," she said as she took another slice. "Two more pieces, and I might forgive you."

◆ ◆ ◆

Milo and Dhabi

In less than fifteen minutes, two tow trucks pulled up and swiftly chained up Neilson's car and Fatima's van and hauled them away.

Milo grabbed his cell phone and called Dhabi. He swiftly turned when he heard the phone ringing behind him.

Dhabi smiled as he wiggled his cell phone. "Milo, this is what I call professional."

"Pretty damn impressive, *lucciola,*" he said, "I didn't even hear the door open."

"It didn't. I scaled down from the balcony on the top floor of the building next door."

Milo nodded his head as he looked up. "That wall is at least twenty feet high. You got a career in the circus if you want it."

"I could," answered Dhabi, "but this is more important. I have sworn to protect Islam and will do that until I die."

"Which could be tonight, *Paisano.*"

"Then I have lived well," Dhabi said, "as have you, my friend."

Milo shrugged. "You die for a lie, or you die for the truth. I learned that in Afghanistan. This time, I'm choosing the truth."

Chapter 42
5:30 P.M.

Pope Peter and Sister Bernadette

I often quote John Paul II when he said [of evolution] that 'truth cannot contradict truth' and if you think you know all there is to know about God, then your religious faith is at fault.

–Brother Guy Consolmagno
Director of the Vatican Observatory

Papal Apartments, Vatican City

Peter spent the entire day praying in his private chapel, searching for the solution to the unthinkable dilemma he unwittingly found himself in. If there was a way to stop *Opus Christos*, he couldn't find it without threatening the survival of the Church. Cardinal De Posada and Superior General Scotti had spun their web tightly.

Returning to the papal apartment, he saw the box of documents that the Cardinal and Superior General had left him lying on his desk. He hadn't remembered removing it from its hiding place, but perhaps, he decided, the stress of the last day had made him forgetful. He made a mental note to call the library after he had showered to tell them to pick them up. He could no longer bear to look at them.

Twenty minutes later, showered and shaved, he heard the front door of his apartment opening. He peeked out of the bathroom door to see one of the nuns standing next to his desk, holding a tray of food. Like most of The Handmaidens of Jesus Crucified, she was an older woman. She seemed transfixed on the spot, a look of shock marring her face. Pope Peter tightened the belt on his robe before he walked across the room and took the tray from her shaking hands.

She stared at the document box before slowly prying her eyes away and turning to look at him. She put her finger to her lips as she turned up the volume on his music. and whispered, "The room is bugged, Your Eminence. Your annoying rock music will cover our voices."

"You know, don't you? We were unsure if you were *Opus Christos,* but I didn't believe it was possible. Cardinal De Posada is using the Church's dirty laundry to blackmail you into doing his evil bidding, isn't he?"

Pope Peter felt like a lightning bolt had hit him.

"Sister Bernadette," he stammered, "I–"

Pope Peter nodded his head and did as she asked.

"When I saw the look of shock and sadness on your face," she said, "I did not doubt the truth. What *Opus Christos* is asking you to do is an abomination to God, but you are not alone."

She lifted the underside of her wimple to show him a small silver dove. "We are the Guardians of the Holy Doves," she said quietly. Judith the Elder founded our order to protect the Messiah's three daughters, who were called the Holy Doves. We have watched over every generation of the Holy Family ever since."

Pope Peter leaned closer to her and whispered, "But why now? Why has the Church hidden the truth for thousands of years?"

Sister Bernadette shrugged her shoulder.

"A better question is why have men denied God's commandments of equality from the beginning of time to satisfy their need for domination and power?"

Pope Peter nodded his head.

"Cardinal De Posada and Superior General Scotti threatened to expose the truth and destroy the Church."

"They won't. Without the power and luxury their positions provide, they are nothing. Unless you bow to their demands, they will likely kill you and usurp the Throne of Peter. They believe it is their right to deny the truth and set themselves above God."

"But the documents-?"

"Are real. They have been hidden from the faithful because they tell a very different story than the Church has preached for two millennia. The Guardians know the truth. We have gathered tens of thousands of early Christian documents to protect the historical records and the truth of the early faith. We have dedicated our lives, generation after generation, to protecting the Holy Doves, the living descendants of the Messiah. We are dedicated to God's truth, not man's."

"But," whispered Pope Peter as he pointed to the documents on his desk, "where did these come from?"

"We can't be sure. The Secret Archives inside the Vatican may have hundreds of documents hidden away that are as damaging to the Church as the ones the Guardians have collected over the centuries. When the Nazis set fire to Marseille in 1942, we were able to save the vast majority of our ancient cache in a cave beneath our monastery, but, sadly, not everything. This casket has the seals of Popes Clement and Pius XII, in addition to those of the Third Reich, so perhaps these are the documents we believed were destroyed during the war."

"The cardinal said the casket and the documents inside were traded for the Church's silence about the Holocaust," answered Pope Peter.

"That explains a great deal. Thank you," she whispered. "Your Eminence, listen carefully, as I do not have time to repeat myself."

"I understand," Pope Peter whispered after Sister Bernadette had finished speaking quietly. "The loyalty of the Guardians is to the Holy Doves and the Christ child. I move forward at my peril."

The Sister stood. "I'm truly sorry, Your Holiness. We are vowed to protect the life of God's Child at all costs. Ultimately, the Church must stand or fall on its own."

Pope Peter was silent for a minute before he spoke. "Sister, nothing, not even our beloved faith, can come before God's commandments. I will do all you request of me."

"For now, do as the cardinal asks," she said before Pope Peter could protest, "without question. He must think you support *Opus Christos'* agenda or, at least, you believe you have no other option. Trust us. We have been preparing for this moment for 2,000 years."

Pope Peter nodded his head. "Then I will be the meek lamb led to slaughter. The Trappist monk, Brother Joseph, is he one of them? Is he *Opus Christos*?"

She paused before she spoke. "We believe he is in the same position as you, Your Holiness, a pawn in their heresy but not a player in the game. He has been fooled, we believe, by their story. He believes he's doing the Church's bidding under your express orders. He does not know who he is."

"What do you mean? Who is he?" asked Pope Peter.

"Forgive me, Your Holiness. I have spoken out of turn. Please understand that some things you do not know are better."

Pope Peter looked at the Sister momentarily and nodded his agreement. He stepped over to the desk, took out the top two parchments, and handed them to Sister Bernadette. "If these documents were given to him," he said, "perhaps he would understand and discover the solution where I have failed."

The nun looked down at the fragile papers in her hands and then handed them back. "Your Holiness, I cannot promise I can get close enough to Brother Joseph to do as you ask. I'm sorry."

"Then I must find another way. May God protect you," he said quietly, "and the Holy Doves."

A startled look crossed the nun's face before she smiled slowly. In her wildest dreams, she would have never expected to hear those words out of the mouth of the pontiff.

Chapter 43
6 P.M.

Cardinal De Posada, Brother Joseph, and Father Richard

The question before the human race is whether the God of nature shall govern the world by his own laws or whether priests and kings shall rule it by fictitious miracles.
—John Adams (1735–1826)

Vatican City

Cardinal De Posada glanced at the mantel clock beginning the first of its six chimes. He pointed at two silk moiré chairs, "You're on time," he said. "May I offer you a Campari or a Dubonnet, perhaps?"

"No, thank you," said Brother Joseph, "It's very kind, but—"

"Yes, of course. I had forgotten that you're a Trappist; chastity, poverty, and all that nonsense," he said, taking the heavy-cut crystal glass filled with ice and Campari from Father Richard. "Personally, I find chastity is not a bad trade-off, but the poverty?" His gaze swept around the luxurious furnishings of his apartment. "That is an unnecessary sacrifice. I suppose I am Benedictine at heart."

Brother Joseph smiled weakly at Cardinal De Posada's attempt at humor.

Cardinal De Posada suddenly noticed that Felix was not there.

"The other man, Agent Blanc? He is not joining us?"

Father Richard bowed slightly, "He was called away, Your Excellency."

"Yes," added Brother Joseph, "Alberto Zayas called earlier. Agent Blanc went to Da Vinci to pick him up. I believe he's come to assist us with the search for the names of the Islamic terrorists."

"And you neglected to inform me of this, Father Richard?" snapped Cardinal De Posada. "You knew that I told him not to come."

Father Richard paled. "Your Excellency, this is the first time I have heard that he is here. Agent Blanc asked me to arrange a car for him, but he didn't tell me where he was going. I–"

"You should have asked! I should have been immediately informed of all developments!"

"You are correct, of course, Your Excellency," said Father Richard quietly as he bent his head in shame. "I failed in my responsibilities."

Brother Joseph tried to defuse the situation and divert the Cardinal's unreasonable reaction to the news of Alberto's arrival away from Father Richard.

"I believe you said there were textiles and a few books in this apartment that were included in the shipment from Cuba?" he asked calmly. "Perhaps I should look at them now?"

Cardinal De Posada fumed quietly before he responded. "Isn't that why you have invaded my privacy? Father Richard, bring the contents of the bottom drawer of my bureau. It's primarily vestments. I have no use for them in my current position, but they remind me of home."

He stood up and gestured to Brother Joseph to follow. "The books are on the bookshelf in the office. Feel free to tear them apart or take them away. They belonged to my parents, so they mean nothing to me," he said as he checked his iPhone. "I must leave you. Something has come up that I must attend to immediately."

◆ ◆ ◆

Alberto Zayas and Felix

The other passengers gave Alberto a wide berth as he stood on that curb at Da Vinci Airport. His Gucci carry-on was lying at his feet, his Tom Ford Cashmere Chesterfield coat resting on his shoulders invited admiring glances. Alberto had spent years perfecting the appearance of being well-bred and, therefore, superior in his mind. It was not true, of course. He had developed this facade to distance himself from his origins as the son of a poor, illegal immigrant family in Spanish Harlem. He was the oldest in a family blessed with more children than beds or shoes. He was just another mouth to feed, an aggravating burden to his overwhelmed parents.

Alberto soon found the attention he craved from the parish priest at St. Teresa's, where he was a charity student. Father Rafael De Posada saw something in the young boy worth cultivating. Perhaps it was that he realized Alberto was willing to do anything to get what he wanted without a single qualm.

As Rafael climbed the Ecclesiastic ladder, Alberto followed him from the parish rectory to the bishop's residence to the archbishop's mansion. His presence was explained away as His Eminence's orphaned nephew. There was nothing improper in their relationship. Archbishop De Posada's only goal was to mold Alberto into embracing *Opus Christos'* ideals. Alberto was willing to do anything to gain De Posada's approval.

Sensing excited whispers growing from behind, Alberto pulled himself together. He turned, his face fixed with a look of studied disinterest, to watch a young man dressed in the traditional *thobe* and *ghutra* exit the terminal. Alberto raised one eyebrow as if to say it was all an incredible bore.

He quietly watched as three shadowy forms covered in the traditional *abayas* scurried forward to enter the cars—one woman into the forward Rolls as the remaining two entered the rear. Turning his head, the young man noticed Alberto watching him. He stared back for a moment before he pursed his lips in a dismissive smirk and climbed into the car.

Alberto stood there, trying to regain his composure, as Felix, a black chauffeur's cap sitting jauntily on his head, pulled up and jumped out of the white Lincoln Town Car.

"Hi, boss," he said.

"You're late," Alberto hissed through his clenched teeth.

Felix nodded as he lifted his carry-on off the curb. "His aide said the cardinal wasn't happy when he learned you were here. He was furious, actually," he said as he threw the bag into the car.

"Father Richard suggested that you lay low until the cardinal calms down. Maybe you can ask Superior General Scotti to explain to the cardinal why he told you to come even after the cardinal ordered you not to. I'm sure that will work," Felix added as he closed Zayas' rear door and turned his head to smirk.

Chapter 44
6:30 P.M.

Milo, Izzy, and Father Patrick

Because it is so unbelievable, the Truth often escapes being known
—Heraclitus

Guardians' Command Center
Abbey Sainte-Victoire, Marseille, France

"Neilson and Fatima were killed this afternoon," said Milo as soon as Father Patrick answered the phone, "outside the *Palazzo Di Luca*. *Opus Christos* knows we're here. It's not much of a leap to figure out they know Bria's here, too."

Father Patrick sighed as he looked over at Izzy. "We have to approach her as soon as we can."

"We're working on it," answered Milo, "but we need a plan."

"I take it that the killings have been covered over?"

"Dhabi had tow trucks remove both vehicles before anyone was the wiser. I don't know where their bodies are now," Milo paused. "Perhaps you could speak with the *Mahdi* and find out so we can give Neilson a decent Christian burial. He would have wanted that."

"I'll take care of that," promised Father Patrick. There was a moment of silence. "Milo, Father Claude, Toshi, and Lucas were able to identify Bria at the Vatican Library with the blond man from the restaurant. It's safe to believe he was the same one at the

Palazzo when you delivered the crates."

"I spoke with Toshi earlier this evening. Brother Joseph and Cardinal De Posada walked past Bria without noticing her. They entered the Sistine Chapel together before Father Claude, Toshi, or Lucas could approach them. Bria and Brother Joseph are alive as of earlier this afternoon."

"That couldn't have been Bria," answered Milo. "Dhabi dropped a GPS device in her jacket pocket when we were delivering furniture. She hasn't left her room all day. We'd know if she had."

"Milo," said Izzy, breaking into the conversation, "her jacket hasn't left the *palazzo* all day. Unlike you guys, we women change our clothes regularly. It was Bria."

"Damn! We were waiting for dark before we would move to grab her."

"It may not be as easy as you think. The blond man seems to stay close to her, and we don't know who he is."

"Wouldn't be fun if it was easy," said Milo, "Are you sure it wasn't Theo?"

"Positive. Her mother, Magdalena, and Theo have reservations on the 8:08 train from Milan to Rome. We believe that Bria may be the chosen one. Her mother is also a Holy Dove and in equal peril. Hold on a minute. Father Patrick has something he wants to ask you," Izzy said.

"Are you positive all the movers left the *Palazzo Di Luca*? No one stayed behind?"

"It was pretty chaotic, so it's possible, I guess. Several crates were large enough for a person to fit inside," suggested Milo, "and the curator's staff didn't arrive until after we left."

"I want you and Dhabi to break in and sweep the entire place. I'll clear it with the *Mahdi*," said Father Patrick. "Jasper says the security system is world-class. The slightest movement will trigger it. He's trying to deactivate it. If someone is inside, we don't want them to know you're coming."

Milo spoke up. "Izzy, besides the security system and possible assassins hiding behind the potted plants, we have no idea where Bria and Blondie Boy are, when they're coming back, or if they're coming back. How do you propose we get Bria out safely?"

"We're working on it. I'm setting up drone surveillance. That should give you a heads up," said Jasper, joining the conversation, "if anyone approaches the *palazzo*. There's a delivery entrance on the north side by the kitchen. It will offer you a bit of coverage. I'll text you the blueprint."

"Just be cautious," Izzy said, "we don't want to lose anybody else."

"I'll talk to Dhabi. He's full of ideas and knows every tradesman in Rome."

"Do that."

"If we find somebody inside?"

"If they're hiding inside the house, we have to assume they're *Opus Christos* and a danger to Bria," Izzy ordered. "Take them out. We'll ask for God's forgiveness later."

Chapter 45
6:30 P.M.

Father Claude, Toshi, Lucas, and Sister Maria Teresa

Angels are in the heavens, I am sure, because there are deeds done by mortals that are difficult to explain by the mortal nature of man.
						—Dagobert D. Runes (1902–1982)

Rome, Italy

Father Claude and Toshi entered the bustling grocery store on the Via Leone IV. The pungent smells of garlic, spices, olives, and cheese assaulted their senses. Behind a barrel of dried cod, they saw a narrow doorway exactly as Izzy had described it. They entered to find Lucas waiting for them next to a quarter-ton delivery truck loaded with crates of fruits, vegetables, and boxes of wine.

"I'm meeting with my 'aunt' Sister Bernadette later to exchange the casket's contents with our forgeries. I'll take the authentic one to *Abbey Sainte-Victoire* for safekeeping," said Lucas. "Orlando's in Milan. He will contact Bria's mother and her friend, Theo, and take them to the Abbey."

"How will he convince them to go with him?" asked Toshi.

Lucas shrugged. "Not my department. I'm sure Izzy knows what she's doing."

"Your inside contact will find you and get you to Brother Joseph. Good luck, gentlemen," he said as he lowered the truck's metal door and pounded on the side of the truck to send it on its way.

Lurching in the darkness toward the front of the truck, Father Claude and Toshi began stripping themselves of their clerical suits and collars. They slipped on the khaki cotton pants and white shirts emblazoned with the grocery store's name silk-screened in green and pink across the front pocket. They tied a stained-white apron around their waists and firmly placed the white cotton cap with the store's name on their heads.

As the truck pulled to the Vatican's gate, they quickly crouched down behind the boxes of produce. They heard male laughter when the driver joked with the security guard. They held their breaths until the truck started moving again toward the kitchen entrance of the Apostolic Palace. With a loud rattle, the metal door slid up and caught in the rails on the ceiling.

The driver stepped onto the truck's bed, pointed to a box of wine, and gestured for Father Claude to place it on his shoulder and follow him as he hoisted a crate of tomatoes. He nodded almost imperceptibly as the second man stepped inside, bent down, picked up a box of oranges, and signaled Toshi to wait.

An elderly nun stood in the kitchen doorway and scowled as she spoke to them rapidly in Italian. The truck driver handed her a crumpled sheet of pink paper. She studied it carefully for several seconds and then moved slowly aside to allow them to enter.

Following the driver's lead, Father Claude crossed the tiled floor to a large, worn wooden table in the middle of the room. He placed the heavy case of wine on the table when he heard the elderly nun scold him in Italian while shaking her head.

"*Aspetti*," she said, searching the pockets of her white apron, "*Ho bisogno mia chiave.*"

He watched in confusion as the elderly nun turned and hobbled across the tiled kitchen floor.

She stopped at a pegboard nailed near the door and looked over her wire-rimmed glasses.

"Ah!" she said, reaching up and grasping the key in her gnarled right hand. "*Mia chiave*," she said, holding the key up. "*Quella direzione*," she said, pointing a crooked finger to a wooden door.

He waited patiently, the heavy case resting on his shoulder, as she fumbled to place the key in the lock. The door swung open to reveal wooden steps leading downward. She reached in front of him and switched on the lights. Holding the rail, she slowly lowered herself down the steep stairway step by step. She stopped at the bottom of the steps and turned to Father Claude.

"Hide well," she whispered in her Irish lilt. "Father Patrick, Izzy, and Jasper send their regards." Her brown eyes twinkled as his face registered surprise at her perfect English.

"It might be a good idea for you to put that case of wine down before you drop it," she said. I'm Sister Maria Teresa, your contact."

He swung the heavy case from his shoulder and placed it gently on the floor.

"Sister Maria—"

The nun brought her finger to her lips. "We shall talk later," she whispered, pointing to a space hidden underneath the stairwell. "I must return upstairs before someone wonders what mischief I am up to."

He could hear the steady progression of feet walking back and forth across the kitchen tiles above his head as the men unloaded the truck. Finally, the cellar door opened, and the heavy footsteps of a solitary man climbing down the stairs echoed throughout the cellar.

"Toshi? Over here!" He whispered as the wooden door slammed shut and the lights switched off. "Duck your head," he said just before he heard a loud thump.

"Thanks for the warning. Do we know who our contact is?" Toshi asked, rubbing his forehead.

"We've already met her. It's Sister Maria Teresa."

"The nun? She's our contact?"

"She'll try to get us into Brother Joseph's room this evening."

"And, meanwhile, we just sit in this dark, cold basement?"

"That seems to be the plan," Father Claude answered.

Chapter 46
7:30 P.M.

Brother Joseph and Father Richard

Ay, what is knowledge among men? Who dares call the child by its true name?

—Johann Wolfgang Von Goethe
Faust

Vatican City

"Brother Joseph," said Father Richard as he tapped on the closed door, "I hope I'm not an interruption."

"Father Richard, of course not," he said as he noticed the basket Father Richard held.

"I thought you might be hungry since Cardinal De Posada was called away before dinner."

"This is kind of you," he said, stepping aside to allow Cardinal De Posada's aide inside.

"It isn't much," said Father Richard as he placed the basket on the small table in the corner of the room, "since I had to prepare it myself. The Sisters have gone into seclusion to pray for the soul of Sister Maria del Carmen. It is always a shock when one of the Vatican family passes away suddenly."

"I'm sorry to hear of her passing. May God welcome her to Heaven."

Father Richard nodded his head. He showed no signs of wishing to leave.

"Would you like to join me?" asked Brother Joseph.

The priest looked around the room nervously. "Perhaps I should go," he said.

"Stay, please," said Brother Joseph as he pulled out one of the two chairs near the table and gestured for Father Richard to sit. "There is more than enough food for us both."

They ate the meal in silence. Brother Joseph finished, wiped his mouth with the linen napkin, and placed it beside the empty plate. "How long have you been Cardinal De Posada's aide?" he asked.

The priest's face grew pale. "For the last year," he answered cautiously. "I was the assistant curator of the Gregorian Pagan Museum before that."

"And you do not like him," Brother Joseph said, more of a statement than a question.

"It is not my place to like or dislike him."

Brother Joseph said nothing momentarily, allowing the air to become heavy with silence. "You came here this evening for a reason, Father Richard."

Just as Father Richard opened his mouth to speak, there was a knock on the door. His face drained of color. Brother Joseph gestured toward the bathroom door. He waited until the bathroom door was closed before he opened the door. He wasn't surprised to see Cardinal De Posada standing there.

He glanced over Brother Joseph's shoulder. "I see that you have eaten."

"One of the Sisters brought me a meal. It was kind of them to think of me at such a time of sorrow."

Cardinal De Posada looked at Brother Joseph. "You mean Sister Maria Rachel's death? It is a great inconvenience. Now I must train another Sister to clean my apartment to my standards."

"It was my understanding that Sister Maria del Carmen passed away. Perhaps I misunderstood?"

"Oh? It is easy to get them confused," said Cardinal De Posada as he waved his mistake, "I have no interest in the lives of women, even nuns." He turned and walked away without another word.

"Brother Joseph?" said Father Richard, his voice shaky as he peeked out of the bathroom door, "The Cistercian Brothers at St. Stephen's honor the Holy Hours. We have missed Compline, but the chapel's side door is left unlocked for those whose official duties might keep us from attending service. I was planning to go to St. Stephen's. Would you like to join me?"

"Yes., Father Richard," he answered, his voice shaking at the callowness of the cardinal's words. "I need the comfort of prayer at this moment. Thank you."

◆ ◆ ◆

Cardinal De Posada and Superior General Scotti

"We had agreed not to speak again until this was over, Enrico," said Cardinal De Posada coldly as he grasped the phone tightly and paced his apartment.

"We agreed not to see each other. I cannot see you nor, I believe, can you see me."

Cardinal De Posada bit his tongue. There was nothing in the world more exasperating than arguing with a Jesuit. They used another's words as swords against them, twisting and turning each statement until the speaker was forced to question his position.

"Any contact between us might jeopardize the mission," Cardinal De Posada said.

"Poppycock!" answered the Superior General immediately.

"You know as well as I do that the only bugs on this line belong to either your people or mine."

"Nevertheless—"

"Has your Trappist found Leah's List?"

Cardinal De Posada spoke curtly, "Not yet, Enrico. I oversaw the packing of my possessions. I seriously doubt that I would have missed seeing it. It does not exist."

"We both know it does. Father Juan swore on his deathbed that it was included in the crates."

"Father Juan could have been mistaken. He was a fool."

"But I am not a fool, Rafael! You may have convinced the others that you are dedicated to the principles of *Opus Christos* and the eradication of the Doves, but I know better. You have loyalty to one thing and one thing only—whatever is profitable for Rafael De Posada."

"I highly resent—"

The Superior General laughed, "Understand me, Rafael. I admire your ruthlessness. If it weren't for the fact that I stood in your way, you would have made an excellent Superior General. It was good that you are not a Jesuit since only one of us would have survived the power struggle. *Opus Christos* would have greatly missed your many talents."

"Or yours," answered Cardinal De Posada.

"I would have ground you into dust." The Superior General's voice was steady.

"We need to come to an understanding, Rafael. I admit that your plan to blame the Muslims for the deaths of the Holy Doves is nothing less than brilliant. It draws the world's attention away from us so we can do what we must to return the Church to its rightful position of power and glory over all people and governments of the world."

Scotti's voice deepened.

"But, understand this, Rafael, if I suspect you care more about your desire to usurp the Papal Throne than ensuring that The Child Who Is Coming will not be born, I will gladly kill you myself. The Doves must be found and eliminated before the Child is conceived!"

"You dare threaten me?" the cardinal asked angrily.

"Threaten you? Rafael," Scotti's voice did not waver. "I am simply reminding you of our mission's true focus. Your ego must be put aside until the Church is no longer in danger. Have you heard from Alberto?"

"He's here in Rome," answered De Posada. "I had told him not to come, but he ignored my instructions."

"Yes, Rafael, he did, but he followed mine. I ordered him to come. He knows who will be left standing if push comes to shove. And Rafael-"

"What?" he asked, unable to keep the fury out of his voice.

"It won't be you," said the Superior General coldly before disconnecting the call.

Chapter 47
6:45 P.M.
Bria and Gabriel

*Coincidences are not accidents but signals from the
universe which can guide us toward our true destiny.*
                                        —*Deepak Chopra*

Rome, Italy

"I like this one," said Bria, holding a glass of white wine, "even
more than the first or the second one. It's slightly sweet without
being cloying. Perhaps a hint of cherry? Or pear?"

Gabriel had switched to a Barbera. He took a drink of the
purple-red wine and then looked at her. "You don't have the
slightest idea what you're saying, do you?"

Bria giggled. "Not even a little bit. I just wanted to sound
European and sophisticated."

Gabriel smiled as he put his glass on the table. "Bria, Inanna
wouldn't have chosen you unless she believed you were perfect
just as you were. I'm shocked to admit that I'm beginning to see
why."

"She seems to think that I'm a better designer than I am. Only
the evening dress, which was the wrong color, the swing coat and
pants, and the lounging pajamas are mine. Theo listens to me, but,
in the end, his decisions are the only ones that matter. Theo's the

one with talent."

"I'm not talking about the collection or your design skills," he said, changing the subject quickly. "How are your mother and Theo enjoying Milan?"

"Oh, Inanna sent a driver to the train station. He's taking them to France to meet some friends of hers. Once they're settled in, I'll meet them in a day or two."

Gabriel choked on his wine. "Where in France?"

"It's a place somewhere near Marseille, I believe. Hotel Sainte-Victory? The phone connection was pretty bad," answered Bria.

"*Abbey Sainte-Victoire?*" asked Gabriel, sitting up straight and leaning toward her.

"Maybe. It's a six-hour drive from Milan. Since there are no direct flights, it's easier to drive. That's why Inanna sent a car. Both Mom and Theo are super excited."

Gabriel slipped deep in thought for a moment. "Of course, no one would expect them to drive. Clever," he said. "That's not a bad solution."

"Solution?"

"Bad word choice. I meant driving instead of flying is a good idea."

"Have you ever been there?"

"To *Abbey Sainte-Victoire?*"

"Isn't that what we're talking about?"

"No, I haven't," said Gabriel, "but I know about the people there, although we've never met."

"And?"

"They believe in what they are doing."

Bria took a sip of wine, "And what is that exactly?"

"Doing the best they can to save the world. I believe Inanna hopes they will succeed. I would care if it mattered to me one way or another.”

“But you don’t?”

“Inanna cares, and that’s all that matters,” Gabriel said as he stood up. “Excuse me for a minute. I need to make a call. Would you order dinner for us? I shouldn’t be long.”

Chapter 48
7:45 P.M.
Dhabi and Milo

*An angel can illuminate the thought and mind of man by
strengthening the power of vision, and by bringing within his reach
some truth which the angel himself contemplates.*

—Thomas Aquinas

Palazzo Di Luca,
Rome, Italy

Dhabi and Milo waited outside the back gate of the *palazzo* until
they saw the drone flying above them. Then, Dhabi pulled the van
marked Petros' Pest Control into the rear service entrance. Dressed
in olive-colored coveralls, he turned to look across the driveway
where Dhabi was positioned, his hand on his weapon and ready to
protect him if necessary.

"Dhabi, what happened to the exterior security guards?"

"They all called in sick, unfortunately, and my uncle's security
firm was unable to find replacement guards at such short notice."

"Of course," answered Milo, "I'm starting to think your family
and friends run this town."

"We have a few investments here and there, but there is still
the alarm system to worry about before we can enter. Is it disabled
yet?" whispered Dhabi.

"Jasper's working on it," Milo said after a moment, "He says it's a go. Let's do this."

"You want to kick it in, or should I?" said Dhabi as he joined Milo.

"I'm thinking that all that noise will destroy any element of surprise we might have. How about we climb through that open window?" answered Milo as he pointed to a window on the second floor.

"Should be a snap for you, Spiderman."

Dhabi nodded as he put his gun in his waistband. He climbed the stonework, slipped through the window, and fell silently onto the deep carpet. Within seconds, Milo was beside him. With their guns drawn, they flanked the doorway and then moved down the hallway, checking each room as they proceeded.

"Not bad, Robin," whispered Dhabi.

"That's Batman's sidekick, *Stupido Merde*," answered Milo as his iPhone vibrated. He brought the phone to his ear, expecting to hear Izzy's voice, but it was a deep voice he didn't recognize.

"There's an armed man in the linen closet twenty-five feet in front of you on the left-hand side, and another is hiding in the music room. Three staff members are locked in the walk-in freezer. Release them once you're finished."

"Who is this?" Milo whispered.

"Clean up the mess and take the garbage with you," the voice said. "I don't want to have to pay the staff overtime." Then the line went dead.

"It could be a trap," said Dhabi as they crept down the hall.

"Yup," answered Milo, "could be, Spiderman. Guess we'll know pretty damn soon."

Chapter 49
8:15 P.M.

Brother Joseph and Father Richard

The Truth is not for all men, but only for those who seek it.
                                                    —*Ayn Rand*

Vatican City

Brother Joseph sat quietly. He stood, genuflected, and left the darkened chapel.

"Brother Joseph?" a whispered voice called from the shadows. He stopped and looked around.

"Father Richard," he said, "I didn't expect to see you."

"The cardinal's upset with me, so he dismissed me for the night. I thought you might have difficulty returning to the Apostolic Palace in the dark."

Brother Joseph lifted his right hand and pointed down the pathway. "It is this way, isn't it?" he said as the priest walked beside him. They had gone several yards in silence before he spoke.

"What do you wish to tell me?" he asked.

"I, I…" Father Richard stammered.

Brother Joseph stopped and turned toward the priest. He placed his hand on Father Richard's shoulder. "It is easiest just to say it. Then it's done and over."

Father Richard took a deep breath and then began to speak. "It's easier if I show you."

◆ ◆ ◆

Sister Bernadette and Pope Peter

Sister Bernadette slipped into the papal apartments with a stack of freshly laundered and pressed sheets. She peeked into the office to see Pope Peter sitting at his desk reading.

"Your Eminence?" she said, her voice at a volume that surprised Peter. "I brought the fresh sheets you requested."

Pope Peter turned toward her. She put her finger up to her lips. He nodded, and she lifted the top sheet to reveal the parchments that Lucas had given her to exchange with the ones in the casket.

"After you put those sheets away, may I ask you to tidy up here? I was drinking tea and eating cookies while I was reading. I'm afraid I've created a bit of a mess."

"I will put these away, then get my cleaning supplies. It won't take a minute."

Pope Peter stood up and walked over to close the curtains; he gathered the documents, keeping a few aside in case he needed them. He turned to find Sister Bernadette standing behind him. She watched as he placed the false documents that Martin and his team at the *Abbey Sainte-Victoire* had created in the wooden box and put his papal stamp to seal it.

He smiled and handed her most of the original documents placed there by Pope Clement in 1266 CE. She gestured for him to turn around and face the wall. He could hear the rustling of the fabric as she hid the documents underneath her voluminous robes.

"I will return in a few minutes to clean up your desk, Your Eminence."

"It can wait until the morning, Sister."

"Of course, Your Eminence, as you wish," she answered as she turned and left to go to the garden where Lucas was waiting.

◆ ◆ ◆

Brother Joseph and Father Richard

Father Richard crossed the paved walkway before quietly slipping into the carefully landscaped garden. Brother Joseph briefly stared at his moonlit face, then followed him. After several minutes, they emerged to the left of the Pontifical Academy near the middle of the Vatican.

They took the curving pathway around the Academy. They entered the Pinacoteca and exited through the doorway into the paved courtyard that separated it from the building that housed the Gregorian Pagan Museum and the Missionary-Ethnological Museum.

Standing at the entrance was a young blond man dressed in the goldenrod and navy-striped uniform of a member of the Swiss Guard—his polished armor chest plate and helmet, topped with red ostrich plumes, glittered in the moonlight. The young man raised his halberd, the four-bladed spear traditionally carried by the Swiss Guard, but lowered it as he recognized Cardinal De Posada's aide.

Father Richard looked around nervously as they climbed the marble staircase and crossed the wide hallway on the museum's second floor. "It's not much farther," he whispered as they crossed the gallery using the dim hallway light as their guide.

Brother Joseph felt Father Richard's hand grab his sleeve and pull him downward. He could hear the priest's raspy breathing and smell the faint odor of Father Richard's body.

"What's wrong?" he whispered as the lights in the gallery flicked on. Father Richard's body tensed as they instinctively pulled their bodies flat against the wall. Brother Joseph slowly turned his head until he could see the main gallery.

Along the walls were glass cases containing gaudily colored statues of primitive and frightening semi-human figures. It took him a moment to notice the man dressed in the crimson cardinal robe standing before a display case. He bowed his head and whispered a prayer in a language neither Brother Joseph nor Father Richard understood before he turned and walked in the opposite direction of their hiding place.

Brother Joseph stood up and brushed off the floor's dust from his robes. "He's gone," he whispered as he reached down to help Father Richard.

"I didn't know he would come here," Father Richard said as he stared nervously at the small anteroom door. "I never expected—."

Brother Joseph walked to the case where Cardinal De Posada had been standing. Inside was a prominent female figure carved out of dark wood. She was naked with full breasts and wide hips; her only ornamentation was a necklace of skulls around her neck.

"It's *Oya*, the Yoruba Goddess of Death," whispered Father Richard. "The cardinal brought her from Cuba."

"She didn't appear on the inventories of the cardinal's possessions."

"The cardinal specifically ordered me to delete all mention of the collection of primitive artwork. He didn't want you to know about it."

"Why was that?"

"The cardinal did not tell me, but it is strange for a man so highly placed in the Church to have such an affinity with pagan deities."

"It is strange that he comes after hours and bows before her. You did not ask why he told you to delete the existence of this collection from me?"

"It is not my place to question my superiors."

"But you're questioning him now."

Father Richard blushed slightly. "I have broken my vow of obedience. It is inexcusable, but after everything I have seen today, I have no choice but to tell you what I have heard. You came here to find the killers. It is whispered that the list of names is women's names, not terrorists. I have been told it was hidden in the cardinal's possessions. This collection was brought to the Vatican from his family's home in Cuba. The Cardinal has gone to great lengths to hide that they are his, and he prays here often."

Brother Joseph as he stared at the statue. "Are the cases locked?"

"They are, but I know where the keys are kept."

"Then it would be a good idea for you to get them, Father Richard."

An hour later, Brother Joseph placed his breviary next to the stack of papers on the desk. He ran his fingers through his short hair. His face was beginning to show the effects of the long hours and little sleep since he had arrived at the Vatican.

"I think we can safely say that the list is not hidden inside one of the pagan statues," he said, "but we may be on the right track." Brother Joseph thought for a moment. "We know that the list was smuggled out of Afghanistan and into Cuba by Turabi's third wife. Perhaps it wasn't hidden with the items that belonged to the Church. Could it have been hidden in something ordinary that might not have been given much consideration? Like dishes or linens?"

Father Richard shuffled through the papers. He shook his head. "There's nothing here like that."

Brother Joseph nodded, "What happened once the crates got here?"

"Anything that was destined for the museums would have been inventoried."

"Anything not destined for the museums?"

"They would have been handed over to the proper departments." Father Richard smiled and tapped the computer on the table next to the desk. "This is the Vatican, Brother Joseph. We've been collecting things for 2,000 years. Everything is recorded. Get comfortable. This is going to take a while."

"Where," asked Brother Joseph, "do we begin?"

"It doesn't matter, does it?" said Father Richard, "It will be in the last place we look."

Chapter 50
9:15 P.M

Izzy and Jasper

Religions do not disappear when they are discredited; it is requisite that they should be replaced.

—George Santayana

**<u>Guardians' Command Center,
Abbey Sainte-Victoire, Marseille, France</u>**

"Milo?" asked Izzy as she picked up the phone. "Is Bria safe?"

"We swept all four floors after permanently neutralizing the two *Opus Christos* agents waiting for her—no sign of Bria or her companion. There were three staff members locked in the walk-in. They're cold and shaken up but fine after we gave them all a shot or two of the Prince's expensive Brandy. We told them it was a simple robbery, but I have no doubt they were waiting for Bria to return."

Milo was silent for a moment. "Izzy, I got a call just as we entered the house informing me of the *Opus Christos* agent's exact locations and asking me to release the staff from the walk-in."

Izzy looked over at Jasper, "Did you call?"

He shook his head.

"Milo, who called you?"

"That's just it. I have no idea. We hoped you might know. Do you have a mole inside *Opus Christos*? It would be good to tell us. We don't want to blow the informant away."

Izzy turned to look at Jasper.

"Give me a second," he said, looking down at his computer. "I'm looking at the logs on Milo's phone. There have been no incoming calls to his phone for several hours."

"How is that possible? Milo says he got a call. Can calls be blocked from being logged?"

Jasper looked over at her. "Are you asking if a call could be blocked from being logged? Yes, it's possible. Could the call have been blocked so I couldn't trace it? Impossible."

"Milo?" Izzy said, speaking into the phone, "We can't find any record of the call. If he calls again, text us immediately, and we'll try to trace it. You haven't responded to the last text I sent you."

"We've been a little busy, Izzy, hunting down *Opus Christos'* assassins and not getting killed. "

"Good excuse. We're trying to bring as many agents to Rome as possible."

"Where's Orlando?"

"He was able to approach Theo and Magdalena before they boarded the train in Milan. He told them that Inanna had asked him to drive them to meet her at the *Abbey*. They should be here in the next few hours. I'll get him back to Rome via helicopter by the morning."

"Good. Orlando's a good man to have on our side. As I remember, he has a bad habit of shooting first and asking questions later. CIA hothead."

"Every time I've heard that comment, people were talking about you, Milo," answered Izzy.

"Oh yeah, that sounds right. It probably is me."

"Anything else you need?"

"We're good. We dropped the packages off at the morgue. Dhabi has contacts everywhere. We're on our way back to relieve his team. Dhabi and I are picking up the graveyard surveillance shifts. "

"The *Mahdi* thinks highly of him."

"So do I. He's one hell of a talented guy. Glad to have him on our side."

"The *Mahdi of Islam* is not on our side," responded Izzy. "We are protecting the Doves, so Christ will return to save us. The *Mahdis* are defending Islam from a potential hostile attack against their faith. Our goals happen to coincide for this moment only. Don't expect this to continue. "

"That's where you're wrong, Izzy. We are never on different sides in God's eyes. The divisions that separate us by skin color, faith, or gender are man's inventions. In God's heart, we are equally loved. There is nothing else worth knowing," answered Milo.

Chapter 51
10:45 P.M.
Bria and Gabriel

Angels transcend every religion, every philosophy, and every creed. Angels have no religion as we know it. Their existence precedes every religious system that has ever existed on Earth.
—Thomas Aquinas

Rome, Italy

"I had a wonderful time," said Bria as they walked back to *Palazzo Di Luca*, "I know you thought the tour bus was tacky, but I enjoyed seeing the building and the fountains all lit up."

"You're right. It was tacky," answered Gabriel, "but Inanna said to indulge you as much as possible without losing my mind. It's been a difficult task, at best."

"You are so full of it," said Bria as she turned to Gabriel. "You had a good time. Admit you had fun, and I'll buy you a gelato."

"I had a miserable time. It was awful: truly awful. It was the worst ever! I barely survived it."

Bria's face dropped as she looked at him. "I'm so sorry. I was being selfish. Forgive me."

"I hope never to do anything that tacky again, but it wasn't the worst thing I've survived."

"You didn't have any fun?" asked Bria sadly, looking up at him with her big hazel eyes.

Gabriel stood there for a second. "Okay, maybe a little bit."

Bria laughed out loud and did a little dance. "I knew it! You had fun!"

Gabriel shook his head. "I said maybe a little bit, but that's not the same as having fun."

"You know what I think, Gabriel? I think you don't let yourself have fun. Do you ever kick back and relax?"

"Never. My entire life is work, work, work."

"So change it."

"I can't. I have tremendous responsibilities. Inanna and His Lordship rely on me. There is no way that I could think of myself first. It's not even in the realm of possibility."

"So you feel like you carry the weight of the world on your shoulders?"

Gabriel looked at her strangely. "I do, actually. You have no idea," he said as a smile almost formed on his lips. "Okay, fine, Bria, you want crazy and unexpected? I can do crazy and unexpected. Did you know there's a secret tunnel into the Palazzo from the far corner of the garden? Maybe I should have another adventure in an evening filled with firsts? It could be fun."

"Why not? It sounds mysterious and a little bit scary. Let's do it!"

"I am beginning to see why Inanna likes you," he said.

◆ ◆ ◆

Milo and Dhabi

"Milo? You in position?"

"Damn straight, Dhabi."

"Jamal picked up Bria, and her guy entered the grounds on Via Delarosa, east of the Palazzo."

Milo swung the binoculars across the courtyard. "I'm not seeing them, Dhabi."

"I hoped that you had a better view from the roof. They were in the courtyard, and then they just disappeared."

"Okay, let's get feet on the ground *pronto*. We have to find her before *Opus Christos* does. We're not the only cowboys out here riding the range, and some of them are wearing black hats."

"That must be another weird American saying, but I get what you mean. Let's do it."

Chapter 52
11:00 P.M.

Alberto Zayas, Felix, and Cardinal De Posada

A few careful people had private records of their own, having either remembered the names or recovered them and took pride in preserving the memory of their aristocratic origin. These included the Desposyni because of their relationship to the savior's family.
—Julius Africanus (160–240 A.D.)

Vatican City

"Alberto, Felix," said Cardinal De Posada sharply as he opened his door, "Alberto, I thought I made it very clear that I wanted you to stay in America."

"Superior General Scotti called and said you had changed your mind and wanted me here."

"From this point forward, you take orders from me and only me. I thought that went without saying. The Superior General is an important ally, but he is disposable."

He turned to look at Felix. "I think brandy is required to calm my nerves. There is a bottle of Rémy Martin in the cupboard," he said as he sat across from Alberto.

"Excuse me, Your Excellency. There's no brandy in the cupboard."

Cardinal De Posada sighed. "Once again, the nuns have ignored my needs. Call the convent and tell them that the wine cellar under the kitchen needs to be unlocked immediately," he said. "My private stock is on the top shelf, Felix. The nun will know where it is."

The elderly nun hurried down the hallway toward the kitchen in less than five minutes; her anger at being woken on the whim of the cardinal was apparent. With a flick of her wrist, she gestured for him to follow her across the kitchen floor. She struggled with the heavy door until she pulled it open with a flourish, causing it to bang against the wall before stomping down the wooden stairs to the cellar. She spoke loudly and pointed to the top shelf where Felix found the Rémy Martin. Without a word, she followed Felix up the stairs, slammed the cellar door, and left the kitchen, leaving Felix to find his way back to the cardinal's apartments.

"Finally," said Cardinal De Posada when Felix returned. "I will wake my aide to accompany you to your room once we finish our drinks. I have a busy day ahead of me, as usual."

"That isn't necessary," answered Alberto, "Felix has already shown me my accommodations."

Felix poured the brandy into two cut-crystal globes and handed one to each man. Alberto drank rather than sipped his Rémy. "It's been a very long day," he said, abruptly standing up, "suddenly, I'm exhausted. Please excuse me, Your Excellency. Felix, are you coming?"

"Cardinal," Felix said, "There are rats in the cellar that need attention. Big rats."

"That is the nun's problem, not mine. Let one of them know in the morning."

"We need to talk about that old nun," Felix said. "Maria de Carmen? I pushed her down the stairs. She broke her fucking neck.

I expect to be paid."

"We've discussed this already. You're not getting paid for her."

"She was a Guardian."

"She was a Handmaiden of Jesus Crucified. Sister Maria de Carmen had worked in the Vatican tending to the popes for nearly forty years. Her devotion to the Church is unquestionable. There is no way she was a Dove or a Guardian. Anyway, the nuns said she died of a heart attack," said the Cardinal.

"I get paid for Guardians and Doves. She was a Guardian. She's dead. That is my deal, Alberto."

Alberto raised his hand and brushed the air as if to wipe away the conversation. "This discussion is over, Felix. Sister Maria de Carmen was not either. What was that about rats?"

Felix felt his anger beginning to build. There was no question that the old bitch was a Guardian. Alberto and De Posada were trying to cheat him, which wasn't right.

"Nothing," he said, "I was mistaken. There's nothing in the cellar, not even a mouse."

Chapter 53
11:30 P.M.

Bria, Gabriel, and Princess Celeste

*I saw tracks of angels in the earth: the beauty of heaven walking
by itself on the world.*

—Petrarch

Palazzo Di Luca, Rome, Italy

Princess Celeste smiled at Bria and Gabriel as they sat in the
Garden Room.

"I'm pleased that the tunnel led you here," she said, "although
I fear Lorenzo may never get over the shock of you emerging from
the trap door in his bedroom."

"It was a surprise for all of us. I'm sorry we scared him," Bria
said as she turned to Gabriel. "I thought you knew where the
tunnel led."

"I assumed we would end up on the Prince's side of the
Palazzo."

"Well," said Princess Celeste, "it was a fortunate mistake. At
my age, sleep is elusive. I find nights infinitely long and lonely.
Don't I, Lorenzo?" She turned to her butler, who had quickly
dressed in his black trousers and mis-buttoned shirt, as he brought
in a tray of snacks and a bottle of champagne.

"I always find our quiet evenings enjoyable," he answered.

Princess Celeste leaned over to Bria and whispered, "He's an accomplished and convincing liar. That's why he gets paid the big bucks."

Bria laughed out loud. "Where did you learn that expression?"

"We often watch old American films at night. Did I use it correctly?"

"Perfectly," answered Bria as she accepted a fresh glass of champagne from Lorenzo.

"Will you need anything else tonight, Princess?"

"I think we'll be fine, Lorenzo. I'm sure Gabriel will be able to find whatever we might need if the occasion arises," she answered.

Lorenzo turned to look at Gabriel. His tone was polite when he spoke, but there was a note of irritation that was impossible to miss. "Will you need access to my quarters again this evening?" he inquired, "If so, I will leave the door unlocked. Please be quiet as you invade my only private space, as I am a light sleeper."

"Thank you, but no. We will find another way to return to our side of the Palazzo."

Lorenzo lowered his head to the Princess and quickly left the room.

"Burn, Gabriel," said Bria.

"Burn? What are you talking about?"

"Burn. Like, burn in hell. He just politely told us to go to hell."

"That makes no sense. Hell isn't hot; it is cold. As Dante said, it is the furthest away from the warmth of God's love."

Bria laughed and took another sip of champagne.

"And you know this because?"

"I've been there on business once or twice."

'Quit teasing the girl, Gabriel," scolded Princess Celeste as she turned to Bria. "He is incorrigible. I don't know why we put up with his silliness."

◆ ◆ ◆

11:45 P.M.
Dhabi and Milo

"Dhabi," Milo whispered as he kicked a large rock, "come over here and look at this."

Dhabi bent down and examined it. "It's fake," he said.

"That part I figured out all by myself, *Paisano*. The question is, why is there a huge fake rock in the middle of a perfectly manicured garden."

"Good question," Dhabi answered as he pushed against it. He leaned over and examined the bark dust and then pointed to the slight indentation as two lines in the dust.

"Those marks look fresh. Could it be?"

"Makes sense."

"Does it scare you that we're already speaking shorthand?"

"We'll deal with this unfortunate development another time. Right now, we have to figure out how to move this damn rock."

Chapter 54
Day Five
12:01 A.M.

Bria, Princess Celeste, and Gabriel

You do not need to know precisely what is happening or where it is all going. What you need is to recognize the possibilities and challenges offered by the present moment and to embrace them with courage, faith, and hope.

-Thomas Merton

Princess Celeste's Apartment, Palazzo De Luca

"Bria, how are your mother and Theo enjoying Milan? Are they returning to Rome soon?" asked Princess Celeste, sipping her wine.

"She's not sure," Gabriel said, speaking for Bria, "Inanna sent a driver to take them to meet some of her friends in France. They're quite excited about the opportunity to see Inanna again."

"Inanna said she's meeting them there?" questioned Princess Celeste.

Bria thought for a moment before she answered. "Mom just said Inanna sent a car to drive them to meet some of her friends in France. I assume she'll be there."

"Strange," said Princess Celeste, "I spoke to Inanna earlier this afternoon, and she didn't mention a thing. Did they say exactly where in France? It's a big country."

"You're going to love this one, Princess," said Gabriel with a smug smile. "Go ahead, Bria. Tell the Princess where Theo and your mother are going."

"Somewhere near Marseille. *Abbey Sainte-Victoire?*"

Princess Celeste leaned forward, looking at Bria. "Are you sure? The *Abbey Sainte-Victoire?*"

Bria nodded. "Pretty sure."

Gabriel opened his mouth to speak when Princess Celeste stopped him.

"Gabriel," she said, "think a minute. It may be a solution that Inanna would approve of, even if it wasn't her idea. If they make it to the Abbey, they will be safe.

Bria looked at them with confusion. "What are you two talking about? If Inanna isn't expecting them to join her, where are they going? And why? I need some answers!"

Gabriel and Princess Celeste both took a deep breath.

"They are safe and among friends at the Abbey," said Princess Celeste, "I would imagine, now that I think about it, that Inanna arranged it. She has a way of making people think that her desires are their ideas. I wouldn't worry if I were you."

"Why," asked Bria, "do I get the feeling there's more to this than you're telling me?"

"Fair enough," said Princess Celeste as she turned to Gabriel, "this is not the moment we had planned, but I think we must agree that the moment has been chosen for us," she said.

"By Inanna?" asked Gabriel.

"It would be my guess. Perhaps you should find us another bottle of champagne. I think Bria will need it. Bring the decanter of Armagnac and three snifters, too. She might want something stronger once she hears what we say."

◆ ◆ ◆

Dhabi and Milo

Milo, lying on his stomach, felt around the underside of the fake rock. A smile crossed his face.

"There's a lever," he said as he pulled it. The rock slid away to reveal a stone stairway.

Dhabi nodded as he spoke with a calm voice on his phone. "Any activity out there?"

"It's clear on this end," answered Jamal, one of Dhabi's surveillance team members. "Besides us, no thermal imaging hits on the grounds, nearby streets, or vehicles."

"In the *Palazzo*?"

"There are three in the Palazzo, but they are in the servants' wing," answered Jamal quietly. They're stationary, so I would venture they are asleep after their frightening experience."

"In the Princess's apartments?"

" I'm showing one static image in the area behind the kitchen. Probably a servant who's asleep, or at least at rest. The area at the southern end of the building shows three images."

" Can you confirm that the alarm systems are operational?" asked Dhabi as he looked at Milo.

"Let me ask Jasper," Milo answered as he punched the Command Center's number.

"Jasper says the Princess's apartments' security system is armed," he whispered to Dhabi before returning to speak quietly with Jasper.

"Jasper, we've discovered a secret entrance, probably a tunnel, under the courtyard. We think it's how Bria and Blondie Boy disappeared," said Milo.

" I'll call you back in three minutes tops. Hold tight." Less than a minute later, Milo's iPhone vibrated.

"Milo, I'm looking at the schematics. The tunnel isn't on the original system. It must have been added later, and the plans weren't revised. Can you see a keypad?"

" Yes, there's one at the bottom of the stairs."

" Go down and show it to me, but be careful. Try not to touch anything until I tell you to," said Jasper. "I can't disarm it without setting it off, but I might be able to reroute the notification."

" Can I breathe?" asked Milo.

" No. Give me a minute. Okay. Press six zeros and then the disarm button."

Milo could hear an alarm going off over the phone, but not in the tunnel.

"So far, so good," said Jasper, "press the six zeros, then the disarm button again."

"The green light is flashing. You're a genius, Jasper."

"It's what I do," he answered curtly before the phone disconnected.

Dhabi turned to Milo. "If we do this, we'll be doing it without backup. We're walking blindly into what could be a dangerous situation. They could be waiting for us."

"Not if they're smart, Dhabi."

"Why," said Dhabi as he descended the staircase, "doesn't your lack of fear surprise me?"

Chapter 55
12:05 A.M.

Father Claude, Toshi, Sister Maria Teresa, and Alberto Zayas

Destiny is something not to be desired and not to be avoided, a mystery not contrary to reason, for it implies that the world, and the course of human history, have meaning.

—Dag Hammarskjold

Vatican City

Once the heavy footsteps stomping across the kitchen floor above them had ceased, Father Claude and Toshi crawled out from beneath the cellar stairs.

"Thank God that nun slammed the cellar door to warn us before she brought Felix down here."

Toshi stretched his legs. "It was too close for comfort. If the sister can't get us to Brother Joseph tonight, we'll have to take the chance that we can find him ourselves."

"Agreed," said Father Claude as they slowly shuffled across the pitch-black cellar, bumping into boxes and crates until he tripped against the staircase.

They climbed up the stairs on their hands and knees until Father Claude's head bumped into the cellar door, and he reached in the dark to search for the knob. They stood up and entered the darkened kitchen as the lights turned on, momentarily blinding them both.

Alberto Zayas leaned against the metal prep table with a Beretta pointing at them.

"I must apologize to Felix, gentlemen," he said. "He told me rats were in the basement, and I doubted him. Throw your weapons over here slowly and put your hands on your heads."

"Let's go," he said as he kicked their weapons away and gestured toward the kitchen door. Toshi and Father Claude looked at each other. Alberto sighed.

"We can do it here, gentlemen. I didn't want to leave a mess for the sisters to clean up, but I bet you two won't be the only dead things found in this kitchen," he said as he raised the gun.

Silently, hovering like a black ghost, Sister Maria Teresa rose from behind the table with a frying pan raised above her head.

"Not in my kitchen, you stinkbug," she said as she swung the pan and hit Alberto soundly against the back of his head, knocking him out cold.

Father Claude moved to check on Alberto as Toshi gathered the guns. He quickly went through Alberto's pockets and removed his iPhone and wallet.

"Is he dead?" asked Sister Maria Teresa.

"No, Sister, but he'll have a hell of a headache in the morning."

"Language, Father Claude!" she scolded as she wagged her finger at him.

Toshi laughed. "Sister, you whacked a man with a frying pan, and you're worried about my language?"

She looked at him sternly, "One was necessary, young man. The other was profanity, which is not. Now pick him up and carry him down to the cellar."

"We can't just leave him there, Sister. He'll wake up sooner or later."

"A secret passage in the cellar leads out to the grounds. My brother is one of the gardeners. I'll call him to meet with his van at the garden door in five minutes."

"You have a plan, Sister?"

"Have you ever met a nun that didn't have a plan for any possible contingency, young man? We have a lot of time to think and few distractions. My family has a small vineyard about fifteen miles east of Bergamo. I will tell my brother to drop him off there."

"I'm not questioning you, Sister, but won't he just get a ride back?"

The Sister got a wicked gleam in her eyes, "He might try. A man with no phone, identification papers or passport, no money, and as naked as God created him might find it difficult to hitch a ride. We're good for a few days, perhaps longer."

Father Claude and Toshi looked at each other.

"Besides that," she said, "my cousin is married to the director of the Refugee Boot Camp in Bergamo. Remind me to call her once we're finished."

Once Alberto Zayas, unconscious, naked, and trussed up, was unceremoniously dropped into the back of the well-used green van, Sister Maria brushed off her hands, and Toshi secured the door.

"That went well, don't you think?" she said as she navigated through the cases of vegetables and wines until she stopped in front of a cabinet.

"Push it to the left," she said, motioning to Father Claude. She took three industrial-sized flashlights off the shelves behind her and handed two of the lights to Toshi.

"Come on and be quick about it. I don't have all night," she scolded as she turned on a flashlight and pointed down the ancient stone stairway.

"Where are you taking us, Sister?" asked Toshi.

"The Vatican was built on top of Roman burial grounds. There are daily tours since many believe Peter the Apostle was buried here. This, however, is an abandoned side tunnel. You will wait here until the first tour is finished and join it at the end. It will be tricky as the guides do head counts several times during the tour, but if you time it right, you should be able to slip out to the street without anyone the wiser. I'll return with fresh clothing as soon as the breakfast preparations are done." She looked them over disapprovingly, "I'll bring disposable razors and combs," she said as she closed the door.

Chapter 56
12: 15 A.M.

Princess Celeste, Bria, and Gabriel

In the flare of torches, I behold the heavens of God. Being initiated, I become holy.

— Clement of Alexandria

Princess Celeste's Apartments, Palazzo Di Luca, Rome, Italy

Princess Celeste pointed at the newly hung painting as they waited for Gabriel to return.

"Do you like it, Bria?"

Bria stood and studied the painting. "I'm not sure," she answered, "It's so different from any Madonna and Child I've seen. She looks a bit wild and uncontrolled. Her hair is a tangle of curls exploding across the canvas, and her expression isn't peaceful or gentle. She looks like a lioness ready to pounce."

Princess Celeste nodded her head.

"Inanna says it's da Vinci. She's never wrong about artwork, but I don't think he finished it. This is the second da Vinci that reminds me of you, Bria. Perhaps he had a vision of the future. Nothing, at my age, can surprise me."

"Me? As the Lioness Madonna? I don't see it."

"It's more like you than you know," answered Princess Celeste. She looked at Gabriel as he filled the champagne flutes with champagne and the snifters from the decanter of Armagnac before he offered the tray of drinks to the women with a flourish.

"Going a little overboard, are we?" Bria asked, "Champagne and cognac?"

"Perhaps, but then again, perhaps not. Time will tell," said Princess Celeste, taking a flute of champagne in one hand and a snifter of Armagnac in the other as Bria accepted the champagne.

"We need to tell you something that may be difficult for you to understand."

"It's not my mom or Theo, is it?" asked Bria. "They're ok?"

"No, dear, your mother is safe, as is your friend, Theo," soothed Princess Celeste as she patted Bria's hand. "Inanna has something to tell you, but she asked Gabriel and I to do it. It's good news, although it might be shocking and difficult to understand. Wouldn't you say, Gabriel?"

He shrugged his shoulders. "As you surely remember, I've been down this road before."

"Then shush, Gabriel. I might handle this better than you, anyway. I…well," she stuttered before she took a sip of the Armagnac. "This is more difficult than I thought. I don't know where to start."

Gabriel leaned forward in his chair. "Told you. Start at the beginning."

"Of course," said Princess Celeste, pausing to gather herself. "In the beginning, there was light."

"Not the beginning beginning, Princess, that will take all night. Cut to the chase."

"With Mary?"

"Perfect."

"Right," she said, taking a deep breath, "two thousand years ago, a young woman named Mary, who lived in Judea, gave birth to the Messiah promised by God."

Bria nodded, "I know the story, of course."

Gabriel looked at her. "You only know a tiny part of the story. Tell her, Princess."

Princess Celeste glared back at him. "Am I doing this, Gabriel, or are you?"

Gabriel raised his hands in surrender.

"The Lady Mary gave birth to a Messiah and a King."

Bria shook her head. "I'm not exactly sure what you're trying to say."

"The basic facts are there, and that's all you need to know now. The important part is that God is real," said Princess Celeste, "and God's love and truth are real. From the beginning, humanity hasn't listened well, and there have been certain misinterpretations of God's message."

Gabriel laughed. "You are such a diplomat, Princess. I would call them flat-out lies."

She shushed him and turned back to Bria. "In the beginning, God was a spark of light in the infinite darkness that grew until the darkness was gone. God is everything, and everything is God, from the smallest virus to the enormity of the universe. God's universe was perfect until–."

Gabriel interrupted, "Until Inanna, on a whim, decided that giving one insignificant creature on one insignificant planet the gift of free will was a creative and interesting idea. His Lordship, Jehovah, vehemently disagreed but accepted her wager, knowing Inanna was bound to lose."

Bria sat there and stared at both of them. "What?"

"For all his great wisdom," answered Gabriel tartly, "Jehovah could never have created the universe. He's more of an administrator, logical and pragmatic. Inanna's the creative one; she's the one with ideas and emotions. She created light, the universe, and all life throughout the vastness of the darkness."

"Inanna's God?"

"Why are humans so dense?" snapped Gabriel impatiently. "We have already explained that Inanna is half of God, and Jehovah is the other half. Opposite but equal in all things. Yin and Yang. Two perfect halves of one whole. She explained all this to you on the airplane. Weren't you listening?"

"Maybe," interrupted Princess Celeste, "it will help you to know that the belief in both a God and a Goddess was accepted for most of human existence. Of course, that wasn't exactly correct. Inanna and Jehovah cannot be separated. They are one."

Bria cleared her throat. "I know most early cultures believed their Gods were married couples. I understand that the idea of a monolithic male deity was developed in the Middle East approximately 5,000 years ago, but I'm having problems with 'Inanna is God.' I know Inanna. She's my friend. How can this be possible?"

"Pay attention, Bria," snapped Gabriel. "One last time: Inanna is not God. She is half of God, regardless of what you've been taught. She existed from the beginning with Jehovah long before humans were created. Denying Inanna's existence only happened when human males decided they were the only ones that mattered."

"Even if I believed you, which I'm not sure I do, I don't understand how you can know this."

Princess Celeste smiled and patted Bria's hand. "We know this because," she glanced at Gabriel, "we've been around from the beginning. We've known God as they emerged from the darkness. We were there when the Earth was formed, billions of years before the first primitive humans were created."

"That makes no sense!"

"Of course it does. Gabriel and I are angels, although I'm retired now."

"Angels? And you're retired?" asked Bria incredulously.

"We're not enslaved. We can retire," said Gabriel, "and I'm not an angel. I'm an archangel."

"As to your other question?" continued Princess Celeste.

"Why are you telling me?" Bria asked.

"Because God," said Gabriel, "has chosen you to be humanity's pathway to salvation."

Bria looked at them both, then began to laugh hysterically. "Right! I see what you're doing! Did Theo set this up? It would be just like him to do something like this to mess with me! Angels? I love Inanna, but she's God? That's the most ridiculous thing I've ever heard! You had me going there for a minute," she said, tears running down her face.

"I'm going to kill Theo. This is the most outrageous prank he's ever pulled, but I've got to give it to you both. You are terrific actors! For just a second, I almost believed you were telling me the truth. But this is ridiculous." she said as she wiped tears of amusement welling in her eyes, "Chosen by God? How gullible do you think I am?"

◆ ◆ ◆

Milo and Dhabi

When Milo climbed out of the trapdoor leading up from the tunnel, he noticed immediately that someone had recently been in the room. The bedcovers were kicked aside, and the pillows were rumpled.

"It's clear," he whispered, "but whoever was sleeping here may be coming back any minute."

"Weapons?"

"Let's keep them handy," answered Milo as he poked his head out the door. "Let's move as quietly as possible toward the thermal images that Jamal saw in the Garden Room. Hopefully, they're still together."

Dhabi nodded as they began creeping through the darkened kitchen. Milo put his arm out to stop him and pointed to the man standing silently in the butler's pantry.

◆ ◆ ◆

Bria, Gabriel, and Princess Celeste

"It's not a prank, Bria," snapped Gabriel as he stood and walked over to the fireplace. "We're telling you the truth. Princess Celeste and I are angels."

Bria raised her glass to him. "Un-huh, Gabriel. You? Princess Celeste, I could believe, almost, if I didn't know this entire conversation is offensive to all things holy! But you, Gabriel? An angel? I don't think so."

"I am an angel, Bria," Gabriel said, more than slightly offended. "I'm one of God's favorites."

Bria shook her head and laughed so hard she snorted. "Nice to meet you, Important Angel Gabriel. I'm Bria the First, Queen of the Universe and Beyond."

Gabriel scowled and shook his head. "You're going to make me do this, aren't you? You couldn't take our word for it. Fine. Let's do this, Miss Queen of the Universe and Beyond."

Slowly at first, only the slightest tips of their iridescent glory showing, he unfurled his wings to their full and magnificent splendor. He stretched them to their twelve-foot spread as a halo of silver light surrounded him. He stepped towards Bria, who had stopped laughing and stared at him.

"Good enough for you? The truth that is clearly before your own eyes. We have much to do before the night ends," snapped Gabriel. "Get with the program before I lose my temper."

"Angels?" Bria looked over at Princess Celeste, her eyes wide.

"Yes, Bria, angels," answered Gabriel. "I am not pleased that you forced me into such an ostentatious display," he said curtly as he ruffled the feathers of his wings.

"Angels?" Bria croaked, her voice shaking.

"Well, duh. I am the Archangel Gabriel," he answered, with a tone of growing frustration, "one of the seven Holy Angels. I am God's messenger."

"God's messenger," said Bria, repeating his words in a monotone.

"You are being quite irritating, Bria," he complained angrily as his eyes took a reddish hue and the feathers on his wings separated into sparkling silver shards.

Without warning, he staggered back; his wings arched above him, and his body became taut and rigid as if hit by an unseen thunderbolt. Almost like a marionette whose strings had been cut, he fell to the cold marble floor, his limbs convulsing and his mouth foaming in a bubbly line of drool.

He lay there twitching as Bria watched him helplessly. Princess Celeste looked down at her hands, ignoring Gabriel's undignified, although deserved, punishment. Slowly, Gabriel raised himself off the floor. He no longer smiled as he wiped a stray tear from his cheek. He cleared his throat and stood ramrod straight.

"Hail, You who are highly favored! You, who is the Daughter of God! The Lord is with you. Blessed are you among all women. Fear not, for you have found favor with God. You shall bring forth a Child who is from the seed of God. The Holy Spirit has come upon you. The Child born of you shall be Holy and shall be called the Child of God."

Bria stared at him momentarily, then raised her hands and clapped slowly.

"The wings and glowing red eyes; bravo! Top-notch special effects. Kudos for the convulsing fit. It was overdone, of course, but strangely convincing. How did you do that?"

Gabriel looked at her in astonishment. "Bria, I just brought you a message from God that you are to be pregnant with God's Child. Your reaction is inappropriate."

"You're right, Gabriel," she said without a hint of humor. "Your behavior is inappropriate, and it isn't funny, you a-hole. It's mean, stupid, and dangerous!" Bria stopped a moment. "Did you drug me? Is that why I'm having this weird hallucination? What did you put in my drink, Gabriel?"

Gabriel shook his head. "Nothing," he said.

Bria looked over at Princess Celeste.

"It wasn't a hallucination, dear, nor did we drug you. It was real. Inanna chose Gabriel and me to tell you the good news," Princess Celeste said gently.

Bria shook her head. "This is beyond crazy," she said as she stood and walked to the window. She turned to look at Gabriel and Princess Celeste. "If this isn't an elaborate prank, then I must be having a mental breakdown. None of this makes sense! Even if it's true, why would God choose me? We all know this can't be true. It's ridiculous!"

"It makes total sense to Inanna," said Princess Celeste as she moved to Bria's side and touched her face gently. "You are a Holy Dove, the descendent of the Messiah. You carry God's blood in your veins. Deep inside, you know it's real. You know it's true."

Bria shook her head in protest.

"Close your eyes and listen to your soul," whispered the Princess.

Slowly, Bria closed her eyes. As Princess Celeste and Gabriel watched, Bria was consumed with the Fire of Divinity. Her face glowed in the way described by those who had seen Joan of Arc or the children of Fatima while in holy ecstasy. Her eyes turned upward, her pupils almost invisible beneath her half-closed eyelids. Her mouth opened slightly, her lips barely brushed each other as her skin developed a luminescence, and an aura of gold surrounded her. She was transformed as she accepted the spirit of God hiding inside her.

As she opened her eyes slowly, Bria knew she had accepted the truth of God's blessing. As had happened to Mary, her many-times-removed grandmother, the Light of God engulfed her, and she accepted her fate as God's chosen vessel.

◆ ◆ ◆

Milo, Dhabi, and Lorenzo

Lorenzo, the princess' butler, had seen it all, as had Milo and Dhabi. He turned to the two men now standing behind him in the pantry. He tried to raise his voice as he fell to his knees. His nerves were on fire, his blood boiled, and his immortal soul crumbled into nothingness. He knew he was dying.

"Holy shit!" whispered Milo as Dhabi muttered a silent prayer to Allah.

Bria's miraculous transformation from woman to Madonna convinced Lorenzo, at last, that God truly existed. In the depths of his being, regardless of his professions of faith, attendance at Church, and disdain for those who ignore their duty to worship God daily, Lorenzo had never truly believed in God. His enlightenment, unfortunately, came too late to save him. Faith that demands tangible proof is worse than no faith at all.

Chapter 57
5:45 A.M.

Brother Joseph and Father Richard

Everybody acts in the interest of good as he understands it. But everybody understands it in a different way.

—G.I. Gurdjieff

Vatican City

Father Richard knocked on Brother Joseph's room at 5:45 a.m.

"This is a surprise," said Brother Joseph, already dressed and finished with his morning prayers.

"I didn't sleep well. An early morning mass might soothe my soul. Would you like to accompany me to my favorite church in the Vatican?"

"I am a simple man, Father Richard. I appreciate the grandeur of St. Peter's, but I fear I would be distracted from my prayers. At the monastery, we hold our service in the barn."

"I understand, but I always go to San Pellegrino in Naumachia when I am free to do so. It's the church set aside for the Swiss Guard, the firefighters, and the other workers. Unlike St. Peter's, it's not as–"

"Theatrical?"

"I was thinking of ostentatious."

Brother Joseph smiled. "Yes, I believe San Pellegrino is exactly what I need. Thank you."

7:45 A.M.
Cardinal De Posada

"Felix, where the hell is Alberto?" said Cardinal De Posada.

"It's before nine. He's probably still asleep," mumbled Felix as he glanced at the clock.

"No, Felix. His bed wasn't slept in."

"I walked him to his room after we left you. Maybe he had a hot date."

"I don't find you amusing, Felix. Find him and find him now."

Felix wanted to respond that he was neither Alberto Zayas' babysitter nor the Cardinal's errand boy but knew about the animosity between Cardinal De Posada and Superior General Scotti. He could think of no better way to get back at him for calling him so early than to answer him innocently. "Do you have the Superior General's number? That's probably where he's gone. They've grown quite close."

Cardinal De Posada slammed the receiver down without a word. Felix laughed before he turned over and fell back asleep.

◆ ◆ ◆

Father Claude, Toshi, and Sister Maria Teresa

The flash of light in their eyes woke Father Claude and Toshi from a restless slumber in the chilly underground chamber. They jumped up, drawing their weapons.

"If possible, you both look even more disreputable than last night," scolded Sister Maria Teresa as she set her flashlight down. "I brought you food. The first tour is at eight. We don't have much time."

"Thank you, Sister," said Father Claude as he reached for the basket.

"Put your guns away," she said firmly as she dropped the basket, "and say grace before you eat. Quickly now, I don't have all day."

"Of course not, Sister."

"'Of course not, Sister,' meaning you don't wish to say grace, or 'Of course not, Sister, you have put yourself in great peril, and we will do as you request?'" she asked, placing her hands on her hips.

Toshi and Father Claude quickly holstered their guns and apologized to the nun.

"After you've eaten, use the razors and moistened cloths. I must return to the kitchen before I am missed. Sister Bernadette will be coming down to bring you clean clothing," she said. "I wouldn't recommend you pull your weapons on her. She is not as kind and understanding as I am."

◆ ◆ ◆

Cardinal De Posada and Superior General Scotti

"Enrico," asked Cardinal De Posada angrily, "where is Alberto?"

"Zayas?"

"Of course, Alberto Zayas. Who else would I be asking about?"

"How would I know?"

"You told him to come to Rome after I had explicitly told him to stay in America."

Superior General Scotti laughed, "Have you lost your little puppy?"

Cardinal De Posada took a deep breath. "Alberto is integral to the success of this mission."

"He's your creature. If he said I told him to come, he was lying. It sounds like he's gone rogue."

"He is loyal to me and *Opus Christos* without question," Cardinal De Posada nearly shouted.

"How, by any stretch of the imagination, is Alberto integral to our success? My agents have killed over a hundred Holy Doves and are actively hunting down the ones that have eluded us."

"Except the Doves on Leah's List. Your Jesuits haven't found them, have they, Enrico?"

"Of course not. Isn't that why we recruited the Trappist monk? Wasn't it because your precious Alberto doesn't have the talent or the connections to find it on his own?" countered the Superior General. "Assigning Father Richard to assist the Trappist was a mistake. He is nothing more than your errand boy."

"He's an errand boy who does what he is told without question," said Cardinal De Posada.

"According to my sources, Alberto disappeared during the night. It could well be that he was kidnapped or killed by the Guardians. Did you think you could hide this information from me, Rafael?"

"Don't be ridiculous, Enrico. I know exactly where Alberto is and what he is doing. It is on a need-to-know basis, and you don't need to know until I decide you do."

"Then, I wonder why you had to ask me where he was. Try to keep your lies straight, Cardinal."

◆ ◆ ◆

Pope Peter and Sister Bernadette

Pope Peter bent to tie his Nike running shoes when he saw Sister Bernadette walking toward him carrying a breakfast tray.

"Your Eminence," said Sister Bernadette, "I will return after you finish your run."

"Thank you, Sister," said Pope Peter as he looked up at her. "How are you this morning?"

"I had an excellent evening, Your Eminence. My nephew, Lucas, was visiting from Marseille. We spent a few minutes together walking in the garden." She raised her eyebrow.

"Your nephew? I hope you had a nice visit."

"It was quite successful. He had brought me letters from my family, and I gave him the requested family mementos. Lucas will deliver them to my family this morning."

Pope Peter nodded his head. "I'm sure your family will appreciate them."

"Yes, Your Eminence, I'm sure they will treasure and protect them always."

◆ ◆ ◆

Brother Joseph and Father Richard

"Thank you, Father Richard," said Brother Joseph as they strolled across the plaza after the mass. "San Pellegrino's was exactly what I needed. Simple and true."

Father Richard looked at his watch as he stepped aside to allow a jogger to pass, but Brother Joseph didn't move aside fast enough. The man's shoulder collided with him, causing Brother Joseph to drop his breviary.

The jogger apologized as he bent over, picked the breviary up, and brushed a leaf off the cover before he handed it to Brother Joseph. They caught each other's eyes and nodded a silent greeting before he turned and ran away.

"Brother Joseph, do you know who that was?" asked Father Richard.

"Unless I am mistaken, that was Pope Peter."

"He swerved away from me but ran into you deliberately."

"I'm sure he didn't see me. Perhaps he has a lot on his mind."

Father Richard smiled, "He is the pope, Brother Joseph. He always has a lot on his mind. I'm sure he worries about things neither of us can imagine."

He looked at his watch again. "I must leave you to attend to the cardinal. Might I suggest that you have breakfast in the dining room? I will meet you here in an hour. I had a couple of ideas during the night where the contents of the Cuban shipment may be stored. I have a good feeling about today. We're going to find the lead that will direct us to the identity of the murderers."

"I pray that you're right," answered Brother Joseph.

"So do I, Brother Joseph. I dread the cardinal's reaction if we are unsuccessful once again."

Chapter 58
8:15 A.M.

Izzy, Jasper, Father Patrick, and Staff

The artist, like the God of the creation, remains within or behind or beyond or above his handiwork, invisible, refined out of existence, indifferent, paring his fingernails.
—James Joyce (1882–1941)

Guardians' Command Center, Abbey Sainte-Victoire Marseille, France

Father Patrick looked over the staff members gathered in the dining hall and smiled.

"Milo contacted me late last night," he started. "His news, while very exciting, will create problems that will task every one of us to our limits over the next few days."

Izzy and Jasper exchanged a quick look at each other.

"Milo and Dhabi entered Princess Celeste's apartment via a secret tunnel last night and saw Bria." He glanced at Jasper. "Jasper was able to re-route the notifications from the tunnel alarm to our server and set up the twenty-four-hour monitoring system. Without his expertise–"

"The expertise of my entire team," interrupted Jasper.

"Correction. The expertise of the entire IT team," said Father Patrick, "I would not be sharing this amazing news this morning without the tireless work of every one of them."

Jasper nodded his head in acknowledgment of the round of applause.

"Can you hack into the main alarm system," asked Father Patrick, "and do the same thing?"

"The system's got a complex firewall. It would be faster to buy my way in."

"A bribe?"

"Yup."

"Do it immediately," Father Patrick said. We need to commandeer all the *Palazzo's* security systems and cameras until we can devise a way to evacuate Bria safely."

Everyone was silent as they tried to digest what Father Patrick was saying. Izzy and Katie stood up at the same time and spoke in tandem. "It's her, isn't it?" they asked, "The fashion designer."

Father Patrick beamed. "Oh, did I forget to mention that Milo and Dhabi were blessed by God and witnessed the Annunciation? God has chosen Bria Tanaka to bear the Christchild."

The room was deadly quiet for a moment, then cheers and laughter exploded as they turned and high-fived each other. Izzy and Katie hugged as Katie whispered, "I told you it was her."

The document department scholars quietly nodded as it made sense to them. Bria Tanaka, the only Dove whose genealogy possibly contained all three bloodlines, would be the chosen one.

Only the computer scientists from the IT Department were apprehensive. They realized that the actual challenges were looming before them.

Father Patrick waved his arms for silence.

"I share your excitement. It is joyous news, but a long, dangerous road will task each of us for years. Learning Bria is the Chosen One is only the beginning."

"The fact that Bria is in Rome is problematic," said Jasper as he, Izzy, and Father Patrick sat around Izzy's desk.

"It makes me question why God brought her there," added Father Patrick. "She's in the storm's center for reasons I cannot quite fathom."

"But, as far as we know, *Opus Christos* is unaware of the Annunciation. That does allow us a little breathing room," said Jasper.

"That may change at any moment," cautioned Father Patrick. "Milo and Dhabi took out two *Opus Christos* operatives hiding in *Palazzo,* so it's safe to assume they know she's there."

"It's just a matter of time until they try again," said Izzy, "and if *Opus Christos* figure out she is the chosen Dove, they'll move Heaven and Earth to kill her."

"Milo and Dhabi are with Bria, as are Princess Celeste and Gabriel. They are all powerful forces," answered Brother Patrick. "The *Mahdi of Islam's* troops are monitoring the perimeters until we can get more Guardians to Rome."

Jasper spoke up. "I'll set up drones to fly over as often as we can without creating public concern or drawing the attention of the police."

"We know she's the Chosen One," added Izzy, "but if we over-protect her, it will signal *Opus Christos* to her special status among the Holy Doves."

"We need to get her to the Command Center as quickly as possible," said Jasper.

"Let's not forget about Brother Joseph. Judith's prophecy says that without the earthly father, the Child will die in the womb. We need to approach him immediately," said Father Patrick.

"Easier said than done, Father Patrick," answered Izzy. "He's in the Vatican, surrounded by *Opus Christos* members. He's constantly surrounded by Cardinal De Posada's staff and Felix."

"Then we'll have to find a way to approach him," said Father Patrick. Who's in Rome, Izzy?"

"Milo, Father Claude, Toshi, plus Dhabi and his team of the *Mahdis,*" she answered. "Orlando should be there soon."

"Lucas?"

"He brought the original documents from Pope Clement's cache here last night, but he's returning to Rome. I can pull everyone we have nearby to join them."

Father Patrick nodded. "Pull in all the European teams you can, but only if no other Doves are unaccounted for in their areas. We can't leave any of the Doves without protection from the *Opus Christos's* assassins."

"Is there any possibility that the *Mahdi* could send us more help?"

'I'll ask. There is another organization I could approach," replied Father Patrick, "I have been reluctant to involve them, but several of their members are in Rome seeking a papal appointment."

"Who? It is not the *Mossad* if they are seeking papal appointments," said Jasper.

"I have already spoken with the *Mossad*. They are unwilling to partner with the *Mahdi*, but I'll try again. I was thinking of a relatively new group, *La Sangre de Maria.*"

"Nicaraguan, right?" asked Jasper, "They oppose Ortega's Anti-Catholic stance."

"I'll make some discreet inquiries," agreed Father Patrick. "We must be assured that their beliefs or dedication to God's true desires align with ours. That may not be the fact."

"I just might be a poor, little, ignorant country boy from Texas," he started, but Izzy interrupted him with a roar of laughter.

He flashed her a dirty look before he continued.

"Protecting Bria and Joseph is important, but so is destroying *Opus Christos* to the last man," he said, "If there's one thing this country boy knows for sure, if you want to be sure the snake is dead, you better cut off its head."

"I'm listening," answered Father Patrick.

"If we neutralize Cardinal De Posada and Superior General Scotti, *Opus Christos* will fall."

"Perhaps, but never discount the viciousness of religious fanatics and their ability to regenerate from the rubble of their misguided causes. I'll listen to whatever you have in mind, Jasper."

"My team and I have an idea. It's risky, but if we discredit Cardinal De Posada and Superior General Scotti, we will bring *Opus Christos* to its knees. It's not exactly up to the Guardian's code of morality, nor can it be considered ethical by any stretch of the imagination, but a snake without its head isn't long for this world."

"Desperate times call for desperate measures," said Izzy.

Chapter 59
8:15 A.M.

Princess Celeste, Dhabi, Milo, & Gabriel

We must be willing to let go of the life we planned so as to have the life that is waiting for us.

—Joseph Campbell

Princess Celeste's Apartments,
Palazzo Di Luca, Rome, Italy

Dhabi and Milo were sitting at the kitchen table when Princess Celeste entered. They both jumped up, slightly nervous in her angelic presence.

"Good morning, gentlemen," she said, "I believe that coffee smells better than the watery brew Lorenzo served me. May I?"

"Princess," said Milo as he pulled her chair out and quickly poured her a cup of coffee.

She took a careful sip. "This is delicious. Did you make it, Dhabi?"

"Yes, M'am. We take coffee very seriously in my culture," he answered stiffly.

Princess Celeste gently put her cup on the saucer and gestured for both men to sit.

"I think we need to clear the air. You must know that Gabriel and I are not the first angels you've met. Most of us come to Earth occasionally. We find humans amusing."

"Yeah," said Milo, "nothing like endless wars, grinding poverty, unchecked greed, social injustice, and systemic hatred to give you a giggle. We're a real kick in the pants."

"Those things were never in Inanna's plan for humanity," answered Princess Celeste. "The depths of your depravity are unparalleled anywhere in the universe, but you can also be kind, loving, intelligent, and creative, which is equally unusual. As a species, you are unique and fascinating."

"Is this where I'm supposed to say," said Milo, "'Ah, shucks, M'am, thank you, M'am?'"

Princess Celeste laughed. "Humans are interesting because choosing good over evil is infinitely easier and more satisfying than inventing new evils, yet you do it repeatedly."

She took another sip of coffee. "Of course, it will soon end in your destruction as a species unless good people stand together as one and refuse to allow evil to continue. That's why Inanna's sending another Messiah. She thinks you'll listen this time."

"Speaking of that, have either of you seen Bria this morning?" asked Milo.

"I was just going to check on her again," responded Dhabi as he walked out of the kitchen.

"She did have two glasses of wine last night. Perhaps that's why she's sleeping in."

"Really, Princess? You think that was it?" said Milo, his personality outweighing his awe of her, "Wouldn't have anything to do with a big-ass blond angel spreading his wings from here to China to announce that she's been chosen to carry God's Child?"

Princess Celeste let out another peal of laughter. "Oh, Milo, you are delightful! I'll hire you in a minute if you want Lorenzo's job. Speaking of that, where did you put his body? I haven't seen it lying around anywhere."

"He's in the tunnel until we figure out what to do with him. It's not high on my to-do list until Bria's safe. Any ideas?"

"I won't mind some toast with jam if you know how to make it," she said to Milo. "My kitchen skills are sadly lacking. Perhaps you missed it, but I'm a retired angel."

"A retired angel?"

"What is it with humans? Of course, I'm retired. Heaven is a pressure cooker. You have no idea how bitchy some of those angels can be."

"I saw Gabriel. I can only imagine."

"Yes, well, he is not the worst by far."

"Thank you, Princess," said Gabriel as he entered the kitchen in his silk pajamas. "I didn't realize that you cared so much for me. It warms my heart."

"That's not what I said, Gabriel," she said as she motioned to the chair beside her. "I meant that you were only slightly less obnoxious than most angels. Don't read more into it than that."

"Are we having coffee?" he asked, turning to Dhabi, who had returned from checking on Bria. "It is one of the few benefits of Earth. I can't think of another creature that has come up with boiling caffeine-laden fruit pips in water. And, just to set the record straight, I am more than 'slightly less obnoxious.' I'm quite charming once you understand my sense of humor. Cream and sugar, please."

"Don't push your luck, Blondie Boy. You'll get what we serve you," said Milo. "Wait, I know your voice. Did you call yesterday to warn us about the men hiding in the Prince's side of the Palace?"

"I thought that being human, you would not be clever enough to figure it out. Inanna wanted me to protect Bria at all costs, and I wanted to finish my wine. You were breaking into the *Palazzo*. It was easier for me to call and let you deal with them."

Milo turned to Dhabi. "That makes sense."

"See?" Gabriel said, turning back to Princess Celeste. "I'm a decent creature, considering the aggravations I've endured for eternity. I'm surprised I haven't turned into a bloodthirsty demon."

"Give it up, Gabriel. I've already explained that demons are a perverted human invention," answered Princess Celeste.

"Fine. Ruin my fun. A few actual demons here and there might be an interesting addition," he said. "It would certainly add a bit of spice to the mix. Believe me, being an angel is never-ending, day after day, year after year, millennium after millennium, pain in the butt. Everybody's so nice all the time. It gets irritating. You can understand that, can't you?"

"I hate people who are nice all the time. You can't trust them," answered Milo. "You know that they're hiding something hideous. Guaranteed."

"Exactly! The Seraphim, Cherubim, and Thrones all think they're so high and mighty. They spend half their time trying to lord their positions over the Dominions, Virtues, and Powers, who, in turn, imagine themselves better than the Principalities, Archangels, and Angels. The entire caste system in heaven leaves much to be desired."

"Kind of like the Marines, right? Rank is everything."

"Exactly! Even among us, The Seven Holy Angels—Michael, Raphael, Uriel, Chamuel, Jophiel, Zadkiel, and myself- there are certain rivalries. Uriel is still sputtering that Michael and I were named in The Bible, and he wasn't."

"Uriel should grow some balls and get over it," agreed Milo.

"Right! It was an accident of fate. Michael ended up being appointed the head of all the Angels. Big rumors about exactly how he got that job, but who knows if they're true."

Gabriel took a drink of coffee and motioned to Dhabi for a

refill. "I was appointed God's Messenger because I have a talent for language. I speak…what?…1,387 or 1,388 human languages fluently. That is on top of everything else I do. I got the job because I did the work. Jophiel, Raphael, and Chamuel couldn't care less. They're career, just biding their time until retirement. You know the type. No offense, Princess."

"None was taken," she answered.

He stopped speaking as he read Dhabi's mind.

"Ah," he said, finally understanding, "you are upset because I'm not all sweetness and light like your Quran promised. Angels are not perfect, Dhabi. We're all flawed in one way or another— not as flawed as humans, of course. Look at me, for instance. I'm beautiful. I'm brilliant beyond imagination, and I'm divinely clever. I'm punctual, neat, and clean. God trusts me."

"It must be his sparkling personality," Milo whispered to Dhabi.

Gabriel shot Milo a dirty look but continued, "God says I have a job for you, Gabriel. I do it. Whatever They want. Whatever words They choose. I'm good at being Their Messenger. Excellent, in fact," He said as he took a bite out of the toast Dhabi set before him.

"And yet, I am flawed in ways I cannot understand or correct. Being an angel doesn't give me any insight regarding myself."

Milo suddenly felt overwhelming sadness for Gabriel. He reached out and touched his shoulder.

"Only God is perfect, Gabriel. Wouldn't make too much sense any other way, would it?"

"No," answered Gabriel, reaching up and covering Milo's hand. "It wouldn't. Thank you for reminding me. God is perfect. We're not."

Milo laughed. "But I get pretty damn close to perfect for a human, right?"

Gabriel rolled his eyes and shook his head. "I wouldn't even go there, Milo, if I were you," he answered as he drank his coffee silently.

Chapter 60
8:30 A.M.

Brother Joseph and Father Richard

A lie doesn't become the truth, wrong doesn't become right, and evil doesn't become good just because it's accepted by a majority.
*   –Booker T. Washington*

Vatican City

Brother Joseph was sitting on a bench outside the dining room, enjoying a quiet moment in the sunlight, when Father Richard arrived, looking harried.

"Sit for a moment," said Brother Joseph. "Tell me what the cardinal said to upset you."

"How did you know?"

He gestured to Father Richard to sit. "Poker is not your game. Your face shows everything."

"My mother always says I am a terrible liar. She can tell the second I open my mouth."

"The cardinal is furious that we haven't found the list."

Father Richard cleared his throat. "He is quite anxious for us to provide the names of terrorists to the pontiff so they can be denounced and destroyed."

"These things take time."

"He demands that we report to him this afternoon with the list in hand."

"We better get started then," said Brother Joseph as he placed his breviary in his pocket. We wouldn't want to disappoint His Excellency now, would we?"

◆ ◆ ◆

Cardinal De Posada and Pope Peter

Cardinal De Posada was waiting impatiently when Pope Peter, dressed in jogging clothes, entered the privacy of his papal apartment. Peter hesitated a second before acknowledging the Cardinal's uninvited presence in his rooms.

"Cardinal De Posada," he said, trying to keep his voice from revealing his irritation at Cardinal De Posada's growing impertinence. "Did I neglect to note we had an appointment?"

Cardinal De Posada reached for the leather portfolio on the table and stood up.

"You are trying my patience, Peter," he said as he walked across the room and stopped inches from Pope Peter's face, too close to be considered anything less than threatening.

"This is the pronouncement you will present at tomorrow afternoon's press conference." De Posada thrust the portfolio into Pope Peter's hand. "You will accuse Islamic fanatics of the ritual murders of 382 innocent Christian women. You will announce that it is an assault against Christianity, and the Western world must avenge this attack."

"And if I refuse?"

"Your mother and niece are presently guests of friends of mine. It would be a shame if you forced us to kill them if you refuse to do as we request."

"Where are they?"

"They are safe for the moment. If you do as you are told, they will remain safe. If not,-."

"I don't trust you, Cardinal De Posada."

"That is immaterial, Your Eminence," he said. "More concerning is whether we can trust you to follow your script to the letter."

"I demand to speak with my mother and niece."

"You are not in a position to demand anything, Peter. You will pronounce the words exactly as written. Your mother and niece's hosts will notice any change immediately: one misstep, one error, one pause where it shouldn't be, and they will be killed without mercy."

"You have left me no choice, have you? I have no option but to do as you demand."

"That is the wisest decision you have ever made, Peter."

"What about the Trappist monk, Brother Joseph?" Pope Peter asked, "Have you threatened his family, or is he one of you?"

The Cardinal paused momentarily as if to decide whether or not to answer Pope Peter's question.

"No, the Trappist has been convinced that Islamic terrorists are responsible for the murders. He believes that the Holy Mother Church is being attacked. He believes he is following your orders. He knows only what we tell him."

With that, Cardinal De Posada bowed in mock humility, which exaggerated his lack of respect for Peter and his position as pontiff.

◆ ◆ ◆

9:30 A.M.
Brother Joseph and Father Richard

Brother Joseph felt his heart drop as Father Richard flipped the light switch. The basement was narrow but seemed to go on forever. The walls were lined with shelves, each crammed with wooden crates and cardboard boxes. Father Richard laughed as he noticed Brother Joseph's face.

"Your Trappist blood is showing, Brother Joseph. This is nothing," he said as he began slowly walking down the corridor between the shelves, "I found six more storage rooms where some of the boxes from Cuba may have been stored. This is just the first one."

"Six more storerooms besides this one?" asked Brother Joseph as he bent down to read the label attached to one of the boxes. "Well, at least everything is well marked." He looked at a box on the bottom shelf. "*Natale* is Christmas, right? Christmas decorations?"

"I forgot that you don't read Italian." Father Richard pulled a pen out of his jacket pocket and carefully printed a series of letters and numbers on one of the labels.

"Here," he said, handing Brother Joseph the paper. "Look for these inventory numbers instead of the names on the boxes. I'll do the right side if you'll check the boxes on the left."

Chapter 61
9:30 A.M

Dhabi, Milo, Princess Celeste, Gabriel, and Bria

For what is it that angels do? They bring us good news. They open our eyes to moments of wonder.

—Joan Wester Anderson

Princess Celeste's Apartments
Palazzo Di Luca, Rome, Italy

When he returned to the kitchen, Milo said, "The Command Center is working on a plan to get Bria to the *Abbey Sainte-Victoire.* Meanwhile, we need to keep her safe."

Dhabi looked up from the newspaper. "That may be more difficult than Izzy believes. After yesterday's events, *Opus Christos* knows Bria's a Dove. It is just a matter of time before they realize she is the Chosen One. They'll assume you'll try to get her to the safety of the Abbey. They'll be lying in wait. I think you should come up with an alternative destination."

"I agree. We need to come up with a plan B," responded Milo. "Have Father Claude and Toshi been able to contact Brother Joseph?"

Milo shook his head. "Their cells aren't working."

I've been told they're hiding in the Necropolis and waiting to sneak out with a tour group this morning. So, I would say the answer is no."

"So we can't count on any assistance from them."

"There's Orlando and me. Lucas is on his way back from the Abbey."

"Is that everybody?" asked Dhabi.

Milo took a deep breath. "I'm afraid so. We've had more casualties than we expected. Izzy's working on bringing everyone she can to Rome. Hopefully, our numbers will increase by mid-day once they get here. Until then, we're all we've got."

Dhabi nodded. "Plus, we have my team of five. Unless Izzy finds some additional support. There are ten of us going up against *Opus Christos*. Not great odds, but doable."

Milo smiled. "Great minds and all that nonsense. Don't discount the nuns," Milo continued. "You might not know about nuns, being Islamic, but anybody attending Catholic school will tell you not to mess with nuns. They'll take you out without batting an eye."

Dhabi laughed. "Sounds like my grandmother and her sisters. Loving as angels, mean as snakes."

"Milo is telling the truth, Dhabi," said Bria as she entered the kitchen wrapped in a floral robe. "My sixth-grade teacher, Sister Mary Rose, could turn your blood to ice with one glance. Your grandmother and her sisters would fit right in."

The two men turned toward the kitchen door. "Bria!" they said in unison.

"Good morning, dear," said Princess Celeste. "Coffee?"

Bria shook her head. "My stomach's upset this morning. Maybe green tea? And some dry toast?"

"Green tea coming up," said Dhabi.

"Where is Gabriel?" Bri nodded her thanks to Dhabi before taking a cautious sip.

"Right behind you," he answered, returning to the kitchen

fully dressed.

"Gabriel," she said, "I had a bizarre dream about you."

"Really?" he said as he leaned against the counter. "Do tell. I love hearing about myself."

"You were an angel with beautiful iridescent wings. They were huge. Like ten feet across."

"Twelve," he corrected, "my wings are twelve feet across."

"Size counts?" asked Milo with a smirk.

"You said I had been chosen to–" Bria faltered. "Sorry, this is just too ridiculous to say out loud."

Princess Celeste leaned over toward her and finished her sentence.

"Chosen to bear God's Child."

Bria looked around the room, quickly catching everyone's eyes before she cradled her head in her folded arms and felt the room spin.

"Oh, crap! I was afraid that's what you said. I mean, it's too ridiculous to be true."

"Ridiculous or not, get used to it," snapped Gabriel

"Sister Mary Rose will have a heart attack when she hears about this. She always predicted I'd end up as a prostitute. Theo's going to freak, and Mom will have a cow when she finds out I'm going to be an unwed mother! This is bad! Really bad."

"Not the reaction I expected," said Gabriel, "but we can work with it."

Chapter 62
9:30 A.M.

Brother Joseph and Father Richard

The more weakness, the more falsehood; strength goes straight; weaklings must lie.

—Jean Paul Richter (1763–1825)

Vatican City

Brother Joseph stood and brushed the dust off his robe. He looked over at Father Richard, who replaced the contents in the boxes before slipping them back into the empty spaces.

"We have to replace each one exactly where we found it. The custodians will notice if even one is misplaced," cautioned Father Richard. "I'll never hear the end of it until my dying day."

"Perhaps it would be best if I handed them to you and you put them in place."
Father Richard nodded his agreement and looked at his watch.

Cardinal De Posada expects us to be at his apartments at one o'clock to report on our progress. Hopefully, we'll have good news for him. We can check a few smaller storage rooms before lunch if you wish."

"As you lead, Father Richard, I will follow."

◆ ◆ ◆

Father Claude and Toshi

Father Claude and Toshi let the first tour of the Vatican necropolis pass by. They were a small group of older Irish women in sensible shoes and gray cardigans. There wasn't a prayer that Father Claude and Toshi could leave unnoticed, hiding among the silver-haired ladies.

They got luckier with the second group, a mixture of American and Australian tourists. Bending low, they waited until the tour guide turned away to answer a question before they slipped into the group unnoticed. Keeping their faces turned slightly, Toshi placed a generous tip into the guide's upturned palm before they hurried up the stairs.

"We're in the clear," whispered Toshi, looking around carefully.

"Let's go to the cafe, order a latte, and see if anybody seems interested in us. I don't want to lead *Opus Christos* to the safe house."

"Right, but let's be quick," said Toshi, "these wool pants are as itchy as hell."

"I don't know where the nuns got these clothes, but they're awful."

"They feed and clothe the homeless of Rome. These pants are the rejects. Even the homeless didn't want them," answered Toshi as he scratched his leg.

Father Claude looked Toshi over. "Yup," he said, "they are even uglier in the daylight. Let's keep our eyes open and our heads down. *Opus Christos* is probably searching for us."

"No 'probably' about it. They are searching for us," said Toshi as he turned and noticed a priest and a brown-robed monk walking toward them.

"That's Brother Joseph," he whispered, turning away to hide his face, "We have to take a chance and try to approach him. We might never have another opportunity."

Father Claude shook his head. "He's with Cardinal De Posada's aide, Father Richard. That can't be good!" he said as he pulled his iPhone out of his pocket. "My phone's dead. Yours?"

Toshi pulled his Samsung out of his pocket and shook his head. "Strangely fitting since we spent the night hiding in a cold, dark necropolis."

"We need to get out of here and call Izzy. She'll know what our next move should be."

◆ ◆ ◆

11:30 A.M.
Cardinal De Posada, Felix, Brother Joseph, and Father Richard

When Father Richard and Brother Joseph entered the Cardinal's apartments, they saw Felix standing beside Cardinal De Posada. The cardinal, as usual, had a scowl on his face.

"Alberto has been called away and is unable to join us," the cardinal said as he dismissed Felix from his side. He gestured for Brother Joseph to sit. "I take it that Father Richard is being helpful?"

"Very much so," answered Brother Joseph.

"I understand you have searched several storerooms that were not your intended focus area. May I ask why you believe our records detailing the locations of the items sent from Cuba are incorrect?"

"I fully trust the Vatican's records, Your Excellency, but it is a standard investigative practice to investigate all possibilities to eliminate those that are not pertinent."

"It is a waste of valuable time, in my opinion," said the cardinal. "The list the pontiff asked you to find will be in the items recovered from Cuba and nowhere else."

"Respectfully, Your Excellency, if there is a list among the items sent from Cuba, our commitment to the thoroughness of our search means we are closer to confirming or denying its existence."

"Perhaps I wasn't clear enough, Father Joseph. I expect you to find the list."

"I understand, Your Excellency. A thorough search must be meticulous and takes time."

"We don't have time! We need the list of Islamic terrorists. His Eminence, Pope Peter, has informed me that he wishes to reveal his accusations against these Islamic terrorists during a press conference tomorrow. The world must know of their vile attack on Christianity and our Church. The righteous Christian nations of the world must respond as one against the Islamic countries who encourage and support these monsters."

"I share your urgency, but we must carefully gather the evidence to prove our accusations without a doubt, Your Excellency."

"His Eminence has no doubt Islamic terrorists are the murderers!" exploded the cardinal. "Are you questioning his wisdom? How far has the world fallen that the Holy Father's word is no longer enough to demand immediate action?"

"With due respect, Your Excellency, I do not question the pontiff's wisdom, but the world will demand concrete evidence. We have reviewed the information various law enforcement agencies collected," Brother Joseph said. "We have confirmed the methods of the women's executions and that the locations of the women's murders were in or near Catholic sanctuaries. This points to a common ideology or group of people. We are learning a great deal, but that is not enough to accuse anyone."

"Even if His Eminence has heard the truth of their guilt directly from God?" asked the cardinal.

Brother Joseph sat silently for a moment, unsure how to respond.

Father Richard spoke up, "Excuse me, Your Excellency. Brother Joseph and I are on the verge of discovering the list, having unearthed several viable clues we are actively pursuing. Perhaps you might consider having Alberto Zayas and Agent Blanc once again review the photographs and reports received from the various police departments worldwide. At the same time, Brother Joseph and I follow the clues and continue searching the remaining storage rooms."

"Do what you must, Father Richard," Cardinal De Posada said, waving his hand to dismiss them. Just find the list and bring it to me. I promise you'll be sorry if you fail me."

They were walking down the steps to the Apostolic Palace when Brother Joseph turned to Father Richard. "You told a lie, Father Richard."

"Yes," he answered proudly, "I must remember to call my mother and let her know I've finally learned to fib. It turns out that I'm quite good at it.

Chapter 63
11:00 A.M.

Izzy, Jasper, Father Patrick, and the IT staff

*I don't see how, without the gift of faith, you would believe he was
the Son of God.*

—John Cardinal O'Connor

Guardians' Command Center
Abbey Sainte-Victoire Marseille, France

Father Patrick interrupted a closed-door meeting between Izzy,
Jasper, and several IT staff members.

"What's going on?" he asked suspiciously.

"We're discussing the team's idea to take Cardinal De Posada
and Superior General Scotti down," answered Izzy. "It's risky, but
Jasper thinks we can pull it off."

Father Patrick sat across from Jasper. "Walk me through it."

Jasper and his team stood up as one. "We don't have time to
chitchat. We have a ton to do and barely enough time to get
everything in place. Izzy can explain."

"So, what are the computer nerds planning?" he asked after
Jasper's team filed out.

Izzy smiled. "We've all agreed that it's better if you don't
know until it's well underway. Our plan breaks every international
banking law and every computer security protocol known to man."

"I'm being cut out?"

"It's for your own good and only for a short while, Father Patrick. Jasper, Milo, Dhabi, Father Claude, Toshi, Orlando, and I will probably be in high-security prison cells if we get caught. You must have plausible deniability that we worked behind your back."

"I don't like it," said Father Patrick.

"I'm sure you don't, but it's how it must be for now. Just like Jasper said 'a snake without its head–.' You're our head. We need you to be safe and able to continue the Guardians' mission."

"Does Jasper's team believe their plan will take Cardinal De Posada and Superior General Scotti down and destroy *Opus Christos*? You believe in it?" asked Father Patrick.

"We all do. Trust us, Father Patrick," she said before she changed the subject to end the discussion.

"Have you met Magdalena and Theo yet, Father Patrick? Have they settled in?"

"Katie's got them situated on the third floor," he answered, "They've asked to see Inanna, but Katie brushed it off by saying they needed to rest after their long journey. I suppose I should be the one to explain what's going on."

"Now works," Izzy said. "They're awake and asking when Inanna and Bria will be here."

Father Patrick sighed. "Go ahead and get them. I guess it's time to face the music."

Izzy returned a few minutes later and tapped on the door frame. "And this is Father Patrick," she said. "He's in charge of the entire compound."

Father Patrick stood up and put out his hand in welcome. "Has Izzy given you the cook's tour?"

"This is so cool!" exclaimed Theo excitedly. "It's like something out of a James Bond movie. You walk into an ancient monastery, but then Bam! It's hiding a secret underground complex. It's fire! Inanna keeps blowing my mind with the outrageous places she invites us to."

"Where is Inanna?" asked Magdalena sternly. "Orlando said she was going to be here."

"Yes, Orlando did tell you that, but Inanna is not here."

"Okay," said Magdalena, crossing her arms across her chest. "I have a feeling there's something you people are not sharing. I want to know where my daughter is, and I want to know right now. Do you understand me?"

Izzy hid her smile as she excused herself. Poor Father Patrick. If he thought Katie was a mama bear, he had no idea of the power of Bria's mother's ire.

"Milo," Jasper whispered to Izzy as he gestured to his phone from outside her office. Father Patrick was standing in the corridor but so focused on Magdalena that he couldn't eavesdrop.

"I need you and Dhabi to find a place where Izzy and I can speak to you without being overheard," he said, watching over his shoulder for Father Patrick.

"Okay, Jasper, answered Milo. "Let me figure it out, and I'll call you back in a minute or two."

"How about the tunnel?" whispered Dhabi, "Except for Lorenzo, nobody's down there. We don't have to worry if he'll listen."

Milo nodded his head. "Sounds like a plan," he said, dialing Jasper back.

Chapter 64
11:45 A.M.
Bria and Princess Celeste

No truth is more certain than this: all that happens, be it small or great, happens with absolute necessity.

—Arthur Schopenhauer

Princess Celeste s Apartments, Palazzo Di Luca
Rome, Italy

Princess Celeste and Bria sat together in the Garden Room, pretending to eat the sandwiches Milo had made for them. Bria pushed her plate aside and placed her napkin on the table.

"Dhabi told me what happened to Lorenzo," she said.

"I'm afraid," answered the Princess, "his faith wasn't strong enough to survive the truth."

"We should tell Lorenzo's family what happened."

Princess Celeste smiled gently. "What would we say, Bria? Lorenzo witnessed the Angel Gabriel announcing that God had chosen you to bear the Messiah and died because his faith was lacking?"

"That's probably not a good idea," Bria conceded.

"Hidden behind his charming facade, Lorenzo only cared what others could do for him. He targeted rich elderly women, hoping they would leave him everything if he flattered them enough."

"I guess that it never happened, right?" asked Bria

"Like most men, Lorenzo never appreciated the cunning of older women. Watching him try to charm me into loosening my purse strings was entertaining." Bria was quiet as she stared out the window, looking toward the garden. "Both life and death have ways of changing one's path in the most unexpected ways," she muttered.

"Bria," Princess Celeste said softly, "I understand this is hard to accept. Only one woman in the history of humanity has shared the experience you are struggling with now. It can't be easy."

"It isn't. I know that you and Gabriel are angels. I know that God exists. I mean, I've met her, but still–."

"Inanna is only half of God," corrected Princess Celeste, "although there are some who consider her the better half. I have no opinion on the subject. It's safer that way."

"I can accept the duality of God. It makes more sense than what I was taught to believe," replied Bria. "But I can't wrap my head around the Mother of the Messiah thing."

"You're wondering why Inanna chose you."

"There are hundreds of Doves, I'm sure, who have never questioned God's existence. Holy Doves who believe in God with their whole hearts, but until a few hours ago, I was never sure I did. In a small part of my brain, I'm afraid that I've suffered a major mental breakdown and hallucinating like a crazy person, and none of this is real. Either way, the truth is that Inanna could have done better than me."

"Inanna made the right choice when she chose you. Trust in both God and yourself to accept that truth. You are the one. Any slight doubt Inanna may have had ended when she had to leave to speak with Jehovah, and you immediately asked what you could do to help her."

"I was concerned. She said her husband was upset with her."

"Exactly. You cared about her more than you cared for yourself. You asked what she needed. It was a response she rarely experienced. 99.9% of the time, humans ask God to help them, absolve them, or grant them favors. It's totally one-sided. You expected nothing, so I understand your feelings of confusion and disbelief. It would be like someone saying I was going to die. It would be hard to comprehend."

"Angels never die?"

"Never. We can't. We might ask to be reassigned to something like counting grains of stardust or dealing with one-celled organisms when we want to slow down and have less responsibility. A few of us ask to retire, but that's unusual. God was surprised when I did it. "

"What's he like?"

"Who? Joe?" Princess Celeste laughed at Bria's expression. "Inanna's not the only one who calls him that. Of course, we would never do it to his face as she occasionally does. He prefers Jehovah, The Lord, or Allah, but he'll answer to Zeus, Ra, Krishna, and a dozen others. He doesn't care what humans call him since God always is and always will be. Names are immaterial. What's he like? He's a mean-looking old guy with a flowing beard and long silver hair."

"Really?" asked Bria in a shocked whisper.

Princess Celeste giggled. "Of course not. Inanna told me you said that. I was teasing you. God is the totality of every living and inanimate object in the universe. They are everything and nothing. They have been and always will be ever-present at all times and in all things. There are no, and never will be, words to describe them. They have no form, as you would understand it. Before you ask, humanity was not created in their physical image. It was another thing humanity did all on its own."

"So, the Inanna I met is like a hologram?"

"On the rare occasions when she chooses to make herself visible, she appears in a way you can understand, as do angels. Inanna was pleased you described God as the wind. It's closer to the truth than anything ever said in humanity's existence."

"But I still don't understand why–."

"She said that you knew a human couldn't comprehend the enormity of God. You knew doing so was futile and selfish and kept you from accepting and loving others as God wanted. She liked that."

"So, the millions of hours mankind has pondered the meaning of God, the countless centuries spent trying to explain God was a waste of time?" asked Bria.

"I wouldn't go that far. Each human who has contributed to forming humanity's religious thoughts did so to the best of their understanding and ability," she said, "but they neglected to consider that each person's relationship with God is divinely personal and individual. Formalized religions demand an unquestioning commitment to a single path, a single way to understand God, which turns your unique relationship with God into a secondhand experience based upon someone else's beliefs."

Bria considered Princess Celeste's comments.

"You're saying it's like watching a movie about climbing a mountain while never attempting to climb it yourself. Listening to another's idea of God can never teach you the pathway to get to the mountaintop."

"Exactly. Building a relationship with God is not a group effort. Read, learn, and think all you want, but ultimately, one's relationship with God is the most private and intimate relationship a human can experience. It can not and should not be shared lightly."

◆ ◆ ◆
2:45 P. M.
Dhabi, Milo, Bria, and Princess Celeste

"Good afternoon, Princess, Bria," said Dhabi, nodding slightly as he and Milo entered the Garden Room a few hours later. "If you have time, Milo and I would appreciate a moment."

"Of course," answered the Princess. "We always have time for you and Milo, don't we, Bria?"

"Always."

Milo looked around. "Do you think that Gabriel can join us?"

"I'm sorry, Milo. He left a while ago," Princess Celeste said.

"Gabriel left?" asked Bria. "He didn't even say goodbye."

"He wouldn't have, dear. He had completed his job. He had to return home."

"I thought he liked me in his weird way."

Princess Celeste reached over and caressed her hand. "He did. Usually, he pops in, makes his announcements, and leaves. He stayed around longer than he should have."

Milo spoke up. "Well, that sucks. We were hoping that he would help us."

"He wouldn't. Even if he would, he couldn't. There's a strict hands-off policy regarding interfering with human behavior."

"Even retired angels?" asked Milo.

"Even the retired ones," Princess Celeste confirmed.

"Are other retired angels living here?"

Princess Celeste smiled at him. "I am one of the few who are silly enough to do so."

"Of course," answered Milo with a flirtatious grin, "that's what I expected. You are one in a million, *Mia Bella Principessa.*"

Princess Celeste shook her head in disapproval of his flattery but smiled happily. "Gabriel and I have pushed the envelope to the limit already. We've gone way beyond the limit. Jehovah will be quite put off if he finds out." She took a sip of her mimosa. "But, what is it, you humans say? In for a penny, in for a pound? What do you need?"

Milo looked at Dhabi before he answered. "Jasper and Izzy have a plan. It can work, but we'll need some help and introductions."

"Tell me what you need and to whom you wish to be introduced. I'll see what I can do while maintaining plausible deniability if I'm busted," she said as she turned to Milo. "Did I say that correctly? I heard it in an American gangster movie in a similar situation."

"Perfect, as always, *Dolce Signora.*"

"We must give thanks to Prince De Luca. I know many powerful people and their naughty little secrets. If I don't, I'll ask Inanna. Once she puts her mind to it, there's nothing she doesn't know or can't do."

Chapter 65
5:30 P.M.

Brother Joseph and Father Richard

There is a great skill in knowing how to conceal one's skills.
—Francois, Duc de La Rochefoucauld

Vatican City

It was late afternoon when Father Richard and Brother Joseph, dirty and tired, finished the fourth of the six storerooms. Brother Joseph slapped his hands together to create a cloud of dust.

"There are only two left. Do you feel up to it, Father Richard?"

"More than I feel up to telling the cardinal that we stopped before we've checked them all."

"Do you remember what you said yesterday?" asked Brother Joseph. "'We'll find the list in the last place we look.' It must be in one of the two remaining storerooms. Our odds are about to improve greatly."

"I hope you're right. We only have to cross the courtyard to get to the next one," answered Father Richard, looking at his watch, "and it's one of the smaller storerooms. We should be finished by supper."

"Brother Joseph," he said as he pulled a dusty ledger off the shelf and flipped through it. "I might have found something. The inventory says there was a gold candlestick with seven arms, but it's crossed out. It's not on the original packing slips, but it shows up when the contents of the Cuban shipment were received here. I don't remember anything like that, do you?"

"No, definitely not," answered Brother Joseph. "Seven-armed? Could it be a menorah?"

"The men who unpacked the crates might not have recognized a menorah."

"Could a menorah be hollow?"

Father Richard bent his head to study the inventory. "The specified weight is low for a piece of its size. That might indicate that the piece is hollow."

"It makes sense," said Brother Joseph, "A menorah—"

"If it is a menorah," interrupted Father Richard.

"Yes, if it's a menorah, it wouldn't be part of Cardinal De Posada's father's primitive art collection or an item a devoutly Catholic family would have used, nor would it be part of the Cathedral's possessions."

"Someone might have put it in a crate without Cardinal De Posada or the Church's knowledge."

"You're thinking like a detective, Father Richard."

Father Richard looked up at Brother Joseph and smiled at the compliment. "It was unpacked, but there's no indication explaining where it went. There are eight museums, several libraries, and numerous storerooms, not counting the public and private spaces. They contain hundreds of thousands of artifacts."

"But certainly, someone would have remembered a large seven-armed candlestick."

Father Richard shrugged his shoulders. "Maybe not."

"Father Richard?" asked a man standing in the doorway.

Father Richard looked up at the slightly portly middle-aged

man. A small nervous smile crossed his face. "Hello, Giorgio," he said. "How are you?"

"I'm fine. I have to lock up the storerooms. This is the last one. Are you finished here?"

"I'm afraid the time slipped away from us. Have you met Brother Joseph, Giorgio? He is visiting Cardinal De Posada from America."

Giorgio nodded his head.

"Giorgio, the cardinal had a large gold candlestick sent here from Cuba," said Father Richard. "He planned to give it as a gift to Brother Joseph's monastery, but we haven't been able to find it."

"A gold candlestick? It could be almost anywhere. Have you checked the museums?"

"We have, but it's not in any of them."

"How about one of the private chapels? It could be in one of them."

"Those are excellent ideas, Giorgio, but we've thoroughly checked all the inventories, and it's not listed as being in any of them."

Giorgio scratched his chin thoughtfully. "A candlestick might have gone to the Household Department, but they're closed now. Go and see them in the morning. Tell them Giorgio sent you over," he said. "My wife serves dinner at 6:00 p.m. sharp. She gets angry if I'm late."

"Of course," apologized Father Richard as they stepped out of the storeroom and watched Giorgio turn the key in the lock. He then hustled them, politely but firmly, back to the courtyard.

"Father Richard," asked Brother Joseph, "would you care to join me for Vespers?"

"I would, very much, Brother Joseph."

Cardinal De Posada and Superior General Scotti

"What is it now, Enrico?" asked Cardinal De Posada sharply as he saw Superior General Scotti's name on his phone, "I was just leaving for dinner. I don't have time for your nonsense."

"The Committee has decided that we will both attend the press conference tomorrow. It will impress Pope Peter with the absolute necessity to adhere to the statement written for him."

"Your appearance is counterproductive. The press will question why the Superior General of the Jesuits is on the dais. No. It's a bad idea."

"Luckily, it's not your decision to make," said Enrico Scotti firmly, "I understand Brother Joseph has not found the list of the Holy Doves. That is quite disappointing, Rafael."

"Enrico," said Cardinal De Posada, "we were never sure that the list of Doves was in Cuba, nor were we positive that Turabi's wife had hidden the list in my possessions. As you remember, we relied on information supplied by Hilmi's men."

"You promised Alberto Zayas could convince Brother Joseph of the Islamic's responsibility for the murders, yet Alberto is missing. When, exactly, did you plan to inform the committee?"

"We are looking for him."

"Who is 'we'?"

"I have several men searching the Vatican grounds as we speak."

"No, Rafael, you don't. Your need for dominance knows no bounds. You bluster and lie to convince yourself you are in control even when you are not. You have Felix and only Felix."

"There are situations, Enrico, that I do not find necessary to discuss with you. I have everything well in hand," answered Cardinal De Posada.

"You can't help yourself, can you, Rafael? I know the location and activities of every *Opus Christos* operative in Rome and the Vatican. No one, except Felix, is aware that Alberto is missing. Felix believes that the Guardians may have kidnapped or killed him. If so, the entire operation may be in jeopardy. You will be held responsible. I promise you."

"Don't be ridiculous, Enrico. The plan was to kill any Dove who might be the Chosen One to bear God's child. I have done that."

"No, you haven't! Some Doves have slipped through your fingers. That little fashion designer and her mother, to name a couple."

"Through *our* fingers, Enrico. Through *our* fingers."

"If the Chosen One has slipped through *your* fingers, the committee will determine who was at fault, and they know it wasn't me," responded Superior General Scotti before he ended the phone call.

6:00 P.M.
Brother Joseph and Father Richard

Brother Joseph crossed himself at the end of Vespers. He was about to inform Father Richard that he would return for Compline at 9:00 when a couple of small pieces of paper fluttered to the floor as he closed his breviary. Father Richard bent and picked them up.

"These fell from your breviary, Brother Joseph."

Brother Joseph stared at them and shook his head. "I've never seen these before. Are you sure they fell from my breviary?"

"I watched them drop to the floor. They fell from your breviary when you took it from your pocket," Father Richard said as he lifted one eyebrow and inspected the parchments Brother

Joseph had handed him. He ran his fingers over their surfaces. "These are the seals of Pope Clement V. If these are authentic documents, they are priceless. How did you get these?"

Brother Joseph shook his head. "I have no idea how they got there, but—." A look of realization crossed his face. "Father Richard, it must have been the pope. We saw him jogging this morning. He ran into me, and I dropped my breviary. He bent down and picked it up before he handed it back to me. I've had my breviary in my pocket all day. I don't think I took it out until the service this evening."

"This is very strange," said Father Richard as he looked at the parchments in his hands. "Why would he give these to you?"

"Not knowing what they are, Father Richard, I am at a loss to explain the meaning."

"Yes, of course," he said, "how would you?"

"Brother Joseph, we need to find somewhere safe so I can look at them more carefully."

Several minutes later, Father Richard carefully laid the sheets of parchment on the desk in his former office at the Gregorian Pagan Museum. He bent over and carefully studied the smaller one.

"Middle-to-late, first century C.E.," he said, allowing his voice to drift away as if he were talking to himself. "Latin, the syntax and language are consistent with other first-century documents I've seen." He paused a moment and stared at Brother Joseph. "It seems to be genuine. This is most extraordinary. If it is a forgery, it dates from before Clement V's reign began in the 13th century."

"If it's a forgery," asked Brother Joseph, "why would Clement have placed his seal on it? Wouldn't a forgery be quickly destroyed?"

Father Richard nodded his head. "One would think so. Even if it is real, I am shocked that it wasn't destroyed centuries ago. I don't understand why Clement kept it."

Brother Joseph sat down next to the troubled priest. "Why? What is it?"

"Don't think I'm overreacting, but if real, this document turns everything we believe upside down."

"Perhaps if you translated it aloud, we could decide a course of action together."

"Yes," answered Father Richard, his voice shaking, "that's a good idea." He brought his eyes back down to the parchment. It seems to be a confession, or a legal statement written by Caiaphas in the year 3799. That would be about the year 35 or 36 CE," he paused to calculate.

"Caiaphas?" said Brother Joseph, "The High Priest who sent Jesus to be judged and condemned to crucifixion by Pontius Pilate?"

"Yes, it appears so," answered Father Richard. "Let me read it as best I can. My translation may not be correct without studying it in more depth, but I should be able to understand most of it."

'*In the year 3799, I, Caiaphas, testify that the Sanhedrin acted on the orders of Jesus, the rightful heir to the throne of David. Jesus, the King of Judea, willingly surrendered himself to Roman justice when his rebellion against their occupation of his lands failed.*'"

Brother Joseph thought for a moment. "Shouldn't it be in Hebrew instead of Latin?"

Father Richard shook his head but kept his eyes on the parchment. "The original was probably in Aramaic. The Temple documents were copied into Latin if they concerned incidents of legal note."

Brother Joseph nodded his head.

"I have seen several examples of court documents from the time in the Vatican Library," continued Father Richard, "but nothing so potentially damaging to the Church. If this is real, it will be the only document from Jesus' lifetime that references him by name."

"This disputes the accepted idea that he was a poor, peaceful carpenter, a victim of the Romans and the Temple," said Brother Joseph. "It clearly says that he was the rightful King of Judea, started a failed rebellion against the ruling governments, and was convicted of treason. The Sanhedrin did not betray him to the Romans but did as their King commanded."

Brother Joseph stood silently, trying to make sense of this shocking new information.

"The question, Father Richard, must be: Why did the Holy Father give this to me secretly? What does he expect us to do with this information? Is it somehow intertwined with the search to discover the mysterious missing list hidden somewhere in Cardinal De Posada's boxes brought from Cuba?"

"It only makes sense if Pope Peter believed that approaching you directly was impossible without endangering you both." Brother Joseph sat down in the chair and rubbed his forehead.

"He is the pontiff, the undisputed head of the Church. I was told I was working at the expressed request of His Eminence. Why is he going behind Cardinal De Posada's back? Could he be afraid of the cardinal?"

Father Richard shook his head. "The inner workings of the Church are a spider web of power struggles and counter struggles; each faction is fighting for dominance. Cardinal De Posada is a dominant force and wisely feared by all. His ruthlessness is legendary. Pope Peter asks us to help him stop De Posada before the cardinal does something unthinkable."

Brother Joseph looked over at the parchment on the desk. "Could it mean De Posada is trying to start a Holy War with Islam by blaming them for the women's murders? Is that what His

Holiness wants us to know?"

Father Richard shook his head. "That seems radical even for Cardinal De Posada, but whatever he's planning, it is something sinister, I fear."

"The pontiff wasn't sure we would discover the truth by ourselves. His Holiness slipped two parchments into my breviary, Father Richard. Hopefully, the two of them together will explain what Pope Peter is trying to tell us.

Chapter 66
6:00 P.M.

Princess Celeste, Bria, Milo, and Dhabi

The second coming of Christ will be so revolutionary that it will change every aspect of life on this planet.
—Billy Graham

Princess Celeste's Apartments, Palazzo Di Luca, Rome, Italy

"Can I ask you a question, Princess Celeste? I've been thinking about the stories in the Bible, the stories we were taught in school and church. They are true, right?"

Princess Celeste put down her magazine, "Why do you ask?"

"I hope the stories are not true, especially those in the Old Testament, which are filled with tales of incest, bestiality, rape, infanticide, and violence. I always found those stories upsetting and scary. Maybe that's why I thought God was frightening."

"Humans will always choose entertainment over enlightenment. I believe that each of those stories in all the holy books contains small grains of God's message," said Princess Celeste. "Since humans first invented religion, countless stories have offered conflicting views of God. Most of the stories were written by mankind in a time of great brutality. Perhaps they were meant to frighten people into good behavior."

"I guess we haven't changed much, have we? We love scary movies and monster stories. We are fascinated by horrific acts, real or imagined," Bria answered. "So what's true? I mean, what exactly does God want us to do?"

Princess Celeste laughed. "That is the problem, isn't it? It is impossible to understand God's vastness, yet humans spend lifetimes trying to figure it out."

"And, yet, it can't be done," said Bria.

"Humans do have a way of making things way too complicated."

"We do, don't we?"

"The answer is quite simple," said Princess Celeste. "The entirety of God's commandment could be typed double-spaced on a single sheet of paper to teach you how to live in God's light."

Bria thought about it for a moment. "The Golden Rule," she exclaimed. "Do unto others as you would have them do unto you."

"Every faith has considered these few words of the utmost importance, but that's not the commandment I was talking about."

"God sent the Ten Commandments to Moses," answered Bria.

"There were eleven commandments, actually, not ten. They were all positive statements originally that defined God's expectation of human behavior. After Moses' death, they were slowly changed by those who believed that people would only follow a Godly path if threatened with punishment and damnation."

"I'm not sure I understand what you mean," said Bria. Please give me an example."

"'Thou shall not kill' was originally 'Respect all life,' which is problematic when you realize God created all life, not just humans. Where's the line between killing and starving?"

"Good question," answered Bria, "I never considered it that way."

'Honor thy Mother and thy Father' was correctly translated, but it was soon taught to mean one's human parents instead of God: Jehovah and Inanna," Princess Celeste said.

"Because they refused to acknowledge Inanna's existence as Mother to Jehovah's Father."

"Exactly. If they acknowledge Inanna as an equal part of God, then how can they justify the continuing and systemic suppression of women?"

"Let me try a couple," said Bria, "'Thou shall not bear false witness' should read 'Be honest in all you do and say.' 'You shall not covet' meant 'Respect the lands and possessions of others.'"

"Perfect. But the most important commandment, the eleventh commandment, has been ignored by man from the beginning as if it never existed."

"The eleventh commandment?" asked Bria.

Princess Celeste nodded her head. "It was quickly ignored as if it didn't exist at all. From the beginning, humans found it difficult, if not impossible, to honor."

Bria shook her head. "I have no idea what it could be. Enlighten me."

"Do you remember the story of the Garden of Eden? What do you think was God's message?"

"Sister Mary Rose said it was about sex."

Princess Celeste smiled. "It's not. God invented sex to be pleasurable to both men and women. It was human's need to control each other that made sex sinful."

"So, it's knowledge?" asked Bria.

"It is not. Think about the story, Bria. Find the lesson, find the Eleventh Commandment."

"The snake told Eve to pick the apple. She did," answered Bria, "Eve offered the apple to Adam. Adam ate it. Then God asked them, 'What happened to the apple?' Is that what you mean?"

"Right. God asked, 'What happened to the apple?'" Princess Celeste responded. "Within seconds, Adam blamed Eve, and Eve blamed the snake. They betrayed each other to proclaim their innocence."

"They got kicked out of paradise because they lied?" asked Bria.

"Bria, who did Adam and Eve think they were dealing with?"

"God?" Bria asked tentatively.

"Right. God knows all things. They got kicked out of Paradise because they broke the eleventh commandment, the most important of all commandments," Princess Celeste said firmly as she leaned forward.

"'Accept responsibility for your actions, thoughts, and deeds.' It's as simple as that."

"That's not simple," Bria answered. "Being responsible for your actions, thoughts, and deeds is the hardest thing imaginable for a person. We humans do our best never to accept responsibility for anything."

"I've noticed," said Princess Celeste, "and so has God."

"Are you hungry, Bria?" asked the Princess, waking from a short nap. "Should we order out? I hear it's quite the thing."

Bria smiled. "Dhabi is preparing a traditional Middle Eastern meal. I'm not exactly sure what it is, but he said we'll sit on the floor and eat with our fingers."

"That sounds interesting as long as you promise to help me. It may not be sitting down, which will create a problem. It may be getting up again."

"Ladies," said Milo, carrying a tray, "Dhabi sent you

traditional Arab drinks, *Limon ou Nana*."

Princess Celeste took a glass off the tray and tentatively took a sip. "Lemon and mint? Delicious! One doesn't even taste the alcohol."

"Because there isn't any," Milo said, gesturing his head toward Bria and raising his eyebrow. "Lemons and mint are directly from your garden."

"Try it, Bria," said the Princess. "It's quite good considering the lack of alcohol."

Dhabi entered the room just as Bria took a sip, carrying a platter filled with fresh vegetables and a bowl of hummus. "You have quite a selection of beautiful vegetables growing in your greenhouse. I hope that it was all right that I'm using them."

"Of course. The greenhouse was Lorenzo's pride and joy," she said sadly. "Remind me that I need to tell the gardeners to take over caring for the plants there."

Milo quickly changed the subject. "Bria, I heard you talked to your mother and Theo. How are they doing at the Abbey? More importantly, how did they take your news?"

"They took the news better than I expected. Theo is totally being Theo, of course. He claims he knew there was something supernatural about Inanna all along. He's planning the baby shower and informed me, in no uncertain terms, that he would be the godfather. He's started to design the layette."

My mother is overwhelmed by the idea of becoming a grandmother in such an unexpected way. Being my mother, she agrees that Inanna, without a doubt, made a perfect choice by selecting me. They are more accepting of the whole thing than I expected, in some ways, more accepting than I am."

"They know in their hearts that it is the truth. They know that God doesn't make mistakes. And they know the Guardians," added Milo, "will die, to the last man, to protect you and the Holy Child."

"But I'm still a little shocked that Theo and Mom are being so blasé. I mean, this is a lot to wrap my mind around. I'm not quite sure how I feel yet."

"I'm sure that Inanna had a hand in steering them into their accepting attitudes," said Princess Celeste, "but it's different for you, Bria. You have to accept, without reservation, that Inanna didn't make a mistake in choosing you. I think she couldn't have made a better one. She rarely makes mistakes."

"Platypuses," answered Milo, "might have been a mistake. Tuna casserole was a major mistake."

"Platypuses were, perhaps, a little creative misstep, but one can't deny they are a conversation starter," Princess Celeste responded, "I promised God had nothing to do with tuna casserole."

Milo looked over at Bria. "That is so true, Bria. I can't remember all of the times we have started conservations with a clever comment about platypuses, can you?"

Bria broke out in giggles. "I think he got you there, Princess."

Princess Celeste put up her hands in surrender and smiled. "Okay, fine. Maybe I'm wrong about platypuses. But God didn't make a mistake in choosing Bria. I know that for sure."

Milo turned to Dhabi as he took a bite of *Maqluba*. "For a bunch of vegetables mixed with rice, this is pretty damn good. I mean, for dinner without any real food."

"It is delicious, Dhabi," said Bria, "I could eat this every day."

"I'm an American male," Milo answered, growling. "Vegetables aren't food. Real food is served medium rare. It doesn't count unless it's dead and served with fries."

"You ate everything except the dishes," said Dhabi as he stood up and started picking up the platters, "Coffee, anyone?"

Bria stood up and helped Princess Celeste to her feet. "It was wonderful, Dhabi, but I think I'll pass," she said, "I'm pretty tired. I didn't sleep well last night. I'm going to bed if that's okay."

"Of course, dear, we'll see you in the morning," the Princess said as she turned her attention to Dhabi, "Arab coffee, thick and black?" asked the Princess. "If so, I'm in."

"Sure, might as well. Cream and sugar?" asked Milo.

"Sugar and cardamom boiled with the coffee, but *no* cream. That is a sacrilege, Milo."

"Sorry," said Milo with a shrug of his shoulders. "After a vegetable dinner, I guess that coffee without cream is just one more indignity I am forced to suffer. "

Dhabi shook his head but turned and walked back toward the kitchen. "You're on dish duty, Milo. Bring everything into the kitchen, and I'll show you how to work the dishwasher. It is German, so it's different from the American junk you're used to. When I return, we can review the plans for the next twenty-four hours."

Bria turned around to stare at them. "Excuse me?" she said, "Excuse me? The next twenty-four hours? Are you three planning to discuss what we will do over the next twenty-four hours without asking for my input? I hate to sound like a stereotypical Southern California girl, but this planning session is about *me*. Let me say that again, so it gets inside your heads: *ME!* This is about *MY* life. From this moment forward, I'm involved in every single decision. You will do nothing. You will make no decisions without involving me! Is that clear?"

"You sounded just like a Valley Girl, Bria. I thought I was watching an 80s movie for a minute," said Princess Celeste. "She's right, you know. This is about keeping Bria safe and healthy for the next nine months. She stays," she said firmly as she patted the sofa, "we listen to her opinions and ideas. Is that understood?"

"Princess, you seem to have forgotten that there are a whole bunch of bad men who will stop at nothing to keep The Holy Child from being born," said Milo. "Bria will be their number one target once her identity is discovered. We're trying to protect her from being killed. This isn't a game for amateurs."

"Hello," said Bria, "I'm right here. I hate it when men talk over me like I don't exist! Wait. Did you say they want to kill me?"

Dhabi and Milo exchanged a glance before Milo spoke. "Unfortunately, I did. As soon as *Opus Christos* figures out you are The Holy Dove, The Chosen One, destined to bear the Child of God, they will move Heaven and Earth to murder you. That's what we're trying to prevent."

Bria slowly nodded her head as she sat down next to Princess Celeste. "Dhabi, I'd like a cup of coffee, a double shot, I think."

Dhabi looked at her sternly. "Correction," he said. "We will listen to your concerns and ideas, but if it comes to making split-second decisions to ensure your safety, then you will do precisely as Milo or I tell you, immediately and without question. We're professionals trained to make life-saving decisions. You're not. We will not negotiate on this issue.

"You'll get a vote on almost everything else, and we promise to respect your opinions. But I'm not negotiating about coffee, wine, or anything else women in your delicate condition should avoid. This isn't about you, Bria. It's all about protecting Allah's child. You'll have warm milk with a sprinkle of cinnamon and cocoa, and that's the end of that," stated Dhabi in a tone that didn't allow discussion.

Chapter 67
7:30 P.M.

Brother Joseph and Father Richard

The great enemy of the truth is often not the lie—deliberate, contrived, and dishonest–but the myth- persistent, persuasive, and unrealistic.

—John F. Kennedy

<u>Vatican City</u>

"Brother Joseph," said Father Richard, glancing up from the document on the table before him, "This document is written in Aramaic."

"Can you translate it?"

"Probably some of it; I studied Aramaic years ago. I'm not sure how much I remember."

"Pope Peter put it in the breviary for a reason."

Father Richard nodded his head. "I'll do my best, but I make no promises."

After a few minutes, he began to speak. "I think it's the story of Judith the Elder, told in the first person. She was an early Christian deacon before the Church decided that women had no place in the faith other than subservient positions or hidden away, voiceless, in nunneries."

"A first-hand account? Is it authentic?"

"As with the first document, without chemical testing, it's impossible to ascertain one hundred percent, but it appears to be first-century CE parchment. It's Aramaic and consistent with the time in Judea. I see no reason to question it."

"Why would Pope Peter go to such dangerous lengths unless he believes it's genuine?"

"That would make no sense," agreed Father Richard, bending over the parchment. "This will be a rough translation, I'm afraid, but I'll do my best."

He studied the document for a minute. "It's just a fragment and starts in the middle of a sentence, *'left their home with…tears,'* I think it's 'tears,'" he said as he bent his head closer to the document. "*'on their faces. They kissed Jesus before the Roman soldiers-'* I'm not familiar with that word—. I'm not sure." Father Richard paused. "*'Beat?'*" He stopped suddenly. "The next section is blurred. I can't make out anything more. I'm going to skip down a bit. It looks like it's in better shape."

"It's something about a garden and a stone. A tomb?" he wondered as he continued to translate, *'I took them to the tomb in the dead of night to say farewell. Their pain and grief hung…on my bones...'* No, that's not right. It's *'engulfed, my soul.'*"

Father Richard stopped momentarily and studied the document before continuing, *'I love the Messiah's three daughters as if they are my own.'*

His face turned deathly white as he read the following line. "I'm not sure about the next line."

"Do your best, please," requested Brother Joseph.

Father Richard stammered as he translated the words. "*'These are our precious Holy Birds–* no*–Doves; who carry the Messiah's blood, as will each generation of their descendants. From one of them shall come a new Messiah to save humanity from destruction.'*"

They were both silent until Brother Joseph spoke up. "Why would Pope Peter give this to us unless he believed Judith's story of the Holy Doves, the daughters of the Messiah, was true?"

"I don't know," stammered Father Richard.

"I don't, either," answered Brother Joseph, "but I need to understand it. I want to go to St. Stephen's for Compline before we continue. I do my best thinking where I feel closest to God."

"Yes," answered Father Richard, "I would like to join you if that's okay with you."

Chapter 68
8:15 P.M.

Bria, Princess Celeste, Milo, and Dhabi

In God's sight we do not fall: on our own we do not stand.
—Julian of Norwich
Revelations of Divine Love (1373)

Princess Celeste's Apartments, Palazzo Di Luca
Rome, Italy

"This is quite delicious," said Princess Celeste after her third cup of Arabic coffee. "A perfect finish to a lovely meal. Please leave the recipe so my cook can make it for me."

"I did find it unusual that Lorenzo was your only staff."

"I sent the staff away when I learned that Inanna and Gabriel were coming. Trying to explain them can be difficult. The staff is scheduled to return tomorrow evening."

"This makes what I'm about to say a little easier. We need to get Bria to a more secure location. The two men Milo and I, uh—"

"Killed?"

"Yes, killed. The men waiting for Gabriel and Bria were Jesuits. We are quite sure they were *Opus Christos* members."

"*Opus Christos*?" asked Bria.

"It's a highly secret, ultra-radical Catholic organization outside the official channels and without the approval of the

Church. Superior General Scotti and Cardinal De Posada are the organization's leaders. *Opus Christos* has orchestrated the murders of more than two hundred Holy Doves so that the Prophecy of Judith could not be fulfilled, and the new Christ child couldn't be conceived."

Bria gasped.

"The drive-by shooting and the bombs at your house in LA weren't random gang violence, Bria. It was just lucky that your housekeeper wasn't hurt. It was intended for you and your mother."

"What you're saying is that," said Bria, "they've tried to kill me at least twice."

Dhabi spoke up. "That's why we were initially so concerned about Inanna and Gabriel. We didn't know who they were."

"The gunshots at the restaurant?"

"No, actually," said Milo, "those were meant for us. *Opus Christos* hadn't figured out where you were at the time."

"But they know now? That's why you are suggesting we move to a new location?"

Milo and Dhabi looked at each other momentarily, then turned to Bria.

"Yes, we believe they know who and where you are. We have an outside team doing surveillance twenty-four hours a day to protect you, but it's just a matter of time before they make another attempt. We need to look at alternatives as soon as we can."

"You can't just sit here and wait for them to make their move," said Princess Celeste. "Bria cannot be put in danger for a single second."

"I couldn't agree more," said Milo. "The Guardians are currently formulating a plan that we believe will work to destroy *Opus Christos*. We need help from you, Princess."

"You understand that I am restricted in what I can do. It just wouldn't be fair."

"Fair to who?" asked Bria.

Princess Celeste shifted uncomfortably. "To Inanna and Jehovah, of course."

"Why would your helping us be unfair?"

She took a sip of coffee. "They made a bet. I can't take sides."

"A bet? What was the bet?" asked Dhabi.

"It was whether or not humans could handle the combination of intelligence, free will, and innate curiosity without destroying themselves. Inanna believed they could. Jehovah disagreed."

Milo shook his head. "Inanna made a terrible bet."

"Perhaps. She is hopeful that humans will choose to turn themselves around," answered Princess Celeste.

"How's that been working?" asked Milo.

"It's been a disaster. Joe will probably win.".

"Princess Celeste, you and Gabriel have helped us already," said Bria. "You've opened your home and your hearts. You helped us understand and accept an unbelievable situation."

"We've been walking a thin line, but when you think about it, we haven't used our powers to do anything. You've made all the decisions yourselves. We're more like technical advisors."

Milo and Dhabi exchanged looks. "I can't argue with that, but what about the Annunciation?" Dhabi asked.

"That was official business, so an entirely different situation."

"Let's see if I've got this. You can help us," said Milo, "but you can't *help* us."

"Exactly."

"If I asked for information, we could use," said Dhabi, "to disable *Opus Christos* or one of its members. You could do that."

"As long as all you want is information, not assistance. That would violate the God-angel confidentiality agreement."

"But if we ask about someone, you could tell their most

closely held secrets?"

Princess Celeste's eyes grew wide. "You want the dirt?"

"The juicier, the better. Illegal and immoral would be a bonus," added Milo.

Princess Celeste smirked. "I might have heard a thing or two."

"If we asked for help to create a diversion to allow us to sneak Bria out of here, could you help us with that?" asked Milo.

Princess Celeste turned her head to look at Milo. "It depends on what you're suggesting. I can't make you invisible or teach you how to fly. I could, actually, but that would grant you an unfair advantage. I would get into serious trouble."

"You're doing it again. You're cutting me out," said Bria, looking straight at Milo and Dhabi. "Inanna wouldn't have chosen me unless I was strong enough to handle it. If you're unwilling to treat me as an equal and share everything you know, I'll take my chances and go it alone. I'm not kidding. I will."

Dhabi and Milo looked at each other, and then Milo smiled. "I think we have what I like to call a meeting of minds. Okay, partner, this is what's going down," he said, looking straight at Bria as he explained their plans for the next few hours. When he was finished, he and Dhabi looked at Bria, waiting for her reaction.

"Yeah," she said after a moment, "we can pull this off, but I think you should start calling me Bri instead of Bria. That's what my friends call me. If we crash and burn, you'll be the last friends I'll ever have."

Chapter 69
9:00 P.M.

Cardinal De Posada, Brother Joseph, and Father Richard

The source and root of all the evils that affect individuals, people, and nations is this: ignorance of the truth and not only ignorance, but at times, a contempt for and a deliberate turning away from it.
—Pope John XXII

Vatican City

Cardinal De Posada slipped into the pew next to Brother Joseph.

"Compline was over an hour ago, but I thought I might find you here. You Trappists," he said as he stared at Brother Joseph, "are creatures of habit. Your unnecessary sacrifices and the hours spent in meditation and prayer are self-indulgent."

"I would not categorize it that way, Your Eminence, but I will consider your assessment. I respect that you are a man well-versed in self-indulgence," said Brother Joseph, unconsciously leaning away from the cardinal, not wanting to be near him, knowing what he now believed of the man's character.

Cardinal De Posada laughed. "Quite witty, Brother Joseph, but you are not wrong. God provides me with luxuries. I see nothing wrong with enjoying them."

"Nor would I, Your Eminence, if it weren't for the fact that so many people struggle just to survive, and you do nothing to help them."

Cardinal De Posada shrugged. "They are not my responsibility, nor the Church's concern. God chose me to be rich and powerful. Why should I deny myself?"

"Because we are responsible for the least among us, I believe."

"And yet, Brother Joseph, we are not that different, are we? What exactly do you do to relieve the misery of others that makes you so much better than me? You hide away in your solitude and prayers. I hide in my silk robes and power. We are the same in the most basic of ways. We have chosen to retreat from the sadness and pain of life, haven't we?"

Brother Joseph bit back any retort he might have considered. "Thank you, Your Eminence. You have given me much to think about."

The cardinal lifted his gaze to catch Father Richard's eyes, sitting on the other side of Brother Joseph. "My desk is stacked high with correspondence. I have phone calls that need to be returned."

"I am at your disposal, Your Eminence."

"Of course you are, Father Richard. Why else would I employ you?" he said as he turned to Brother Joseph. "Have you found the list of the Islamic terrorists?"

"Not yet, Your Eminence, but there are a few more storerooms we have yet to search. I assure you that if there is a list, we will find it."

"I'm under great pressure from His Holiness to produce results. There is a press conference scheduled for tomorrow afternoon. He wishes to announce the Islamic attack upon Christianity."

"A statement to the press, at this point, would be irresponsible," stuttered Brother Joseph.

Cardinal De Posada interrupted him, "Brother Joseph, His Holiness is adamant. Have you forgotten your vows of Obedience to the Church, or are you questioning his authority and wisdom?"

"No, Your Excellency," Brother Joseph answered as he bowed his head in supposed submission. "I understand my position and vows. I will do exactly as Pope Peter requests."

Cardinal De Posada smiled. "That is excellent, Brother Joseph. I will inform His Holiness."

Chapter 70
9:30 P.M.
Milo and Bria

God greatly underestimated mankind's capacity for perfidy. They will lie and then convince themselves that they have done it for the greater good.

—The Secret Gospel of Judith the Elder

Princess Celeste's Apartments, Palazzo Di Luca
Rome, Italy

"Izzy?" asked Milo as soon as she answered the phone at the Command Center, "I was supposed to speak with Jasper, but he's not answering his phone. Princess Celeste gave us the information that Jasper had asked for. I think it's explosive enough to do the trick. You're going to have to write this down."

Izzy grabbed her laptop and began typing. "This is exactly the stuff Jasper was hoping for, Milo," she said. "We'll call you back within fifteen minutes." She stood up and quickly gestured to Jasper and his team to join her behind her closed office door.

Milo's phone rang exactly fourteen minutes later. "Izzy? I'm putting you on speaker. Bri insists she's included in all our plans from here on out."

"Fair enough. Hi, Bria," she said, "Jasper and the IT team are here, too."

"My Mom and Theo said I can trust you. I already trust Milo and Dhabi to protect me."

"We will never lie to you, Bria. You must know that the next twenty-four hours are critical and very dangerous, but the Guardians will protect you and The Child-Who-Is-Coming with our lives if necessary. We will not fail you."

"I appreciate your honesty, Izzy, but time is short, and we need to prepare to leave the gracious hospitality of Princess Celeste," answered Bria. "What is the plan to wipe *Opus Christos* off the map?"

Chapter 71
9:30 P.M.

Brother Joseph and Inanna

I don't believe in God, but I'm very interested in her.
                                        —Arthur C. Clark

Vatican City

Cardinal De Posada's words had upset Brother Joseph beyond measure. He sat alone on a bench near St. Stephen's long after Compline was over, wondering if the cardinal was correct about him. Had he joined the Monastery to hide from the world's pain to ease his own? Had every decision he had made in the last nine years been a mistake?

"The cardinal is an odious man, but he is not wrong, Joseph," said a woman's voice. "He cares only for the power and wealth his position provides him. You hid from your guilt and pain in the silence and seclusion of your monastery. Both of you have been selfish in your way."

Brother Joseph turned toward the voice but saw nothing but mist and shadows. Slowly, as he watched, Her form became cleared. Her hair fell in gentle waves of gold and silver around her shoulders as the smell of cinnamon and roses filled his nostrils. Slowly, she lifted her face, her brown eyes warm and gentle, to smile at him.

"All life is intertwined, Joseph. Godliness is not what you do to ease your burdens, soothe your fears, or carry your sorrows. It is what you do to help others ease their burdens, fears, and sorrows that honors God."

"Are you an angel?" asked Brother Joseph as she walked toward him, her scent engulfing him.

"Would you mind if we walked in the garden, Joseph? I don't often get a chance to do so. I would
enjoy it," she said as she slipped her hand under his arm and lifted him from the bench.

"Who I am? I'm surprised you haven't figured it out yet," she said as she steered him toward the graveled path. "I am air and light, mist and shadows. I am mystery and magic. I am loved and yet forgotten. I am everything and nothing. I am Inanna, who sits at the right hand of Jehovah. We were one in the darkness before I created the light and all things in the Universe. We are two halves of one whole. We are opposites and, yet, equals. Together, we are God."

Brother Joseph turned to look at her.

"Hello, Inanna," he said calmly.

"You're not afraid of me, Joseph. That surprises me."

"If you are God, there is nothing to fear. If you are not, then God will protect me from you."

Inanna stared at him for a moment and then laughed.

"Such unquestioning faith is dangerous, Joseph. If I were not God, I would destroy you for it."

"I don't understand," said Joseph quietly.

"I gave humans the intellect to think and to question everything. I bestowed them with free will to choose their destinies. I blessed them with an insatiable curiosity unparalleled in the universe because I wanted them to question everything. Your unquestioning faith denies the most important gifts I gave to humans: intelligence, free will, and curiosity."

"Forgive me, Inanna," said Joseph. "I don't know what to say."

"You are wondering if I am God because God is a stern old white guy with a flowing beard and a coarse cotton robe surrounded by adoring angels."

"I've always believed that God is Our Father in Heaven."

"Why do men insist upon believing they were created in God's image?" asked Inanna, her tone showing her aggravation. "Of the billions upon billions of life forms I have created, only human males have the unparalleled egotism to dare to believe they are replicas of God."

"The Church teaches us that we were created in God's image."

"You're not. I promise you are not," she said firmly, "but if humans had to choose between us, why did you choose him?" She didn't wait for him to answer. "If you knew him better–," she muttered as she tightened her grip on Brother Joseph's arm. "Together, we are one. We are God. He's logic and rules, reason and order, judgment and wisdom. He's rather dull. I am not criticizing him. For what he is, he is perfect. He is, after all, God. As am I."

Brother Joseph nodded his head slowly.

She smiled sweetly, almost flirtatiously, and smoothed her gown with her free hand. "Truthfully, I would be lost without him. He sets the boundaries so my imagination can roam freely without fear. To be responsible for one's creativity and emotions is a heavy burden."

Brother Joseph finally found his voice. "I suppose it must be."

"If I had left it to him, the universe would still be an endless, empty black void of nothingness. Everything that exists is because of me. I have always been full of new ideas. He has no imagination," she shrugged. "But, equally, I have too much. I create, and he administers the universe with his cold, logical mind. Luckily, we balance each other perfectly most of the time."

"But not always?"

Her chest heaved with a soft sigh, "Almost always." She looked away for an instant. "Humanity has been a problem. I thought creating the only creatures in the universe with intelligence and free will would be interesting."

"And?" asked Brother Joseph.

She returned Her eyes to his. "He hated the idea. From the very first, he said it was my worst idea ever. He said it would be a disaster with unimaginable consequences since no creatures could handle such enormous responsibility that it would entail."

"He's probably right."

A flash of anger crossed Inanna's eyes but faded immediately.

"He usually is," she said as they walked along silently.

Brother Joseph looked at her. "I am comforted to know those I love are with you in heaven."

Inanna stopped and faced him, taking his hands in hers. "Oh, Joseph," she said gently, "There isn't a Heaven or a Hell. They are human inventions to calm the fears of the inevitable and to frighten people into behaving."

She saw the stricken look on his face and tried to comfort him. "Joseph, you have always been, and always shall be part of God. You will always be part of those you love through God. The essence of their uniqueness and their spirit cannot be forgotten. They live forever through me."

"And Jehovah?" asked Brother Joseph.

"Of course, when I speak of myself, I speak of him. We cannot be divided. I know that death is frightening to humans. How can I explain what happens when your time on Earth is over," she mused, "in a way that you will understand?"

"Close your eyes, Joseph. Imagine you are at the most

beautiful beach imaginable. Can you see the beach, the palm trees swaying, the sky deep blue and dotted with white fluffy clouds?"

Joseph did as Inanna asked. After a second, he nodded his head. "I can."

"Good," answered Inanna. "Do you see every individual grain of sand, or do you see hundreds of billions of grains of sand coming together to become one glorious sight?"

"Yes," answered Brother Joseph, "everything flows together to create perfection."

"Good. That is as it should be. Now, look a little closer at the sand, Joseph. Do you see that the grains are not identical? Some are sparkling on the beach, shining in the sunlight. Those are the ones who lived righteous lives. They choose good over evil, acceptance over hatred, and kindness over cruelty. These shining grains of sand are imperfect, but each one has struggled to be the best they could be. Those grains of sand are beloved by us and will always be a part of us, part of God."

Joseph smiled weakly as Inanna's beach continued to form in his mind.

"There are other grains of sand," Inanna continued, "are dull and unremarkable. They live in apathy and ignorance. They willingly accept another person's ideas and beliefs. They lived without caring for the lives of those around them. They are further from us since they ignored the spark of God within them."

Joseph silently nodded his head. "I do. I see them."

"Good. Now, search for the grains of sand that are dark and sharp. Many of these grains lived privileged lives of wealth and power. They believed it was their rightful due and forgot their responsibility to all humanity."

They were often politicians or religious bigots who forgot about the people they were to serve. They judged others and disdained those who disagreed with their ideas. They are those who have no respect for others. They thought only of themselves. Those grains of sand will soon wash off the beach and disappear into the eternal ocean. At that moment, they ceased to be a part of us, and it was as if they never existed." Inanna paused a second. "There is no greater punishment than to be forgotten by God," she said quietly.

"Nothing," whispered Joseph, "could be worse than to be forgotten by God."

Inanna was distracted momentarily as she looked over his shoulder. She nodded her head before she pulled her attention back to Brother Joseph. "You must listen carefully to what I am about to say. The fate of humanity lies in your hands."

"I will do as you ask of me," Brother Joseph whispered.

"I have one chance, Joseph, to prove to my husband that the humans can choose, as one, to use their free will for the good of all creatures on this insignificant planet."

"They never have before, Inanna," said Brother Joseph quietly.

"Which is not my fault, Joseph," Inanna answered sharply. "Millions of years of existence, and you, as a species, haven't learned a thing. I created humans with the ability to choose enlightenment over evil, but humanity has made one disastrous decision after another."

"It must be frustrating," sympathized Brother Joseph.

"It is. My greatest creative experiment will fail if I don't move decisively," she sighed. "My husband, Jehovah, is threatening to annihilate humanity one and all."

"But you have a plan to save us, don't you?"

Inanna smiled. "You are quite perceptive, Joseph. I do. I am sending another savior to walk among you, a child, to bring our simple message of love, acceptance, and equality to the world."

Joseph looked at Inanna. "And if humanity refuses to hear

your message?"

"I have no choice," she said as she lowered him to the ground, "but to allow Jehovah to destroy you all."

"Inanna, I have no power to change humanity. I wouldn't know where to start."

"Joseph," she said as she began to fade away. "You carry the blood of the first Messiah in your veins. You will be the earthly father of the new Christchild. You must find the Holy Dove, the Holy Mother, who also has God's blood flowing in her veins. Unless you are one together, our child will not quicken in her womb. The Christ-child will die, as will humanity's hope for salvation."

"The Holy Mother? Who is she? How do I find her?"

"Her name is Bria," she said, her voice a mere whisper, "Open your heart, Joseph."

Then she was gone, leaving only the slightest aroma of cinnamon and roses in the midnight air.

Chapter 72
9:30 P.M.

Jasper and Father Patrick

Everyone has his own idea of good and evil and must choose to follow good and fight evil as he conceives them. That would be enough to make the world a better place.

—Pope Francis

Guardians' Command Center,
Abbey Sainte-Victoire
Marseille, France

"Jasper," said Izzy, "is the intel on Paolo Mandini accurate? Can we use it?"

"A few posts on various social websites indicate that Princess Celeste is right about his 'secret' interests. True or not, even the hint of a scandal of this magnitude would ruin his life."

"The IOR has been plagued with scandals for years. It won't take much to convince the world that a new scandal is true," Izzy answered. "Mandini will betray Cardinal De Posada and Superior General Scotti to save himself. If this works, we will destroy *Opus Christos* once and for all."

Jasper stared at Izzy. "My plans always work. Is Father Patrick up to speed?"

Izzy thought about it for a moment. "Not quite yet. I want to protect his deniability until we are too deep to let him pull the plug. If everything goes as planned, I'll tell him tomorrow morning after it's too late to stop it. Are they ready to move Bria?"

Jasper looked at his watch. "Orlando, Lucas, and Bakir will be at the *Palazzo* with the trucks once it's dark. We've got video surveillance, drone coverage, and *Mahdi* snipers on the entire route. Gabriella and Lilliana just arrived at Da Vinci. They'll provide additional backup once Milo and Dhabi start moving Bria out of Princess Celeste's apartments. We're ready as we can be for anything *Opus Christos* throws at us."

Chapter 73
9:45 P.M.

Milo, Dhabi, Bria, Princess Celeste, Lucas, and Orlando

We should not be simply fighting evil in the name of good but struggling against
the certainties of people who claim always to know where good and evil are to be found.

—Tzvetan Todorov

Princess Celeste's Apartments, Palazzo Di Luca
Rome, Italy

"Milo?" asked Dhabi as he knocked on the bathroom door. Dhabi suppressed a laugh as Milo exited.

"I feel like a fool," Milo complained, wiggling uncomfortably in Lorenzo's tuxedo tails. He turned to Princess Celeste. "We'll talk about this penguin suit when I come to work for you, Princess."

Princess Celeste giggled. "You can wear as much or as little of it as you like, Milo."

"Enough, you two. It's showtime," said Bria as the doorbell chimed.

Orlando, Lucas, and Bakir were standing in olive uniforms and caps with a local plumbing company's logo on the front and back of their shirts. Over Orlando's shoulder was a plumber's snake, while Lucas and Bakir carried two canvas tool bags. As soon as the door closed, they dropped the snake and the tool bags. Lucas pulled a black body bag out of one of them.

"Izzy, Jasper, and Father Patrick send their regards," he said as he bowed his head to Bria and Princess Celeste. "It is an honor to meet you both," Orlando said before turning to Dhabi and Milo.

Jasper has this planned out to the microsecond. We need to get moving."

"What's left of Lorenzo's body is in the tunnel," said Dhabi. "Once Bri is at the new location, we'll need to drop the body somewhere so it can't be traced back to the Princess."

Orlando nodded his head.

"We've got it covered," he said as he and Bakir unbuttoned their shirts and unzipped their pants to reveal another plumber's uniform under their garments. "Throw these over your clothes," he said to Dhabi. "Anybody watching will see the same number of plumbers who came in leave. I will stay until the Princess' staff returns tomorrow morning. Then I'll join you in the Vatican."

Orlando turned to the Princess and took her hand in his. "I've heard you are quite a delightful companion, Princess," he said with a toss of his shiny black hair. He smiled widely, showing a mouthful of gleaming white teeth.

"Okay, young buck," said Milo protectively, waving Orlando away. "Don't get any ideas. The Princess's heart belongs to me. Right, *Mia Cara Principessa*?"

Princess Celeste laughed out loud. "The best thing about being my age," she said, "is knowing ridiculous flattery when I hear it. I don't believe a single word, but it makes me feel wonderful."

"Milo, stay in the butler's uniform for now. We'll need you to walk us across the courtyard and show us the location of the sewer line clean-outs," said Orlando.

"I have no idea what a clean-out is or where they are," said

Milo.

"Luckily, I do, but if *Opus Christos* is watching, it will look like the butler is showing us the location of the clean-outs, which would be expected. Lucas," he continued, "help Barik bundle up the package in the tunnel and get it by the tunnel entrance. Once we start cleaning the line, there will be enough noise from the generator for you to slide back the rock and open the vans' side doors without anyone noticing. We've removed the interior light bulbs, so be careful."

"Okay," said Bria, "what do you want me to do?"

Orlando looked over at Milo questioningly.

Milo shrugged. "She's a team member whether we like it or not."

Orlando looked between Dhabi and Milo uncertainly.

"Give her a job," they said together as one.

"Ok, Bria. You can help Dhabi and me clean out the sewer," Orlando said as he pulled another plumber's shirt out of the tool bag, "or you can help us bag what's left of Lorenzo's body. It's up to you."

"Two inviting choices. I've been in the tunnel before, so I know the layout and remember how to open the hatch. That should be helpful. I'll help with Lorenzo's body."

"Fine," said Orlando. "Milo, return to the house once you've shown us the clean-outs, and we'll trade uniforms. I'll become the beautiful Princess' butler, and you'll return outside as a plumber."

"Dhabi, call the surveillance team and tell them to be on their toes. We should be ready to move out within twenty minutes. Unless anyone has a question that can't wait, it's go-time."

Princess Celeste turned to Bria and engulfed her in a hug. "I shall miss you, my dear Bri. Please come and visit one day when it's safe. And promise me you will listen to Milo and Dhabi. They both want the best for you."

"I will. I promise," said Bria as she hugged the Princess back.

Princess Celeste let go of Bria and turned to Orlando. "I believe I heard something about your talent in making margaritas," she said. "When you return, I'm willing to find out if they are as good as I've heard."

"Oh, *Principessa*," moaned Milo, "you're cheating on me already? My heart is breaking."

"Only until you return, Milo," she answered with a laugh, "then I promise I'll be faithful again."

Chapter 74
9:45 P.M.

Cardinal De Posada, Father Richard, and Felix

The only thing necessary for the triumph of evil is for good men to do nothing.

—Edmund Burke

Vatican City

Father Richard looked up from stacks of new correspondence at a knock on the door.

"I need to talk to the cardinal," said Felix as he stepped inside.

"We'll finish in the morning, Father Richard." He waited until his aide closed the door. "What do you want, Felix?"

"I haven't been able to find Alberto. He hasn't answered his phone all day."

"Is it suddenly necessary that your superiors check in with you?"

"No, but—."

"What Alberto does is none of your business. I heard you spoke to Superior General Scotti without my permission. I will not tolerate you plotting with Scotti. You report to me and only to me."

"Are you forgetting that Brother Joseph trusts me? You need me if you want him to show up at the press conference and say what you want him to say."

"Father Richard is controlling Brother Joseph. I doubt you have anything to offer other than your talent in killing defenseless women. Without Alberto keeping you in line, I question your value."

Felix was furious. After slamming the door, he stomped toward his room on the floor below Cardinal De Posada's quarters. *Opus Christos'* plan wouldn't have worked without him, he thought angrily. No one else could have killed so many women so quickly and efficiently without leaving a trace of evidence. How dare Cardinal De Posada speak to him with disrespect? It wasn't right, and it wasn't fair. He didn't notice the ancient nun until he almost ran into her as she climbed the steep stairs.

"Scusi!" she shouted as she nearly dropped the small package she held in her clawed right hand. She stood rooted in her spot, expecting Felix to step back to let her pass.

Her eyes caught Felix's, and an electric spark flew between them. In that second, they recognized each other for who they were. For a moment, Felix and the nun were transfixed by that knowledge. Then, as Felix watched her, he saw fear grow in her eyes. She was afraid of him. Fearful of his power, terrified of his evil. It excited him.

Felix silently closed the small gap that separated him from the nun. Her arthritic left hand gripped the wooden railing; her eyes grew wide as she saw him smiling down at her. He kicked out with his right foot and caught her squarely above her right temple. She reeled from the blow, but her clawed hand held tightly to the rail.

He kicked out again, and her fingers loosened their hold on the railing. Her eyes caught his as Felix winked and blew her a kiss as she tumbled down the ancient stone steps to her death. Another Guardian down, he thought proudly. It was just too easy.

◆ ◆ ◆
Brother Joseph and Pope Peter

After Inanna's visit, Brother Joseph found sleep impossible, so he sat quietly on the bench near the spot where she had faded away when he felt someone nearby. He kept his eyes down, almost afraid to look up, when he heard a man's voice whispering his name.

"Brother Joseph, pull out your breviary. Read it as if you are unaware I am here. Enemies surround us."

He did as he was told; too much had happened this evening for him to question anything. Bending his head, he focused his eyes on his breviary before he spoke.

"Your Eminence?" he whispered.

"Yes," Pope Peter answered as he bent down to tie the laces on his running shoes. "I saw her talking to you. She looked at me and nodded before she faded away into nothing. Was she an angel?"

"You saw her? How is that possible?" whispered Brother Joseph.

Pope Peter stood up and began doing stretches.

"I have no idea, but she wanted me to see her. Perhaps it was because the Guardians told me the truth about your identity."

"The Guardians?"

"The Guardians is a two-thousand-year-old organization vowed to protect all the Doves, including you. I know that God chose you to be the father of the new Messiah."

"That is what she said," said Brother Joseph quietly. "I don't know how to react, honestly."

Pope Peter nodded to one of his bodyguards, watching him anxiously. "You are in grave danger if Cardinal De Posada and Superior General Scotti discover your true identity," he whispered as he removed his windbreaker and placed it over the back of the bench.

"Stay here reading your breviary, Brother Joseph. I'll do a lap and return to speak with you if possible. I am being carefully watched. The Guardians of the Holy Doves are devising a plan to protect you and the Dove chosen to carry the Holy Child."

It was fifteen minutes before Pope Peter returned. He turned away from his bodyguard and began going through a series of stretching exercises to cool down after his run.

"Everything that Cardinal De Posada has told you," he said quietly, "is a lie. The Islamic terrorists do not exist, and the list–."

"Is not a list of assassins," interrupted Brother Joseph, "it is a list of potential victims."

Pope Peter smiled at Joseph as he shook his arms and bent over, pretending to stretch.

"Yes. The list is the names of the blood descendants of Leah, the eldest of the Messiah's three daughters, which was lost during the war. Without the list, Opus Christos can't find and murder Leah's Doves," Pope Peter said as he gripped the bench's back to continue his wind-down stretches.

"I am a descendant of Leah?"

"I don't know. Possibly. If *Opus Christos* discovers your true identity, they will kill you. The new Christ child will die in the womb of the Holy Dove. Cardinal De Posada and Superior General Scotti must continue to believe that you are working in their interests, and you believe their lies. The Guardians will do everything they can to eradicate them one and all. Until then, both you and I must play our roles perfectly. Trust us, Joseph. We will, I have no doubt, win in the end."

"I will do as you wish, Your Eminence."

"I believe that God's true desire will prevail. There is no other possibility."

Chapter 75
11:30 A.M.
Toshi and Father Claude

All good moral philosophy is but a handmaiden to religion.
—Francis Bacon

<u>Rome, Italy</u>

"Are you sure this is the right place?" asked Toshi as he looked around the filthy alley.

Several teenage boys in black leather leaned against the brick walls, trying to look unconcerned and yet alluring as Father Claude walked toward them. He pulled his ID out of his inside jacket pocket, ensuring his shoulder holster with his SIG Sauer P365 was revealed.

"CIA," he said.

They started to scatter until Toshi pulled his weapon and pointed it at them.

"Where can we find him?" said Father Claude as he flashed a photo of Paolo Mandini.

Toshi reached out, pulled the boy into a chokehold, and put the gun to his head.

"We're going to ask you nicely one time. Where's Paolo?"

Slowly, the boy raised his hand and pointed to a door at the end of the alley.

"Get the hell out of here," Toshi said, walking down the alley next to Father Claude.

◆ ◆ ◆

Bria, Dhabi, and Milo

"Are you okay, Bri?" asked Milo as they sat next to each other in the back of the van.

"Not an experience I'd want to have again," she said as she shrugged. "We bagged up what was left of Lorenzo and carried him down the tunnel. It wasn't as bad as I thought, but it was still pretty gross. You?"

"It was just another day in the wonderful world of Milo, cleaning out sewers while waiting for a sniper's bullet to blow my brains out."

"But it didn't happen. We got away with it."

Dhabi turned his head to look at her. "Let's not jinx it, Bri. We're not safe yet."

"Are the other cars in place?" asked Milo.

"Gabriella and Lilliana, two of the Guardian's top marksmen, are in the black Fiat behind us. Samil and David are in the white Mercedes, two cars ahead."

"What about the plumbing truck with Lorenzo's body?" asked Bria.

"Jamal and Lucas will drop it off at the dump and set it on fire. Barik and Freddie are following them. They'll join us as part of the security detail at the hotel once we get there." Dhabi answered, "Milo, you and Bria need to get out of the plumbers' uniforms and into these," and threw a bundle of clothing into the back of the van. "We're going to switch vehicles in a few minutes. You need to be ready and dressed."

"You must be f-ing kidding, Dhabi," said Milo, holding up the clothes Dhabi handed him.

"Get over it, Milo. It was the best we could come up with, considering *Opus Christos* knows what you look like. Just shut up and put it on."

◆ ◆ ◆

Toshi, Father Claude, and Paolo Mandini

"Get your pants on, Mandini," he said as the two Sudanese boys screamed, jumped from the bed, gathered their clothes off the floor, and ran out, still naked, into the alley.

Father Claude waved his badge as Toshi pulled out the handcuffs. "We're taking you in."

"On what charges?" asked Mandini.

"Whichever damn ones we decide to pursue. We will start with running a child prostitution ring, money laundering for the Mafia and various terrorist groups, and embezzlement of IOR funds, but those are just for starters," said Toshi as he forced Mandini's arms behind his back to handcuff him.

◆ ◆ ◆

Dhabi, Bria, Milo, Lucas, and Jamal

"Lucas, Jamal," Dhabi said as they parked their vehicles in the employee parking lot hidden behind the Hotel Artemide as Gabrielle and Lilliana set up their surveillance positions.

"We'll change behind the dumpster over there. Bri, hand me the plumbers' uniforms. I'll get rid of them in the dumpster. We'll enter the hotel from the side entrance."

Dhabi returned dressed as a Saudi Prince, while Jamal and Lucas wore the somber black suits of professional bodyguards. A dark-haired older man dressed as a hotel's doorman slipped out the back service entrance and approached the van. He bowed to Dhabi and spoke quietly in Arabic. Dhabi handed him the keys and ordered that the van disappear permanently.

"The Rolls has arrived," he said as he placed a traditional *ghuthrain* over his head and tied the *agal* to secure it. "We're going to walk through the hotel lobby. Lucas, you stay slightly ahead of me by my right side. Barik, flank my left side. Milo, You and Bri will walk silently ten feet behind me. Samil and David will join us in the lobby and walk behind you. If anything goes down, they will return you to the employee parking lot, where Gabriella and Lilliana will be waiting. They'll get you away."

"Are you forgetting that Father Patrick made me in charge?" asked Milo.

"You're in my world now. I'm the Prince. You're my second wife. You will allow Samil and David to protect you. You and Bri must stay in character."

Milo was silent.

"Right?" asked Dhabi firmly.

"Fine," answered Milo grudgingly.

Barik and Lucas took their positions with Dhabi between them, their jackets open to allow a subtle glimpse of the weapons readily available if needed, as Samil and David entered the lobby to join them, standing respectively behind the Prince's two veiled wives as the group walked calmly toward the waiting Rolls Royce.

With a sigh of relief, Samil opened the rear door, and David took his place as driver. Once the limo's doors were closed, Barik tapped the roof before entering the black Escalade waiting in front of the Prince's Rolls while Lucas and Samil entered the matching Escalade parked behind the Rolls. As the caravan began moving, Dhabi spoke.

"So far, so good," he said. "We're going to drive around for a while just to assure ourselves that we're not being followed. Milo?"

"Yes, my worthless shit-dog of a husband."

Dhabi laughed. "I was going to say that you can take off the *Abaya, Hajib,* and *Niqab* until we reach our destination, but I think you look better this way. Best you leave them on."

"Screw you, Dhabi."

"Silence, wife number two," laughed Dhabi. "You've never looked better, and I have never loved you more."

◆ ◆ ◆

Toshi, Father Claude, and Paolo Mandini

The office building on Vittorio Veneto Street was modern and stark. The guard nodded to Toshi and Father Claude as they entered, with the handcuffed Mandini between them. Toshi pushed the elevator button to the fourth floor, which brought them to a reception area with the seal of the United States of America emblazoned on the wall behind the vacant desk.

"Take him into the first interrogation room. I'll see if the chief wants to sit in," said Toshi.

Father Claude pushed Mandini into a small, stark room. "Should we call your wife and get her down here, Mandini?"

Mandini's face lost its color. "No, please don't call her. I want my attorney."

Father Claude laughed. "Mr. Mandini, you are being held by the United States government on charges of international money laundering and embezzlement in connection with terrorist factions. What you want is immaterial. You'll be offered legal representation in the good old US of A."

"I'm an Italian citizen," he said.

"Let me make this clear; we don't give a shit."

Toshi came into the room. "The chief says the extradition papers will be here within the hour," he said. "He's royally pissed

311

off at you, Mr. Mandini, furious you're responsible for another scandal that will seriously damage the Church's reputation. How did you think you'd get away with it?"

"But I didn't!" Mandini shouted. "I didn't do any of it!"

Father Claude laughed at him. "The two Sudanese boys were what? Fourteen? Fifteen? How many do you have in your prostitution ring?"

"But I don't!" said Mandini with tears, "I enjoy the company of young men. I treat them well, which is more than I can say for some of their other customers who are important men in the Church. I could give you names. I could help you."

Toshi shook his head. "Paolo," he said as he leaned over Mandini, "the United States government doesn't give a rat's ass who or what you diddle. Screw snakes if that's what gets you off. We, however, absolutely do not tolerate financial crimes. America takes the almighty dollar very, very seriously. Fuck with our money; we fuck with you. Never forget that."

"But, I—"

"Shut up, Mandini! We have indisputable proof you have been the lynchpin in an international money laundering scheme funding terrorism, drug dealing, and organized crime. There is more than $186 million missing from IOR deposits. As the bank's director, all the evidence leads to you."

"But I haven't. I didn't. I know nothing about improprieties regarding either our funds or our depositors. Someone has set me up. I swear, I'm innocent."

"If it wasn't you, then who would have access to the bank's operations and pull off something like this? Who, Mandini?"

Mandini shook his head.

"Think hard."

"Cardinal O'Malley?"

"Wrong! He's been in a nursing home for the last year. It's not him, and you know it. Try again!"

"Cardinal De Posada is a director on the board. I've heard rumors–"

"What kind of rumors?" Toshi placed his hands on the table and hovered over Mandini.

"I heard that De Posada and Superior General Scotti are involved in a secret organization that plans to return the Church to traditional values. I imagine they would need a lot of money to do that."

Toshi and Father Claude looked at each other.

"Interesting," Father Claude said, "as bank directors, De Posada and Scotti would have access to the bank's most sensitive information. It's possible. He might be telling the truth, Agent Toshi."

Toshi turned back to Mandini. "There is a terrorist group that we have indisputable evidence is laundering money through the IOR. Perhaps you will recognize it."

"I'll try," Mandini said.

"*Sangre de Dios.*"

"Yes!" answered Paolo Mandini. "Cardinal De Posada and Superior General Scotti of the Jesuits are co-signers on their account. But they're not drug dealers. *Sangre de Dios* is a charity providing housing and education for Latin America's most desperately poor people."

"No, Paolo, it is not a charity," said Father Claude, slamming his hand against the table, "It's a large drug cartel based in Miami Beach, Florida, a group of Cuban expats dedicated to overthrowing the Cuban government."

"But I was told it was a charity. I believed it was a charity."

"How is the cardinal involved?"

"He's their sponsor," said Mandini, "If Cardinal De Posada is involved with criminal activity, then Superior General Scotti must be involved, too. They regularly move funds in and out of that account, but I knew nothing about their activities. I swear."

"Interesting," answered Father Claude. "Agent Toshi?"

"It fits," said Toshi after a moment. "If it's true and you're innocent, then we'll need your help to get the proof to charge the cardinal and the superior general with their crimes."

Mandini nodded his head. "I'll do whatever you want."

"We'll need access to all their accounts."

"Yes. I'll do whatever you want; keep my name out of it. I have a reputation to protect."

"We need to get the chief's okay. I'm ninety-nine percent sure he'll drop all the charges against you if you help us nail the real culprits: Cardinal De Posada and Superior General Scotti."

Chapter 76
11:58 P.M.
Izzy and Father Patrick

Mankind is not likely to salvage civilization unless he can evolve a system of good and evil which is independent of Heaven and Hell.
—George Orwell

Guardians' Command Center,
Abbey Sainte-Victoir
Marseille, France

"Izzy?" asked Father Patrick as he walked into her office. "It's the middle of the night."

"I hadn't noticed," she answered. "The next few hours are critical. I couldn't sleep if I tried. "

"I think you should try. Jasper can let me know what's going on," answered Father Patrick.

"We already discussed this. It's too dangerous for you if things go wrong. The Guardians would be in serious trouble without you at the helm. We all agree it's for the best. In a few hours, once it's too late to back away, we'll tell you everything. Trust us, Father Patrick. "

"Fine. I wouldn't say I like it, but I'll accept it. Can you at least tell me if Bria's okay?"

"Bria's in the process of being moved to another location.

Milo will call once they're settled in."

"Have you spoken with Toshi or Father Claude yet?" asked Father Patrick.

"They haven't contacted Brother Joseph if that's what you're asking, but everything's good so far. I'm not going to jeopardize your ability to disavow our actions if something goes wrong at this point. You'll know everything tomorrow once it's too late to stop. We'll either be heroes or felons on the run. Either way, you'll be safe to carry on the good fight."

"It's better than nothing, I guess," answered Father Patrick.

Chapter 77
Day Six
12:12 A.M.
Milo, Dhabi, Bria

Fate often saves a doomed warrior when his courage endures.
—Author unknown
Beowulf (c.1000 CE)

Rome, Italy

"Milo," said Dhabi as he signaled the caravan to pull over on a deserted street, "if you're ready to become part of the security detail, I will gladly divorce you. Take the *Abaya, Hijab,* and *Niqab* back to Freddie, the driver of the rear car, and change places."

Milo couldn't get out of the limousine fast enough. He watched as Freddie, the rear car's driver, stepped out of the driver's seat and removed the chauffeur's hat. Long, wavy black hair escaped from the cap. Milo stared at her as she walked toward him before he turned and spoke to Dhabi.

"Couldn't' we have just done this to begin with?"

"We could have, but you're too recognizable if *Opus Christos* was waiting for us, and, honestly, it was fun." Dhabi laughed and blew a kiss, "I will miss you, my little buttercup."

Milo shook his head as he pulled the clothing off and threw

them at Dhabi.

"If it's the last thing I do, Dhabi, I'll get you for this. Once Bri's safe, you better find a hole and hide."

The ancient caretaker slumped quietly just inside the apartment building's foyer door. He bent his head quickly in greeting and then stood straight.

"Your Highness," he said, catching Dhabi's eyes for a second before he lowered his own again. "This is a welcomed surprise. Mr. Aziz, your father's secretary, informed me you would arrive just two hours ago. Please excuse us if the accommodations are not meeting our usual standards."

"It was an unexpected stopover. The jet had a mechanical problem. We will continue to Zurich in the morning with Allah's blessings."

"This is your first visit to Rome, I believe? I thought I had met all of your father's sons in the years I have worked for him. Perhaps I was wrong," the concierge said as he studied Dhabi's face.

Dhabi didn't flinch under the man's critical eye. "My father," he answered calmly, "has been blessed with many sons, but I met you years ago. I was on my way to boarding school at Eton."

The concierge squinted his eyes and stared at Dhabi with intense concentration. Suddenly, his face lit up. "Of course," he said. "You were much younger then, but I would recognize you anywhere."

"And I you, but the night air is chilly," Dhabi said, "and my wives are tired."

"Of course, Your Excellency. Your father would never forgive me if you caught your death of cold while in my care," he said to the Prince while ignoring the veiled women exiting the Rolls Royce.

"If you need me, dial 1-2-3 on the house phone. I am at your disposal," the concierge said as he led them to the private elevator to the penthouse.

"We're leaving as soon as the jet is repaired," Dhabi replied, pushing the button to close the elevator door. Thank you. I will inform my father that you were gracious and helpful."

Minutes later, Milo and Dhabi carefully checked the vast apartment for intruders and recording devices before setting up a security schedule inside the penthouse. Lucas and Barik guarded the balconies against the possibility of sniper fire while Gabriella, Lilliana, Samil, and David secured the perimeter of the building. After the all-clear, Milo gestured to Bria and Freddie to remove the black garments and relax.

"We did well, don't you think?" Bri asked as she smiled at Dhabi and Milo.

Milo opened his mouth as if to speak and seemed to think better of it.

"Very well, Bri," said Dhabi. "Your idea that Milo and you wore traditional clothing once we were away from Princess Celeste's was perfect."

"I read about it once in a book. It said that it would be unthinkable to ask to see the face of a veiled Saudi woman. Even customs officials won't ask them to remove their face covering. They switch passports sometimes, especially when meeting someone for a secret romantic dalliance."

"But," said Dhabi, "If they're caught—"

"They're executed," said Bria. "But sometimes, death is better than living without love or hope."

"As long as there is life, there is hope," answered Milo.

Bria looked at him and then at the jumble of discarded black fabric at her feet.

"You haven't lived long enough as a woman, Milo. For many women in this world, there is no hope," she snapped as she took two steps toward the center of the room. "I need a bath and sleep."

Dhabi glanced at Milo. Milo shook his head. He was going to allow Dhabi to field this one.

Dhabi blushed. "Well, the main bedroom, but," he said, "Milo and I thought that—"

"What?"

"It's best you don't sleep alone."

"We're not as safe as I want to think, are we?" she asked.

"No," answered Dhabi quickly. "We're perfectly safe for the moment. It's just—"

Milo stepped forward. "It's just that we can't forget that our enemies will stop at nothing. If they suspect you are the Chosen One, they will turn over Heaven and Earth to find you."

"And kill me."

"And kill all of us, but you are the primary target."

"Thank you, Milo, for telling me the truth."

Chapter 78
7:30 A.M.

Father Richard and Brother Joseph

I love you when you bow in your mosque, kneel in your temple, pray in your church. For you and I are sons of one religion, and it is the spirit.

—Khalil Gibran

Vatican City

"Brother Joseph," whispered Father Richard, slipping into the pew. "Accept my apologies for being late. The cardinal is in quite a mood."

"Upset that we haven't found the list of terrorists?"

"He's mostly unhappy with Felix, plus Alberto Zayas has disappeared."

"Alberto is missing?"

Father Richard looked around to see if anyone was listening. "He thought Alberto and Felix could find the list with or without our help. He's fed up with all of us."

"We can only do what we can do."

"He said Pope Peter is relying on him, on us."

Brother Joseph started to speak and then thought better of it. That was not what the pope said last night. As much as he liked Father Richard, he wasn't sure he could be trusted. Still, he promised Pope Peter he would act as if he was pliant to the cardinal's every wish.

"Brother Joseph, are you all right? You have a strange look on your face."

"I'm sorry, Father Richard. I have been up all night praying for guidance. I understand now that we must do all we can to help Cardinal De Posada. Shall we continue our search for the missing list?"

"The cardinal would like to speak with you as soon as it's convenient, meaning immediately."

"I will take him at his word. It will not be convenient until we finish the last few storerooms."

Father Richard smiled. "He will not be happy, but what can I do? I was explicitly ordered to help you however I could and do everything you asked. My hands are tied."

Brother Joseph was looking through a ledger. He was sitting in a narrow cubicle in the Acquisitions Office when Father Richard spoke.

"May I ask you a personal question, Brother Joseph? You can tell me to mind my business, but why did you become a Trappist monk?"

"It wasn't a decision taken lightly. Why do you ask?"

"It's something, I'm sure, many people have wondered for years."

"Many people? You've lost me, I'm afraid."

Father Richard looked at him incredibly. "Four days after the terrorist attack on the Walker Tower in Chicago, you had discovered the names of the nineteen terrorists responsible for the deaths of 3,000 Americans and quickly had them arrested. You were a media sensation and a hero to all Americans. Then you just disappeared. It was rumored that the CIA silenced you or terrorists assassinated you, but no one ever mentioned you again. What happened?"

Brother Joseph sat quietly as Father Richard sat beside him, waiting for a response.

"A bomb that was meant for me killed my wife and child," he said, his voice cracking, "It was put in my car by friends of the men I accused of religious terrorism. My family died because of my ego; I needed to tell the world about my success. I failed my family and my promise to God to protect them."

Father Richard reached out and held his hand. "I'm so sorry," he said, "it wasn't your fault."

"But it was, Father Richard. It was my fault."

◆ ◆ ◆

Father Claude, Toshi, and Paulo Mandini

Rome, Italy

"Wake up, Mandini," said Father Claude. "Agent Toshi made breakfast, and you need a shower. You smell pretty rank from last evening's 'entertainment.'"

Paolo sat up and rubbed his eyes. He looked around the shabby apartment. "What time is it?"

Father Claude looked at his watch. "It's time to get cleaned up and dressed, Mandini. That's what time it is. We want to be at the bank by 10:00."

"The bank doesn't open until 11:00," Paolo said.

"We know that."

Paolo blanched. "I was wondering-."

"Toshi," Father Claude yelled. "Paolo's changed his mind. He's decided not to cooperate. Call the chief and tell him to courier the extradition order here. Paolo wants to spend the rest of his life in an American federal prison. Leavenworth, I would imagine."

"No!" shouted Paolo. "Tell him not to call! I don't want my wife to learn about this!"

"Paolo, we already agreed to protect you. After all, if you can't trust the CIA, who can you trust?" said Father Claude, trying to keep a smile from his face.

Cardinal De Posada and Superior General Scotti

Vatican City

Cardinal De Posada looked at the number flashing on his cell phone. The last thing he needed was a call from Superior General Scotti.

"I expected to hear from you this morning, Rafael," the superior general said, "Have you forgotten that the press conference is scheduled for noon?"

Cardinal De Posada took a deep breath to control his desire to hang up in Scotti's ear. "No, Enrico, I have not forgotten. The press conference will happen as planned. Pope Peter and Brother Joseph will testify that a list has been discovered that proves a group of Islamic terrorists have been murdering Christian women as an attack on Christianity and the Western world that can't be ignored."

"Oh really?" said Scotti, "I understand your Trappist hasn't found the list."

"Of course not, Enrico. It was destroyed years ago," said Cardinal De Posada.

"What if Brother Joseph refuses to verify our story during the press conference?"

"Brother Joseph will say what I tell him to say. I have

threatened him with eternal damnation. Pope Peter will do as he's told if he wants to see his family stay alive," answered Cardinal De Posada. "In the unlikely event that they refuse to speak, I'll speak to the press. It's not inconceivable that a man in my position might discover this information."

The Superior General laughed. "That might make sense if you ever spent time in the countries under your jurisdiction. You have no credibility with the press. No, we'll use one of my Jesuits, perhaps my aide, Father Michael."

"Enrico, I will consider that option if—"

"Perfect, Rafael, then it's settled. Once again, my Jesuits succeed when your men fail. I hope you remember this. The Council and I certainly will," the Superior General said before he ended the call.

Chapter 79
9:55 A.M.

Brother Joseph and Father Richard

One of the greatest tragedies of mankind is that morality has been hijacked by religion.

—Arthur Clarke

"I saw something earlier while scanning the household accounts," Father Richard said as his fingers moved quickly across the computer's keyboard. "It just didn't click at first."

Brother Joseph stood and peered over Father Richard's shoulder. "What am I looking at?"

"The inventory of the Pre-Seminary, the school for altar boys. When it was remodeled last year, the electric power to the school was disrupted multiple times. The priests and sisters gathered every candlestick and lantern judged to be of no historical value. I've suddenly realized that I haven't seen they were returned."

"Certainly, someone would have recognized a menorah."

"The boys come from rural towns in northern Italy and from devout Catholic families. They wouldn't know a menorah if they saw one."

Brother Joseph nodded his head. "Then it would still be at the school?"

"If the menorah was taken to the Pre-Seminary, it's still there. I'll call the housekeeper."

"Tell her we'll be there in half an hour. Let's recheck the logs to see if we missed something else the first time."

◆ ◆ ◆

Toshi, Father Claude, and Paolo Mandini

"*Signore* Mandini," said the security guard as he opened the main door of the IOR, "Is there a problem? It's not even 10." He cautiously looked at Toshi and Father Claude and lowered his hand to touch the gun handle resting on his right hip.

"Everything's fine, Franco. My friends," he said, using the excuse that Toshi had suggested, "are forensic auditors with the American government. The bank's supervisors and the pontiff have approved that they are given access to several American-owned accounts believed to be drug money."

"But the bank isn't open yet."

"I decided it is best done before opening. The pontiff agreed. We don't wish to make our other clients uncomfortable, now do we?"

The security guard removed his hand from his weapon. "Of course not, *Signore*."

"We're glad you agree," he answered.

"You did well, Paolo," said Toshi as the three men entered Mandini's private office. "I wouldn't be surprised if you end up with a medal from the American government."

"I would like that," Paolo answered, imagining himself with an impressive medal decorating his lapel at the next large dinner party his wife planned.

"Fire up your computer while I call headquarters in D.C. to set up a remote link. Our agency needs access to several accounts that we know belong to the *Sangria de Dios*. Our forensic IT agent will explain exactly what you'll need to do."

Father Claude pulled out his cell phone and punched a code to divert the call through several locations before connecting to Jasper at the Command Center.

"Agent Ellis," he said, "I have Paolo Mandini here at the Vatican bank. He will cooperate with every request you make. Once we're finished, can you please rescind the extradition order? We did assure him that the US government would issue *Signore* Mandini a letter of commendation and, possibly, a medal. Can you see to that? Excellent!" he said as he put the phone on speaker.

"*Signore* Mandini," said Jasper, "My name is Robert Ellis. Thank you again for being a valuable partner in the fight against the drug cartels who prey on innocent children. You are a hero."

"We must all do our part to protect our dear children from the evils of drug addiction."

Toshi made a face behind Mandini's back like he was throwing up. Father Claude shot him a warning look.

"*Signore* Mandini," said Jasper, "I need you to log in to the computer. I believe you have a two-factor identification system. Please take your SecureID and put in your PIN. A numeric passcode will be generated. Do you see it?"

"Yes."

"Good. Now enter that passcode."

"I'm in."

"Great. *Signore* Mandini, there are two ways we can do this. I can explain what I need step by step and give you directions, or you can give me remote access, and I can do it for you."

"I'm not good with computers. How do we do the remote thing?"

"I'll walk you through it step-by-step. Do you see the pop-up box I just sent you?"

"Yes."

"Click 'accept.' Perfect. This will take less than an hour since we know what American accounts we are targeting. You can sit on the couch, relax, and drink an espresso, but I'll need you to stay nearby since the program might request another code from your SecureID."

"What happens then?"

"I will ask you to enter another passcode. I am well acquainted with this system. It may request a second password or confirmation. It rarely happens, but occasionally it does. Before we begin, I want to thank you from the American government. Without people like you, we wouldn't be able to fight international drug dealers and the horrible destruction their activities inflict upon the world's children."

"Agent Ellis is correct, Paolo. You are a hero," added Father Claude as he patted Mandini's shoulder. It was overboard, but flattery worked well on Mandini.

It was barely forty-five minutes before he heard Jasper speaking to him through his earpiece. "We're good," he said, "there's a new account in the cardinal's name and another in the superior general's name. They are both filled with embezzled funds. They are now both co-signers on the *Sangria de Dios* account. I've assigned a vacant safe deposit box, 342617, to Cardinal De Posada. Ask Mandini for the keys. He may balk but get them anyway. He'll have them back before the bank opens. It's all up to you and Toshi now. Break a leg."

"Excellent work, *Signore* Mandini," said Father Claude, "we've identified all the accounts tied to the drug dealers. All I need from you are the safe deposit box number 342617 keys."

"The bank keeps one key to be used for security purposes. We never give clients both keys."

"That's good practice, but I need both keys briefly. I understand that in the case of the aforementioned safe deposit box, the bank has retained possession of both keys."

"We do occasionally retain both keys for special clients."

"We will return them to you by eleven at the latest. No one will know you provided them to us. It will be our secret."

Toshi interrupted, "We have just one more thing we'll need, Paolo, and then we'll authorize repealing the extradition order and all charges pending against you."

Chapter 80
10:00 A.M.
Milo, Dhabi, and Bria

If a man hasn't discovered something that he will die for, he isn't fit to live.

—Martin Luther King, Jr.

<u>Rome, Italy</u>

Milo was enjoying the spectacular view of the Dome of St. Peter's as the door leading into the kitchen opened, and Dhabi backed into the breakfast room. He had a large tray firmly gripped in his hands. A teapot, a white china cup, and an assortment of pastries sat on the tray.

"Good morning, Milo," Dhabi said, "Did you get some rest?"

"I haven't slept. Lucas and Barik were out cold. I covered their watches. Kids these days," he said, shaking his head.

"Excuse me. I need to get this to Bri. We don't need to be at the bank until 11:00, but I want to review our role in Jasper's plan with everyone one last time."

"You haven't changed your mind?"

Dhabi looked at him sternly. "We're not going to discuss this again, are we? Jasper, Izzy, and the *Mahdi* agreed it was the best solution."

Milo threw up his hands in the air in mock surrender. "I'm just checking, Dhabi."

◆ ◆ ◆

Brother Joseph and Father Richard

Vatican City

High-pitched adolescent male voices filtered down the hallway as the sound of Father Richard's leather soles hit the marble floor, announcing their arrival. The middle-aged nun seated at a desk in the center of the room looked up.

"Are you Father Richard from the museum?" Sister Mary Margaret asked without waiting for an answer. "We're performing next week for the Curia. I don't understand why those silly candlesticks are so important. We've had them for the last two years. Suddenly, you have to have them back this morning."

Father Richard shrugged his shoulders. "I don't know, Sister," he said. "I do what I'm told. Maybe they're doing an inventory or something."

"Hmm," she answered. "They're probably in the basement, but you'll have to find them. I can't leave the office unattended, and Father Cosmos is busy with the boys."

"Yes, Sister," said Father Richard, hoping he sounded deferential. "Thank you."

"Go back outside to the courtyard. You'll see the stairway," she said as she handed Father Richard a large ring of keys. "You're just going to have to go through them. I don't know which one unlocks the basement door. Don't make a mess down there."

Father Richard meekly nodded. "Yes, Sister," he said.

Chapter 81
10:30 A.M.

Brother Joseph and Father Richard

I do not feel obligated to believe that the same God who has endowed us with sense, reason, and intellect has intended us to forgo their use.

—Galileo

Vatican City

"You're sure?" asked Father Richard as they finished searching the Pre-Seminary's basement.

"There isn't a single candlestick on the shelves I've checked. Where else can we look?"

"We've searched all the storerooms," said Father Richard disappointedly as he reached over to turn off the lights.

"Then," said Brother Joseph, "we're going to have to tell the cardinal that we've failed."

"I'm not looking forward to his reaction. Cardinal De Posada doesn't take other people's failures well," answered Father Richard. "What fools we've been!" he said as he slapped his head. "If the power went out, Brother Joseph, you wouldn't want to stumble around a dark basement looking for candlesticks. You'd want them handy. They've never been in the basement. They're in a cupboard or closet inside the school."

"Yes, of course, Father Richard. You're right. Why didn't we think of that before?"

Chapter 82
10:50 A.M.

Father Patrick, Izzy, and Jasper

How can we expect another to keep our secret if we have been unable to keep it ourselves?

—Francois de la Rochefoucauld

Guardians' Command Center Abbey Sainte-Victoire Marseille, France

"Toshi and Father Claude have done their part," Jasper said as Father Patrick and Izzy entered the Command Center. "Now it's up to Dhabi, Bria, and Milo."

"I thought we were waiting until the press conference before we told Father Patrick everything."

"I've given him a broad overview. We can go into greater depth as needed," answered Jasper.

"Are you sure your idea will work?" asked Father Patrick.

"My end is foolproof. I was in and out of the Vatican Bank like a ninja," answered Jasper, "I cleaned up any trace of Mandini logging in this morning. Now, it's up to Dhabi, Milo, and Bria to do their part. Then it's on to the grand finale."

"Once they're done. Milo will let us know," added Izzy. "I've spoken to Tavano Fiore, the Minister of the *Guardia di Finanza*. He's ready to have the search and arrest warrants at the Vatican as soon as we give him the go-ahead. It's in God's hands now."

"Yes," said Jasper, "but God helps those who help themselves."

"Have you located Pope Peter's mother and niece?" asked Izzy.

Jasper didn't bother to pull his attention away from the computer screen. "I traced the girl's cell phone to a beach house in Virginia. If you plan to send in the calvary, the team's already there and ready to rumble. We should have them safe in the next few minutes."

"Let me know as soon as we have them," said Father Patrick. "I'll call Sister Bernadette so she can let Pope Peter know they're safe. She'll need to approve the pontiff's statement to the press."

Izzy turned her head toward Father Patrick as they returned to her office.

"Sister Bernadette?" she asked. "Why do we need her approval?"

"For one thing, she has easy access to His Holiness."

Izzy stared at Patrick. "For one thing?" she questioned him, "Is there another?"

Patrick motioned for her to sit. "The Abbot promised Pope Peter, through Sister Bernadette, that we would rescue his family from *Opus Christos* before he attended the press conference. He won't speak to the media until he knows they're safe."

"There's something you're not telling me, Father Patrick."

"I could say the same about you and Jasper. You kept me in the dark about what you were doing until this morning."

"It was for your safety, Father Patrick."

"Fair enough. I told you I don't know the Abbot's identity. That's true; I don't. But I do know the identities of the members of the Grand Council. I report directly to them."

"So, what connection does Sister Bernadette have with the

Grand Council?"

"Sister Bernadette is the Senior Member of the Grand Council," Father Patrick answered. "She is the only Guardian who speaks directly to the Abbot. That means that we all, myself included, report to her in one way or another. She's the most powerful woman in the Guardians unless the Abbot is also a woman, which is very possible. They often are."

Chapter 83
11:15 A.M.

Felix, Cardinal De Posada, and Superior General Scotti

No man is justified in doing evil on the grounds of expedience.
-Theodore Roosevelt

Vatican City

With less than an hour until the papal press conference, the camera crews were busy inspecting equipment, checking satellite feeds, and taking sound levels as the on-screen personalities were nestled in their trailers, surrounded by their make-up artists and dressers. All the activity created an atmosphere of barely contained chaos.

A pair of uniformed security guards struggled to maintain order by blowing whistles and waving their white-gloved hands. Like the media members, Felix ignored them as he carefully stepped over the black cables running snake-like across the street in front of the Papal Audience Hall.

He flashed his Vatican Employee Pass to the Swiss Guard as he entered the large auditorium. He spotted Superior General Scotti and Cardinal De Posada standing in the center of the stage.

Their faces were turned away, but even from a distance, Felix knew they were in a heated dispute. He held back for a second before walking toward the dais. He wasn't looking forward to their reaction when they learned he hadn't found Brother Joseph or

Father Richard.

"I don't find this humorous, Enrico," said Cardinal De Posada as the superior general noticed Felix. The two men turned as one to face him.

"Where's Brother Joseph, Felix?" Scotti asked. You were supposed to bring him.

Felix never considered telling the truth that he had not seen the monk since yesterday.

"He asked me to leave him in the big church so he could pray."

"St. Peter's?"

"Yeah," answered Felix, "he wanted to have a few minutes alone before the press conference. I told him I'd let you know he was coming."

The two men stared at Felix for a moment without speaking. The superior general started to say something, but Cardinal De Posada stopped him with a firm grip on his forearm.

"Felix, I need you to go back and wait for Brother Joseph at St. Peter's," he said, keeping his voice level, "then I want you to bring him here. Can you do that?"

"Sure," said Felix, relaxing a bit.

"Did he seem upset when you spoke with him?" asked Cardinal De Posada.

"No," Felix lied smoothly. "He was fine. I waited for him in his room while he showered and shaved. He wanted to stop and pray at the church."

The Cardinal put his arm around Felix's shoulder. Liars of Felix's ilk were easy to fool. While often cunning, they are rarely intelligent enough to see through another's lies.

"I am concerned about Brother Joseph," commented the cardinal. "The Trappists are a funny lot. They don't even read the newspapers or watch TV. Brother Joseph might find speaking in front of the world's press too much to handle. He might try to back out of the press conference. Is it possible that Brother Joseph asked you to leave him at St. Peter's so that he could give you the slip? He didn't mention that he had changed his opinion about the Islamic terrorists being involved in the killings, did he?"

Felix shook his head vigorously. "No, he has no idea what's going on. I make sure of that," he answered. "He trusts me."

Cardinal De Posada nodded his head. "Why don't you look in the Basilica to see if he's still there? If not, check his room and the basement office. Perhaps he forgot something."

Felix nodded his head thoughtfully as he walked away with a smug smile.

"He's lying," hissed Scotti.

"Of course he is," said Cardinal De Posada in a low voice.

"Felix?" he called out. Felix, ready for a trap, turned quickly to face the cardinal.

"If Brother Joseph has changed his mind about his testimony during the press conference -."

Felix understood immediately. "No problem," he said, patting the Beretta under his jacket.

Chapter 84
11:15 A M

Bria, Milo, Dhabi

The God who existed before any religion counts on you to make the oneness of the human family known and celebrated.

—Desmond Tutu

Rome, Italy

Milo wiggled uncomfortably inside the expanses of black gauze covering his face and body.

He looked back to ensure that Lucas and Barik, who were in the rear Escalade, had barely made it through the traffic light. Samil and Freddie were in the lead, and the Escalade slowed to allow them to catch up. Jamal drove the Rolls Royce between the Escalades and carried Bria, Milo, and Dhabi.

"Dhabi," he said, "we need to inform the drivers that we'll enter the Vatican through the *Porta Sant'Anna.* We'll be stopped, but that shouldn't be a problem once they see us. If they ask, we're on the way to the IOR."

"Thanks, Milo. I wouldn't have known what to say if you hadn't coached me," answered Dhabi sarcastically.

"Okay, guys, cool it. We're going to go right into the lion's mouth, so we're all on edge," said Bria. "Let's all breathe and chill out a bit."

"Bri's right. Let's not forget that a single mistake can blow our operation out of the water," answered Dhabi. "Milo, you must stay in character no matter what happens."

"Got it," he answered. "I'll be the model of a modest little wife."

"I'll believe it when I see it, but," said Dhabi, "our lives may depend on you doing just that. Toshi and Father Claude will be outside the bank for us. Toshi will put his hand out to offer me a handshake and pass me the safe deposit keys. Then they will leave us to find Brother Joseph and get him out of the Vatican."

"Wait a second!" said Bria. I thought we were conducting a sting operation to bring down Cardinal De Posada and Superior General Scotti. Who is Brother Joseph?"

"I guess it slipped our minds being busy and all saving your life," answered Milo. "Father Claude and Toshi are pitching in to help us pull this operation off, but they are the Guardians assigned to contact and protect the Son of the Dove. "

"Son of the Dove?"

"Yes, Bri, there is a Son of the Holy Doves. There are probably three, but one from Sarah's line is an infant. Leah's List was destroyed in WWII. We cannot discover who the present son from her line could be. Brother Joseph is from the middle daughter Rebecca's line. I thought I explained about the Sons," he said.

Bria shook her head. "No, this is the first thing I've heard about male Doves."

"Every generation, the oldest female Dove of each branch of the family, gives birth to a single male child, one of whom will be chosen to be the Christ child's earthly father."

"Did you call him Brother Joseph? He's a priest?"

"No. He's not a priest. He's a Trappist monk. It's a long story." answered Milo.

"Let me see if I've got this right. He's a monk, and he's related to me?"

Milo laughed. "I had never thought about it, but the

genealogists figure thirty-five years per generation, approximately two thousand years, so," he answered after doing the math on his phone, "he would be your cousin seventy-second times removed. Not kissing cousins for sure."

"But he's a monk? Are you telling me Inanna chose a monk as the earthly father of my child?"

"If it makes you feel any better, he hasn't taken his final vows, so he's kinda a monk-in-training, not a committed-for-life card-carrying monk. I think that's different."

Bri rolled her eyes. "Yeah, Milo, that makes it all better, a monk and a distant cousin."

"A very, very, very distant cousin, Bri. You do trust that Inanna made the right choice in picking him to be the earthly father of the Christ child, don't you?"

"Of course I do. There's no question of that," said Bria. "If he's Inanna's choice–I was just a bit surprised there were sons, I guess. Sarah was my ancestor then?" said Bria.

"Yes and no," answered Milo. "We believe you are a Dove of all three lines: Leah, the eldest; Rebecca, the middle child; and Sarah, the youngest. It is highly unusual and probably unprecedented, but our genealogists believe it's true."

"Ok. So where is the Son of Rebecca, this Joseph? How do we find him?"

"We know who he is. We know where he is. We just haven't been able to get to him."

"I'm missing something," said Bria, "if I am already carrying the Child Who Is Coming, why do we need the Son?"

Milo looked at her. "The prophecy says that the Child will not quicken in your womb without the presence of the son chosen as the earthly father. The Child will die before its birth."

Bria unconsciously moved her hand to her stomach to protect the new life inside her. "My baby could die? Milo, we have to find

Joseph immediately!"

Milo reached out and touched her hand. "We're working on it. Contacting him is not as easy as you might think. He's in the Vatican and surrounded by *Opus Christos*."

Bria gasped. "This Joseph," she said, "he's involved with *Opus Christos*?"

"Highly unlikely," answered Milo. "We've been watching over him since the day he was born. We have no evidence that *Opus Christos* knows who he is. They are using him. He was a world-renowned expert in Islamic terrorist groups when he was with the CIA."

"If *Opus Christos* knows who I am, then why don't they know about him?"

Milo hesitates a moment. "His biological mother, Anja Romanoff, was one of the Russian Doves. He was raised by an Italian family in New York, Franco and Stella Pirelli."

"An Italian family? How did that happen?"

"For the last 300 years, the Guardians have switched the Sons at birth with another child. That way, if anyone had discovered the True Son's identity and tried to murder him, they would have killed the wrong child. The True Son would survive."

She shook her head in disbelief. "That is inexcusable. Why would you take a child from his parents?"

"There are only three sons in each generation. We had to take extraordinary measures," said Milo, "to protect them and the Child you are now carrying."

Bria was silent for a moment as she digested this information. "What the Guardians did was horrible to do to a family, but perhaps they did a wrong thing for a good reason."

"Right or wrong, Joseph is alive because of it."

"So, you're saying we have to save him before *Opus Christos* figures out who he is," said Bria.

"That's our plan," answered Dhabi, "but right now, we must focus on destroying *Opus Christos* and protecting you. Toshi and Father Claude will approach Brother Joseph before the press conference and get him away before *Opus Christos* knows he's gone."

"We'll be out of the Vatican before the final act begins," added Milo. "Everyone will be focused on the papal press conference scheduled for noon, so their attention will be elsewhere. We'll create our own diversion with the Rolls, two Escalades, two drivers, four bodyguards, and a Saudi Prince with two veiled wives trailing behind him. We're putting on such a flashy show that, with any luck, *Opus Christos* will completely ignore us."

Chapter 85
11: 30 A.M.
Superior General Scotti and Cardinal De Posada

Rivers, ponds, lakes, and streams—they all have different names, but they all contain water. Just as all religions do—they all contain truth.

—Muhammed Ali

Vatican City

"This isn't good," Superior General Scotti hissed into Cardinal De Posada's ear as his eyes swept over the reporters streaming into the audience hall. "I said from the beginning that relying on a crazy Trappist monk was a bad idea. Now both he and Alberto are missing."

Cardinal De Posada bristled. "The Committee agreed with me if I remember correctly."

"With great reservation. Rafael, I'll throw you to the wolves if your plan fails."

Cardinal De Posada's voice was icy as he spoke. "The pope and the Trappist will say what I tell them to say. The world will believe that Islamic terrorists are committing the murders because the Western media has convinced people that Muslim people are all want-to-be terrorists."

"And if they don't believe it?"

"It doesn't matter, Enrico. Have you forgotten that this is just a magic show to pull any hint of responsibility for the Dove's murders away from us? Have you forgotten that Brother Joseph is looking for the mythical Leah's List, not a list of terrorists that never existed in the first place? We have one focus and one focus only: to find the Doves and eliminate them so the expected Christ child will never be born, and if non-Christians can be blamed for the murders, so much the better for the Church."

"I have not forgotten, Rafael, but I no longer trust that the Trappist will do as you demand. Someone else will have to speak," said Superior General Scotti.

"Fine. I will speak. I will testify to the Islamic involvement in the women's murders."

"Absolutely not!" whispered the Superior General with equal venom. "The last thing we want is to bring you into the spotlight. What if the press discovers your connection to the rest of us? I cannot allow you to play such a prominent role."

The cardinal was not convinced. "Alberto and I have put years into setting this up. We built a web of police officers willing to look the other way when needed or manipulate crime scenes by planting evidence pointing to Islamic terrorists. If anyone deserves—"

"You misunderstand me," placated Superior General Scotti, changing his tactics. "I meant to say that we can't take a chance of sacrificing you, Rafael. If we are to destroy the Doves, we need you. But, if you alone sit next to the pope, it will seem strange. However, no one would dare question the three most powerful, respected men in the Church standing together to make the pronouncement as a sign of unity and commitment to the truth."

Cardinal De Posada nodded his head in acquiescence. He wasn't fooled and disagreed with the superior general, but he understood that Scotti was right on a certain level.

◆ ◆ ◆
Bria, Dhabi, Milo

The Swiss Guards stationed at the *Porto Sant'Anna* were not impressed by the black Rolls Royce cradled between matching black Cadillac Escalades stopped at the checkpoint. Nor were they surprised that the passengers were a Saudi prince and his two veiled wives on their way to the IOR.

Jamal parked the Rolls in front of the bank, ignoring the no parking signs, and slowly walked around the car to open the rear door. Bria's hand snaked out from under her *abaya* and grasped Milo's.

"Dhabi?" Milo asked quietly, "Should we review it again?"

Dhabi shook his head. He reached up and touched the *agal*, the black cord worn on top of his *ghutra*, and his cloth headdress to hold it in place. "I'm good," he said.

"You ready, Bri?"

She nodded her head in agreement.

"Milo," said Dhabi, holding them back as Jamal opened the door. "No matter what happens, you will act like a proper Muslim wife. You will be quiet and show no interest in my business. If things start to go sideways, you must not react in any manner. Let me deal with it."

"We have twenty-five minutes and not a second more," reminded Dhabi quietly as he stepped over Milo and Bri to exit the car. "Toshi will leave once we're inside the bank. He'll go to the Audience Hall and try to find Brother Joseph. He'll bring Brother Joseph here and hide him in one of the Escalades if he can contact him. No one would dare check the cars of the Saudi royal family."

Milo spoke to Jamal.

"If Dhabi is in the bank longer than expected, I will bring Bri out. You will take her to Da Vinci. There will be a private plane waiting to take her to Marseilles."

Dhabi's voice was stern when he spoke. "You will wait until I dismiss you, Milo. Walking out on your own would blow our cover. You are a Muslim woman. I will tell you when you can leave."

He slipped out of the car without giving Milo a chance to respond. He stood outside for a second, waiting for the chauffeur to hand him his black-leather briefcase. "Jamal, I doubt if anyone will insist you move the cars as the Saudi royal family is one of the Vatican Bank's largest depositors. If it does happen, stand firm and refuse to move. Pretend you don't understand them, but stay here no matter what."

Dhabi quickly looked to see if his bodyguards exiting the Explorers were in position, but he did not turn to help the two veiled figures depart the Rolls. Such a thing would be beneath the dignity of a Saudi prince. He paused momentarily to straighten the folds of his *thobe,* and then, looking neither left nor right, he walked swiftly into the bank.

◆ ◆ ◆

Brother Joseph and Father Richard

Brother Joseph was kneeling on the storage closet floor on the Pre-Seminary's third floor, pulling boxes off the lowest shelf, when Father Richard stopped him.

"Brother Joseph," he said as his voice wavered. "I believe–." Father Richard took a deep breath. "I believe that Cardinal De Posada has lied to us."

Brother Joseph stood up. "Why would he do that?"

"I'm not sure, but I overheard a call between the cardinal and the superior general last night. I was returning some documents last night to the cardinal for his signatures. His door was slightly open and – I didn't mean to eavesdrop, but–"

"What did the cardinal say, Father Richard?"

"He said he would have no problem convincing you that Islamic terrorists were responsible for the murders of the Holy Doves even if we could not find the missing list."

Brother Joseph stared at Father Richard. "He called the women the Holy Doves? Are you sure?"

"Yes, but I turned and walked away before he saw me. I know this sounds crazy, but I don't think the list has anything to do with Islamic terrorists."

"It doesn't. They're potential victims," said Brother Joseph as he leaned against the wall.

"But why? I don't understand."

"I don't have the time to explain it fully, Father Richard, but I believe the list is the names of the descendants of the Messiah."

"Jesus's children? That's impossible. He never married."

"It's more complicated than that, believe me." Brother Joseph pinched the bridge of his nose as he gestured for Father Richard to follow him into the hall.

"What do you know about Felix?"

Father Richard shook his head. "I never saw him before I picked you up at the airport, but he wears a cross that matches the ones that the cardinal, the superior general, and Alberto Zayas wear." He paused a second, gathering his courage. "Before I accepted the job as the cardinal's aide, another priest told me that the cardinal was a dangerous man with dangerous ideas about the future of the Church."

"What did he mean, Father Richard?"

"He said the cardinal was a member of *Opus Christos,* an ultra-right Catholic society intent on returning the Church to the absolute power it held during the Middle Ages."

Brother Joseph shook his head. "I've never heard of them."

Father Richard stammered, "I hadn't either."

"Is the pope a member of *Opus Christos?* Is that why he ordered me to find the list?"

"I don't think so. I think that Cardinal De Posada threatened him," answered Father Richard.

Brother Joseph stood without saying a word as the truth became frighteningly clear.

"Father Richard, I will understand if you say no. I need your help to stop *Opus Christos.*"

"What do we need to do?" asked Father Richard hesitantly.

"We must find and destroy the list before *Opus Christos* can get their hands on it. The lives of hundreds of innocent women depend upon us."

"But the cardinal expects us at the press conference in half an hour. He expects you to condemn the Islamic terrorists to the world."

"I guess the cardinal isn't going to get what he wants," answered Brother Joseph firmly.

Chapter 86
11:30 A.M.

Dhabi, Toshi, Paolo Mandini Milo and Bria

Look at how a single candle can both defy and define the darkness.
–Anne Frank

Vatican City

Dhabi faltered slightly as he entered the Vatican Bank. He recovered quickly and walked confidently toward the largest of the offices. As he crossed the lobby, a dark-haired man approached and extended his hand. Milo discreetly poked his back to let him know it was Toshi.

"Your Highness," the man said as he shook Dhabi's hand and slipped the keys he had made on a small laser cutter from the original into his hand. "Mathias Sugar," Toshi said, "I met you at the Cannes Film Festival last year. Davis and Philomena Cooke's party?"

"Yes, of course," said Dhabi as he slipped the keys into his briefcase and continued walking.

He ignored the young man sitting behind a small desk outside Mandini's office. He knew, without thinking, that a Saudi Prince would not even consider dealing with any of the lesser employees. Without invitation, he entered the most prominent office, placed his black briefcase in one of the two chairs, and sat on the other.

A balding, middle-aged man dressed in a somber black suit and blood-red tie was seated behind the desk. He looked up from his paperwork and let out a yelp of surprise.

"*Signore* Mandini," Dhabi said with a dignified nod.

The man's eyes quickly shifted from Dhabi to the two veiled women standing outside his office door, flanked by two burly men dressed in Western suits. He slowly snaked his hand toward a security button hidden beneath his desk's center drawer, ready to push it if necessary. After the night and morning, he had had, Mandini was understandably on edge. The last thing he needed today was a robbery or a demanding Saudi prince. He wasn't sure which was worse. He forced himself to smile at the robed figure sitting smugly in his visitor's chair.

"Prince Al Sa'ud," Paolo Mandini answered as he stood. It was a calculated risk, but as far as he knew, all of the bank's Saudi depositors were members of the ruling family. Fortunately, he thought, money knows no religion.

"This is an unexpected honor," he said in a tone that held only the slightest hint of reproach that the Prince had not called for an appointment. He smiled to soften the unspoken message. One didn't offend one of the bank's largest depositors. "May I offer you coffee or tea?"

Dhabi shook his head slightly and slowly lifted his right hand with his palm facing the bank manager. He imagined this was an aristocratic acknowledgment. *Signore* Mandini thought so, too.

"How may I be of service, Your Highness?"

"I wish to access my safe deposit box. Your predecessor, Signore Zattini, personally handled all my family's transactions. He has retired, I take it."

"Yes, he left the bank last year. The stress–."

"Please offer him my regards," said Dhabi as he leaned over and removed a thick sheet of cream-colored paper embossed with the Al Sa'ud family crest from his briefcase.

"I assume you have your key?" Paolo Mandini asked deferentially as he skimmed the letter.

"As mentioned in the letter, *Signore*, the bank retained both keys in its private box in the vault. This code is all that you need to provide me access to my safe deposit box."

Signore Mandini bristled. "This is highly unusual."

"The world is full of unusual situations, *Signore* Mandini. I would suggest you research this one before you question it further," Dhabi's tone was calm, but there was no missing the implied threat. "Perhaps a call to *Signore* Zattini?"

"No, no," stuttered *Signore* Mandini, suddenly mindful of the $850,000,000 of Al Sa'ud money in his care. "If you'll excuse me for a moment, I will get the keys."

Dhabi nodded as he bent and closed his briefcase. He began counting silently backward from a hundred—anything to keep his mind occupied so that he wouldn't start to imagine that Mandini had seen through his ruse and was calling the authorities or, even worse, *Opus Christos*.

◆ ◆ ◆

Brother Joseph and Father Richard

"It's not here," said Father Richard as he stood up and pushed the last box into place.

"Then we'll search all the closets in the residence hall and school," said Brother Joseph. "The menorah has to be here somewhere."

Father Richard placed his hand on the wooden shelf behind him. "His Holiness is holding the press conference at noon. We're expected to be there. Cardinal De Posada will realize we know the truth if we don't show up."

"You may leave if you wish, but I cannot stop because I fear what Cardinal De Posada may do."

Father Richard straightened his shoulders. "You're right, of course. We can't quit."

"Equally, we can't report the truth of *Opus Christos'* heresy if we're dead. Even if we do not find the menorah, we have one chance to get out of the Vatican alive, and that will be during the press conference." Brother Joseph checked his watch. "Twenty minutes more, and then we have to stop."

◆ ◆ ◆

Dhabi, Paolo Mandini, Father Claude, and Toshi

A muted cough brought Dhabi back from his thoughts. He turned to see *Signore* Mandini standing quietly beside him with a small manila envelope in his right hand. "Your Highness," Mandini said, "Would you please be kind enough to accompany me to the vault?"

"Of course," answered Dhabi as he retrieved the black leather briefcase from the chair.

With Bria and Milo standing behind him, Dhabi stood inside the vault as *Signore* Mandini opened the envelope containing the two keys. He put out his hand and accepted one of the keys. Mandini inserted the other key into the box and stepped aside, allowing Dhabi to place his key in the lock. Dhabi turned the keys together, and the metal door swung open to reveal a large box.

"If you will kindly remove the box," said *Signore* Mandini, "I will take you to a private office."

"I prefer to stay here with my wives," answered Dhabi. "This should only take a few minutes."

"Bank policy states that," started *Signore* Mandini, but stopped as he remembered that the Al Sa'ud family was one of the

IOR's largest depositors.

He quickly modified his original comment, "Normally, the bank doesn't allow clients to be left alone in the vault, but I'm sure we can make an exception in your case. I'll stand outside with your bodyguards until you're finished."

Once *Signore* Mandini stood with his back to the vault, Dhabi placed the box on the narrow metal table dividing the room and opened it. Inside was a stack of bank books and thick banded piles of $1000 bills. He retrieved the keys Toshi had given him from his briefcase and handed them to Milo, who quickly located the two boxes Jasper had indicated and used keys to unlock them before he brought them to the table.

Dhabi removed the first box's contents, and Milo filled the two empty boxes with cash, bank books, and several official-looking forgeries created by the Guardian's Documents. He returned the boxes to their cubicles and locked them. He turned and wiggled the keys in his hand.

"Let's get the hell out of here," he whispered as he hid the extra keys under his *Abaya*.

Dhabi allowed a small gust of air to leave his lungs. He picked up the briefcase, walked to the vault's door, and stepped outside. Bria and Milo followed silently behind him.

◆ ◆ ◆

11: 45 A.M.

Dhabi tapped *Signore* Mandini on the shoulder. "I am finished," he said as he returned the other keys to the bank manager. "Please continue, as the bank always has, to retain the keys to my box."

"Thank you, Your Highness. If I can be of any assistance in any other matter—"

"I shall tell my father that you have been accommodating. I shall not forget."

Signore Mandini beamed at the vision of Al Sa'ud money endlessly streaming into his hands. "Allow me," he said, "to walk you to your car."

Dhabi lifted his hand in protest, but Mandini ignored it. "No, I insist. It's the least I can do for one of our most valued clients."

Dhabi thought Italians had as hard a time saying goodbye as Arabs. Mandini kept pumping his hand and thanking him repeatedly for his family's patronage.

"*Signore* Mandini," he said quickly. "My private jet is waiting on the runway as we speak. You understand how difficult it is to get takeoff clearance at Da Vinci."

Mandini had no idea about flight procedures but understood that the prince had politely dismissed him. He dropped Dhabi's hand, allowed his body to bend slightly in a bow, and then backed away several steps. Dhabi looked over to where Bria and Milo were waiting.

He nodded to one of the two bodyguards, who quickly moved them to the waiting cars. He quickly dialed a code into his iPhone while smiling at Mandini. "We are leaving the IOR now. We are on the way to the jet. Please have everything ready to go," he said as he walked away.

Father Claude stepped up to Mandini to stop him from following Dhabi's entourage.

"Paolo, who was that?" asked Father Claude.

Mandini stammered. "A member of the Saudi royal family. They are one of our largest depositors. I couldn't ignore him, and he refused to deal with anyone else. I had no choice."

"Fine. No harm done. The *Guardia di Finanza* will be arriving at noon. Stay calm and do everything they ask of you," Father Claude said quietly.

"You're not going to stay?" asked Paolo Mandini nervously.

"There are jurisdictional issues," said Toshi, "The Italian authorities will take over at this point. It would be best if you didn't mention the US government's involvement. Take all the credit for yourself like the hero you are. You still want the medal, correct?"

"*Signore* Paolo Mandini?" asked the distinguished, silver-haired man in the front as he pulled out his identification. "I'm *Ispettore* Granucci with the *Guardia di Finanza.* We have been informed of several serious infractions of international banking laws. I have the written permission of the pontiff," he said as he handed Mandini a leather portfolio with the Pontifical Seal embossed in gold.

"Subpoena," he said as he snapped his fingers. One of the men surrounding him quickly passed him another folder with the legal documents. "It is all legal and approved by the Court."

"*Signore* Mandini, please excuse us," said Toshi, bowing his head at the Inspector as he and Father Claude excused themselves and walked across the lobby to exit the bank.

Granucci looked at them for a moment and then turned back to Mandini. "There has been a serious breach of your operation. We seek evidence of drug money laundering, embezzlement, and computer manipulation of your depositor's funds."

"The entire bank and our records are at your disposal," answered Mandini. "The IOR, under no circumstances, condones illegal activities."

Granucci smiled.

"Thank you, *Signore* Mandini. We will be in and out without inconveniencing your clientele unnecessarily," he said as he handed him the subpoena. "As you can see, we have the authority to seize safe deposit boxes numbered 342617, 122527, and 863746. We have a court order to seize the records of the accounts held by *Sangre de Dios,* Cardinal Rafael De Posada, and Superior General Enrico Scotti."

"At your service," said Mandini, taking a wistful look at Toshi's and Father Claude's receding backs.

Chapter 87
11:45 A.M.

Felix, Father Richard, and Brother Joseph

The simple step of a courageous individual is not to take part in the lie.

- Aleksandr Solzhenitsyn

Vatican City

Felix felt a thin line of sweat forming on his shirt collar. He considered removing his jacket but realized it would reveal his shoulder harness and Beretta. He stopped a moment to get his bearings. The Audience Hall was behind him, so if he circled the back of St. Peter's and took the shortcut across the *Sala Regia,* he'd end up in the Belvedere Courtyard outside the library. He kept his eyes out for Father Richard and Brother Joseph as he moved quickly, scanning every person walking by.

Where the hell could they be, he wondered, as he made it through the complicated maze of buildings. It would have been faster, he thought, if he had been able to cut through the Piazza in front of the Basilica, but the hordes of photographers waiting there for the press conference to begin made him shy away. His continued success as an *Opus Christos* assassin was because no one knew exactly what he looked like. He planned to keep it that way.

He should give up and return to Superior General Scotti and Cardinal De Posada. They would be upset that he couldn't find Brother Joseph, but he'd tell them it wasn't his fault. He'd say he saw Father Richard and Brother Joseph enter a black car and leave the Vatican. They would believe his lie. He was that good.

◆ ◆ ◆

Pope Peter and Sister Bernadette

Sister Bernadette slipped quietly into the papal apartment. She put her finger to her lips and gestured for Pope Peter to follow her into the bathroom. He started to speak, but she gave him a don't-you-dare look perfected by Catholic nuns. She turned on the shower full blast before she pulled an iPhone out of her habit.

"Please trust us," she whispered, handing him the phone. "We're going to get you safely out of this situation. The operation is already underway. Father Patrick will explain exactly what you must do."

Pope Peter nodded his head, took the phone, and put it to his ear.

"Father Patrick?" he said quietly as Sister Bernadette stepped back and bent her head, the essence of womanly modesty.

"Your Eminence, I apologize that we haven't contacted you directly. It would have been dangerous to our operatives, the Holy Parents, and would have put you and Sister Bernadette in jeopardy. The Guardians carried out a raid on a house in Virginia Beach approximately fifteen minutes ago. Your mother and niece are unharmed and in our protection. We will arrange a call with them as soon as we end this conversation."

"Thank you, Father Patrick. You have no idea how I have been praying they would be safe."

"As were we," Father Patrick. "Your Eminence, we have

devised a plan to take down *Opus Christos*. It is well underway as we speak. We are now at the point where your cooperation is imperative. We need you to know what will happen so you can respond properly."

"I'm listening," whispered Pope Peter, turning the sink faucets and flushing the toilet. Hopefully, the noise would block the microphones hidden in his apartment.

When Father Patrick was finished speaking, Pope Peter reached over and flushed the toilet.

"Yes," he whispered. "I will do everything you ask."

"I hope you can come up with a new speech quickly. The one *Opus Christos* wrote for you will be useless. Sister Bernadette can provide help if you wish. She has a way with words."

"We don't have time to write a new speech," whispered Pope Peter, "we're supposed to leave for the Audience Hall in a few minutes."

Father Patrick chuckled. "I wouldn't worry about that. The press will wait. You are, as they say, the star of the show."

◆ ◆ ◆

Dhabi, Milo, and Bria

With Bria and Milo trailing him, Dhabi walked out of the IOR. He stopped short as he saw five black sedans with the seals of the *Guardia di Finanza* blocking the Rolls and the two Cadillac Escalades. The whispered words 'What the hell?' escaped from one of the veiled women walking behind him. Dhabi turned quickly and shook his head at Milo.

"I asked them nicely to move, " Jamal said quietly. "but the Italian response translated roughly to 'go fuck your camel.' "

"They weren't supposed to be here for another fifteen minutes," answered Dhabi. "We hadn't planned for such efficiency from the Italian authorities."

He looked over at Milo. "Let's stay calm. We're stuck here until the *Guardia di Finanza* is finished. Jasper sent Inspector Granucci the digital files with the evidence incriminating De Posada and Scotti and the numbers of the safe deposit boxes that he needs to confiscate, so it shouldn't take them very long. Luckily, the Rolls is bulletproof. We have no choice but to wait it out."

◆ ◆ ◆

Cardinal De Posada, Superior General Scotti

The noise level inside the Audience Hall was deafening. More often than not, the reporters from the *L'Osservatore Romano,* the daily Vatican newspaper, knew the pope's deepest thoughts long before the rest of the world and held themselves aloof from the rest of the media. But, this time, they were as much in the dark as everyone else. They joined in the gossip and conjectures swirling around the room, trying to guess what this press conference could be about.

The presence of Cardinal De Posada and the Superior General of the Society of Jesus, Enrico Scotti, standing on the stage raised more than one eyebrow. The whispered comments grew as Cardinal De Posada led the superior general to the seat to the left of the papal throne and then took the corresponding chair to Pope Peter's right.

The energy level in the hall jumped up a notch as the reporters and photographers pushed, as one, closer to the stage. They didn't know what would happen once the pontiff arrived, but seeing the Red pope, the Black pope, and the White pope together in any setting, much less appearing as a united front in the Audience Hall, was unprecedented. Something big was about to happen.

Chapter 88
11:50 A.M.

Brother Joseph and Father Richard

No one ever became extremely wicked suddenly.
            —Decimus Junius Juvenalis

<u>*Vatican City*</u>

Brother Joseph watched as Father Richard removed the candlesticks one by one off the top shelf of the pantry closet and handed them to him.

"Hurry, Father Richard. We can't stay much longer."

Father Richard stopped suddenly. His hands began to shake as he pulled a golden candlestick from the back of the shelf. Only three of the seven branches were still intact, but there was no doubt it had been crudely altered. He held the menorah, or what was left of it, in front of him as he handed it wordlessly to Brother Joseph and climbed down the short ladder.

"We found it," he said excitedly.

"How do we break it open to see if the list is inside?"

"Twist the base," Father Richard answered, pointing to a line on the base, "It's in two pieces."

Brother Joseph nodded as he turned the menorah over and placed the three branches between his thighs to hold them firmly. He grasped the base and twisted it clockwise, but it didn't budge.

"The other way," said Father Richard, "sometimes the threads run the opposite way."

Brother Joseph repositioned the candlestick and began to turn it counterclockwise. At first, there was no movement. Then he felt the base shift slightly, moving a quarter of a turn before it stopped. A thin stream of sweat ran down the side of his face.

He wiped his hands on his pants legs, grabbed the base firmly, and twisted with all his strength. He nearly lost his balance as the base broke away. Father Richard's hand shot out to steady him.

"Quickly," he said as he handed the menorah to the priest while tightly holding onto the base.

"Something's inside!" Father Richard exclaimed, "I can feel it but can't grasp it. I need tweezers or something to reach it. There's a toolbox behind you. See if there are needle-nose pliers."

Brother Joseph rummaged through the toolbox, found the pliers, and handed them to Father Richard. He carefully slipped the tool into the cylinder and smiled as he drew a rolled parchment from the candlestick.

"I think we've found it!" Father Richard said as he dropped the menorah to the floor and carefully unrolled the parchment. Father Richard smiled. "It says *'The Line of Leah, Firstborn Daughter of the Messiah.'*"

"We need to get this to the pontiff for safekeeping."

Father Richard looked at his watch. "He'll be at the Audience Hall by now. If we enter by the stage door, we might be able to approach him without the cardinal seeing us."

Felix turned to get his bearings. The Audience Hall was to his right, directly behind the Pre-Seminary. If he cut across the park in the back of the Pre-Seminary, he could make it by noon to let

Cardinal De Posada know that Brother Joseph had disappeared through no fault of his own and wouldn't be at the press conference. It seemed as good a plan as any.

At first, he discounted the man he noticed walking past the third-floor window of the Pre-Seminary as one of the priests working as teachers here, just one more of the scores of men scurrying around the Vatican grounds dressed as priests or monks. Then he realized the priest in the window was Father Richard, and if Father Richard was there, Brother Joseph couldn't be far away. He hesitated a second before he turned on his heels and ran across the courtyard toward the school.

12:00 P.M. Noon
Signore Mandini and Ispettore Granucci

Signore Mandini had difficulty sitting at his desk without fidgeting but had taken Toshi's warning to heart. To the casual observer, he seemed the model of calm professionalism.

"*Signore* Mandini?" asked one of the younger men who had been in the group of forensic examiners. "*Ispettore* Granucci would like to speak with you."

"Of course," the bank manager responded, his mouth suddenly dry as he stood up.

"Follow me, please."

"*Signore* Mandini," *Ispettore* Granucci said as he gestured to the chair across from him. "I find that there is nowhere more private than a bank vault, don't you agree?"

"Yes," he stammered, "it is very private."

Ispettore Granucci stared at him a moment. "You have nothing to worry about, *Signore* Mandini. Your records are immaculate. I will have no problem using them to prosecute the guilty parties."

"That's good to hear," answered Paolo Mandini, not knowing what else to say.

"I just have a few questions."

Paolo felt his stomach turn. He didn't trust himself to speak, so he nodded his head.

"*Signore* Mandini," Granucci said as he pushed a stack of papers across the table. "To your knowledge, are these the documents and accounts we requested?"

Paolo looked over the documents. He hadn't seen them before but immediately realized that the Americans must have sent them to the *Guardia di Finanza.* He decided it was best to go along with everything the CIA had done instead of questioning their methods. He certainly didn't want the agents to come back again.

"Yes, these are the documents and accounts requested," he answered cautiously.

"Do they appear to have been altered since you provided them?"

"No, I didn't–" he quickly corrected himself, "don't see any alterations."

"Thank you," *Ispettore* Granucci said as he pointed to the three safe deposit boxes on the table. "Are the box numbers 342617, 122527, and 863746?"

"Yes," he said, "they appear to be."

Signore Granucci took the master keys and opened the boxes one by one. Mandini's eyes grew larger as he stared into the box and saw the large stacks of bills and several passports inside. Granucci unzipped three large blue pouches. With his assistant's help, he emptied each box's contents into the individual pouches.

"*Signore* Mandini, can you testify that you observed me remove the contents of safe deposit boxes numbered 342617,

122527, and 863746 and place the contents in the three blue pouches I am now passing to my assistant?"

"Yes," he answered as his palms began to sweat. He didn't think he could take much more.

Ispettore Granucci put out his hand. "Thank you for your cooperation, *Signore* Mandini. We will need a formal statement to verify the evidence chain of command, but you can come to our headquarters in the next day or two. One of my assistants will contact you."

"Of course," said Paolo, starting to relax, "we must all do our duty to protect the integrity of our financial system."

◆ ◆ ◆

12:00 P.M. Noon
Brother Joseph, Father Richard, and Felix

Brother Joseph recognized the sound of the silencer as a small circular hole formed in the center of Father Richard's forehead. The bullet's impact tore off the back of his skull as Father Richard's body crumpled to the pantry floor.

Brother Joseph turned his head as his hand tightened on the candlestick base to see Felix standing outside the pantry door.

"Felix," he said calmly as he stepped over Father Richard's lifeless body. Years of experience he had taught him that dealing with a sociopath was tricky. One false move, one sign of fear, and Felix would kill him without a second thought.

"I was hoping you'd make it in time, Felix. Father Richard kidnapped me. He tried to stop me from speaking at the press conference against the Islamic terrorists. We must hurry. The cardinal is waiting for me to appear. There is no time to waste."

Felix stared at him briefly, then returned the Beretta to his shoulder holster.

"The cardinal was concerned about you," he said as he moved away from the door. "He was worried that you were not going to speak to the press about the terrorists."

"We must hurry if we are going to make it on time," Brother Joseph repeated as he stepped past Felix and then quickly turned his body, lifting the candlestick base high over his head. He brought the heavy metal circle down on Felix's skull with as much power as he could muster.

With his animal cunning, Felix felt the blow coming and moved so swiftly that the base glanced off his left shoulder instead of connecting with the back of his head, but the blow's force knocked him to his knees.

Brother Joseph turned and sprinted down the stairs.

Chapter 89
12:00 P.M. Noon
Pope Peter

Madness is rare in individuals, but in groups, parties, nations, and ages, it is the rule.

-Friedrich Nietzsche

Vatican City

As he stepped from the Lincoln Town Car, Pope Peter noticed the significantly increased security forces surrounding the side entrance to the Audience Hall. The Swiss Guard, in their traditional bright uniforms, flanked the town car, flanked by several men in black suits.

"Who are all these extra men?" he asked as he stepped onto the pavement.

The Captain of the Guard bowed his head. "Cardinal De Posada has provided increased security, Your Eminence. He was concerned for your safety," he said as De Posada's men fell in beside the Swiss Guard. One of the somber-suited men spoke to him slowly; his voice was barely audible.

"We have memorized every word of your address. You'll die before your body hits the floor if you change a word. We have no problem becoming martyrs to our cause. Don't test our devotion."

The tinge of anger in Pope Peter's voice when he spoke

surprised even himself. "I will read the statement as it is written. I have no other option. I will blame Islamic terrorists for your crimes."

"Then we have nothing to worry about, do we?" the man answered calmly.

◆ ◆ ◆

Felix and Brother Joseph

Felix struggled to his feet, ignoring the pain in his shoulder, as he raised his Beretta. He had Brother Joseph in sight when the school bell directly over his head rang. It was enough to cause him to waver slightly, and the bullet flew off target. He swore as the classroom doors began to open. Ignoring their adolescent shouts as he pushed the kids out of his way, he sprinted down the stairs.

Brother Joseph pushed open the exterior entry door as Felix pulled the trigger. Brother Joseph fell only to pick himself up before he stood and staggered through the crowd of tourists walking across the courtyard toward St. Peter's. The smile left Felix's face. Son-of-a-bitch, he thought, as he began running after his prey.

The throbbing pain in Brother Joseph's left arm had subsided into numbness by the time he entered the cool darkness of the Basilica. He scolded himself silently for refusing Cardinal De Posada's offer to take him to worship in the Basilica. If he had accepted, he would have had a better idea of the layout and how to use the space to elude Felix. He gingerly touched the wound on his left arm, which sent another wave of pain through his body.

Felix couldn't be that far behind, he thought as he looked around. If he was going to cross the vast open interior of the Basilica, he couldn't wait. He spun his head around, searching for an escape route. He turned to stare at the Altar of St. Peter's Chair on the opposite side of the building. There had to be an entrance to the Sacristy nearby, the rooms where the priests and altar boys prepared for Mass.

Taking a deep breath, He forced himself forward, trying to skirt the groups of tourists wandering around. Expecting to feel the searing pain of another bullet ripping through him, he ran across the marble floor. Each step he took rang out and echoed in the stillness of the Basilica.

As he touched the door handle, the wood above his head exploded. He quickly pulled the door open and slipped inside. He could hear the voices of the altar boys preparing for the noon Mass straight ahead, and he rushed toward them.

The boys, dressed in black robes with white-lace over-tunics, turned at the sound of his footsteps. Their expressions of surprise turned into shock as they noticed the gaping hole in the sleeve of his robe and the blood trickling onto the floor from his fingertips. The silence was broken as they all began shouting excitedly in Italian as he pushed past the boys.

"Porta!" he shouted over their combined voices as they turned as one and pointed to a hallway on the left side of the room. *"Grazie!"* he shouted as he ran toward the door.

Felix wasted precious seconds doing damage control. He pulled out his fake CIA badge and identity card. At the same time, he shouted, *'Polizia!'* as he swept the badge in a slow semicircle like he'd seen Clint Eastwood do in the *Dirty Harry* movies. The security guards' hands moved away from their holsters. He began to run with the Beretta in one hand and the badge in the other toward the doorway where Brother Joseph had disappeared. He kicked open the Sacristy door and raced down the hall. The altar boys' faces went white as they saw the gun.

"Polizia!" he screamed. It had already worked once, so he wasn't worried that some snot-nosed kids in lacy dresses would see

through him. They turned as one to point toward the door at the side of the room. Felix pushed through them roughly and ran to the open door.

He emerged from the Basilica and swore out loud. Where the hell did that damn monk go? He couldn't see him anywhere as he moved toward the Apostolic Palace. Brother Joseph could run, but sooner or later, he would catch up with the monk and finish the job.

◆ ◆ ◆

Milo, Dhabi, and Bria

The drivers were leaning on the side of their cars when the men from the *Guardia di Finanza* walked out of the IOR and quickly jumped to attention.

"It's about time," complained Milo from behind his veil. "These damn things are hot. I don't know how women do it. I'm dying here."

"Try high heels, Spanx, and underwire bras," commented Bria. "Suck it up, Buttercup."

Dhabi impatiently watched the financial examiners place the folders and pouches into the car's trunk. An older, silver-haired man stepped into the car before they started their engines and pulled away in the opposite direction of the *Porto Sant'Anna,* the nearest way out of the Vatican.

"Where the hell are they going? Jamal," said Dhabi to the Rolls' driver. "Tell Samil and Freddie we need to follow them. I think the *Guardia di Finanza* is heading toward the Audience Hall."

The driver nodded his head and picked up his cell phone.

"Dhabi," said Milo, "we must get Bri out of here now. Your curiosity be damned. It doesn't matter where the *Guardia di*

Finanza is going or what the fuck they're doing."

"Trust me, Milo. If they are heading to the Audience Hall, this is about to go down. We need to back up Father Claude and Toshi if this all goes to shit."

"Bri, lay on the floor. I need to move freely without worrying about where you are."

Bria began to speak, but Milo cut her off.

"Don't argue! We don't know what we're getting into. Dhabi may be as crazy as a junkyard dog, but he's right. Brother Joseph will be at the press conference, as will God knows how many members of *Opus Christos*," he said as a siren bleated behind them and blocked their cars in. Police officers approached their three cars to order them to stay in place as an ambulance and several police vehicles, sirens blaring, rushed past them toward the Pre-Seminary.

Milo put his face in his hands in exasperation. "What the hell is going on now?"

Bria looked at him sternly as she rose from the limo's floor. "Bet it's more upsetting, Milo, for the people who need the ambulance and the police. A little compassion might be in order."

Milo sighed. "Bri, all that matters right now is ensuring you and Brother Joseph are safe."

"I need to be alone for a minute," Bria shouted as she grabbed the door handle and pulled the door open, "because, right now, someone has been seriously injured or killed, and all you can think about is how you're being inconvenienced! Every life is equally precious to God. At this moment, there is something more important than getting Brother Joseph and me out of here so you can be heroes!"

"Like saving all humanity from annihilation?" asked Milo quietly as Bri slammed the car door and walked away from the Rolls.

"Let it go, Milo," answered Dhabi. "She isn't entirely wrong."

Chapter 90
12:10 P.M.
Pope Peter

All truth passes through three stages. First, it is ridiculed. Second, it is violently opposed. Third, it is accepted as being self-evident.
-Arthur Schopenhauer

Vatican City

Pope Peter stood backstage for as long as possible while Sister Bernadette stood silently behind him.

"It's time," she whispered as she touched his elbow to propel him forward.

Without looking left or right, Peter walked solemnly to the chair in the middle of the stage and sat without looking at the two men sitting smugly in the smaller chairs hastily placed on either side of him. He nodded at Monsignor Danti, the Vatican's Public Information Officer, who walked to the podium.

"The pontiff," he announced firmly once the members of the press quieted down, "will not be available for questions after his address, but–" Monsignor Danti stopped mid-sentence as the exterior doors of the Audience Hall were thrown open loudly.

Six dark-suited men, followed by a dozen Italian police officers, swarmed the stage to stand on either side of the three popes and guard the exits as an older, silver-haired man climbed the stairs and crossed the stage.

He glanced at Monsignor Danti before speaking quietly to Pope Peter, who nodded. Cardinal De Posada and Superior General Scotti attempted to rise but were stopped by a police officer's firm grip on their forearms.

"I am *Ispettore* Granucci of the *Guardia di Finanza,*" said the silver-haired man, taking the Monsignor's place at the podium. "I apologize to the pontiff for commandeering his scheduled address." He turned to tilt his head respectfully to Pope Peter. "But I'm sure you will soon understand why I am compelled to do so."

He paused a moment. "We at the *Guardia di Finanza* take the violation of our financial and banking laws very seriously, especially those involving money laundering and criminal activities. We have worked closely with the Vatican for several decades to monitor the bank's transactions. We are especially concerned when the criminal elements use the IOR to launder their ill-gotten gain."

The room was deadly quiet as the reporters and photographers leaned forward. Each set of eyes in the audience was focused so intently on Granucci that few noticed the quick look of shock and fury that passed between the Cardinal and the Superior General.

"For the last several months," he said, "we have been investigating several serious violations of international banking laws committed against the IOR. This investigation has revealed that over $980 million have been embezzled from unsuspecting depositors. We have also uncovered a money laundering scheme being used by international drug cartels and evidence of the human trafficking of both women and children. With the cooperation of the pontiff, we have been able to identify those involved in this criminal endeavor."

A loud gasp of shock echoed throughout the audience as

Granucci gestured for silence.

"As soon as these heinous crimes were brought to the pontiff's attention, he contacted us immediately. We also commend *Signore* Mandini of the IOR for his invaluable assistance. To my great shock, trusted men within our beloved Church used their powers and positions to commit these unspeakable crimes," he said as he turned to look behind him.

"Those men are Cardinal De Posada and Superior General Scotti. May justice be served and God forgive them for their unpardonable sins." Inspector Granucci turned to the police officers standing on either side of them. He nodded to them as they pulled Cardinal De Posada and Superior General Scotti to their feet, handcuffed them, and led them, struggling, from the stage.

"His Eminence," he said, "would now like to make a statement." He bowed to the pontiff and left the stage. "I will leave you to it, Your Holiness."

◆ ◆ ◆

Felix and Brother Joseph

With Felix closely behind him, Brother Joseph turned on the balls of his feet. He slipped around the curved entrance at the rear of St. Peter's just as he heard the outside door of the Sacristy slam shut and cut him off from that escape route. He had seconds before Felix rounded the corner and saw him.

Brother Joseph frantically searched for an escape route. He hesitated momentarily before moving toward the steep stairway from St. Peter's to the Apostolic Palace when he heard the pop of the silenced Beretta and felt a second bullet rip into his side. He stumbled and fell, slamming his wounded arm against the doorway. Pain coursed through his body as he struggled to his feet. A bright red smear of blood stained the white wooden door as he forced himself forward. He had no choice but to keep moving if he wanted to live.

Pope Peter

The Audience Hall was deadly silent as Pope Peter approached the podium. He stood looking over the crowd for a moment. "I speak to you," he started, using the speech that Sister Bernadette had written for him, "with a heavy heart to deliver a statement that, I had hoped, no pontiff would ever have to share."

The reporters leaned forward as the photographers let their cameras sit in their hands unused. They intently listened to Peter's words, unable to do anything else in their shocked condition.

"The laws of God are simple, yet some men chose to ignore them to pursue power and wealth. We see this defiance of God's laws among government leaders as they fight for dominance over other nations. We see this defiance of God's laws by corporations that poison the Earth and exploit workers to increase their profits. Nothing, however, is more unforgivable than men who use their positions as representatives of God to satisfy their greed for wealth and power. These men betray us all."

The reporters and camera operators pushed forward as one.

"Cardinal De Posada and Superior General Scotti are such men," Pope Peter continued, his voice tinged with anger. "May they be judged by the laws of man and God accordingly."

The room erupted into shouts and questions as the police officers marched the cardinal and superior general out of the Audience Hall and into the waiting police cars. Pope Peter stood with his head bent before he turned and left the dais.

He knew it was his duty to bind the wounds inflicted upon the Church by *Opus Christos*. He knew it was up to him to return the faithful to the path of righteousness as God intended.

But, at this moment, he needed to be alone in the Papal Chapel to try and understand how anyone could betray God and humanity so egregiously in the first place.

◆ ◆ ◆

Brother Joseph, Felix, Milo, and Bria

Brother Joseph lost his footing as he hurried down the marble stairs leading to the courtyard. He hit the pavement with a loud thud. He scrambled to his feet, ignoring the pain, and frantically began moving toward the *Porta Sant'Anna,* where he knew there would be a police presence.

He could hear the clatter of Felix's feet on the marble stairs as he stumbled away, expecting another bullet to rip him apart. He pushed forward, leaving a trail of bright red blood behind him. He could see the *Porta Sant'Anna* in front of him as he took several steps toward a group of people standing beside a Rolls Royce outside the steps to the Vatican Bank.

He watched as the rear doors of the Rolls opened, and a single veiled figure stepped out of the car, quickly bringing four bodyguards to surround her.

Brother Joseph tried desperately to catch their eyes as he stumbled toward them, but the men were watching their charges and took no notice of him. He took two more steps before he collapsed unconscious a few yards away from the cars as Bria turned her head toward him.

Without realizing it, she had felt Joseph's presence as soon as she exited the vehicle. As she spotted him, she didn't stop to think. She broke away from the group, ignoring Dhabi and Milo's cries as they exited the Rolls.

"Joseph!" she screamed as she ran toward him. "It's him; it's Joseph!"

Felix skidded to a stop as he saw the veiled woman run toward Joseph. Another woman and five men took up the chase, getting closer to him by the second. He turned and ran away as fast as he could. *Opus Christos* didn't pay him enough to face these odds.

Bria fell to her knees and covered Brother Joseph's body with her own, trying to protect him. She felt his blood soaking through her black garments as he lay on the ground. She had seen the assassin as he turned and ran away, and in a surge of anger, she stood up and began to run after him.

"You bastard, you murdering son-of-a-bitch!" she screamed as she felt Milo's strong hands grab her and pull her to the ground. She lashed out at Milo with her fists, "Why did you stop me, Milo? I could have caught him!"

Milo held her tightly. "And then what? He has a gun! What the hell were you thinking?"

"I don't know!" yelled Bria, pushing him away.

"Damn it, Bri!" said Milo, pulling her to her feet. "He could have killed you! How can you forget that you're carrying Our Savior!"

"And have you forgotten that without Joseph, it doesn't matter," she cried as tears streamed down her face. "The Child will not quicken without him, and it will die!"

"Joseph isn't dead! He's shot!" said Milo.

"He's not dead?"

"He's hurt, Bri, but he's alive. I promise you," Milo answered as he bent over, picked Brother Joseph up, and carried him to the Rolla, where he gently placed him on the back seat while Dhabi hustled Bria into the safety next to Brother Joseph. The four bodyguards gave chase, trying to catch Felix.

"If you don't believe me, you can ask him yourself," Milo said as he jumped inside and shouted to Jamal to drive. Dhabi reached over and closed the door before the Rolls and Escalades turned around and sped out of the *Porta Sant'Anna.*

Milo spoke to Bria, who was suddenly shy, and Brother Joseph, who was bleeding and in pain but conscious.

"Bri," he said in the most formal voice he could muster, "meet Joseph. I hope you both appreciate everything we've done to arrange this blind date."

Chapter 91
5 P.M.

Brother Joseph, Bria, Dhabi, and Milo

Healing takes courage, and we all have courage, even if we have to dig a little to find it.

— Tori Amos

Rome, Italy

The clinic, hidden in one of the valleys created by the Seven Hills of Rome, has the most exclusive clientele in the world. Its security and secrecy level was one of two reasons Father Patrick directed Milo and Dhabi to take Joseph there. The second was that the clinic director was from a Guardian family and could be trusted to protect Bria and Joseph with his life if necessary.

Joseph was in surgery before Bria, Dhabi, and Milo had settled into the three-bedroom suite hurriedly prepared for them. Still dressed as a Saudi prince, Dhabi spoke quietly on his phone with the *Mahdi*, who had already contacted the Saudi royal family.

Milo sat with Bria as one nurse after another came into the room bearing flower arrangements.

Milo shook his head. "Let me guess. Princess Celeste?"

"Who else? She has spies everywhere," answered Bria.

"I do love that woman…angel."

"Retired," corrected Bria as she shifted in her chair. "Milo,

I'm sorry. I don't know what got into me. But when I saw Joseph, I just responded without thinking. I put us all in danger."

"Shock can make us do stupid things. Just don't pull a stunt like that again, okay? You almost gave me a heart attack, and we both know I'm too young and handsome to die." He turned to Dhabi.

"Don't fight me about this, Dhabi. I'm just saying it before you start your damn eternal arguing."

Dhabi raised his hands in a gesture of innocence. "Any chance you will tell me what we're not arguing about?"

"You must leave on the prince's jet as soon as possible. The Royal family expects you in Riyadh this evening," Milo said. "Brother Patrick and the *Mahdi* have agreed that we need to break up the team for a short while."

"Pope Peter's shocking indictment of Cardinal De Posada and the superior general is worldwide news. Joseph being shot has been ignored as if it didn't happen," said Dhabi.

"It won't be long," said Milo, "A shooting inside the Vatican? It's too juicy to be ignored by the trash press."

Dhabi's cell phone rang. He listened carefully before disconnecting and turning to Milo and Bria.

"The *Mahdi* has informed the king," answered Dhabi after he hung up. "but he was already aware of the situation. They have worked out a plausible story."

"How could he have learned about it so quickly?" asked Bria.

"Never underestimate the *Ri'asat Al-istikhbarat Al-Amah*," answered Dhabi. "Their ability to ferret information is on par with my ex-wife or the *Mossad.*"

The story that will soon be released to the press is that I, Prince Amahi bin Abdulaziz Al Saudi, grandson of King Abdullah, will be accompanying the body of my second beloved wife, Fatima, who died later of a heart attack after bravely trying to save the life of her bodyguard, Yosef. He was murdered outside the IOR in an attack against the Saudi royal family by an ultra-right American Christian radical. The assassin escaped but is being actively pursued by the Italian police."

"Turnabout is a bitch," said Milo.

"Two coffins are being loaded on the jet as we speak," continued Dhabi, "The Saudi government has already sent a strongly worded diplomatic sanction to the Vatican. The Western governments will feign outrage and launch an investigation, but the incident will be forgotten quickly. Oil is too essential a commodity to Western industry for the governments to react in any other manner."

"So there will be a lot of yelling and flag waving, but it will all be for show," commented Bria.

"Your pope has already agreed to the story," said Dhabi, "as have the Guardians. It will all be soon forgotten except for a bit of posturing by both sides. Freddie and Samil will stay here as they both have nursing backgrounds. They will be explained as your private nurses. Jamal and Orlando," Dhabi added, turning to Milo, "will be my wives tonight, but I shall miss you, my Buttercup."

"I wish everyone would quit calling me that," Milo said in mock anger. "But better Orlando than me, I guess. Those outfits are miserable and restrictive. Just send Orlando back here once you're safely on the jet. He needs to relieve Lucas, Toshi, and Father Claude on security detail until we can get more Guardians here. Gabriella and Lilliana are resting now, but they'll cover the night shift with Orlando."

"I will be back within a day or two with a few others from our membership. You will need all the help you can get to protect Bri and Joseph until *Opus Christos* is destroyed to the last man."

"Thank you, Dhabi," Milo answered, thrusting his hand toward Dhabi. "Go with God."

"You need to get them out of Rome as soon as possible. If *Opus Christos* can regroup without De Posada and Scotti, this is the first place they'll look. Maybe they should go to Marseille?"

"Izzy and Father Patrick are working on a plan, but we're safe here for now," said Milo.

"We will be at your side as long as you need us. You are not alone. Know that, my friend."

"The Guardians started with a handful of women with nothing more than their love of God to sustain them." Milo smiled as he placed his hand over Dhabi's, "But with the help of the *Mahdi*, the world is a better place for all people. You're a good man, my friend."

Dhabi reached out and hugged Milo. "You are as brave as my grandfather told me your great-grandfather, Merle, was. I believe you are just as fearless and just as crazy."

"Now, if you'll admit I was the best fake Muslim wife you ever had, my life will be complete," Milo said as he hugged Dhabi back.

Chapter 92
9:30 P.M.

Father Patrick, Izzy, and Jasper

All great truths begin as blasphemies.

—George Bernard Shaw

Guardians' Command Center,
Abbey Sainte-Victoire Marseille, France

Father Patrick knocked on the glass window of his office to gesture to Izzy and Jasper to join him. They looked at each other with sinking dread, worried that something had gone wrong after Joseph's surgery.

"With your permission, Your Eminence," he started as Izzy's eyes grew as big as saucers, "I would like to put you on speaker. Izzy, ah, Isabella, and Jasper are here."

"Isabella and Jasper, Father Patrick informed me that the two of you were instrumental in the planning and success of the operation."

They looked at each other before Izzy spoke up. "Your Eminence—," she started.

The pope interrupted her. "Peter," he said, "is what my friends call me."

Izzy stammered, "Peter?" She took a deep breath. "Peter. My friends call me Izzy."

"Izzy? I like that. Isabella is lovely but quite formal."

Izzy smiled. "Jasper and the entire IT department deserve the majority of the credit for the operation's success," Izzy said, "but, equally, so do the field operatives who risked their lives. They deserve equal credit, especially Milo, Father Claude, Lucas, Orlando, and Toshi. And, of course, Dhabi and his team from the *Mahdi of Islam*."

"Our documents department has been instrumental in protecting centuries of valuable ancient documents and relics. But without Father Patrick's guidance and experience," added Jasper, "it never could have worked. He's the glue that kept us all focused and moving forward."

"And you, Izzy? What was your role?"

Jasper laughed. "She's our traffic cop, Your Em— Peter. She makes sure everyone is doing what they're supposed to be doing when they're supposed to be doing it. She's like a chess master moving the pieces to stop *Opus Christos* from winning a single advantage."

"I may have to borrow her to straighten out the Vatican. I will need a master chess player/traffic cop."

Father Patrick spoke up. "I have spoken to the clinic. Joseph is out of surgery and doing well. Bria is doing fine, considering all she's gone through."

"Please keep Sister Bernadette informed of all new developments," answered Peter. "As you know, Father Richard was killed, as were two of the Handmaidens of Jesus Crucified. We believe that Felix is responsible. The police are searching for him now, but he seems to have slipped away."

"He has escaped capture for years," said Izzy, "Alberto Zayas was able to stop investigations and bury evidence to protect him. Now that Zayas is missing in action, Felix will surely slip up, but until then, Bria, Joseph, and the remaining Doves are still in mortal danger. We must make sure *Opus Christos* is destroyed from the ground up."

Sister Bernadette spoke up. "Alberto Zayas is interred in a camp for illegal immigrants in Bergamo. Somehow, the authorities believe he is an illegal alien from Syria. The Council has decided to leave him there for the time being. With enough persuasion, he may decide to provide valuable information needed to eradicate the last vestiges of *Opus Christos*."

"I'm not going to ask, Sister Bernadette, how you know that," said Peter.

"That's probably best. We had Cardinal De Posada's quarters searched," she continued. "A ledger containing the names and locations of *Opus Christos* members was discovered. I had a copy couriered to you. It has also been shared with the Saudi royal family, the *Mahdi*, and Interpol."

"My new *aide d'camp*, Sister Bernadette, is a wonder to behold, " said Peter.

"Did I hear you correctly?" asked Izzy, "Sister Bernadette is your *aide d'camp*? The pope's never had a female aide in the history of the Vatican."

"It was time for a change, and Sister Bernadette has proven her worth. Her new position will be announced tomorrow afternoon. The Curia will scream bloody murder, but ultimately, it is my decision. It's the first of many changes I plan to make within the Church. I am committed to bringing God's message of love and equality for all humanity regardless of skin tone, gender, nationality, sexual orientation, or faith to the world."

"And to the multitude who lack faith," added Izzy.

"God does not discriminate in their love of their creations," said Pope Peter. "It is not acceptable for humanity to do so."

"The Guardians are ready, Peter, to help in anything you need of us," said Father Patrick. "We've waited two thousand years to bring God's true message to the world."

"I had hoped you would say that because," answered Pope Peter, "I have several requests."

"You only need to ask."

"I would appreciate the help of your documents department. I know that you have the majority of the contents of the casket sealed by Pope Clement. The ones returned to the Vatican Library are clever forgeries, but I expect the originals to be returned."

"Of course," answered Father Patrick.

"I also believe that there are other documents in the Secret Archives equally important in proving God's message to humanity. I understand from Sister Bernadette that Martin and his team are the most skilled translators of ancient manuscripts worldwide."

"It is fair to agree that they are," said Father Patrick. "I have a feeling that I know where this is going. I want Martin and Fran to be included on the call with your permission, Peter."

Once the documents department was on the line, Peter explained his request more fully. Martin was momentarily speechless before he spoke, his voice laden with excitement. "Your Eminence, access to the documents in the Vatican Library would be a dream come true. We will probably need considerable time, decades, and a secure place to translate the documents we believe are in the Secret Archives, but the collection is highly restricted. How–?"

"There happens to be a single exception to that restriction, so that will not be a problem."

"Of course, Your Eminence. You have total access to everything in the Vatican collection."

"And you will be working under my direct supervision. It will ruffle a few feathers, but, in the end, they have no option but to do as I request. Send Sister Bernadette a list of your requirements, and we will set up a lab in the Apostolic Palace. We'll transform one of the apartments on my floor to ensure maximum security for your workspace."

"Thank you, Your Eminence. I don't know what to say. Thank you isn't enough."

"I am looking forward to meeting you and your team," responded Pope Peter before Jasper disconnected Fran and Martin from the call.

"Sister Bernadette has an idea that involves Isabella... Izzy," continued Pope Peter.

A look of confusion crossed Izzy's face.

"We would like to request," continued the pontiff, "that, with Patrick's permission, Izzy is reassigned for a short time. Izzy has proven both resourceful and insightful."

Father Patrick looked over at Izzy, pride shining in his eyes. "You just have to ask."

"While the men guarding Bria and Joseph have repeatedly proven their skills and dedication, Sister Bernadette has wisely pointed out that Bria needs a female companion during the coming months. We would appreciate it if–"

"It will be my honor," answered Izzy, "My loyalty is to the safety of the Holy Mother and the Christchild. I will protect her and my Savior with my life if necessary."

Father Patrick looked at Izzy and smiled sadly. "I can think of no one better to be Bria's companion. Thanks be to God," said Father Patrick.

"Thanks be to Jehovah and Inanna," answered Pope Peter as he disconnected the line.

"Did he just say what I think he said?" asked Izzy as she hugged Father Patrick.

"Yes," said Father Patrick, hugging her back. "He did. He really did. He acknowledged Inanna."

Chapter 93
Five Weeks Later

Bria, Brother Joseph, Father Claude, and Milo

The first step towards getting somewhere is to decide you're not going to stay where you are.

— John Pierpont "J.P." Morgan

Rome, Italy

It had been five weeks since fate brought Bria and Joseph together. His recovery was progressing well, although he faced months of intensive physical therapy. It was decided that while being at the clinic would continue to ensure Bria and Joseph's safety, staying longer would create questions from the staff that the Guardians would prefer not to have raised.

During the weeks of seclusion in the clinic, Bria and Joseph began to develop a trusting and close friendship. They both secretly wondered if it would turn into something more, but neither was ready to discuss their growing feelings toward each other.

Father Claude entered the room with Milo directly behind him. "Whenever you are ready," said Father Claude. "At the request of the *Mahdi*, the Saudi royal family has offered us the use of one of their private jets. It is waiting for us at Da Vinci."

"Bri," added Milo, holding back his laughter, "you and I will revive our roles as dutiful Muslim wives. Joseph, we have an extra

Burka. You'll be the third wife."

Joseph looked at them. "You're kidding."

"Orlando and I will be dressed as the security force," answered Father Claude, "but you, Bria, and Milo are potentially too recognizable if any remaining *Opus Christos* members are looking for you."

Bria laughed as she turned to Joseph. "It's not that bad. We can stick out our tongues and make faces at Dhabi and Orlando without them knowing."

"I'll wear the *Burka*. I'll do anything to keep you safe and happy, Bri," answered Joseph.

Milo rolled his eyes. "Are we done with this mushy stuff? Let me give you the rundown. Dressed as a Saudi Prince, Dhabi will be here at three o'clock with the black limousine flying Saudi flags. He and two veiled women will enter the clinic to pick up his wife, who's been here for the last two weeks."

"The woman in room 243?" asked Bria. "I heard rumors a Saudi Princess was here for a facelift, but she never came out of her suite the entire time. She brought a private nurse for after-surgery care."

Milo laughed as he said, "It's Gabriella. I'm sure she enjoyed a relaxing two-week vacation with Lilliana. They were the snipers covering us when we left my darling Princess Celeste's apartment, the hotel, and the Al Saudi family's apartment."

"They're changing into surgical scrubs as we speak," added Dhabi. "They will leave the clinic through the employee entrance before the three o'clock shift change. They'll join the bodyguards as snipers when we move you, Bri, and Joseph."

"We'll only have a few minutes between the shifts to get you into her room, change into *Burkas*, and gather the mountain of the luggage the Saudi princess brought," Father Claude added. "The director is calling an impromptu, mandatory staff meeting in the break room to empty the hallways and nurse's station as soon as possible. We should be able to pull this off without anyone noticing you're gone until after we're in the air."

Joseph looked at Bria fondly. "We can do this, right?"

"We can do about anything if we do it together," she answered as she reached for his hand. Joseph lifted it to his lips and kissed it gently.

"Please, you two!" said Milo as he pretended to gag. "I think I just threw up in my mouth a little. Can we focus on getting you safely out of Italy first? You can play kissy-face or whatever you're doing later."

Bria packed the Italian leather suitcase secretly sent over the day before by Princess Celeste. Once again, the retired angel was ahead of everyone else when it came to knowing what was happening. She watched as Joseph carefully folded his Trappist robes and packed them in a smaller matching bag. Her eyes caught his.

"I'll mail them back to the Abbey," he said, "once we're settled in the States."

"We're going home to the States?" asked Bria, "I thought the Guardians wanted us to go to the Command Center where they could watch over us."

Joseph walked over to her and held her hand gently. "I've told Father Patrick that we can't start a life together as a family like that. We need our own home with a yard for our child to play in. We need a place to plant a garden in the spring and a porch with rocking chairs so we can sit in the evenings drinking tea and sharing our hopes and dreams. That's not going to happen in a secure underground fortress."

Bria's eyes teared up.

"But I'll call Father Patrick back if that's not okay. I'll tell him you want something different. We can go anywhere you like and do anything you want. If you're safe and happy, I have everything I need for the rest of my life."

Bria's eyes put her hand over his. "That's the sweetest thing I've ever heard, Joseph. It sounds perfect. Thank you."

Chapter 94
December 25th

Felix and Milo

The end and perfection of our victories is to avoid the vices and infirmities of those whom we subdue.
                    —Alexander the Great (356–323 BCE)

Magdalena, New Mexico

Felix was sitting in Cookie's Cafe, drinking lukewarm coffee and finishing the last bites of his chicken enchiladas smothered in green chili. It was not a typical Christmas dinner in most of America. Still, it was expected, considering he was in a small, rural town in New Mexico and wasting time until the DOT station north of Socorro was closed, and he could sneak by undetected.

Driving a 15-year-old rusted truck for a fly-by-night trucking company in El Paso was a long step down from his life as a highly paid assassin for *Opus Christos*. After returning to the US with no money, no references, and a fake ID, it was the only job he could get. It wasn't all bad, he admitted to himself. He didn't have to put up with Alberto's constant bullshit and De Posada and Scotti looking down at him like he was worthless slime.

If he could figure out how to access his accounts at the Vatican Bank without alerting the Guardians of his whereabouts, his life would be almost tolerable. Killing prostitutes and druggies who were always hanging out at the truck stops didn't pay like hunting down Doves, but they would have to do when his urges got too much to contain.

He turned at the sound of the front door opening.

"Mike!" the young Hispanic waitress exclaimed cheerfully, "Merry Christmas! Your order's ready. That will be $57.93." She leaned over the counter and whispered to him, "Don't tell Cookie, but I threw in half a dozen cherry empanadas for dessert at no charge."

"Thank you, Rosie. I know they'll be appreciated," he said as he lifted a bag of chips off the rack and stuck it in the bag, "Things got a little crazy, and we forgot to stick the turkey in the oven. I'm glad you were open, or we would have eaten peanut butter sandwiches for Christmas dinner."

"It's a crazy time of the year for everybody. How's your boss's wife doing? Any minute now?'

Milo started to answer when his eyes met Felix's. A shocked expression of recognition crossed his face as Felix stared at him, trying to remember how he knew him. Waving a quick goodbye to Rosie, Milo grabbed his car keys from his jacket pocket, grabbed the bags of food, and left the restaurant without another word.

◆ ◆ ◆

Bria, Joseph, and Izzy

Joseph nodded to Izzy as she climbed on one of the super-quiet Coolster ATVs perfect for perimeter checks in the desert, where sound traveled for miles.

"Bria and the little one are sleeping," she said. "Be quiet when you get into the house."

"Are you sure you're up to doing the perimeter checks?"

asked Joseph.

"They need to be done, and I'm the only game in town. Orlando and Toshi are sleeping after doing 18-hour shifts last night and this morning. Milo's in town picking up Christmas dinner since I forgot to cook it," she said. "We lost a few surveillance cameras, monitors, and trip wires. I think the darn coyotes are chewing on them. Father Claude and Toshi replaced them all this morning, but I want to check they're all working while it's still light out."

"Aren't one of the other guys available? You must be exhausted."

"Father Claude and Dhabi are patrolling the Mesa and Western parcels. Anyway, I'm still on an adrenalin high. I couldn't sleep if you paid me."

Joseph smiled. "Thank you for everything, Izzy. The guys are great at keeping the ranch going and protecting all of us, but this morning was outside our comfort zone. I'm glad you are here."

"I just listened to the midwife and did what she told me," said Izzy.

"Bri was amazing, wasn't she?" Joseph asked. "I'll never understand how women do it."

"She was, but so were you. You kept her focused and calm. That's one lucky kiddo to have you two as parents," Izzy said as she watched Joseph turn and walk back to the house before she pulled the ATV onto the gravel driveway.

Bria was sitting in the antique rocking chair near the fireplace. Her eyes were closed as she cuddled the newborn in the soft blanket her mother had knitted. Joseph bent to remove his boots.

"I wasn't sleeping," she whispered, "Just resting my eyes."

He walked across the room and bent to kiss her on the top of her head.

"Can I make you a cup of herbal tea?"

"I'm good," she said, pointing to the teapot and cup on the small table at her side. "Izzy brought it when you were in the barn feeding the horses."

"I'm getting used to caring for them, but I'm a city boy at heart. At least Jasper couldn't talk us into a herd of cows that needed to be milked at the crack of dawn."

Bria laughed. "Remember what he said, 'can't call yourself a rancher without animals.'"

"He has a point. Having a ranch without them would look strange to the neighbors."

"I was so happy," said Bria, "that Jasper set up a video chat with Mom and Theo. They are both positive that no one has ever given birth to a more beautiful and brilliant child in the history of the world."

"They are one hundred percent correct," answered Joseph. "Izzy mentioned that she spoke with Father Patrick, Princess Celeste, and Pope Peter. They all sent their love and congratulations."

"We're lucky to have so many loving people surrounding us, aren't we?"

"Speaking of loving friends, Milo's picking up dinner at the cafe. It's going to be a casual meal," Joseph teased as he stroked the newborn's cheek, "since I heard the women folk forgot to cook the turkey dinner. What have you been doing all day?"

Bria laughed. "Nothing much. Just giving birth to the Christchild."

◆ ◆ ◆

Felix and Milo

Felix turned to the woman behind the counter of the cafe. "I know him from somewhere."

"Mike?" she answered, "He manages a ranch south of town.

The new owners are billionaires or something. Maybe movie stars. All kinds of rumors are floating around. They have guards everywhere. They never leave the ranch, as far as I know. They all moved into the ranch about seven months ago."

"They?"

"The couple owns it and Mike. He's like their bodyguard or something. Then there's the housekeeper, the ranch hands, and the security guys. I heard the owner got shot in a hunting accident. I guess that's why they keep to themselves," she said as she looked out the window.

"Milo!" Felix shouted. He dropped money on the counter and flew out the door in one fluid movement. Milo looked up, and their eyes met as the Range Rover's engine roared to life, and he pulled out of the parking lot. Without hesitation, Felix ran across the lot, climbed into the cab of his truck, and threw it into gear. Milo! It all made sense. The husband and wife had to be Bria and Joseph.

He wasn't even sure how to contact *Opus Christos*. Superior General Scotti died while awaiting trial. Cardinal De Posada was in prison. Albert Zayas was probably dead and buried. But this wasn't about the money. It was a matter of principle. They had ruined his life.

Joseph had hit him with a candlestick base after lying to him by saying Father Richard had kidnapped him. He had a headache for days. He had to flee the Vatican without a passport or money. He had to sleep in fleabag hotels and break into cars to get enough to eat. It was disgusting, beneath his dignity. His months of misery were Joseph's and that woman's fault. He wasn't about to forgive or forget. They were going to pay for what they did to him.

Milo had pulled several blocks ahead, but Felix quickly worked through the gears and closed the gap between them. The Range Rover had a definite advantage. It was smaller and lighter, but the narrow country roads dotted with snow and ice were too dangerous to take at high speeds. Milo struggled to get his iPhone out of his jeans pocket to warn Joseph and Bria without slowing down or driving off the road.

Felix pulled the truck up and tapped the Rover's rear bumper. Milo turned the steering wheel sharply and kept the Rover on the pavement. Felix smiled. He wasn't ready to finish him off quite yet, anyway. He backed off a few yards to allow Milo to get the Rover under control as they began going through a series of curves. The ground on either side of the pavement sloped downward toward a series of ditches. He didn't have to rush. There was time.

◆ ◆ ◆

Bria and Joseph

Joseph smiled as he took the baby from her arms.
"I reminded Milo that you didn't like green chilis."
"They do take some getting used to," said Bria, stifling a yawn. "Milo says that if we don't want to stand out as 'foreigners,' I must learn to love them."
It was Joseph's turn to smile. "As if being the parents of the Messiah isn't going to be enough to make us stand out," he said as his cell phone rang, "Probably Milo, asking if we want extra green chili."
Milo didn't wait for Joseph to say hello. His voice was ragged. "Felix's here," he shouted, "I led him away from the ranch, but you and Bri need to…shit!" There was an earsplitting roar of metal scraping against metal. Then the line went dead.

◆ ◆ ◆
Felix and Milo

Felix pressed down on the gas pedal, and the truck surged forward. He hit the Rover solidly, and it skidded across the pavement. The amber plastic taillights exploded as the bumper crumpled, and the Rover slid sideways. Felix sped up and rammed the Rover squarely on the rear passenger side. The windows shattered as the Rover slid across the blacktop.

Milo slumped into the steering wheel as bright red blood flowed down his face. Felix pressed down on the gas pedal, then quickly pounded his foot on the brakes. The truck shivered before the brakes took hold, pushing the Ranger Rover off the pavement and into the ravine.

Felix lost sight of it as it plunged down the steep embankment. He considered exiting the cab to search the wreckage for a second but then changed his mind. Milo was a minor player, so the hike down the muddy ditch was not worth it. He had to get back to town to ask the girl at the Cafe for directions to the ranch. Milo sure as hell, wasn't going to be able to tell him.

◆ ◆ ◆
Bria and Joseph

Joseph tossed the phone on the table, rushed across the living room to the gun cabinet, and pulled out a high-powered Winchester 30.06 rifle. He quickly inserted five rounds of soft-point hunting ammunition and closed the bolt, chambering a round.

He heard Bria gasp as he turned around, motioned her to the floor, and went from window to window, looking for any movement outside. If Felix was on his way, he wasn't here yet. He felt, rather than saw, Bria slip beside him, cradling their baby protectively in her arms.

"*Opus Christos* found us, haven't they? Where's Milo?"

Joseph shook his head, "I don't know. Felix ran him off the road. I think he's seriously hurt."

"Izzy?"

"She's doing the interior perimeter check. Father Claude and Dhabi are doing security checks on the Mesa and the Western parcel. Orlando and Toshi are sleeping after covering everyone's shifts for the last twenty-four hours. We must wake them and send them to find Father Claude and Dhabi."

"Joseph, we can't leave without Milo. We have to go find him!"

"We have no choice. If Milo were here, he would insist that we get away now," Joseph answered, "I'm going outside to start the car to warm it up. I'll wake Orlando and Toshi. Call Izzy and Father Claude and get them back here."

"I'll try, but cell coverage is spotty when you're too far from the house."

"Do your best, but if you hear shots, grab the baby and run out the back door, Bri. Hide in the desert. I'll find you when it's safe."

"Call Jasper. Tell him we need a jet ready to leave Albuquerque within the hour." Joseph stepped forward and held her briefly. "It's going to be okay. Whatever happens, we can get through it together. I love you, Bri."

"I love you, too, Joseph. Inanna was correct. I did find my Mr. Right-Forever."

Felix

Felix was less than 100 yards away and moving silently

toward the house when Joseph stepped outside onto the front porch. He quickly dropped flat on the ground and patted his rear pants pocket to ensure his extra clip was there before he screwed a silencer onto the Beretta's barrel. For a second, he was afraid that Joseph had spotted him. He slowly raised his head to look at the ranch house. Joseph was moving forward toward the SUV parked in the driveway. Sunlight reflected off the barrel of the Winchester that Joseph held tightly with his right hand.

Felix ducked his head and waited for the blast of the Winchester, but when it didn't come, he released his breath. Silently, he slithered forward on his belly, propelling his body with the force of his legs. He moved swiftly, ignoring the small stones and brambles that poked through his clothing. He pressed himself to the ground as Joseph's head turned to look in his direction before he laid the Winchester across the SUV's roof to reach down and open the driver's door.

It was now or never. Felix jumped up and quickly crossed the driveway. His Navaho boots muffled any sound his feet made on the gravel. Joseph didn't look up until it was almost too late.

Milo

Milo panted with raspy gasps. Two ribs on his left side were broken, and a thin stream of blood was seeping from his mouth. He was hurt far worse than he was willing to admit, and he wasn't sure how long he had been unconscious or how long it had taken to extract himself from the wreckage. Pausing at the top of a slight rise, he could see the lights of the ranch house, but he had no idea how far away it was. It could be yards or miles. Distances in the desert were deceptive.

He tripped over a rocky outcropping and fell, cutting a wide gash across his temple. Blood cascaded down his face. He lay still for a moment, trying to catch his breath and focus on the lights coming from the ranch. He forced himself to his feet and bent his body so that his head was level with his hips to steady himself.

A sharp ringing sound suddenly broke the silence, and it took him a moment to realize what it was. He looked around and picked up his cell phone on a rock near his feet.

"Milo? Where are you?"

"Bri?" he croaked, forcing a stream of blood to trickle out of the side of his mouth.

"Milo, where are you?" she repeated.

"I don't know. I can see the house. I don't think it's too far."

"In which direction?"

"Direction?" It took a second for the meaning to sink in, "I'm east of the house, I think."

"Stay where you are. We'll find you."

"No!" he shouted, causing a jet of blood to spray over his phone. "Felix is on his way."

"We won't leave you, Milo!" she said as she placed the newborn in the Baby Bjorn and tied it on her back before she ran across the room. "Stay where you are. We'll be there as soon as we can."

◆ ◆ ◆

Felix, Joseph, and Bria

By the time Joseph whirled toward Felix, it was almost too late. Their eyes met as Joseph reached for the Winchester. Felix smiled as he lifted the Beretta. He kept his eyes on Joseph, imagining Joseph's head exploding in a crimson river as his corpse crumpled to the ground.

It was only a second of hesitation, but it was enough. Joseph dropped to the ground and rolled beneath the SUV. Felix screamed in fury as he emptied the clip into the fender and grill. He heard bullet after bullet hit metal. He pressed the trigger wildly, and the windshield exploded. He waited a second for a scream or a whimper, but it never came. He released the empty clip and reached into his pants pocket for another when he heard the crunch of footsteps on the gravel behind him.

He quickly spun around and dove into the narrow ditch on the side of the driveway. Scrambling like a crab, he moved away as fast as he could while struggling to insert the new clip. He felt the searing pain of the first shell slam into his shoulder, pushing him forward so that he faced the empty desert when he regained his footing. Whipping his head, he saw a figure silhouetted against the setting sun.

"Don't even think about it," shouted Bria as she slowly walked toward him, the Winchester rifle planted firmly against her shoulder. "I will take you down like the rabid dog you are."

Felix slowly raised his hands. "I'm not armed," he said. "You can't kill an unarmed man."

Bria hesitated for a split second. That was all he needed. Felix dropped into the ditch, found his weapon, and inserted the clip. With the gun in his left hand, he jumped out of the ditch and pointed it at Bria.

"Big mistake, little girl. It would be best if you had shot me when you had the chance. Drop the rifle. And Joseph," he shouted, "I suggest you do the same and get your butt over here unless you want to watch your little lady die while you're hiding under the car like a pussy."

"I'm here," shouted Joseph, his hands raised. "Leave her alone, Felix. Your fight is with me."

Felix gestured with his gun for Joseph to move to Bria's side. "I was nice to you, Joseph. I helped you. Then you hit me with the candlestick. I had to leave the Vatican without my passport or any money. Do you have any idea how difficult that was on me?"

"You were trying to kill me, Felix. You killed Father Richard. Did you forget that part?"

Felix shrugged. "That was business," he said as he raised his gun. "This is personal."

Bria slipped her hand into Joseph's and closed her eyes. Felix hesitated, enjoying seeing them silhouetted against the final rays of sunlight falling behind the mountain.

"No," shouted Izzy as she jumped the ATV over the ditch and placed herself in front of Bria and Joseph. Orlando and Toshi burst out of the casita, their Sig Sauers pointing at Felix's head.

Felix whirled around at the sound of footsteps dragging across the gravel to find Milo standing just feet away, bruised and bleeding, his Glock extended in front of him and pointed at Felix's head.

Felix's face registered shock as he looked over Milo's shoulder. He turned his eyes, looking for an avenue of escape as Gabriel descended from the evening sky, his wings fully extended, his face red with fury. He set himself between Felix, Bria, Joseph, Izzy, and Milo.

"It's not my fault," croaked Felix, cowering before Gabriel's relentless gaze. "I did what I was told to do. I had no choice."

Gabriel looked at Felix with disgust burning in his eyes.

"God has already forgotten you ever existed, Felix," he whispered as Felix crumbled lifelessly at his feet.

Chapter 95
Earlier that Day
Pope Peter and Sister Bernadette

The church is a woman, and if we cannot understand what a woman is, what is the theology of women, we will never understand the church. One of the great sins we have witnessed is the 'masculinizing' of the church.

> *–Pope Francis*
> *International Theological Commission*
> *November 30, 2023*

<u>The Vatican</u>

"Your Holiness?" Sister Bernadette said, "The press is waiting."

Pope Peter stood from the *prie-dieu,* crossed himself, and brushed nonexistent dust from his vestments. "Thank you, Sister. I needed a moment to thank God before I shared a message of hope and joy on this most wonderful day."

A look of concern crossed the nun's face.

"Not too much hope," he laughed, "I will do my best to contain my joy."

"As must we all, Your Holiness. We can do nothing to endanger Bria, Joseph, and the Holy Child. You must be careful in both your words and actions."

"As must we all, Sister," he repeated as he reached to touch the nun's shoulder.

His appointment of Sister Bernadette as his *aide de' camp* had sent a tidal wave of concern over his unprecedented departure from the Church's male-centric hierarchy and patriarchal traditions that had defined Western religions for six thousand years.

Many lay Catholics, especially those younger and more liberal, found Pope Peter's pronouncement to be more in line with their modern ideals of equality as he called upon the faithful to clear their hearts of fear and hatred and to open their hearts to all people with love and acceptance. However, There was no argument that Peter's vision for Christianity was one more in line with the Messiah's message of love, acceptance, and forgiveness for all, especially those in need.

"Today," he began as he stood at the podium looking out over the members of the world's press, "my heart is filled with joy and hope. This is the day we celebrate the birth of our Messiah." He paused and glanced over at Sister Bernadette.

"This is the day we embrace a new beginning for our faith and a new vision for humanity," he continued, his voice growing stronger with every word. "This is the day I call upon every man, woman, and child to open our hearts as one and accept that God's infinite wisdom, love, and mercy extend to all of us equally, regardless of faith, nationality, race, gender, or lifestyle choices. With God's blessing, this is the day we will strive together to become as God, from the beginning, intended us to be."

His eyes caught those of Sister Bernadette, who discreetly flashed him a thumbs-up before he smiled at the audience. He raised his right hand to give the press members his benediction before he turned and left the stage.

Chapter 96

Bria, Joseph, and Inanna

Sometimes, the strength of motherhood is greater than natural laws.

—Barbara Kingsolver

Magdalena, New Mexico

The golden light of the winter day had surrendered to the star-filled night as Joseph and Izzy quietly gathered their belongings in preparation for the move to a yet undecided location. Milo, battered and bruised with a split lip, two broken ribs, and a loose tooth, was resting in Izzy's room. She and Dhabi had treated his injuries as best they could using the available supplies. Dhabi and Orlando patrolled the grounds closest to the house until they were ready to leave.

Father Claude, followed by Toshi in the pickup, had abandoned Felix's rig at the truck stop outside Los Lunas. They left his body in the sleeper compartment before they drove to the airport in Albuquerque to set up a security perimeter. With luck, it would be several days before anyone noticed the smell of Felix's decomposing body.

"Izzy said we're going to leave in twenty minutes. We don't know if Felix reported our location to the few remaining *Opus Christos* members. It's too dangerous to stay. But," said Joseph, "if I had ever questioned God's unfailing sense of justice, Felix having a heart attack as he was ready to murder us all would be enough to remove my doubts."

Bria looked up at him. "Didn't you see–." She stopped mid-sentence, realizing Joseph hadn't seen Gabriel. None of them had. He had revealed himself only to Felix and to her. She wondered if Inanna had sent him or if he had come on his own. She smiled as she realized it was the latter. He did care.

"Didn't I see what?" Joseph asked.

"The shocked look on Felix's face," she answered quickly. "He knew he was dying seconds before it happened." She glanced across the room at the hours-old baby sleeping peacefully in a small antique bassinet in the corner of the room near the warmth of the fire. "Has it been decided where we're going?"

"There's a private jet waiting for us at the Sunport in Albuquerque. Father Patrick and Izzy have suggested that we come to the Abbey," said Joseph. "Your mother's and Theo's shop in Milan is closed for the twelve days of Christmas, so Father Patrick has invited them to join us. We all agree that going to the Abbey is the best short-term solution, but we'll do anything you want."

Bria stood up and gently stroked Joseph's face as she looked around the room. "Going to the Abbey is perfect for now. Besides Mom and Theo, I want everyone who worked so hard to protect us to meet our little miracle, but Joseph, I'm going to miss this place," she said, tears forming in her eyes, "This is where we became a family."

Joseph kissed the top of Bria's head. "My home is wherever the two of you are."

"So small to have such a burden on its shoulders," said a voice from the corner of the room where the tiny form, bundled in soft blankets, was lying in the cradle. "I had forgotten how frail and defenseless humans are when they are born. They are quite ugly and ridiculous looking."

Bria and Joseph turned as one, watching Inanna

materialize from the mist.

"Inanna," they said as they walked to her side.

She turned her head to look at them. "Have you chosen a name?"

Bria smiled. "We have."

"If you approve, of course," interjected Joseph quickly.

"I'm listening."

"Lilith Inanna," said Bria tentatively, watching for a reaction.

"It is too strong a name for a human," Inanna said as she bent over to stroke the baby's soft cheek, "but she will need our strength for the task ahead of her," she said, fading slowly into the mist of lights and shadows. "I approve. Lilith, after the strong woman I first created, and Inanna after me."

"Joelle Inanna," suggested a deep voice as Jehovah materialized and became one with Inanna.

"After us," he said. "You know, Grandma Inanna and Grandpa Joe."

He made a short barking sound that Inanna understood was as close as he ever came to laughter. "They think I don't know that they all call me Joe behind my back. The joke's on them."

"You came," exclaimed Inanna with a catch in her voice.

"How could I not come? We are one. Where else would I be if not to meet our beloved grandchild?"

He turned to look at Bria and Joseph, his ruddy face relaxed and his dark eyes softening as he reached out and gently stroked Joelle's soft cheek. "Raise her well," he said as he faded into the mist an instant before Inanna followed him.

"It will be as you intended from the beginning," promised Bria as the last spark of God's light faded. She picked up her newborn daughter and held her against her chest as Joseph wrapped his arms around them.

"We expect nothing less," answered the wind.

The End and the Beginning

Background Information/ Footnotes

The Holy Doves is a work of fiction, but historical facts are sprinkled throughout the story. While there have been and probably are multiple 'secret' brotherhoods within all religious faiths, the Guardians of the Holy Doves, *Opus Christos*, and *the Madhi of Islam* are figments of the author's imagination... probably.

Prologue:

The earliest religious representations of humans as God-like figures may be from the Upper Paleolithic period, approximately 40,000-10,000 BCE. Over 200 of the 'Venus' figurines have been found, all obese females, suggesting that their similarity may be the earliest known example of religious depictions of a Supreme Being.

Polytheism, the belief in multiple gods, was popular in early cultures: Greco-Roman, Viking, Egyptian, Sumerian, and MesoAmerican faiths. Buddhism, Hinduism, and several nature-based faiths like Wicca are based on polytheism. Akhenaten, an Egyptian Pharaoh (1353-1336 BCE +/-), abandoned traditional Egyptian polytheistic beliefs to solely worship Aton or the sun as God. Upon his death, the old Gods were quickly reestablished.

The idea of a single male deity is a relatively recent development in human religious history originating in the Middle East. Zoroastrianism originated in ancient Persia 4,000 years ago and, still in existence, is considered by many scholars to be the first recorded example of monotheism. Zoroaster is believed to have been born in southwestern Afghanistan or northeastern Iran in a polytheistic culture but had a mystic vision of a supreme being, Ahura Mazda, at age thirty. The faith was spread along the Silk Road to Europe, China, and the Middle East. It helped shape the foundations of Abrahamic religions: Christianity, Judaism, and Islam.

There are several major branches of Islam: Sunni, Shi'a, Ibadi, Ahmadiyya, and Sufism. Most Jewish people tend to align themselves with one of the three branches: Orthodox (traditional), Reform or Progressive (liberal), or Conservative (middle ground). Christianity has a long history of schisms. The six main groups are Church of the East, Oriental Orthodoxy, Eastern Orthodoxy, Roman Catholic, Protestantism, and Restorationism, each with its own beliefs and rituals. Combined, it has been estimated that 41,000 different denominations consider themselves Christians.

Chapter 1

Light in Judeo-Christian scripture often symbolizes God's presence or divine intention, starting with Genesis when light was created. When Moses met God, God was depicted as a burning bush and in a beam of light when Moses descended from Mount Sinai. The connection to light continues in the New Testament. Paul's conversion is described as a flashing light from heaven.

Chapter 4

The Order of Cistercians of the Strict Observance is a group of cloistered monastics. Following the Rules of Saint Benedict, the brothers take vows of stability, obedience, and fidelity to the monastic life. They speak only when necessary but otherwise live in silence. While most monasteries support themselves with work like bookbinding, their days are filled with prayers and religious services.

Chapter 7

In 1492, Queen Isabella gave the 200,000 Sephardic Jews a choice: convert to Catholicism or leave Spain. Many Jewish families fled to the New World, posing as devoted Catholics. When the Spanish Inquisition came to New Spain (Mexico), many of the *Marranos* (secret Jews) fled north to what is now the state of New Mexico. Most of these families, many of them now deeply devoted Catholics, were unaware of their Jewish heritage until the advent of DNA testing. For the purpose of the story, there are Holy Doves from the bloodlines of Sarah and Hannah, the descendants of the Messiah, among the *Marranos* families in New Mexico, including Izzy of the Guardians. The Guardians are scholars and warriors who have been waiting two thousand years for the Light of God.

Chapter 9

Religions have had a long history of secret organizations working in the background to impose their views upon both the laity and religious community. Catholic secret societies such as The Knights Templar were blessed by Pope Urban in 1095 to seize Jerusalem. Pope Gregory VII sanctified the idea of Holy Wars by altering the Church's idea of 'justified' violence.

Opus Dei, founded in 1928 by a Spanish priest, Josemaria Escriva, was canonized by Pope John Paul II in 2002. Noted for being ultra-right wing in its beliefs and influence, Opus Dei is estimated to have over 100,000 members and is noted for their religious and political leverage. *Opus Christos* comprises men with such radical ideas that Opus Dei considers them too dangerous to remain members. Opus Christos is a figment of the author's Imagination, as are the Guardians of the Holy Doves.

Chapter 22

The pontiff is chosen by a vote of the Papal conclave, consisting of eligible members of the College of Cardinals, upon the death or retirement of the previous Pope. While the majority of Popes have come from the highest echelons of the Church, the only requirement for the office is that the person be a male baptized in the faith. Women cannot be considered for the position.

In their 500-year political power and influence history, the Jesuits have been a formidable adversary to the power of the Papacy. It was rumored that more than one Pope had tried to disband the Jesuits and died for the effort. Their power in both the temporal and secular worlds cannot be taken lightly, as they are active as educators, researchers, and cultural liaisons. They conduct evangelization missions in 112 nations. The present Superior General is not Enrico Scotti but Arturo Sosa, the 31st leader of the order since it was founded by Ignatius of Loyola in 1541.

Chapter 25

Pius XII's silence on the Nazi crimes against humanity has long been questioned. In 1942, a US diplomat gave the Vatican a secret report about the mass murder of 150,000 Jews in Poland and Ukraine. The Ukrainian Greek Catholic Archbishop, a month earlier, had also reported the deaths of 200,000. Pius XII made no acknowledgment or rebuke of the Nazi atrocities. While often denied by Vatican apologists, in 2020, a portion of the Vatican's archives were opened to researchers. Multiple documents prove the long-held allegations that Pius XII knew the truth and did nothing.

Chapter 28

Pope Clement V reigned as Pontiff 1305 - 1314 CE and moved the Papal Court to Avignon, France, to be protected by the French Royal Court. He was considered by many as a puppet of Phillip IV, a concern significantly increased when Phillip IV, deeply in debt to the Templars, moved against the Order in 1307 C.E., when he had the Templars arrested, tortured, and burned at the stake. Clement V did not protest Phillip IV's treatment of the Templars; in 1312, he ordered their perpetual suppression.

St. Malachy, an Irish saint (1094-1148 CE), is best known for his Prophecy of the Popes, detailing the subsequent 112 Popes, the last of whom would be Peter of Rome, before the Final Judgement. Modern scholars question whether Malachy wrote the prophecies. Many believe them to be 16th-century forgeries. It has been suggested that Nostradamus wrote them based on the similarity of literary style.

Chapter 33

The Quran mentions the Christian Messiah more than any other person; twenty-five times by the name Isa, forty-eight times in the third person, and the first person thirty-five times in addition to other attributions and is considered a great prophet of God. Mary (or Maryam) is mentioned thirty-four times in the Quran, while only mentioned nineteen times in the Greek version of the New Testament.

Chapter 39

Lilith was Adam's first wife and was made by God from the same clay at the same instance as Adam (Genesis 1:27). When Adam demanded that she submit to him as they submit to God, Lilith refused, claiming her equality. In a fury, she left the garden and refused to return until Adam accepted her as an equal. He refused to do so. Jewish mythology remembers Lilith as a demon, as is any woman who refuses to accept male domination. Eve was Adam's second wife and did not appear until a chapter later (Genesis 2:21). As she was created from Adam's rib, Eve meekly accepted Adam's dominance without question. In doing so, Eve denied that the Spark of God resided within her, and she was condemned to never-ending derision and disregard by man.

Chapter 43

The Benedictines, Cistercians, and Trappists follow the Rule of St David to different degrees. Typically, Benedictines follow the Rule the least strictly, involving themselves in both the parish and academic worlds. Cistercians led a middle path while the Trappists are still, for the most part, true monastics, cloistered and retired from the world.

Chapter 49

The daily Monastic Liturgy, a Roman Catholic faith service, consists of eight scheduled prayer times. The hours of the Liturgy are modified according to the year's season.

Matins (2:00 a.m.), Lauds (dawn /5:00 a.m.),
Prime (6:00 a.m.), Terce (9:00 a.m.),
Sext (noon), None (3:00 p.m.),

Vespers (Sunset/ 6:00 p.m.), Compline (7:00 p.m.).

Western African beliefs were brought to Cuba in the 16th century when many of the Yoruba people were transported to the Americas as enslaved people. The owners demanded allegiance to Catholicism. Santeria is a blending of the Yoruba and Catholic beliefs. It is reported that roughly 70% of Cubans observe some *Santeria* rituals or other religious practices based upon African religions.

Chapter 55

Since 2014, the number of illegal immigrants from Middle Eastern and African countries has approached 1 million. The Boot Camp at Bergamo is considered one of the most progressive internment camps. They teach the immigrants Italian and other skills that will allow them to integrate into Italian society. This is a controversial approach in the minds of many Italians who have growing concerns over the surge of illegal immigration from non-Catholic countries.

Archeologists excavated the necropolis beneath Saint Peter's Basilica from 1940 to 1949 after Pope Pius XI's death in 1939 and burial in the Grotto of St. Peter's Basilica. While digging the grave through two levels of the area, bones from an early internment were discovered. They were quickly declared St. Peter's, which was somehow missed during the 120-year construction of the new St. Peter's Basilica in the 16th century. They are still revered as such.

Chapter 57

San Pellegrino in Naumachi, built in 800 CE, is the second-oldest Church in the Vatican. In the 1700s, Pope Clement granted the Church to the Swiss Guards. The original Saint Peter's Basilica was built over the location of the Circus of Nero by Constantine in the fourth century. Pope Julius III replaced the entire structure in the 1500s.

Chapter 61

Attacks against the Catholic Church by governments have a long history. The Roman Empire executed thousands of Christians, as did Genghis Khan, the Huns, and others. Martin Luther's ex-communication led to religious conflicts throughout the Western Christian nations during the 16th, 17th, and 18th centuries. The Wars of Religion in France (1562-1598) between Protestants and Catholics claimed up to four million victims. The War of Three Kingdoms saw religious-based conflicts (1639-1653) in England, Ireland, and Scotland. The Act of Settlement (1701) forbids a Roman Catholic from being King or Queen. Ortega, who has been in power in Nicaragua since the late 1970s, has closed Catholic TV and radio stations and ended the legal status of nunneries, Catholic civic organizations, and charities.

Chapter 66

The first written version of this concept, which is currently known, was a quote from Ma'at, the ancient Egyptian Goddess in The Eloquent Peasant: 'Now do this is the command: Do to the doer to make him do.' All major faiths have very similar sayings.

Chapter 72

The Institute for the Works of Religion (*Istituto per le Opere di Religione*) is commonly called The Vatican Bank or IOR. It is a private bank run by a Board of Supervisors who report to a Commission of Cardinals and the Pope. It has been plagued with scandals of financial impropriety, embezzlement, and money laundering for decades. In 1974, Michele Sindona used more than £20 million of IOR's funds to shore up Franklin National Bank and his private investment. He was murdered in a US prison. Archbishop Paul Marcinkus was charged with being an accessory to fraudulent bankruptcies in 1987. Banker Roberto Calvi was convicted of violating Italian currency laws and was murdered in London in 1991. The IOR paid £23 million in 2011 to the Italian government for violations of anti-money laundering laws. In 2017, two former top IOR officials were charged with £60 million of illegal money transfers. A year later, a former IOR bank president was charged with embezzling £62,000,000.

Chapter 75

Many Arab women wear traditional black clothing, including the Ayaba, a long robe, the Hajib, a headscarf, and the niqab, a face covering. The more severe *Burka* covers the entire body and face, often with only a mesh screen to see through.

Chapter 86

The *Guardia di Finanza is* the Italian law enforcement agency under the Ministry of Economy and Finance. It is a military police force essentially responsible for financial crimes, smuggling, and the illegal drug trade. The *Guardia di Finanza and the Italian*

Judicial system have worked with the Vatican to investigate and prosecute financial crimes at the Vatican Banks.

Founded in 1942, the *Banco Vaticano* operates at a level that puts Swiss banking to shame. The bank's policy of unrestricted import and export of funds and utmost secrecy, its depositors include a wide range of ecclesiastic funds and a scattering of private corporations, governments, and the richest of the world's private individuals. It is rumored that both the King of Brunei, one of the wealthiest men in the world and a Muslim, and Tsumu Kawasaki, the Japanese multi-billionaire and a Buddhist, strongly influenced the Vatican's policy of unrestricted import and export of funds, an attractive draw. The fact that the funds are untaxed is the frosting on their financial cake.

Chapter 91

One of Saudi Arabia's intelligence bureaus is the Ri'asat Al-istikhbarat Al-Amah. The Mossad is one of the leading entities of the Israeli Intelligence network. While its methods and actions are often criticized, its ability to gather information cannot be denied.

Author's Acknowledgements

The idea for the Holy Doves began at the Trappist Monastery in Lafayette, Oregon. I was there for a simple reason: I was trying to understand the divide between the Church's religious teachings and humans' spiritual history, which has been filled with violence, hatefulness, prejudice, greed, and dominance of others.

If God was loving and created the Universe, then the stories I was told about an angry, vengeful God must be wrong. Humanity must have invented a version of God to justify their control and power over the people. It was at that moment I had a flash of clarity. God was different than I was led to believe.

I am not alone. An increasing number of younger people and women in Western society have turned away from formalized religions. They no longer reflect modern society's scientific knowledge and social ideas of equality for all. Whether God-given or a coincidence of natural selection and evolution, humanity has the unique gifts of free will, curiosity, and intelligence. We can think and question. Sadly, we have used our gifts poorly, more often than not. Hopefully, it's not too late to learn how to live with respect and love for all.

Special thanks to Jan, Gabriella, Maggie, Fiona, and Linda, who have endured countless revisions, rewrites, and discussions. Thanks also to Hawker Vanguard for his assistance on cover art. Also, thanks to my writer's group members, Michael, Oliver, Maxine, Chuck, Mark, and Jose, who have supported me through this journey. I also want to express my love and thanks to my two wonderful daughters and sons-in-law, who have patiently tolerated me while researching and writing this book.

When the Universe is filled with a brilliant flash of blinding light, Bria Tanaka and Joseph Pirelli have no idea their lives are about to change in unimaginable ways. Chosen by Inanna to become the parents of the new Messiah, Bria and Joseph are soon the focus of a secret and bloody conflict between two rival Catholic Brotherhoods for the soul of the Church and the continued existence of all humanity. A captivating religious thriller.

9 781735 185521